Blowing up the
High Street

THE STORY OF HEATHFIELD SILVER BAND

First published in 2021

ISBN: 978-1-3999-1044-6

Illustrations © Lee Hunt

Published by:

Mark Learey
13 Cator House
44 Pevensey Road
Eastbourne
Sussex BN21 3HP

mark.learey@icloud.com

Front cover: 1904 East Hoathly Hospital Parade (image supplied by Norman Edwards).
Rear cover: 2019 Uckfield Bonfire (image supplied by UckfieldNews.com).

Blowing up the High Street
THE STORY OF HEATHFIELD SILVER BAND

MARK LEAREY

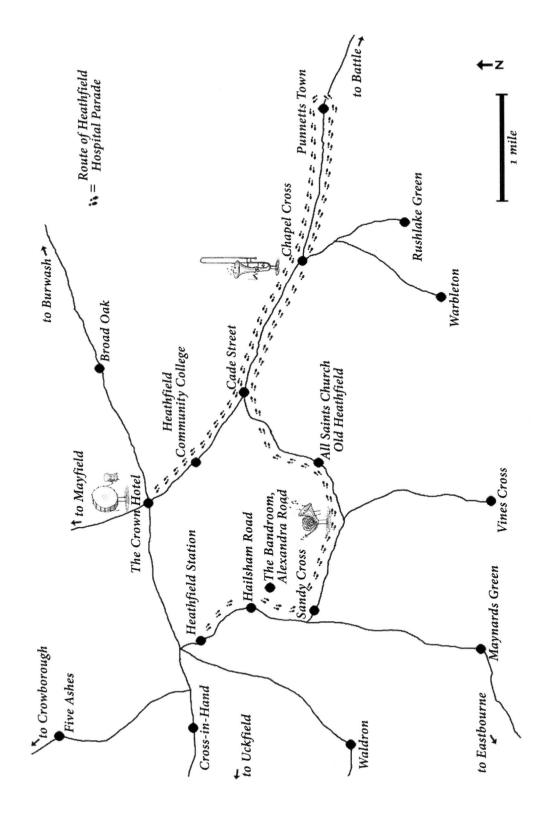

N

1 mile

to Battle →

Punnetts Town

Chapel Cross

Rushlake Green

Warbleton

to Burwash →

Broad Oak

Heathfield
Community College

Cade Street

All Saints Church
Old Heathfield

to Mayfield ↑

The Crown Hotel

Heathfield Station

Hailsham Road

The Bandroom,
Alexandra Road

Sandy Cross

Vines Cross

to Crowborough ↖

Five Ashes

Cross-in-Hand

to Uckfield ↓

Maynards Green

Waldron

to Eastbourne ↓

⋮⋮ = Route of Heathfield
Hospital Parade

For Ted

Contents

Foreword by Philip Harper   8

Introduction History in the Making   10

What's in a Name? Becoming a Silver Band   13

Brass Banding A Way of Life   16

1890s Establishing a Rural Community Band   20

Members of Note Edward Bean   30

Interlude The Team Strip: The Uniforms of Heathfield Band   32

Members of Note Charles "Charlie" Pettitt   42

1900s Now is the Time for Marching   44

Members of Note George Mepham Snr.   52

Interlude Earning Our Beds: Sussex Hospital Parades   54

Members of Note Jack Mitchell   58

1910s The Great War   60

Members of Note Arthur Frost   70

Interlude Bold As Brass: The Instrumentation   72

Members of Note George Mepham Jnr.   78

1920s Like a Phoenix: Recovery, Collapse and Rebirth   80

Members of Note Jack King   94

Interlude Contesting Times   96

Members of Note Cyril Leeves   114

1930s Changing Times and Financial Struggles   116

Members of Note Jeff Hobden   130

Interlude It's the Music That Matters: The Repertoire   132

Poem Our Village Band by Len Thorne   144

Members of Note Bert Wise   146

1940s World War II: The Boys from the ATC   148

Members of Note Roy Elphick   156

Interlude Blaze Away: Celebrating Sussex Bonfires   158

Members of Note Bob Lee   170

1950s Rising to Giddy Heights   172

Members of Note Lloyd Bland   182

Interlude With a Little Help from Our Friends: The Band Supporters   184

Poem *The Band Social Dinner* by Bob Lee   194

Members of Note Dennis Guile   198

1960s Creating a Modern Band   202

Members of Note Ben (Bernard) Guile   212

Interlude The New Recruits: Training Future Bandmembers   214

Poem *The Bandsman* by Bob Lee   228

Members of Note Tom Kelly   230

1970s Activity & Achievement, Friendliness & Fun   232

Members of Note Mostyn Cornford   246

Interlude Continental Adventures: The Band Tour   248

Poem *Bless 'em All!* by Bob Lee   260

Members of Note David Threlfall   266

1980s Comradeship, Craftsmanship and Showmanship   268

Members of Note Cedric "Sid" Forward   280

Interlude Room for Improvement: The Story of the Bandroom   282

Poem *David Threlfall and His Band* by Bob Lee   296

Members of Note Graham Farley   298

1990s Serendipity and the reinvention of a Sussex Institution   300

Members of Note Fred Richardson   314

Interlude Fame and Glory: Celebrity Encounters   316

Story *The Silver Band* by Dennis Guile   324

Members of Note Eric "Animal" Kemp   332

2000s Music for a new Millennium   334

Story *The Silver Band Committee Meeting* by Dennis Guile   352

Interlude Inter-Band Relations: The Heathfield Band Family Tree   356

2010s Amateur Banding Today   366

Members of Note Ted Lee   380

Coda The Story Continues…   382

Select Bibliography   386

Index   388

Foreword by Philip Harper

It gives me great pleasure to contribute a short introduction to this wonderfully evocative book, which I am certain all band history fans will enjoy reading.

Having been the Musical Director of the World's Number One Ranked Band, Cory, for the last nine years, you may think that there would be no comparison between what we do at Cory, and what the good folk of the non-contesting Heathfield Band have been doing for the last 130 years. Cory is used to winning national and international competitions, undertaking long-haul tours around the globe and playing to thousands of people. You won't read about these kind of activities in this book.

However, I would argue that, on the contrary, if you look below the surface, what Heathfield Band does is exactly the same as what Cory Band does – which is to create, nurture and celebrate a community of seemingly disparate, but like-minded people who come together for their own enjoyment, their inter-personal connections, their sense of purpose and achievement in life.

Of course the community stretches much further than just the musicians in the band, as this book fondly demonstrates. Family is a great pillar on which the band leans, supporters can include fans from every walk of life – from philanthropic benefactors to members of Joe Public who are addicted to the brass sound – and these days there is a sizeable online community of friends and followers too. The community comes together to share in music-making, particularly brass music with its unique uplifting qualities, and makes the world a better place.

Every word in the preceding paragraph can equally describe Cory Band or Heathfield Silver Band or any number of the thousands of brass bands at all levels across the world. What is absolutely true is that the very existence of Cory Band at the top of the tree would be impossible without all these other bands providing the integrated network of support further down the pyramid – bringing through the next generation and keeping the sound of brass very much alive in so many towns and villages.

This book chronicles the highs and the lows of the Heathfield Silver Band, and the theme of resilience shines through. To read about how the Band survived through cataclysmic events such as two world wars has taken on a special relevance in this immediate post-pandemic world of 2021. At no point in any previous catastrophe was live music-making forced to stop for as long as it was by the coronavirus. You could argue that this would have been the biggest challenge to face any music-making organisation in its entire lifetime, as rehearsals went online and amateur musicians had to dig deep to find the mental reserves required to persevere with their passion having had the joy of social interaction stripped from it. But I have no doubt whatsoever that the community in the Heathfield Silver Band will remain strong and resolute, as it evidently has done for well over a century.

I congratulate the Band on all its achievements, and I particularly congratulate Mark Learey on this fascinating insight into 130 years of Sussex banding history. Whether you are reading this from cover to cover, or just dipping in and out, you are certainly in for a treat over the following pages!

Philip Harper, October 2021

Introduction History in the Making

The story of Heathfield's own Band has been 130 years in the making, and the very existence of this book is tangible proof, if any were needed, of its enormous value as a local institution and charitable organisation. The book draws on thousands of sources, the content the result of kind and generous input from several dedicated researchers and dozens of Band *alumni* who have kindly donated their time, memories, thoughts and memorabilia to the project.

Image supplied by Heidi Watkins

Many of the sources survive purely through the efforts of certain forward-thinking individuals. Bandmember Anna Farley saved countless documents from one bandroom clear-out, and former musical director Frankie Lulham who boxed up and kept everything from her time with the Band: video and audio recordings, emails, letters, personal notes, and even her baton. These and other personal collections would be generously loaned to me for this research. What is perhaps difficult to imagine, however, is the extent of sources which are now sadly lost to future generations. Even as I wrote, various items were destroyed or misplaced, and others became inaccessible, much to my despair. The resulting book, then, represents a feat of sheer determination somewhat rare in the amateur banding world.

Indeed, the immensity of the task was to defeat two previous attempts at a written history. Preliminary research was undertaken by bandmember Peter Cornford, a descendant of Edward Bean, the Band's co-founder, during the late Seventies and early Eighties. In addition to archival research, Peter recorded some fascinating oral histories with surviving Band veterans, whose memories stretched back to the early twentieth century. The next wave of research was in 2012, in preparation for the Band's 125th anniversary celebrations, during which Shineen Galloway and other local historians were to document various personal collections, record a further batch of oral histories, and begin cataloguing the surviving written records.

I became involved with the project in 2018, whilst fulfilling the role of bass trombone player with the Band. By then, the research had stalled and, as I had already shown an interest in curating and preserving the Band's historic materials, the committee enquired whether I might consider writing the book. As I was embarking upon an MSt at the University of Oxford, I agreed to take a look at the project on the understanding that it would be some time before it could be completed.

The work recommenced in the Autumn of 2019, following my graduation, my daunting first task being to reconstruct the Band's early years, prior to the existence of any official records. The remaining ninety years would – theoretically, at least – be somewhat easier to tackle, as a wider range of sources became available. Writing began in September 2020, just as the Band was turning 130 years old.

It quickly became apparent that the original intention for a lightweight publication, comprising photographs, a timeline of important events and some themed articles, would simply not do the project justice. A more comprehensive approach would be necessary. The final publication now contains chapters for each decade of the Band's history, themed essays, and a selection of poems and stories. Also included is a variety of short biographies; whilst these have been chosen somewhat arbitrarily and the list could never be comprehensive, the intention here is to bring to life some of the more colourful characters from the Band's past.

The book which you hold in your hands is very much a patchwork of disparate source materials. The quality of photographs reflects the variability of archive sources. However, they have been restored wherever possible (if you know of better sources, I would be very glad to hear from you). Despite making all reasonable attempts to identify and credit copyright owners, I have not always been 100% successful, and where it has not been possible, I extend my humble apologies. All sources are included for their historical significance, in the spirit of enriching the academic work, and no infringement is intended. I will gratefully receive any information regarding uncredited sources, and shall endeavour to update such references in future editions of the book.

Writing a history of the Band has been a most satisfying and enlightening challenge. Retelling the story is very much a balancing act, and the task would require much soul-searching, questioning, and out-of-the-box problem-solving. Many memories are hearsay or contradictory, rumours are rampant, and tall tales bountiful, and there are no first-hand accounts or minutes from the Band's formative years. As a result, I have had to think long and hard when attempting to make sense of things. Any errors are all my own, but I have aimed to achieve a faithful, honest, and respectful representation of the people and institution whose story is told. All prices adjusted for inflation have been estimated using the Bank of England's online inflation calculator.[1] As the author of this work, I bring my knowledge of the Sussex brass banding world, and several decades of experience as an amateur bandsman. I also offer my passion for the heritage of the Band, which I hope is reflected in this volume.

My thanks are extended to everyone who contributed to the book, but special appreciation is due to the following: to Philip Harper, for his foreword, Mostyn Cornford, for his generous financial support towards this self-funded and independent project; Peter Cornford, for his encouragement, suggestions, biographies, and for access to his original research; Pauline McIldowie and the late Richard Ayres, invaluable sounding boards and eagle-eyed proof-readers; Shineen Galloway, for permission to use her 125th anniversary research; the families of Bob Lee and Dennis Guile, for providing access to their stories and poems; Gary Francis, Sarah Tate, Keith Pursglove, and everyone who kindly provided such a rich selection of photographs; Lee Hunt, for his glorious illustrations; and all the interviewees who gave their valuable time to share such wonderful memories.

It is hoped that this book will provide a lasting tribute to what is undoubtedly a vital piece of Heathfield's social life. It is dedicated with love and respect to the Band's legions of members and supporters – past, present and future.

Mark

Mark Learey, October 2021

---

[1] www.bankofengland.co.uk/monetary-policy/inflatin/inflation-calculator

What's in a Name? Becoming a Silver Band

The *Heathfield Silver Band* that we know and love today has had many names, and several faces, since its founding in 1888. The press frequently refers to it by alternative and interchangeable names. In 2012, for example, when the Band appeared in a music video for pop group Keane, it would be acknowledged in a full-page notice in *The Observer* as *Heathfield Marching Band*. Although it is possible that the collective publicly presented themselves as several different bands in the early years, there is absolutely no evidence for this, either in the press, in existing Band records or, more importantly, in the oral recollections of veteran bandmembers (with the exception of a brief division in the late 1920s).

If we return to its roots, historic news reports normally refer to the Band as *Heathfield Band* or *Heathfield Town Band*, and this is sometimes the case even today. Prior to becoming *Heathfield Brass Band*, it was formally known as *Heathfield Drum and Fife Band*, and less-formally as *The Chicken-Fatters' Band*, having attracted financiers, and members, from the booming poultry industry. Sometimes, it was simply referred to as *Heathfield's Own Band*.

The most accurate appellation, certainly in its formative years, is *Heathfield Brass Band*, the name which would most commonly be used from the early 1890s. This should not to be confused with *Heathfield Brass Band*, Somerset, formed in 1899, or *Heathfield Brass Band*, Lanarkshire, which was formerly *Garnkirk Brass Band* but changed its name in 1902 because it was rehearsing in Heathfield Square at the time.

During its association with the Artillery Volunteers, the Band was sometimes referred to as the *2nd Sussex Artillery Volunteers Band*. This can prove confusing to modern researchers, as it was not the only volunteer band attached to the same regiment; for example, the *Fairlight Artillery Volunteers Brass Band* would also be given the same title on occasion. The Heathfield Band was therefore sometimes distinguished as *Heathfield Volunteer Brass Band* (incidentally, due to its close association with the ATC, the Band was known as *Heathfield ATC Band* during the Second World War). Other names associated with the Band around the turn of the century were *Heathfield Friendly Societies Brass Band* and *Heathfield Friendly Brass Band*, which reflect the important social role it fulfilled during that period.

In the early 1920s, success on the contesting scene would lead the Band to follow a trend already set by other Sussex brass bands; we therefore see mentions of *Heathfield Prize Band* (and *Prise Band*). Soon afterwards, the Band then rebranded itself as *Heathfield Silver Band*. It would be convenient to assume this title distinguishes the newly-formed offshoot from the original brass band. However, it was in fact the original Heathfield Band, under bandmaster Charles Pettitt, who first used the name, which is first recorded in 1927.

The original Band collapsed in 1928, and when its offshoot won the Christie Challenge Trophy at the Tunbridge Wells Contest in 1930, it would immediately publish postcards with the caption: "*Heathfield Silver Prize Band*." It seems that the Band's public persona during this era remained as flexible as it had been in previous decades. This final development poses a question-mark over the Band's switch from a brass band to a silver one. Interviewed in 1981, bandmember Bert Thompson offers one explanation: "Every other band seemed to be changing to *Silver Band*." Gordon Neve, a contemporary of Thompson's (also speaking in 1981), adds: "As more silver instruments were added, so the Band changed its name."

Received wisdom amongst Sussex brass banders asserts that silver bands were largely a southern innovation, reflecting a perceived class distinction between the grass-roots brass bands of the north and the wealthier, silver-plated counterparts of the south. In reality, this is far from the truth, as silver bands had actually originated in the north of England during the late nineteenth century; for example, we find mention of [George] Stephenson's Operatic Silver Band, based at the famous locomotive works in Newcastle upon Tyne, as early as 1872.[1]

Silver Bands became popular nationwide during the Twenties and, whilst Heathfield Band's switch can most plausibly be explained by a simple case of embracing the trend, it is nevertheless intriguing that it did so precisely when it was most successful on the contesting scene. Could the "silver" in *Heathfield Silver Band* in fact be a long-forgotten reference to the prestigious trophies it was winning at the time, a remnant of the variant *Heathfield Silver Prize Band?* Perhaps not, but I like to imagine that it does indeed survive in this way, to honour the Band's phenomenal achievements and distinctive history.

---

[1] Holman, G., 2018a. Brass Bands of the British Isles: a historical directory [online] Available at: <https://gavinholman.academia.edu>

Brass Banding A Way of Life

Brass banding is a great force for equality, regardless of the personal identities or social backgrounds of members. Within the collective, such individual traits as age, class, or gender become irrelevant to the goal of bringing music to the masses. a brass band instead becomes a key part of the wider social landscape, contributing to the culture and identity of its community. It performs important outreach, linking different facets of society and fostering connections further afield through initiatives such as band contests and tours. However, the constituent parts of a band – the musicians – remain an important part of its story. Heathfield Silver Band has welcomed several hundred playing members and touched the hearts of thousands of people during its expansive lifetime. It is hoped that this book, in addition to exploring the Band as an institution, will also introduce you to some of the individuals behind its success.

For many members, inclusivity is the most important part of the amateur brass band. "Heathfield Band is a community band that takes all-comers, young and old, and no one is turned away because they are not very good," says cornet player, Keith Pursglove. "it took me away from some difficult times at home, helped me to become more independent and built my confidence... It was all mine," believes Lesley Dann (née Bray), Bb cornet and soprano player during the Sixties and Seventies. "The Band is very inclusive. Many, like myself, are largely self-taught, and like me, well into their fifties or so before taking the plunge to play an instrument," adds Richard Ayres (writing in 2019). "What's so nice for me, as an octogenarian playing bass trombone, is to have beside me another bass trombone player just less than half my age, together with a first trombone player in his early teens, and a second trombone player even younger."[1]

Newcomers are immediately embraced as part of the extended band family, and this philosophy fosters a sense of belonging, a love of music, and an appreciation of teamwork. "One of the great aspects about being a part of Heathfield Silver Band is the opportunities it opened up for me, specifically when I was younger," recalls horn player, Charlotte Butcher. "There have been many highlights [...], whether it has been performing at Heathfield's annual agricultural show or Heathfield Silver Band's Christmas Concert, no two events are ever the same. The variety of places and events we have played at has been a privilege, whether it has been at a donkey sanctuary, the Band's 125th anniversary celebrations or at a wedding, they have all been extremely enjoyable [...]. I am eternally grateful for all the friendships and opportunities it has given me."[2]

Sarah Leeves, the Band's current musical director, joined in 1990 at the age of 10, when a family friend (and bandmember) invited her along to a rehearsal. She fell instantly in love and returned home clutching a battered old euphonium. For Sarah, a key part of banding is the social aspect. "Playing in a brass band is all about getting together and having a good time," she says. "Whether you can play two notes or whether you can play a million notes at a million miles an hour, Heathfield is the sort of Band where you should be welcomed and embraced. It's as much about people, having a good laugh, as the music."

Peter Cornford joined the Band in 1976, at the age of 11 and became its principal cornet player, before leaving to attend university. Inspired by the camaraderie he experienced, he remained active in the brass band fraternity, playing for village and town bands, a championship section band, and nowadays conducting bands in the Bristol and Gloucester area; he also writes and arranges music. "It has been one long pleasurable experience of lifelong friendships, playing and conducting an extremely wide range of music, and generally being part of something which produces such fun and enjoyment amongst those who take part and for the listening public," he says.

The dedication required of bandmembers can be difficult for non-musicians to appreciate. "An instrument is for life, not just for Christmas," offers Sarah Leeves with a grin. Former musical director Frankie Lulham elaborates: "You have to be very committed. There are engagements every weekend and weekly – or more – rehearsals. It's a consuming hobby," she says. "Every weekend I was away playing with a band somewhere, and You had two practices a week," adds cornet player, Ken Russell. Gordon Neve, who says he knew nothing when he took up a battered old tenor horn in 1926, played with the Band for over sixty years. "Before the Second World War, I missed about ten practices in 20 years," he says (speaking in 1981). "We used to go in the front room to blow, but there was [rarely] time in the old days to practise. Very often I was late from work, so I missed my dinner not to be late to practice."

Euphonium player, George Mepham Jnr., considered brass bands to be the poor man's orchestra. This was not a derogatory sentiment, but rather an acknowledgment of the movement's working-class origins. However, Heathfield Band is much more interesting than the average orchestra. "The diversity of music is one of the best things," says Sarah Leeves. "You can go from *1812 Overture* to *Bohemian Rhapsody* and *Final Countdown*. Kids love this. We have fun mixing it all into one concert. What motivates me is helping young people do their best in order to develop a life-long love of playing music. Enjoyment and enthusiasm is just as important as progress; in fact, inextricably linked!"

The key to the Band's longevity, says Mostyn Cornford, percussionist and treasurer for almost forty years (and father of Peter), is that it encourages youngsters with free tuition, an instrument and a uniform, ensuring music-making and appreciation is accessible to all.

Anna Farley, horn player for over four decades (and daughter of long-time member Ted Lee), recalls: "There wasn't a lot else to do round the village. it was nice because we used to get out to go to different fêtes and that. I loved the marching and outside jobs. With the schools, it wasn't the '*in thing.*' one minute they were teasing you but when they actually saw you play, when you did Heathfield Carnival and you was actually marching in the Band, they would say, 'Oh, we saw you… you were really good!' " Sarah Leeves played with the Band all through school: "It's what everybody associated with me. It was never negative, there was no stigma. Now some youngsters don't want to be seen wearing band uniform!"

Family is an integral part of the Heathfield Band. Founding member and euphonium player John Mitchell remained with the Band until the outbreak of the Great War. His son, Jack, a cornet and horn player, whose pride in his father's music-making drew him into a lifetime of banding, remained a member for seventy years; as did tenor horn player, Ted Lee, whose wife, Clarice, always said that marrying him was like marrying the Band. "It is the band most like a family," observes Heidi Watkins who, in addition to playing cornet, has headed countless parades as its very own drum major. In addition to attracting existing families, players have often fallen in love and begun new families together.

"Brass banding is a way of life," concludes Frankie Lulham. "If you are in a brass band, it will take over your life." According to her daughter Danielle, a member for seventeen years, there were many lasting, joyous and sometimes bittersweet memories to be made. "I started out on triangle, aged 8, and ended on drum kit, aged 25, and played most things in-between," she says. "We used to play out with the Band nearly every weekend, sometimes multiple times over the weekend. We did a lot of marching, for remembrance when I used to play Last Post/Reveille, and especially bonfire marching. It sounds silly but Band was LIFE at that time, it was hard to leave it behind." Paula Brooks, cornet player during the early Eighties, remembers her time with nostalgia: "Those were the best days of [my] brass banding. some great achievements and fun was made and great memories too."

Heathfield Silver Band means many things to its members, past and present, but Frankie Lulham perhaps sums it up best: "To me it's about the people who come to Band, their funny little ways, their little quirks, the things they say, the fact that they are my friends and I spend a lot of my spare time with them. I care about them and hope they care about me. It's about all the new people who have come along to join us making music and having some fun. I care about them too. It's about all the people who belonged to the Band right from the start up to the present day, but also it's about the people who will belong to the Band in the future. I care about them too."[3] One thing is certain, within the community band, it is undoubtedly the people who matter most.

---

[1] Heathfield Magazine, February 2019: 35

[2] Heathfield Magazine, November 2018: 17

[3] MD Report, Frankie Lulham, 27th February 2007

1890s Establishing a Rural Community Band

Heathfield Brass Band (appearing as 2nd Sussex Artillery Volunteers Band), ca. mid-1890s.
(Back Row, L–R) G.R. Pettett, John Mitchell, Fred Stephens, Edward Bean, William Harmer, Mr. Relf, Bob Roberts.
(Middle Row, L–R) Herbert Harmer, Charles Pettitt, Mick Bassett, J. Gorringe.
(Front Row, L–R) Ben Haffenden, Sam Gurr.
Photograph by J. Frisby of Uckfield.

How does a popular brass band come to exist in a tiny, rural community located in the heart of the Sussex High Weald? The story of Heathfield Silver Band would very much parallel that of its community. The town of Heathfield that we recognise today did not even exist in 1888. There were no buildings in the High Street, save for *The Welcome Stranger Inn*, on the corner opposite the current fire station.[1] Kelly's Directory of Sussex describes it as: "a large village and parish on the road from Lewes to Battle, with a station two miles west on the branch from Tunbridge Wells to Eastbourne," and gives the permanent population at around two thousand.[2] The surrounding countryside would have been mostly woodland and farmland, worked by a handful of families clustered around Heathfield Park and Cade Street, in the area we now refer to as Old Heathfield.

The demise of the Sussex iron industry during the previous century had led to a certain amount of stagnation, but by the latter end of nineteenth century the area was again beginning to thrive. Cade Street was set apart from any major commercial centres; however, situated along the main road between Battle and Mayfield, it was fast becoming an influential locus. The district had already plenty to offer a growing community: there was the Parish Church, a school, a windmill, inns, workshops, and essential shops such as a blacksmith's, a wheelwright, a bakery, a post office, a slaughter house and a butcher's. In addition, there was a weekly market at *The Crown Hotel*. The majority of the male population would be concerned with agricultural work, primarily for local smallholdings, while the parochial nature of everyday life would dictate that most people had limited time, money or means to travel far from the community.[3]

However, the sleepy proto-town could not avoid change for long: a communications revolution was in full swing and the advent of better roads and the growth of the steam railway would lead to faster, safer, and more reliable connections to the big cities.[4] Although it was mostly self-sufficient, the community of Heathfield was thus presented with increasing opportunities to expand and export produce beyond the parish. The arrival of the railway in 1880, by way of the *Cuckoo Line* to Heathfield and Cross-in-Hand Station, would place the London markets effectively within reach for the first time. This was to prove a boon to agriculture, and especially to the poultry-rearing business, which was becoming a major local industry at the time.[5]

The colonial system's huge demand for produce was to lead to an influx of relative wealth to the region, and improved connectivity would suddenly make political, social and technological advances relevant on a local scale. [6] Rapid developments in mass-production, coupled with radical improvements to labour rights, health and sanitation, education, and social welfare, would gift the working and lower-middle class populace with better living conditions and an extended life expectancy.[7] Indeed, such advances were so significant that the population of England and Wales would triple during the 1800s.[8]

With improved living conditions would come increased leisure time and new opportunities for self-improvement and there was a growing appetite for art and leisure activities. In the final quarter of the nineteenth century, the community would see sports clubs (including golf, cricket and football), night classes, and myriad opportunities for music making and appreciation spread rapidly beyond the preserve of the wealthy. The people of Heathfield would create a music lending library, a glee club, a violin club, a string band, and a choral society, and, sometime in 1888, local carrier Edward Bean would recognise a niche for a community band to more fully cater to the community's wider musical needs.

Edward Bean's family were well-established in the parish and would have lived in reasonable comfort. He would have enjoyed some personal leisure time and would also have been stimulated by new ideas and cultural developments as he travelled around on business. Thus it was that, whilst still in his early twenties, Edward would team up with his thirty year-old friend and neighbour, Fred Adams (a stableman at the *Half Moon Inn*, just a stone's throw from the Bean residence at Cade Street), to form a community band.

The initial idea was to found a drum and fife band (comprising drummers and pipers), as such ensembles were extremely popular at the time and it would be fairly straightforward to put one together. The idea would quickly gain the support of the community: "The Parish looks forward to a time when it will have a band of its own, and it must be confessed that the drum and fife band have been very industrious and painstaking and are getting on very well," reports the Parish Magazine in August 1888. "Perhaps by Winter time they may feel able to give a public performance."[9]

The earliest bandmembers, of whom there were perhaps a dozen or fewer, would all learn to play from scratch, by the light of oil lamps at the Heathfield National School (now All Saints & St. Richard's Primary School in Old Heathfield). The Band was tutored by Stephen Saunders, an accomplished cornet player and musician from Little London, who had connections with Hadlow Down School.[10] Stephen would sometimes conduct the Band for engagements and was to maintain some involvement until at least the outset of the Great War. The Band's co-founder Fred Adams was its first bandmaster, a role that would have entailed deportment, discipline and taking the baton as and when required.

The drum and fife band worked hard, quickly proving itself "capable of better things than many people supposed."[11] By June 1889, it would successfully stage a fundraising concert at the National School and, in September, it entertained patrons at a busy local bazaar.[12] This favourable reception meant it would rapidly be accepted as a blossoming local institution. Indeed, the Heathfield Parish Magazine frequently refers to it as "our own Band." Edward Bean and Fred Adams soon gained the support of the Parish Committee and attracted subscriptions from local businesses and landowners, and through his work in the poultry industry, Edward would even obtain finance from contacts at London's Leadenhall Market.[13]

Almost all the Band's founding members came from well-established Heathfield families, and were born and lived locally. Many would have spoken with a strong Sussex accent, which has become much rarer today due to greater mobility and easy access to worldwide media. It was a young band too; most players were aged somewhere between their late teens and early twenties. Members' vocations reflected local industries, suggesting the Band's origins lie very much in an informal network of working-class tradesmen, whose paths crossed from time to time as work dictated. Bandmembers would therefore possess a good mixture of practical specialisms: by day, they were farm and nursery workers, blacksmiths, bricklayers and carpenters.

But a drum and fife band is not hugely versatile in terms of performance style or entertainment potential, and this severely limited its appeal to townsfolk with a growing range of musical requirements. Brass bands, on the other hand, provided an attractive alternative, and were fast approaching the

East Hoathly Hospital Parade, 1904.
Includes: Edward Bean (trombone), George Mepham Snr. (euphonium),
Charles Pettitt (behind Mitchell), and Ben Haffenden (side drum).

peak of their popularity (there would be approximately five thousand brass bands active across Britain during the final decade of the twentieth century).[14] By this time, brass band contests had become a popular national spectator sport, firmly cementing the movement as a "vital part of the new Victorian leisure industry."[15]

Brass bands could produce a wide repertoire, were eminently suited to formal engagements, such as garden parties and park and bandstand concerts, and were also able to add to the atmosphere of seasonal events, such as bonfire parades and Christmas celebrations. Increased musical literacy would mean that a network of suitable music teachers was becoming readily available, even in rural locations such as the Sussex High Weald, and the advent of mass-production made brass instruments relatively affordable for the first time. In addition, arrangements for brass were beginning to appear in music journals.[16]

In September 1890, the decision was therefore taken to transform Heathfield Band into the more versatile ensemble that it is today: a brass band for every occasion.[17] The Heathfield Brass Band would comprise about a dozen musicians, and even included clarinets until the 1920s. Its tutor was Mr. G. Cuthbert, bandmaster of the old 2nd Sussex Artillery Band, at Eastbourne, and its first conductor (and longest-serving to date) would be Charles Pettitt, a labourer who lived next door to Edward Bean's brother in Cade Street. Rehearsals took place at Cade Street, in the Drill Hall beside the *Half Moon Inn*.

Heathfield Brass Band quickly established itself as an essential part of local social life, and many engagements would become annual fixtures. It contributed two pieces to a Wednesday night village concert in the Spring of 1892, and enlivened proceedings at the Burwash Common Provident Society Fête later that Summer.[18] By the Winter, the Band was ready to lead bonfire parades at Mayfield and Hailsham.[19] "The village is becoming celebrated for the success of its concerts," enthuses the Sussex Express in November 1892. "Heathfield Band must be a source of real pride to the villagers; its contributions were so good, both as to time and execution."[20] Another review states: "Of our local talent [including] our own Band, we may always speak with pride."[21]

However, the cost of setting up a brass band was not insignificant. Early concerts attracted large audiences but financial success could not happen overnight. In addition to renting a practice hall, the Band had to pay for a tutor, purchase instruments, and rent or buy sheet music. The opening of Heathfield's music lending library in November 1892 must have encouraged the fledgling Band but, by February 1893, it still owed a considerable sum towards the purchase of its instruments. It would therefore stage a fundraising concert at the National School.[22]

From the very beginning, a core part of the Band's *raison d'etre* was to support local charities. The latter half of the nineteenth century had seen the growth of Friendly Societies and Benefit Associations, as the general public sought to insure itself against illness, unemployment and misfortune, and the Band would find itself devoting much time to such causes. In July 1893, for example, members of Heathfield Benefit Association formed up at *The Crown Hotel* and, headed by their band, "which is now, we are glad to see, the Heathfield Band, and which we may congratulate on its steady advance," marched around Heathfield Park, calling at the houses of principal subscribers on the way.[23] The entourage paused for a service at the Parish Church, before returning for dinner in the grounds of *The Crown*. This was then followed by speeches, a rousing performance of *Rule Britannia,* and open-air sports and games.[24]

Since its earliest days, patriotic events were to prove a mainstay of the Band's work. In July 1893, the gaily decorated village of Mayfield celebrated the wedding of Prince George, Duke of York, to Princess Mary of Teck, with a festival of sports, fireworks, and music which would be provided by the Heathfield Band and Mayfield Drum and Fife Band.[25] The same month, the Band helped to launch the annual fête of the Ancient Order of Foresters, heading a parade from the Parish Church to *The Half Moon Inn*.[26]

Many of Heathfield's traditions have grown hand in hand with the town band. In August 1893, it "rendered excellent services" at a forerunner to the modern Heathfield Agricultural Show,[27] and assisted the Heathfield Lodge of Oddfellows with celebrating its anniversary at the *Star Inn*. The Band once again headed Hailsham's Guy Fawkes Celebrations in November, and it would perform some "splendid selections" at a packed smoking concert (or *smoker*) at the *Star Inn* in March 1894.[28]

Further concerts and other engagements trickled in, but the Band would rarely travel far from home. Indeed, getting to *away gigs* must have proven irksome prior to the ready availability of motor transport. It was fortunate that Edward Bean worked in the carrier trade, as the Band was sometimes able to make use of his horse-pulled vans. In this way, it could travel as far as Goudhurst, a one-way journey of three and a half hours (which today takes about half an hour by car).[29] Interviewed in 1981, George Mepham Jnr. recalled the early years, during which his father was a bandmember: "Went to Hailsham and East Hoathly, my father did. They used to get up early to get to jobs on time and they were gone all day. Not all blokes could get away from work. There was only one solo cornet sometimes, so all the bands used to help one another. There were a lot more bands about then."

Despite having progressed enormously as a community band, an association was built with the 2nd Sussex Volunteer Artillery Corps, and the earliest evidence for this appears in the Eastbourne Gazette, dated 8th August 1894. At that time, it was fairly common for the Volunteer Corps to sustain amateur bands, as the arrangement would be a mutually beneficial one.[30] From the Band's point of view, the association provided it with excellent fundraising opportunities, by way of officers' subscriptions and community fundraisers. Instruments and uniforms were also provided, and it could use the spacious new Heathfield Drill Hall in Station Road for rehearsals.[31] The Volunteer Corps also gave valuable tutoring, which would further enhance the Band's performance capabilities. In return, the Band would lend a much-needed sense of authenticity and occasion to military events, and promote good relations between the Volunteer Corps and its local community.[32]

Heathfield Band thus found itself leading the Volunteers at church parades, entertaining the troops, and providing the *Reveille* and other music for martial parades. It could even be seen playing selections for cricket matches at Windmill Hill Place, through "the kindness" (for which we must surely read "permission") of Captain J.G. Knight.[33] The repertoire was in many ways similar to that of civilian bands,[34] though its performance may have proven more tedious at times. Bandmember Jack Mitchell (interviewed in 1981) remembers playing a march called *Love Not* seventeen times at one parade!

As part of the arrangement, members were required to attend training camp at Lydd, the most southerly town in Kent, for two weeks each year. Here, they trained as stretcher bearers and medical orderlies, practised marching technique and performed military music, in addition to training with 64-pounder guns (John Mitchell, Jack's father, was to blame these for his deafness in later years). By 1899, the Volunteer Artillery Corps had transferred to the Royal Garrison Artillery and the 2nd Sussex RGA (designated "heavy" artillery), to which the Band was attached, was based at Eastbourne, where training would also take place.[35]

Because the association was part-time, the Band was also free to pursue other engagements, such as fêtes, flower shows and Friendly Society club days, and provide dance music for the community's end-of-hop-picking festivities. It was therefore an incredibly busy Band, and its musical ability would accordingly improve in leaps and bounds. "Our village concerts are now in progress and giving much pleasure," reports the Parish Magazine in Spring 1897. "At the first concert of the season, it was generally noticed that our Heathfield Band had made immense progress during the last year, and all will unite in wishing them success."[36]

The Second South African Anglo-Boer War broke out in October 1899 and, although no bandmembers were called-up, they would nevertheless play an important part in the war effort back home, supporting the military and boosting morale. The return of one CIV to Heathfield Station in November 1900 was naturally heralded by the Band, accompanied by an enthusiastic and cheering crowd. The growing entourage then escorted the soldier to his parents' residence, where thanks were given and speeches made. "On leaving the residence the Band played *Home, Sweet Home*, and all the crowd marched through the grounds giving cheer after cheer for our gallant defender."[37]

The exceptional work of the Band's founding members during its first decade had paid dividends. It had quickly progressed from a small drum and fife band to a much larger, more accomplished brass band, and its links with the military served to strengthen and legitimise the Band as a real source of pride, and even patriotism, for the community. As it entered the twentieth century, the Band would grow from strength to strength, supporting charities, enhancing social events, and maintaining morale during the challenging times which lay ahead. In little more than a decade, community life without the Heathfield Band was already inconceivable.

[1] Heathfield Horticultural Society, 2021. *Our History* [online]. Available at: <https://heathfield-horticultural.org.uk/our-history/>

[2] Kelly's Directory 1899: 408

[3] Galloway et al, 2008. *Old Heathfield And Cade Street*. Heathfield: Old Heathfield and Cade Street Society: 19–24; Gillet, A. & Russell, B., 1990. *Around Heathfield in old photographs*. Stroud: A. Sutton

[4] Galloway et al, 2008: 21

[5] ibid: 26; Foord, F., 1982. *The Development Of The Tilsmore Area Of Waldron Parish From 1874*. Heathfield: F. Foord: 25–7; Gillet, A. & Russell, B., 1990

[6] Galloway et al, 2008: 20

[7] Diniejko, A., 2014. *A Chronology Of Social Change And Social Reform In Great Britain In The Nineteenth And Early Twentieth Centuries* [online]. Available at: <www.victorianweb.org/history/socialism/chronology.html>

[8] Galloway et al, 2008: 20

[9] Waldron, Heathfield and Warbleton Parish Magazine, August 1888

[10] Sussex Express, 26th December 1919

[11] Waldron, Heathfield and Warbleton Parish Magazine, September 1889

[12] ibid

[13] Kent & Sussex Courier, 7th January 1955

[14] Holman, G., 2018a. Brass Bands of the British Isles: a historical directory [online]. Available at: <https://gavinholman.academia.edu>

[15] Herbert, T., 2000. Nineteenth-Century Bands: Making a Movement. In: T. Herbert, ed., *The British Brass Band: A Musical and Social History*. Oxford: Oxford University Press: 34

[16] Blythell, D., 1994. Class, Community, and Culture – The Case of the Brass Band in Newcastle. *Labour History*, 67 (November 1994): 145; Herbert, T., 2000

[17] Sussex Express, 10th January 1913

[18] Waldron, Heathfield and Warbleton Parish Magazine, May 1892; Sussex Express, 3rd June 1892

[19] Sussex Express, 11th November 1892

[20] Sussex Express, 26th November 1892

[21] Waldron, Heathfield and Warbleton Parish Magazine, December 1892

[22] Waldron, Heathfield and Warbleton Parish Magazine, October 1892 & February 1893

[23] Waldron, Heathfield and Warbleton Parish Magazine, July 1893

[24] Sussex Express, 10th June 1893

[25] Kent & Sussex Courier, 7th July 1893

[26] Sussex Express, 28th July 1893

[27] Sussex Express, 12th August 1893

[28] Sussex Express, 2nd March 1894

[29] Kent & Sussex Courier, 7th January 1955

[30] Herbert, T., 2000: 37–43

[31] ibid

[32] ibid

[33] Sussex Express, 14th July 1899

[34] ibid

[35] Litchfield, N. and Westlake, R., 1982. *The Volunteer Artillery, 1859-1908*. Nottingham: Sherwood

[36] Waldron, Heathfield and Warbleton Parish Magazine, ca. March 1897

[37] Sussex Express, 9th November 1900

MEMBERS OF NOTE...

Edward Bean

founder & trombone player,

1888–ca.1935.

E dward Bean was born in March 1865, on the family farm in Hellingly. By the time he was 16, the family had moved to Cade Street, Old Heathfield, where his father, Charles, would begin a business as an agent and carrier for local breweries. This was to gradually shift focus towards the thriving chicken-fattening industry, and Edward would soon become involved, first as an assistant and later a clerk. However, he was no ordinary workman, and would regularly undertake errands of importance, such as travelling to Eastbourne to do the firm's banking (a round trip which would take an entire day).

Edward was to marry Alice Jane Rusbridge in March 1886.

Along with Fred Adams, a blacksmith from Hailsham, Edward would co-found the Heathfield Band in 1888. To raise the necessary funding, the pair were to make made use of his far-reaching connections in the poultry trade, along with contacts in the Old Heathfield Parish Committee and other local businesses. "Heathfield's own band" was born.

Edward would not enlist in His Majesty's Forces during the Great War, and was instead to serve his country at home in "work of national importance." He would leave the neighbourhood for a few years, but was to return in the early Twenties. The economic effects of the war were to cause a sharp decline in the chicken-fattening industry, and the Bean family business would again be transformed, this time into a coal merchants operating from premises on the High Street.

Edward and Alice Jane lived opposite the Band's rehearsal room in Cade Street and, from time-to-time, his carrier van and a pair of horses would be used to transport bandmembers to engagements. He became an accomplished trombone player, despite being something of a "foot-tapper;" indeed, he would "cuff" one young musician – Jack King – for laughing at his habit. At engagements, he would sometimes perform solos, and was occasionally known to perform as part of quartets and quintets. He would even win a gold medal at the Tunbridge Wells Contest.

Edward would go on to be a highly-regarded member of the community, and was to become a popular worker at a chicken-fattening mill on Mutton Hall Hill. He would often be spoken of as if he *was* the Band, though by now it was controlled by an organised committee and Edward was to have little to do with its running. However, from time to time he would personally finance the Band and was made an honorary life member in 1930, continuing to play for at least another half a decade.[1]

In later years, Edward and Alice Jane are thought to have lived in humbler circumstances, certainly making do without the live-in maid they enjoyed during the pre-war years. Edward died in June 1942, at the age of 82.

---

[1] Sussex Express, 28th June 1935

Interlude The Team Strip:
The Uniforms of Heathfield Band

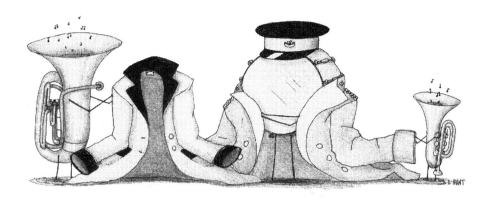

Appearance can subtly alter an audience's perception, for better or worse, and so every serious band requires a uniform (or, as the Band's musical director calls it, the "team strip"). It is easily recognisable, a mark of identity, and a token of professionalism. "You usually tuck it over your arm on the way home," says Sarah Leeves. "People have asked me, 'Have you been to a hunt?,' 'Do you drive a bus?,' all sorts of things, because they don't understand what it's all about… despite the big euphonium on my back!" The uniform thus signifies an individual's proud belonging to a valued social collective.

Indeed, the Heathfield Band means so much to its members that some are buried with their uniform. Others have been known to attend the funerals of former members wearing the full Band uniform. The funeral cortege of founding member William Harmer, who died in 1913 at the age of just 41, was marked by a coffin upon which, in addition to floral tributes, rested his uniform and cap, and several of his band colleagues acted as bearers.[1] The coffin of Cyril Leeves, member from 1928–79, was interred with his peaked band cap placed carefully on top.

However, this is not to say that members will not sometimes attempt to assert their individuality. Describing one posh engagement in 2002, former musical director Frankie Lulham writes: "Flaps were checked on jacket pockets, then it was discovered that Mike had come out wearing odd socks – one black, one blue – not to mention Geoff's socks had patterns on them! A strict lecture ensued on dress code…"[2] There were also occasions when young members would attempt to appear in public without their ties, or wearing other non-regulation garb!

The Band's uniform has evolved quite considerably, from stuffy and formal to relatively casual, in line with changing expectations and social norms. Evidence from its formative years is scarce and, consequently, it is uncertain whether the Band even possessed a uniform at the outset. My feeling is that it would not have done, since raising the money for such a significant investment would have taken some time, and most likely would have been achieved by staging fundraising concerts. It is also possible that the desire to obtain uniforms could have been the early Band's motivation to associate with the Artillery Volunteers.

There are just three surviving photographs of the Band from the turn of the century, though precise dating is difficult and has been derived primarily from the memories of second-generation bandmembers. Two are portraits and the other depicts East Hoathly Hospital Parade. The Band wears a different uniform for each, but all are more or less militaristic in style. So, what clues do we have? A newspaper from late 1903 tells us the Band has recently severed its connection with the Volunteers and is busy raising funds for a new uniform.[3] The martial appearance might therefore suggest that all three photographs predate the end of the association, though it is believed that the picture from East Hoathly dates to 1904. However, civilian uniforms from this period would very possibly have resembled military uniforms, and may have been purchased from army surplus stores to save money.

The oldest photograph (see page 20) probably dates to the mid-1890s. In it, bandmembers wear pillbox-type caps, which were always worn slightly askew. Bandmaster Charles Pettitt's has a coloured band, which is probably gold, and Sam Gurr, who is lying to the front right of the picture, has chevrons on his hat and right arm, signifying his role as a bombardier. The uniform consists of dark shoes and trousers, and virtually plain tunics with brass buttons (Charlie's includes the full nine, indicating that he is the senior officer). The tunics do have braiding on the arms and piping around the collars, though Charlie's is a different colour, again very probably gold. The Band's bass drum bears the coat of arms of the United Kingdom, with *Heathfield Brass Band* and the motto *Dieu et mon Droit* (God and my right) emblazoned across the front.

The second photograph (see page 44) dates to around 1900. Flat-topped forage caps with narrow visors were fairly common in the late Victorian military and, although it is uncertain what colour they would have been, midnight blue seems likely, as this was in popular use at the time. The players' caps would be trimmed with yellow bands, whilst that of bandmaster Charles Pettitt would be gold with an eight-pointed star above the cap band (unfortunately detail is poor, so it is difficult to determine the design of the star). Those of the Royal Sussex Regiment normally display a feathered plume, but Charlie's does not. It might instead signify his one-time affiliation to the Coldstream Guards, though we may never know the true story. The rest of the uniform comprises tunics with elaborate braiding on the front and piping around the edges, which would most likely be red in colour, with dark trousers and black shoes. The bass drum is the same as that depicted previously.

The photograph from East Hoathly (see page 23) shows a dark and relatively plain uniform. No brass buttons are visible and the caps are now of the "Kepi" variety, with flat tops and thin peaks, each decorated with a badge of an eight-pointed star surmounted by what appears to be a crown. The tunics of contemporary Artillery uniforms would generally include red piping and stripes down the trousers, which may fit with surviving reports of Band appearances. At the 1907 Hadlow Down Hospital Parade, for example, the Band contributed "both colour and cheerfulness to [...] proceedings with their bright uniforms and music."[4] The 1909 Heathfield Hospital Parade is described thus: "There was just sufficient breeze to keep the pretty banners floating which, with the bright coloured uniform of the bandsmen and regalia of the members of the various societies, and the glittering instruments, went to make up a pretty and imposing procession."[5]

Heathfield Band, and life in general, was to come suddenly to a halt for the Great War, and social and economic recovery at its conclusion would take many years to achieve. Photographs from this period are scarce, so it is difficult to characterise the contemporary Band uniform. However, it seems likely that the well-worn outfits seen in the 1922 portrait (opposite) are, in fact, those same surviving uniforms from 1904, albeit with the addition of wider-brimmed caps. The cap badges now depict eight-pointed stars surmounted by the crown of St. Edward.

One thing is clear: by the Twenties there was a pressing need to replace the uniforms. In September 1923, the Band held a fundraising social at Heathfield's Recreation Hall, attracting an impressive two hundred attendees. In addition, the Parish Council granted permission for it to perform Sunday afternoon concerts on the village green and other locales in the district, in order to take collections. By the Summer of 1924, enough money had been raised to purchase new uniforms for all eighteen bandmembers. These were dark blue, with gold around the collar and red vertical stripes running down both breasts and each trouser leg, and they would be complemented with white music satchels. The cost was about £66 (equivalent to over £4,000 today), but it would undoubtedly be a worthwhile investment, helping to propel the Band proudly to success in the fourth section of the Tunbridge Wells Contest that July.

By 1929, the number of bandmembers was on the rise, and the committee determined to recall the uniforms of "late members."[6] It is uncertain whether this is a reference to actually deceased players, or whether it in fact refers to members of the original Heathfield Band which had now disbanded. George

Heathfield Brass Band, August 1922.
(Back Row, L–R) Bill Jarvis, Tom Upfield, Edward Bean, Frank Upfield, Arch Knapp, Jack Mitchell, Lleyland Upfield, Fred Mitchell, Charlie Woodgate, Les Taylor.
(Middle Row, L–R) C. Adams, Bob Roberts, George Mepham Snr., Charles Pettitt, Nelson Harriett, Sam Upfield, Jim Paine.
(Front Row, L–R) Arthur Relf, Mrs. T. Upfield, Horace Mepham.
Photograph by Bray of Heathfield.

Mepham Jnr. (speaking in 1981) claims the uniform was lost when the old Band broke apart; however, we know that the new Band was in possession of eighteen very worn uniforms at this time. Gordon Neve, who joined the Band in 1926 (also speaking in 1981), believes that the uniforms did indeed come from the old Band. In December 1929, the Band – now with twenty-five playing members – made it known that its carolling efforts would aim to redress this unsatisfactory situation. "The committee are anxious to fit the remaining seven members with uniform, and solicit the generous support of the public," reports the Sussex Express.[7]

The looming economic depression dictated that, unlike in 1924, fundraising would be slow. By 1930, the Band was forced to abandon its tattered uniforms altogether, performing and competing in "civvies"; it is immortalized on one postcard *sans* caps and wearing an ill-matching array of lounge suits and ties (see page 99)! Another carolling season would come and go and still sufficient funds had not been forthcoming. By February 1931, the Band's committee would ask members to make up the difference by way of a loan, and Messrs. Beevers and the Army and Navy Supply Stores were approached for patterns and quotes.[8] Players collectively advanced a total of 15 guineas (over £1,000 today), and the new uniforms could finally be purchased in the Spring of 1931, at a cost of almost £98 (about £6,800 today).[9] It would take the remainder of the year, and a further Christmas appeal, to clear the deficit. "The members devote many hours during both Summer and Winter months for practice, and they also give their services unstintingly," writes the Sussex Express. "It seems rather hard on the men that they should have to advance money to pay for their uniforms."[10]

The new jackets would represent a move away from the militaristic style, towards a more familiar brass band look that we might consider "traditional" today. They had splashes of red and blue, stiff arms and collars, elaborate gold braiding on the shoulders, and brass buttons on each cuff and down the front and back. Wide-brimmed caps with badges were reintroduced, complemented by the usual dark trousers and shoes. Cyril Leeves (speaking in 1981) recalls how his father would not let him leave the house for engagements until he had brushed his uniform clean and polished all the buttons. He also remembers looking so smart that he once caught the eye of the daughter of the *Barley Mow*'s landlord, who immediately offered him a pint! The new uniform was given its first outing in Cross-in-Hand, at the

Easter Monday Humble-Crofts Cup Final between Heathfield United and Uckfield.[11] The Band can be seen pictured in this uniform just one week before the outbreak of the Second World War (see page 126); several members wear medals but they are not, as one might imagine, for services to King and Country… they are, in fact, medals commemorating musical achievements at brass band contests!

During the Second World War, the Air Training Corps introduced their own uniform to the Band (see *1940s World War II: The Boys from the ATC*). It was not, therefore, until 1949 that replacement uniforms would be required. However, the cheapest options were priced at about £10 each (£360 today), and there was now also a need to source some larger-sized jackets. As a result, the Band seems once again to have made do whilst it was raising the necessary funds. By early 1953, it would finally own a set of replacement uniforms, an acceptable second-hand solution having been found. These were very dark blue, with gold and red belts and a red stripe down each trouser leg (see overleaf). Gordon Neve describes the fabric as "so thick it nearly stood up!" Bert Thompson (speaking in 1981) believes they were re-conditioned busmen's uniforms, but they might possibly have been ex-police garb, as the Band became informally dubbed *The Police Band* for a time (would that in fact make it a copper band?!).

But these uniforms were only a temporary measure, as the Band was once again expanding. By early 1955 it had twenty-nine playing members. However, despite the clear need to purchase new uniforms, no further progress would be made until October 1956, when a dedicated fundraising committee was finally established. A thermometer-target was installed on the bandroom wall, prices and patterns were sought, and the cost of a complete set estimated at between £300–400 (roughly £7,600–£10,200 today). Fundraising, this time in association with the newly-established Heathfield Band Supporters' Club, would take three years to complete.

Things became so desperate that bandmaster Bert Wise proposed taking out a mortgage on the bandroom. However, the Supporters' Club would come to the rescue, promising to donate £200 (about £4,750 today) towards the cost. The new uniforms were finally purchased in 1959. Again, they would be dark blue, with the addition of very light blue lapels, and had thick silver braiding on the shoulders and silver buttons down the front. They were

The "Police Band," Civic Way, near the Assembly Hall, Tunbridge Wells, ca. 1953–57.
Bandmaster Bert Wise.
Photograph from www.ibew.org.uk/vbbp-ukh.html

complemented with peaked, badged caps, straight black ties and black trousers. "They were really thick but smart," says bandmember Lesley Dann (née Bray). "Good for the cold bonfire parades but sweltering in the Summer!" Gordon Neve adds: "Bandsmen didn't like [the] coloured uniforms as they needed cleaning!" The jackets were of such high quality that they continued to be used long after they were retired as the Band's primary uniform, becoming the attire of choice for bonfire parades until the 1980s.

By November 1963, the Band's membership had dropped significantly, leading Uckfield Band to request some of its surplus uniforms for their learners to wear. This was duly agreed, but would lead to a uniform shortage a few years later when new members were to arrive on the scene. Several new jackets were purchased over the following few years, but only whenever the Band became desperate. In the late 1960s, these uniforms were augmented slightly, with the introduction of air hostess-style hats for female members. These were worn for a while, but interest would quickly fade.

As the 1970s dawned, there was a desire to revamp the Band's appearance. "They wanted to update and be more modern," says Lesley Dann. "I think that it was difficult and expensive to replace the others, and many were getting old, but I also seem to recall they wanted something thinner and cooler." Once again, the significant expense involved meant that this would be another long-term project. By 1974, the Band had banked over £700 (about £7,460 today) and it felt ready to proceed. Patterns and quotes were obtained, a short-list drawn up, and a ballot of possible styles put to members. The outcome was the purchase, in 1975, of the red jackets that we associate with the Band today. "They were plain, they removed all the braid, absolutely nothing on the cuffs; I don't think they even had brass buttons," says Peter Cornford. "It was like a dinner jacket, really, but red with black lapels. They were light to wear, too." The new jacket was complemented with a black skirt or trousers, a white shirt, and black bow-tie, and was very much a "concert-style" uniform, more suited to the variety of engagements that the Band was now undertaking (see image overleaf).

Consideration was also given to having distinct male and female versions; however, it was ultimately decided that a single design would be more cost-effective and give added flexibility for outfitting guest players and newcomers. There was, however, no question of females being allowed to wear trousers, and a debate would even rage regarding the acceptable colour of ladies' tights. "There were quite heated discussions," remembers Peter Cornford. "There was general agreement that they should not be brown(ish). It was at this time that I learned the expression 'nearly black' as a tights colour! There were also periodic grumbles from some of the lady members that they should not have to wear tights at all on hot Summer engagements." Hats were to have been included but the additional cost – £104 (or about £1,100 today) – meant that the idea was ultimately dropped.

The signature red uniform persists to this day, albeit with occasional minor pattern changes, such as the reintroduction of silver piping to the shoulders and cuffs from the end of the 1980s.

By December 2003, membership was growing once again and there were just not enough uniforms for everyone. "I had cornets coming out of my ears and not enough jackets to fit," recalls Frankie Lulham.[12] In 2006, a new set of thirty jackets (costing around £200 each), waistcoats and bowties were purchased and, thanks to a donation from Heathfield and District Lions, the training band would also receive its own uniform, comprising black-fronted/red-backed waistcoats.

Whilst continuing to honour its past, at no point has the Band allowed itself to become bogged down by tradition. "We must try to be fun and attractive to everybody," says Keith Pursglove. "It doesn't have to be stuffy, collar and tie." In line with this ethos, in 2007 a Band crest and logo was created, by principal cornet player Adam Kearley, and crested straight ties adopted for most engagements. In August 2009, crested polo shirts and fleeces were introduced for bonfire parades.

It has also become more acceptable to remove jackets (and, occasionally, even bowties) on especially hot days. This trend would foster desire for a bespoke

Assembly Hall, Tunbridge Wells, November 1975.
(Back Row, L–R) Jack King, Ted Lee, Trevor Rood, Dave Sutton, Roy Elphick, Bert Thompson, .
(Middle Row, L–R) Albert French, Ben Guile, Cyril Leeves, Dennis Guile, Julie Seymour, Dave Dunk, ?, ?Phil Dickenson.
(Front Row, L–R) Sue Guile, Sue Sutton, Wendy Guile, Tom Kelly (bandmaster), Lesley Bray, Gerald Dann, Bob Mayston, Bob Lee.
Photograph supplied by Kent & Sussex Courier/Tunbridge Wells Advertiser.

Summer uniform, which finally came to fruition in 2019 with the introduction of black polo shirts. The previous attempt a year earlier had not been so well-received. "Our current idea is to have red polo shirts along with black shorts and this would be what we'd wear to most of our Summer fête jobs," writes the Band secretary to players. "Does anybody already have black shorts which they think would be ideal? Can you wear them to Band next week?"[13] The response was lukewarm, prompting bass trombonist, Richard Ayres, to comment: "The mystery that exists under people's long trousers is rightly understood by the wearer alone, and is generally healthily not wondered at by others. Let's retain the mystery of nice warm longans!"

---

[1] Sussex Express, 10th January 1913

[2] MD Report, Frankie Lulham, 8th August 2002

[3] Sussex Express, 5th December 1903

[4] Sussex Express, 3rd August 1907

[5] Sussex Express, 20th August 1909

[6] Minutes, 13th April 1929

[7] Sussex Express, 13th December 1929

[8] Minutes, 2nd February 1931

[9] Accounts, 1931

[10] Sussex Express, 4th December 1931

[11] Sussex Express, 3rd April 1931

[12] Press Release, Frankie Lulham, ca. 15th December 2003; MD Report, Frankie Lulham, 21st December 2003

[13] Correspondence, Band Secretary to Bandmembers, 6th July 2018

MEMBERS of NOTE...

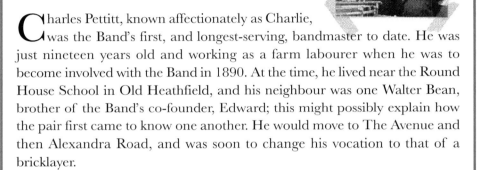

Charles "Charlie" Pettitt
bandmaster & cornet,
ca. 1890–1935.

Charles Pettitt, known affectionately as Charlie, was the Band's first, and longest-serving, bandmaster to date. He was just nineteen years old and working as a farm labourer when he was to become involved with the Band in 1890. At the time, he lived near the Round House School in Old Heathfield, and his neighbour was one Walter Bean, brother of the Band's co-founder, Edward; this might possibly explain how the pair first came to know one another. He would move to The Avenue and then Alexandra Road, and was soon to change his vocation to that of a bricklayer.

Charlie was a pleasant, gentle man, and an excellent bandsman. According to a Heathfield Band contemporary, Jack Mitchell (speaking in 1981), he was the best cornet player the Band has ever seen, and probably the finest all round musician; he would sometimes conduct and play cornet solos at the same time. He also had a great sense of fun; in 1912, he was to come third in a bandmembers' race, behind Francis Greenaway and Jessie Oliver, at the annual Framfield Flower Show.[1]

During the Great War, Charlie was one of a handful of bandmembers who would be left behind, and he was to spent the duration on munitions work. He would later lead the Band not only to a full recovery, but also to success on the contesting scene. When the original Band was to collapse in 1928, Charlie would briefly step away as its frontman. However, he was soon to become one of the original four trustees with the *new* Heathfield Silver Band.[2]

In early 1930, the Band was to persuade him to return as bandmaster, and he would proudly conduct their winning performance in the fourth section of the Tunbridge Wells Contest that May.[3] At the 1932 contest, he would be honoured to carry the wreath in the massed bands parade to the War Memorial.[4]

Contemporary bandmembers have fond memories of their time under Charlie's leadership, and clearly shared a happy and fruitful relationship with him. However, by 1934, forty-four years after he first took up the baton with the Band, his health was beginning to wane. He would sadly be forced to resign as bandmaster, although he would continue to work as a bricklayer, until the Second World War was to necessitate a move to Carlisle for bomb disposal duties. Despite this, Charlie would maintain a connection with the Band until his death in 1943.

---

[1] Sussex Express, 23rd August 1912

[2] Minutes, 15th May 1929

[3] Sussex Express, 9th May 1930; Minutes, 28th August 1930

[4] Sussex Express, 13th May 1932

1900s Now is the Time for Marching

Heathfield Brass Band, ca. 1900.
(Back Row, L–R) William Harmer, Jim Paine, Mr. Sinden, Charles Pettitt,
Herbert Harmer, Mr. Dinnage, Fred Stephens.
(Front Row, L–R) Edward Bean, Mr. Curtis, Sam Gurr, Ben Haffenden,
John Mitchell, Bob Roberts.
Photograph by A.E. Stickells, Cranbrook.

The new century dawned with a sense of hope in the air. Real social improvements had been achieved during the long reign of Queen Victoria, and the community of Heathfield was expanding rapidly. The Heathfield Band was now firmly integrated into the social scene, appearing at all manner of public events, from charity fundraisers and sporting occasions, to church services and military parades. As the decade progressed, its association with the Volunteers was to come to an end, but the Band's growing confidence would lead it to become a self-sufficient community band, closer in character to the one we know today.

Brass bands were very much in the public eye in 1900, at least among the working classes, bridging as they did the social divide between high art and popular music.[1] The arrival of *"mechanical music,"* in the form of gramophone and phonograph recordings, would further erode that gap, giving practically everyone access to a wider range of musical repertoire. In addition, the brass band contest at Crystal Palace (which originally ran for just four consecutive years during the 1860s), would be successfully revived, now offering a one thousand guinea first prize (about £132,000 today) and further popularising the movement.[2]

Demand for brass entertainment therefore continued to grow. In Heathfield, as more shops and local amenities appeared on the scene, so too would the possibilities for musical performance and rehearsal. The Union Church was erected around 1900, as was the Agricultural Hall in the High Street (now *Trading4U* but originally used by Natural Gas Fields of England following a discovery of local gas in 1895). In addition, the Recreation Hall in Station Road (now State Hall) would open towards the end of the decade, providing townsfolk with a cornucopia of social entertainments, including dances, theatre, and even roller skating.[3]

Heathfield Band continued to support the Artillery Volunteers (until the latter were absorbed into the territorials in 1909), heading church parades from the Station Road to All Saints Parish Church, Old Heathfield, and back again, and also lending its support to prizegiving concerts at the Drill Hall. It would sometimes even be referred to as *Heathfield Volunteer Brass Band*. However, the official association was to end in the Summer of 1903.

The exact reasons for the split are lost in the depths of time, but it seems likely that the demands of both military and community functions, along with vocational and family commitments, were just too much for amateur bandmembers to cope with. We know, for example, that founding member John Mitchell was reluctant to go to training camp when his wife was pregnant with their son Jack. Nevertheless, the Band continued to support those who were serving their country. In 1901, for example, it hastily put together an impromptu homecoming celebration for one Imperial Yeoman returning from Africa. The Band "paraded at Cade-street, and accompanied by a large crowd marched to Park House, where appropriate airs were discoursed."[4]

But the split from the Volunteers would not be without its consequences. For one thing, the Band would once again have to find and rent its own rehearsal room. It has been suggested that it briefly moved into a building in Alexandra

Road, but the evidence for this is limited. We know with more certainty that it was soon to return to the Drill Hall at Cade Street, and here it would remain until about 1928 (see *Room for Improvement: The Story of the Bandroom)*. Another challenge was the sourcing of uniforms, which would no longer be provided by the Volunteers.

The Band needed to attract funding, and the immediate solution was to stage a series of benefit concerts, a tradition which persists to this day. The first such concert was held at the Cade Street Drill Hall in December 1903, when the Band more than proved its worth, tackling music such as contemporary test piece, *Crown of Victory,* and *My Colleen*, which the crowd so enjoyed that they immediately demanded an encore.[5]

Another fundraiser was to take place at Cade Street in February 1906, when an even more varied programme – including cornet solos by Charles Pettitt and trombone features by Edward Bean – would be attempted.[6] Also that month, the Band performed "a first rate programme of dance music" for a fundraising ball at the new Drill Hall in Station Road.[7] This event was such a success that dancing would continue until 2.30am! There were also similar fundraising efforts in early 1908.[8] Such concerts would often take place on Tuesday evenings, as many businesses had half-day closing on Wednesdays, no-doubt to the relief of workers who had been partying late into the night!

Arguably the greatest barrier to the wider acceptance of brass bands was class snobbery. The upper echelons of society generally considered making and listening to brass music an *improving activity*, something to educate the unwashed masses and keep them from the ills of intemperance and other vices.[9] Brass bands were often involved with church activities, which could only serve to encourage the music-loving working classes towards a purer existence. However, the coronation of King Edward VII in 1902 (during which the Band would head local community celebrations) finally heralded the beginnings of social change. Kings Cross Band and Besses o'the Barn were commanded to play at Buckingham Palace and, having discovered the King's love of brass music, high society soon began attending open-air concerts and inviting brass bands to private functions.[10] Heathfield Band was to suddenly find itself in great demand at agricultural and flower shows, sports events, garden parties, fêtes, and other social occasions, and its range of repertoire would necessarily have to expand to suit the growing variety of venues.

Perhaps the biggest social phenomenon was the rapid growth of cottage gardening and flower shows which, according to Sussex Express, were a way of "brightening the lives of those who live and work in the country villages [...], encouraging rural hobbies and giving the people a greater interest in their everyday lives."[11] Naturally, the Band was a regular attraction at such events, alongside poultry shows, sports, and even horse and motor gymkhanas. Initially, such occasions were held on Wednesday afternoons to take advantage of half-day closing, but would soon switch to Bank Holidays to capitalise on the custom brought by visiting holidaymakers. Heathfield Band went down a storm at the 1902 Framfield Show and, at its conclusion, were given "hearty cheers" by the adoring public.[12] It would play several afternoon sets at the 1909 East Hoathly Show and, according to twelve year-old Ivy Keel: "In the evening there was dancing on the cricket pitch, while the Band played heartily."[13] However, the pinnacle of such events was arguably Heathfield Agricultural Show, now hosted by William Cleverley Alexander at Heathfield Park, during which the Band could be seen playing beside the Gibraltar Tower: selections by day and dance music in the evenings.[14]

From its very beginnings, Heathfield Band was a strong supporter of charitable events, and in the early 1900s hospital parades would emerge on the scene (see *Earning Our Beds: Sussex Hospital Parades*). These were a combined initiative of local churches and Friendly Societies, intended to help people to help themselves, by raising funds for hospitals before the existence of a National Health Service. Heathfield Hospital Parade normally raised money for the *Princess Alice Hospital* at Eastbourne. The marches were long, hard work, but the Band duly played its part, undertaking several such parades each year.

Whilst brass bands often worked in association with churches, they were not always embraced by them. The growth of Sabbatarian ideology would see clergy from several denominations roundly condemn the increasingly popular trend for Sunday afternoon park concerts, asserting that such entertainment actively competed against the sacred and sober efforts of the Church on the

Lord's Day.[15] *The British Bandsman* believed that it was nonsense to claim that only church music could be morally or spiritually beneficial.[16] In 1907, the editor Herbert Whitely would be moved to write: "How can it prevent people going to church on a Sunday when according to statistics published by the Church authorities, only FIFTEEN out of EVERY THOUSAND go to church on a Sunday anyway?"[17]

The Sabbatarian debate was to rage on and off for decades, and it is true to say that the outlook of Heathfield folk remained somewhat more traditional than the more cosmopolitan city-dwellers. During speeches at Hadlow Down Club Day in 1907 (for which Heathfield Band naturally provided the music), some would feel compelled to declare that society was going in the wrong direction, with "religious indifference" and "Sunday pleasures" now holding sway.[18] Such parochial views are possibly the reason that the Band did not perform Sunday concerts until the 1920s, by which time its own committee was more forward-thinking in their approach.

Contemporary engagements very much reflected the growth of leisure time within the community. The Band was in especially high demand for club fêtes, annual all-day affairs held by Friendly Associations and Benefit Societies (who insured their members against illness and unemployment, offered pensions, and even covered the costs of their funerals). In fact, such was the demand for its services that the Gibraltar Arms Slate Club would have to make do with rather distant "second-hand" music at its 1906 fête: the Band was already committed to perform at a nearby flower show for the Horticultural Society.[19] At a planning meeting for another club fête, the Cross-in-Hand Foresters were presented with the choice of four possible bands: Blackboys, Battle, Tunbridge Wells or Heathfield. According to the Sussex Express, their preference reflects the high regard with which Heathfield Band was held at the time: "Heathfield Volunteer Brass Band was selected and a compliment was paid to bandmaster Pettitt for the excellent way in which he had catered for the musical programme on previous feast days."[20]

The Band played far and wide for club fêtes, from Upper Dicker to Chiddingly, Cross-in-Hand to Hadlow Down. Such gigs were the particular favourites of many bandmembers. In addition to enjoying a free meal and a fun, sociable day out, each player would earn 5 shillings for attending. This was double the daily farm labourer's wage at the turn of the century, and was to prove a great boon to bandmembers when economic depression took hold in 1905. Jack Mitchell, the son of founding member John, remembers departing early for such events in Edward Bean's horse-drawn vans, the Band dropping him at school *en route*. Club fêtes usually began with a parade to the Parish Church for a suitably topical sermon. The entourage would then enjoy a club feast, often held in a large marquee in a convenient field, after which the Band would perform various musical selections. In the evening, there were outdoor sports and amusements, and the Band would play waltzes and other dance music. One such fête is reported thus: "The Heathfield Brass Band, under Mr. C.E. Pettitt, played for dancing and a goodly number of people tripped the light fantastic toe on the green sward until a late hour."[21]

The Band was also in demand for a variety of other engagements. For one day in August 1902, it entertained spectators attending Heathfield Cricket Week and, in June 1905, it enlivened the sports day at Mayfield Xaverian College.[22] In 1904, Mr. Langdale of Heathfield House held a rearing supper at the *Star Inn*, for the contractors who had been renovating his home. Together, the company celebrated the completion of the works with tobacco, cigars, nuts and seasonal fruits whilst "the Heathfield Brass Band added greatly to the evening's enjoyment."[23] Other engagements would include the opening of a new club room at the *Cross-in-Hand Hotel*,[24] a benefit concert for Heathfield United Football Club,[25] and Heathfield Equitables Juniors' Treat (a fun day for the children) on the Heathfield Tower Cricket Ground.[26]

The Band's contribution to social life cannot be understated. In 1908 it played for a New Year's Ball at the Heathfield Agricultural Hall, where dancing was to continue until 3am![27] The following Easter, it gave a successful "Cinderella" at the Cade Street Drill Hall.[28] By November 1909, the Recreation Hall (now State Hall) was finally complete. The Band would launch its grand opening in style, with performances of *The Regiment Comes* and, appropriately, *Jubilation*.[29] The decade drew to a close on New Year's Eve 1909, as several hundred people crowded into the Recreation Hall to enjoy a roller skating carnival and fancy dress ball. At midnight, attendees joined hands to sing *Auld Lang Syne*, with the accompaniment of their town band, of course.

For the people of Heathfield, the new century had undoubtedly brought a higher standard of living and greater opportunities for social activities. The community was growing, local industry was productive, and the Heathfield Band thrived. The sheer demand for its services is conclusive evidence, if any were needed, of the Band's entertainment potential and musical capability. Above all else, its diverse activities provide solid proof that it had really arrived, and could function successfully as an autonomous community institution. However, the ensuing years would test its resilience to the very limits.

---

[1] Herbert, T., 2000. *The British Brass Band: A Musical and Social History*. Oxford: Oxford University Press: 5

[2] ibid: 7; Hailstone, A., 1987. *The British Bandsman Centenary Book*. Baldock: Egon

[3] Foord, F., 1982. *The Development Of The Tilsmore Area Of Waldron Parish From 1874*. Heathfield: F. Foord

[4] Sussex Express, 4th February 1901

[5] Sussex Express, 5th December 1903

[6] Sussex Express, 3rd February 1906

[7] Sussex Express, 24 February 1906

[8] Sussex Express, 8th February 1908 & 11th April 1908

[9] Herbert, T., 2000

[10] Hailstone, A., 1987

[11] Sussex Express, 8th September 1906

[12] Sussex Express, 19 August 1902

[13] Sussex Express, 17 September 1909

[14] Pryce, R., 1996. *Heathfield Park: A Private Estate and a Wealden Town*. Heathfield: Roy Pryce: 129–30

[15] Hailstone, A., 1987: 60

[16] ibid

[17] ibid: 77

[18] Sussex Express, 15th June 1907

[19] Sussex Express, 11th August 1906

[20] Sussex Express, 1st April 1902

[21] Sussex Express, 11th June 1909

[22] Sussex Express, 16th August 1902; Kent & Sussex Courier, 30th June 1905

[23] Sussex Express, 31st December 1904

[24] Sussex Express, 21st November 1903

[25] Sussex Express, 20th April 1907

[26] Sussex Express, 27th August 1909

[27] Sussex Express, 8th January 1909

[28] Sussex Express, 16th April 1909

[29] Kent & Sussex Courier, 5th November 1909

MEMBERS of NOTE...

George Mepham Snr.
cornet, euphonium & trombone,
1902–35, 1938–40.

George Mepham Snr. was an extraordinarily versatile musician and a dedicated brass bander. He was born in 1880 and would begin making music after receiving a mouth organ for his birthday one year; before long, the young lad was busking for pennies around Bodle Street village. He would soon begin experimenting with other instruments, such as improvised drums, flutes and penny whistles, and by the age of sixteen he was taking cornet lessons.

Almost immediately, George was to become one of the founding members of Warbleton Brass Band. "We were a pretty rough lot of musicians in those days," he would later recall, "but we improved slowly thanks to studying our tutor books, and picking up tips from some of the old 'uns!" By 1900, George had also joined Herstmonceux Band.

George worked as a gardener, and in 1902 his work was to take him to Heathfield, where he would naturally join the town band, playing euphonium and later trombone. He was to marry and have children, and would serve in France and Belgium during the Great War as part of the 2nd Royal Fusiliers, for whom he was duty bugler and stand-in flautist. He would proudly play with the 29th Divisional Band during a visit from King George V, for a grand march-past of the regiments.

Following the war, George would return to Heathfield Band, soon to be followed by his sons; George Jnr. would play euphonium (from 1919) whilst Horace would play the cornet (from 1922). There was a short break from the Band during the Thirties when the family moved briefly to Eastbourne and, whilst there, George Snr. would play for the Artillery Band. In 1938, they were to return to Heathfield and its Band, and George would remain an active member throughout the Second World War. Indeed, he was one of the few bandsmen who would be fortunate enough to do so, as he was now serving his country as a part of the Home Guard.

George would retire to Hailsham in 1946, and upon leaving the Band he was proudly made a life member. He would continue to make music, however, first with Hailsham Brass Band and later with Hailsham Orchestra (as a violinist). When interviewed in 1969, George was to recall fond banding memories of trips round the countryside in horse-drawn vans, playing at church fêtes and club festivals, contesting with the Band at Tunbridge Wells, and the time he won a silver medal for his euphonium solo. "We really enjoyed ourselves," he said. "Almost every village in the county had its own band of one sort or another, and we were proud of our playing."

This tribute is based upon a 1969 local newspaper article, source unknown.

Interlude Earning Our Beds: Sussex Hospital Parades

Arguably the Band's most important engagements during its early years would be the annual hospital parades, which were held in almost every large parish in the Sussex High Weald, becoming popular at the beginning of the twentieth century. Heathfield Hospital Parade would collect for Eastbourne's Princess Alice Hospital, whilst others contributed to the League of Mercy, Tunbridge Wells Hospital, and Sussex Hospital, among others. Thus, as communities realised the value of working together for the benefit of their hospitals, the Band would find itself marching at Hadlow Down, Burwash, Warbleton, Waldron, Mayfield, and Brightling & Dallington. In 1931, it even ventured as far as Eastbourne, marching through the town to take part in an Amalgamated Societies' open-air service at the Recreation Ground in Seaside.[1]

Each parade was a heavy undertaking and, according to bandmember, George Mepham Jnr. (interviewed in 1981), they were "sweat and toil in the Summer." Gordon Neve (also speaking in 1981) agrees: "Bandsmen used to earn their hospital beds," he says. The processions were headed by members of Friendly Societies, carrying their colourful banners high and collecting donations in the streets. The entourage would begin by visiting the houses of affluent residents, before attending a thanksgiving service at the Parish Church. Indeed, the phenomenal support given to hospital parades by the community was, for many, a moral duty. Speaking at Hadlow Down Hospital

Parade in 1907, the Vicar proclaimed that "their work that day had been no mere holiday or parade, but holy work done on a holy day."[2]

"The villagers all marched along with the bands, them who liked a bit of music," recalls Bert Thompson (interviewed in 1981), who took part in countless hospital parades during the Twenties and Thirties. "There weren't other entertainments then like there is now. As soon as you strike up a march, a lot of people get carried away don't they? They wave their arms… There used to be a lot of that. Then we used to have a feast at the end." Bert continues: "The old Foresters and the Equitables, they all used to have a hand in. They used to collect quite a lot of money, you know. All that used to go to the hospitals, every penny of it. The men used to run about with collecting boxes and there was a man – Mr. Barton his name was, came from Waldron – he'd got a dog with him with a money box strapped on its back. He used to lead it round. It was just the kiddies delight to get a penny off their father to put in the dog's box." In the days prior to Mr. Barton, local fireman Hayward would make similar collections with his own celebrity dog, *Hospital Jack*. One can't help but feel a little sorry for the dogs, the boxes becoming heavier and heavier as each parade advanced. Nevertheless, the combined efforts of human and beast produced considerable results.

Heathfield Hospital Parade was a complicated affair, with several processions led by different bands. In 1905, for example, there were four: Heathfield, Warbleton, Black Boys and Burwash. Each band commenced from a different location around the parish, before marching to the railway station to combine forces. From there, they marched to Hailsham Road and Sandy Cross, to All Saints Parish Church, and thence to Punnetts Town and back to the *Crown Hotel*, a circuit of nearly seven miles. Here, the bands performed together for the gathering crowds.[3] Hadlow Down Hospital Parade was even longer, at nearly twelve miles from start to finish. "They were long marches, but I used to enjoy them," says Bert Thompson. "Used to make you a bit tired, but we never used to care nothing about it. There was always someone who had something funny to say when you weren't blowing, it shortened the journey."

There was never a shortage of refreshments to make the long marches more tolerable. Many would be alcoholic, such as cider, beer and even home-made bee wine, which participants carried with them in jars. Bert has an amusing memory of one Waldron Hospital Parade: "We went in the *Star Inn* in

Waldron and had a bit of tea in there before we marched back to Cross-in-Hand. They wanted us to give them a tune in there, you see. But the roof being low pitched, they had oil lamps hanging down, and directly we started all the lamps went out. The flame went right up through the globe and we were in darkness. It was the vibration of the instruments, you see!"

Warbleton Hospital Parade was a staggering sixteen miles long and would have presented quite a challenge to bandmembers who had to simultaneously march and play their instruments. "We wanted some tea at the end of that," says Bert. Heathfield Band would return with Warbleton Band to the latter's rehearsal hut for refreshments, and then the pair would mass together to play on Rushlake Green. "We were about to play *La Traviata*," remembers Bert. "Arch Knapp – he was the comedian of the Band – he was the only person with the word 'DIM' written in his music, all the other bandsmen hadn't got it, you see. Well, Charlie [Pettitt, bandmaster] had got his stick up, and Arch suddenly shouted, 'Charlie! Charlie! What about my DIM?!' Everybody collapsed… we couldn't play!" To return the hospitality, Heathfield Band's chairman (and, later, its president) F. Howard Martin would host both bands at his home, *Spring Lodge*, following the Heathfield Hospital Parade. Here, the bands would enjoy tea and then stage a concert together.

In 1921, it was proposed that a separate parade be introduced to the Waldron Parish, whose population had grown quite considerably.[4] This was introduced the following year, and Heathfield Hospital Parade was also expanded from the standard two processions to three, now headed by Heathfield Band, Warbleton Brass & Reed Band, and Mayfield Brass Band. These would merge together and process to Heathfield Park Cricket Ground, whereupon a united service was held. From there, the company paraded to the new War Memorial at Cade Street where, to the embarrassment of all concerned, it was discovered that none of them had brought along music for the *Dead March*![5]

By 1930, hopes were being pinned on the prospect of "a medical service to which every human being in the land should have access" – a National Health Service.[6] Such a system of universal health care would be funded by taxation and free to everyone at the point of use, but it was to take another eighteen years to implement, no doubt in part delayed by the Second World War. In the meantime, hospital parades would continue to raise huge sums with the support of local bands. However, from the 1930s they began to amalgamate with local carnivals to offer a broader appeal, and would fade completely as the country headed to war. When day-to-day life started to return more than a decade later, communities would primarily focus their attention on rebuilding infrastructure and the economy, trusting the state to implement a suitable healthcare solution. With the ultimate realisation of a National Health Service, Sussex hospital parades were destined to become just another happy memory of a bygone age.

---

[1] Eastbourne Gazette, 26th August 1931

[2] Sussex Express, 3rd August 1907

[3] Sussex Express, 9th September 1905

[4] Sussex Express, 23rd September 1921

[5] Kent & Sussex Courier, 1st September 1922; Sussex Express, 1st September 1922

[6] Sussex Express, 1st August 1930

Jack Mitchell
cornet & horn, 1914–1983,
librarian, 1936–8,
deputy bandmaster, 1930–7 & 1940–57.

by Peter Cornford

Jack Mitchell is, to date, the Band's longest-serving member. He played his first engagement in July 1914, the day after war was declared, and would finally retire in 1983. He was descended from good brass banding stock, as his father, John, and uncle, William, were both founding members of the original Heathfield Band.

As a boy, Jack and his father were to spend Sunday mornings practicing in their wood shed, and together they would walk the two miles to and from rehearsals at Cade Street. Jack would go on to play a significant role in the Band, as its principal cornet during the inter-war years, as librarian in the 1930s, and as a semi-permanent committee member over the ensuing decades.

I first knew Jack when he was 75 and on the final lap of his long banding career. His playing abilities had faded by then, but his enthusiasm for everything to do with the Band was to remain undimmed. At rehearsals, he would frequently deputise as conductor, and was one of the first to help Mostyn Cornford in renovating the bandroom, despite the fact that Jack was, by then, aged about 80.

Jack lived with his sister just a few doors down from the bandroom. He was a small man, introverted, very serious, and he rarely smiled. He always struck me as someone straight out of the mould of the long nonconformist heritage of the Heathfield-Warbleton area, staunch supporters of the Strict Baptist and other godly established-church-rejecting tradesmen. These were men and women who were to lead unremarkable lives insofar as the national picture was concerned, but who locally would have been influential characters.

I doubt that Jack touched a drop of alcohol all his life; he and his father, John, were committed teetotallers. He would be very vocal about this and was forever berating Bob Lee, his great nephew trombonist, about drinking to excess. "Forsake the drink and fear the Lord," Jack would say to Bob, to which I remember Bob once retorting: "I would rather die happy than be a miserable old fool like you!"

Jack was to take his banding as seriously as he took his religion. From his scrupulous appearance at engagements to his punctuality for band practice and impeccable manners whilst in the bandroom, Jack would command admiration and respect. He was very encouraging to me as a young player, as I worked my way from 3rd cornet towards the principal cornet seat. He and I share a common ancestor, so he was an interesting source of anecdotes about my family history and particularly its nonconformity.

In Jack's final years, he and I would sometimes provide Sunday afternoon musical entertainment at Heffle Court old people's home. He used to say very earnestly that it was important to encourage the people in the home to sing hymns. We were an incongruous duo; Jack in his eighties, scraping atrociously at his old cello, and me, a lanky teenager doing my best on the home's battered piano. Jack would warble the tune as we played. The old folks would sit silently or sleep through the sessions in the main, but Jack got a lot out of it.

Jack's memories form an important part of this book, especially concerning the early years of the Band. As I interviewed him in the early Eighties, it struck me that I was, by means of Jack's reminiscences of his father and uncle, experiencing almost first-hand the dawn of its creation and the Band's fledgling years.

1910s The Great War

As the 1910s began, things looked extremely positive for the town: the economy was thriving and many residents had arrived at an acceptable work-life balance. The Band would contribute to and share in this success, providing great cheer and entertainment to the masses. Engagements were varied, spanning a range of flower shows and hospital parades, and expanding to include school sports days, ladies' entertainments, and other *ad hoc* appearances. The coronation of King George V in 1911 would increase demand for the Band's services still further. However, a dramatic and devastating change of fortunes lay just around the corner. During the Great War, a quarter of Heathfield Band's members would die or be killed, and it was even suspended for two years, very nearly collapsing altogether.

The Band had begun the decade with a successful New Year's Eve roller skating carnival and it would appear at similar events over the ensuing months. Indeed, the nationwide craze was so popular that the floor of Heathfield's new Recreation Hall ("one of the finest Rinks in the South"[1]) had been specially constructed from maple to accommodate it. Thrice-weekly skating evenings were held there[2] and skating carnivals typically drew about a hundred participants and five hundred spectators.[3] The carnivals hosted fancy dress competitions and activities such as egg & spoon and

A 1910 Sussex Express Advertisement

wheelbarrow races, and musical chairs, whilst music was provided by Heathfield Band.[4] Hailstone suggests that the main reason brass bands were engaged for such events is because their music was loud enough to cover the collective din of the roller skates![5]

1910 was perhaps the most productive year in the Band's short history, a culmination of the founders' hard work and proof that it was now very much embedded as a local institution. The Band was even to dip its toes briefly into the world of theatre. *Caste*, a three-act comedy drama examining social class-structures, was enjoying something of a revival at the time, and would no doubt have proven especially interesting to the folk of Heathfield. The play, by Thomas William Robertson, was staged at the Heathfield Recreation Hall in January 1910, with musical accompaniment by the town band.[6]

Also in 1910, "a thoroughly enjoyable time was spent in Tottingworth Park, where sweet music was discoursed by the Heathfield Brass Band."[7] The event in question was the annual Ladies' Entertainment for Mothers of the Ecclesiastical Parish of Burwash Weald. In early August, the Band performed for an evening dance at Heathfield Tower Cricket Ground, to conclude the Junior Equitables' Annual Treat.[8] Its community outreach was further advanced at the Mayfield Hospital Parade: "For about an hour after the evening church service the Heathfield Band played selections of sacred music in the High-street by the fountain, and further collections were made for the same good cause."[9]

One activity which enjoyed something of a boon was competitive sports, and the town band would support such events at every opportunity. Sports played an important part in almost every social occasion, and the community embraced them with enthusiasm and good humour, the games becoming progressively sillier with each subsequent event. At the Framfield Flower Show in 1911, for example, there was a 200 yards flat race for men with umbrellas (dressed in women's skirts and hats), and a 150 yard race for bandmembers carrying their instruments (a risk to which no self-respecting musician would subject their prized instrument today).[10] Eccentric races were also part of the annual sports days at the Mayfield Xaverian College (a distinguished boys' school) which the Band would attend in 1910 and 1914.[11]

Town bands were in great demand in June 1911, as the country collectively celebrated the coronation of King George V. However, the loyalty of Heathfield Band was torn between two parishes: Heathfield Parish would ultimately secure its services for the day, causing some ill feelings from the parish of Waldron .[12] The occasion would commence with a jubilant peal of the bells at All Saints Church, followed by a programme of athletic sports and a public tea. At dusk, the Band led a procession to Sky Farm, where a bonfire and fireworks display were given.[13] The Parish Church remained proudly decorated with its coronation Union Flag several months later, which flew majestically over the fashionable wedding party of Stella Langdale of Heathfield House to Charles Antram of Cachar, India. Guests attending the reception at Heathfield House were to be warmly greeted by the music of Heathfield Band, who performed on the lawn outside.[14]

In April 1912, the *RMS Titanic* disaster brought brass bands back into the popular imagination, as talk spread of the ship's band playing *Nearer My God To Thee* as it sunk beneath the waves; the reality would almost certainly have been less romantic.[15] Meanwhile, Heathfield Band undertook a six-week tour to raise its profile and generate funds, playing at locations such as Broad Oak and the *Station District* every Saturday evening.[16] It was also active in Hadlow Down, appearing before the Bishop and resident gentry at the vicarage on a rainy evening in June,[17] and at the annual Hadlow Down School Treat in August, the latter comprising a church service, tea, amusements and sports.[18] The children then sung songs and gave hearty cheers and the evening would conclude with the National Anthem.[19] As the year drew to a close, the Band continued its tradition of *Christmassing* around town with "appropriate and seasonable music."[20]

By 1913, industrial strikes and general poverty became a growing concern and brass bands across the land contributed more than ever to charitable causes.[21] Heathfield Band would naturally play its part, marching at hospital parades in Mayfield, Hadlow Down and Heathfield, and performing its regular gigs at fêtes and flower shows. It also entertained members of Cross-in-Hand Women's Club at Little London Farm in July, and played at a children's fête for *Campaign Against Consumption* (the widely prevalent tuberculosis), at Heathfield Park in September.[22] The latter included tea on the lawn, old English songs, dancing, and singing games.

Earlier in the year, the first major tragedy had struck the Band with the death of 41 year-old solo cornet player, William Harmer.[23] In addition to being a member of the Ancient Order of Foresters, William had been a founding member of Heathfield Band and undoubtedly had music-making in his blood. His loss would be deeply by the local banding community, whose musicians turned out to his memorial service in full dress uniform. "On either side of the hearse were the members of the Heathfield and Warbleton brass

Public Notices.

HEATHFIELD EQUITABLES'
ANNUAL SPORTS
WILL BE HELD ON THE
Heathfield Tower Cricket Ground
ON WEDNESDAY, JULY 9TH, 1913,
Commencing at 3 p.m.
The Heathfield Brass Band
will be in attendance.
DANCING IN THE EVENING.
ADMISSION FREE.

CHILDREN'S FETE
AT
HEATHFIELD PARK.
WEDNESDAY, SEPT. 24th, from 2 p.m. to 8 p.m.
ADMISSION FREE. TEA ON THE LAWN, 1.- & 6d.
OLD ENGLISH SONGS,
DANCES AND SINGING-GAMES
by Children at 3 p.m. and 5 p.m. Seats, 1'-. 6d. and 3d.
THE HEATHFIELD BRASS BAND
will play throughout the Afternoon.
The Proceeds will be given to the Campaign against
Consumption. Reserved Tickets for the Entertainments can
be obtained in advance if preferred from Miss R. F. Alexander,
Heathfield Park. A limited number of Shilling Tickets can
be obtained in advance in packets of Six for 5/-, and Sixpenny
Tickets in packets of Seven for 3/-.

Two 1913 Sussex Express
Advertisements

bands, and members of the former acted as bearers in their turn at the house and at the church."[24] But nature abhors a vacuum and a replacement player was soon to present himself in William's thirteen year-old nephew Jack, the son of bandmember John Mitchell. Jack was to become one of the Band's longest-serving members, playing his first engagement in July 1914 and finally retiring in 1983.

The Summer of 1914 was glorious and happy-go-lucky. "The sun shines benignly on brass bands," writes the British Bandsman, as bands nationwide played fêtes and promenade concerts, took part in contests, and even attended a large music festival at Dieppe in France.[25] Sports days and pleasure fairs had now become firmly associated with Bank Holidays, and the athletic sports at Warbleton was no exception, taking place on Whit Monday of that year. "A large crowd assembled on Rushlake Green and watched with interest the athletic sports and cycle carnival," reports Sussex Express, "whilst the Heathfield Brass Band, under the conductorship of Mr. C.E. Pettitt, dispensed lively music and provided the music for the dancing in the evening."[26] Ominously foreshadowing the coming war, the winner of the *Best Decorated Bicycle* contest was *HMS Warbleton*, a replica of a man-of-war with actual smoke rising from its funnels.[27]

The assassination of the heir presumptive to the Austro-Hungarian throne, Archduke Franz Ferdinand, in Sarajevo in June 1914, would initially seem of little consequence to the small, rural town of Heathfield. However, as a network of interlocking European alliances began to take sides, tensions quickly escalated. By late July war seemed inevitable, and it was soon apparent that there would be devastating knock-on effects to every aspect of British life, even within the agricultural communities of the Sussex High Weald.

Although the Band would continue, many engagements were delayed or cancelled, as townsfolk filtered away to serve King and Country in the war effort. The 1914 Heathfield Hospital Parade was delayed from early August until the end of September and, when it did finally take place, attendance was significantly reduced.[28] In addition, many residents shunned the church service for "conscientious" reasons, though quite what these were is now difficult to ascertain.[29] It could be that the Parish Church had simply fallen out of favour with some, though it seems more likely that the advent of war was calling people's faith into question. In order to improve attendance in the future, it was suggested that parades might culminate in an open-air service, and that "nonconformists" (which one takes to mean atheists, agnostics, and those who worshipped outside the Church of England), local Brotherhoods and branches of the Church of England Men's Society, should also be invited.[30]

As the war progressed, the primary role of brass bands would be to boost morale and raise money for war funds and charities. One novel initiative was the *Heathfield Tobacco Fund*, a charity which existed to send tobacco and cigarettes to the front line. The charity staged a variety concert at the Cade Street Drill Hall in December 1914. "Something to smoke is perhaps the only happiness and real enjoyment a soldier can possibly get on the battlefield," says the concert programme. "Help us to keep the brave men happy."[31] In addition to musical acts, a duologue, recitals, and a comedian, Heathfield Band opened each half with topical music selections – *It's A Long Way To Tipperary* and *Soldier Hero*.[32] It appeared again, at a follow-up concert in May 1915, during which all eligible men were urged to sign up or, if too old, to join the Volunteer Training Corps (VTC).[33] By this time, the fund had already sent over seventeen thousand cigarettes and 435 packets of tobacco to Heathfield soldiers, which would undoubtedly have been greatly appreciated. A letter from Private W.E. Tyler from nearby Burwash reads: "I shall be glad to be back and hear the old village band again. It is hot stuff out this way. [But] if a fellow is hit and he can manage to hold a cigarette in his mouth he is happy."[34]

One way for Heathfield Band to boost morale was by directly supporting the local militia. In November 1915, for example, it paraded with the Heathfield and Waldron company of the VTC from Heathfield Tower Post Office to Cade Street, and one report of the event even mentions its earliest known performance of the county's unofficial anthem: "The smartness of the Company was generally commented upon as they proceeded down Hailsham Road to the strains of *Sussex by the Sea.*"[35] It also brought much-needed joy to the community by playing at garden parties. In Hadlow Down, for example, Mrs. C. Lang Huggins decorated her garden at *The Grange* with colourful flags and opened it to the public for a "few happy hours" of sports, singing, and brass band music.[36]

Ultimately, attempts to keep the Band together were against the odds: by the end of 1917, eleven bandmembers had joined up to serve in the forces.[37] Of the eight players left behind, Edward Bean, Fred Buss, John Mitchell, Jack Mitchell, Fred Mitchell and George Roberts were mostly engaged in work of National Importance, while Charles Pettitt and Tom Upfield would be busy with munitions work. "These eight could make up a quartette band if need be," suggests the Sussex Express, "although in these busy times it is very difficult to find the necessary time for practice."[38]

Over 8 million soldiers were killed in the Great War. Among them would be three members of the Heathfield Band: Sapper Francis Greenaway, Private Alfred Hopkins and Private George Baker. In addition, Edgar Jarvis, serving with the Royal Sussex Regiment, was seriously wounded and discharged, and George Mepham Snr., of the Royal Fusiliers, was also slightly wounded.

Francis Greenaway, aged about 26, originally from Wiltshire, had been an active member of the Heathfield community. He was a member of the Oddfellows, the St. Phillips Church Choir, the Burwash Church of England Men's Society, and played cricket for *Tottingworth Park Estate*, where he had also worked as a painter. He had joined the Royal Engineers as a Sapper (military engineer) in 1915, and would take part in the Battle of Loos on the Western Front. In May 1916, the house in which he was billeted was hit by a shell burst. Francis suffered serious injuries to the legs and head and died just hours later. He is commemorated on War Memorials at Wootton Bassett (his birthplace), St. Phillips Church in Burwash, and at Cade Street.[39]

Alfred Hopkins, aged about 21, from Burwash Common, had also played cricket for the *Tottingworth Park Estate*, where he worked as a gardener. He was married two weeks after the war broke out and would enlist in the Coldstream Guards in the Summer of 1916. He was killed in October 1917 at the Battle of Poelcappelle in Belgium, and is commemorated on the War Memorial at Cade Street.[40]

George Baker, aged 30, was originally from Warbleton, where he had been a keen sportsman, playing cricket and football. He had later married, and lived and worked as a gardener at *Barfield*, before joining the Labour Battalion around 1916. He sadly died from heart trouble at Rouen, France, in April 1918, after previously suffering from trench fever and wounding.[41]

The arrival of peacetime brought with it economic woes and a devastating flu epidemic, and the misfortunes of the Band would continue. In 1919, co-founder Edward Bean left the neighbourhood, and another founding member, John Mitchell, died whilst staying at Hellingly Psychiatric Hospital.[42] He was just 55 years old and had been ill for some months, perhaps brought about by the horrors of the war.

Just a day before John Mitchell's death, in July 1919, the country had enjoyed a national holiday: "Heathfield was gaily decorated with flags and bunting on Peace Day," writes Sussex Express. "The Union Jack floated from the ancient church spire and a new red, white and blue flag hung from the flagstaff on the historic Gibraltar Tower in Heathfield Park."[43] Heathfield Band had re-emerged to take part in the celebrations, and the bells of All Saints would peal at intervals throughout the day. In the afternoon, the Band had led a procession of schoolchildren from the fountain near Heathfield Tower Nurseries to Heathfield Park Cricket Ground, where there was a short united service, singing and playing of the National Anthem, sports, and a sit-down feast for about a thousand residents. Mr. Groves, the owner of Heathfield Park, remarked that he hoped they could "have many festivities in the park, but not to celebrate peace again."[44]

In the Autumn, the Band made its return to the Heathfield Hospital Parade, held as usual in aid of Eastbourne's Princess Alice Hospital. There were now two processions, beginning from Cross-in-Hand and Cade Street, which were led by Heathfield Band and Hailsham Drum & Fife Band respectively. They then joined together in the High Street and marched to an open-air service at Heathfield Park Cricket Ground, where the former would accompany the beloved hymns: *Stand up, Stand Up For Jesus*, *O God, Our Help In Ages Past*, *All People That On Earth Do Dwell*, and *All Hail The Power Of Jesus' Name*.[45]

But the Band had fallen on hard times. Although its annual expenses were only a mere £12 (about £630 today), its finances were nevertheless precarious. Membership was considerably weakened, weekly rehearsals had ceased, and the instruments were in desperate need of repair.[46] As a result, a crisis meeting was held at the National School, during which "the members of the Band expressed themselves willing to endeavour to continue the Band if the necessary public support was forthcoming."[47]

To address the situation, the Band made an urgent public appeal, with the backing of the Sussex Express: "For the last twenty-nine years public festivities and celebrations have owed much of their success to the efforts and zeal of the Heathfield Brass Band. At this moment the desire of the members to continue its existence is practically frustrated by the urgent need of funds for its reconstruction. […] Consequently the Band feels that if the public will respond to an appeal […] toward the repair of the instruments and other necessaries and the purchase of new music, instruments and requisites, a task quite beyond the power of the members themselves, what is really an absolute necessity of public life can be supplied."[48]

In a short space of time, the Band had become more than just a highly-regarded entertainer; many now considered it essential to the town's social well-being. Having supported the residents through thick and thin, it was one of the constants of community life. Together they had weathered immense challenges, and together they had celebrated the joyous occasions. It was almost inconceivable that the Band would not now play a role in Heathfield's post-war recovery. After three decades as a local institution, it was make or break time for the Heathfield Band…

———————————————————————

[1] Sussex Express, 7th January 1910

[2] Sussex Express, 5th November 1909

[3] Sussex Express, 13th May 1910

[4] Sussex Express, 15th April 1910 & 13th May 1910

[5] Hailstone, A., 1987. *The British Bandsman Centenary Book*. Baldock: Egon: 96

[6] Sussex Express, 28th January 1910

[7] Sussex Express, 8th July 1910

[8] Sussex Express, 5th August 1910

[9] ibid

[10] Sussex Express, 18th August 1911

[11] Sussex Express, 1st July 1910; Kent & Sussex Courier, 3rd July 1914

[12] Sussex Express, 31st March 1911

[13] Sussex Express, 23rd June 1911

[14] Sussex Express, 29th September 1911

[15] Hailstone, A., 1987: 111

[16] Sussex Express, 7th June 1912

[17] Sussex Express, 21st June 1912

[18] Sussex Express, 16th August 1912

[19] ibid

[20] Sussex Express, 20th December 1912

[21] Hailstone, A., 1987: 110

[22] Sussex Express, 25th July 1913 & 19th September 1913

[23] Sussex Express, 10th January 1913

[24] ibid

[25] Hailstone, A., 1987: 120–1

[26] Sussex Express, 4th June 1914

[27] ibid

[28] Sussex Express, 24th September 1914 & 2nd October 1914

[29] ibid

[30] ibid

[31] Russell, B., 2004. *From Heathfield to East Hoathly*. Leyburn: Tartarus: 44–5

[32] Heathfield Tobacco Fund Charity Concert Programme, 16th December 1914

[33] Sussex Express, 14th May 1915

[34] Kent & Sussex Courier, 20th August 1915

[35] Sussex Express, 5th November 1915

[36] Sussex Express, 25th August 1916

[37] ibid; Sussex Express, 19th April 1918

[38] Sussex Express, 28th December 1917

[39] Walker, N., 2018. *Here Dead We Lie*. CreateSpace Independent Publishing Platform: 42

[40] ibid: 93

[41] Sussex Express, 19th April 1918

[42] Hailstone, A., 1987: 143; Sussex Express, 26th December 1919 & 25th July 1919

[43] Sussex Express, 25th July 1919

[44] ibid

[45] Sussex Express, 5th September 1919

[46] Sussex Express, 26th December 1919

[47] ibid

[48] ibid

MEMBERS of NOTE...

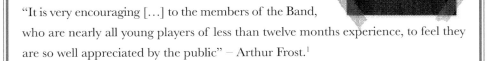

Arthur Frost
bass drummer, Eb bass & trombone,
secretary, 1924–1957.

"It is very encouraging [...] to the members of the Band,
who are nearly all young players of less than twelve months experience, to feel they
are so well appreciated by the public" – Arthur Frost.[1]

Arthur Frost, who lived in Cross-in-Hand, joined the Band around 1924 and would remain a keen member for the rest of his life. In addition to being a talented and versatile musician, playing the bass drum, Eb bass and trombone, he was to demonstrate efficient (if pompous) organisational skills, serving as the Band's secretary for an impressive thirty-three years, and also acting as treasurer for a time. However, he was only human and there would be occasional hiccups; whilst carolling around town one Christmas, the Band was to surprise the residents of *Heathfield House* by showing up to play unannounced. It was assumed that the secretary's letter had been lost in the post, but he would later confess: "I forgot to post the bloody thing!"

Arthur was one of the constants who survived from the original Band into the founding of the *new* Heathfield Silver Band in 1928, when he was to become one of its first trustees. He was liked by (and argued with) most people, and there is no doubting his love of the brass banding movement. He would be closely involved with the Tunbridge Wells Amateur Band Federation (serving as its joint secretary) and was one of the main driving forces behind Heathfield Band's initial foray into the contesting scene, during the 1920s.

In May 1930 Arthur would marry his sweetheart, Ms. Flossie White, at All Saints Church in Old Heathfield. The following year, both he and a work colleague were to have a lucky escape from deadly poisoning, whilst tapping a gas main in the High Street.[2]

During the mid-Thirties, when the Band would be without a permanent leader for several years, Arthur was to find himself sharing conducting duties with deputy bandmaster, Jack Mitchell. As well as attending countless meetings on behalf of the Band, he was to travel to Boosey & Hawkes in London to buy and sell instruments, and would even provide storage for unused ones during the Second World War (he was, in fact, one of just three members who would not be called up to serve in the army).

During the Fifties, through his involvement with the Southern Counties Band Contest, Arthur was to forge a friendship with the successful Callenders (Electric Cables) Band. This would endure for several years, during which time Heathfield Band was to visit the Callenders' practise room in Dagenham and accept donations of their old music; the pair would also stage a number of joint concerts in Heathfield.

Arthur would keep the Band running smoothly until the very end of his life in 1957, by which time he was now also treasurer. He was hospitalised in March of that year, and would sadly die in the Autumn. At the Band's AGM that October, a moment's silence would be held in his memory.

---

[1] Sussex Express, 28th December 1928
[2] Sussex Express, 16th May 1930 & 31st July 1931

Interlude Bold As Brass: The Instrumentation

Although Heathfield Band began as a short-lived fife and drum ensemble, the many benefits from becoming a brass band were quickly realised. Brass repertoire is better suited to a much wider range of engagements and, perhaps more importantly, the relative ease of learning to play a brass instrument, and to make fast progress, makes them appealing to those with no prior musical background (i.e. precisely the demographic of many amateur players). The transition therefore made complete sense and today Heathfield Band tends to adhere to the accepted brass band instrumentation. However, there have been some variations and compromises to this line-up during its long history.

The growth of the brass band movement was arguably made possible by Adolph Sax, who capitalised on existing valve technology to bring about a revolution in brass instrument mass-production.[1] Prior to this, keyed instruments had to be crafted by hand, and were prohibitively expensive to those from working class backgrounds. Mass-production enabled a growth in manufacturer competition and led to a significant reduction in prices. Community bands thus became a viable prospect for the first time. Adolph Sax simply consolidated what had come before to create a coherent and graded family of valve instruments, covering the full range required by a brass band. His instrumentation, which would become known as the Saxhorn family, was patented in 1843 and rose rapidly in popularity.

The Saxhorn family adopted by brass bands is relatively simple to learn. With the exception of the trombone section, music is written in treble clef, with instruments pitched in Bb or Eb. This results in identical fingering across the Band, enabling musicians to move between sections and interchange sheet music as required.[2] "It also means you can at the same time teach a group of people playing different instruments at different pitches, and helps amateurs playing in groups when the conductor is wanting to explain a myriad of musical issues," says Peter Cornford. In recent years, tenor trombones have also moved to treble clef, though the bass trombone continues to be notated in concert pitch bass clef, in line with classical orchestras and wind bands.

During Heathfield Band's early years, in addition to cornets, horns, euphoniums, trombones and basses, there were also clarinets. Today, this might seem a little strange to the brass band purist, but it should be remembered that the movement in part evolved from wind orchestras. Many community bands would therefore have been something of a hybrid at the time.[3] "Most local bands had clarinets," recalls George Mepham Jnr. (interviewed in 1981). "I started on one and my father played one… he could play anything! They played the melody, a great help to cornets, particularly on the march." Clarinets did not alter the essence of a band, but instead would reinforce the principal melody. They also added brightness to the upper register in lieu of a soprano cornet.[4] Although much of the early repertoire would have been taken from brass and reed journals, the Band abandoned clarinets by the mid-1920s. Whether this change was a conscious decision or happened organically is unknown, but perhaps it manifested from a move to a "purer" brass sound more in keeping with its contesting ambitions.

The instrumentation of amateur brass bands has, in a sense, never been precisely pinned down. It is subject to the availability of players and instruments, and even the repertoire within a band's music library. Nevertheless, most bands today, Heathfield included, tend to adhere more or less to the current requirements of the National Brass Band Championships of Great Britain, namely a combination of Eb soprano cornet, Bb cornet, Bb flugel horn, Eb tenor horn, Bb baritone, Bb euphonium, trombones, Eb and EEb bass, Bb and BBb bass.[5] According to Harold C. Hind, writer of the seminal book *The Brass Band* (1934): "This standardisation has proved a great boon to the arranger for brass bands as he always knows the size of the musical combination for which he is writing. There is no parallel in either the military band or orchestra."[6] Unlike contesting bands, which are usually limited to 25 brass musicians plus percussion, amateur community bands may be tiny, perhaps because membership is going through a lean period, or enormous, as is frequently the case with the growing number of university brass bands. Heathfield Band has variously ranged from a dozen members in its early days, to occasional peaks of thirty or more players. However, it usually defaults to the ideal size of about two dozen musicians.

Though fashions and production techniques have evolved, instruments have changed very little since the Band's beginnings. The most obvious difference today is a general move from brass to silver-plated instruments, which may be reflected in the change of name to Heathfield Silver Band. To maintain a smart appearance, brass instruments require considerable elbow-grease, but silver-plated instruments tend to look smarter, are easier to clean and, at least according to manufacturers, are more hygienic. Gordon Neve (interviewed in 1981), explains: "[The silver] saved cleaning. Brass needed *Brasso* [but] silver just had soapy water." A contemporary of Gordon's, Bert Thompson (also interviewed in 1981), once believed he had come up with an ingenious solution: "I cleaned my instrument up one Sunday morning, the church parade was in the afternoon, and I thought, Well, I dunno, I've bought a bottle of brass lacquer, so I painted it over with this brass lacquer, and stood it outdoors in the sunshine to dry. When I came to collect it, 'twas covered in gnats and flies! They were attracted by the sweet smell – like pear-drops – and they'd gone and stuck on it, you see. I hadn't got a lot of time so mother went and got some paraffin and she washed it down for me. All that work for nothing!"

Silver-plated instruments became extremely popular during the Twenties, but it is something of an urban myth that silver bands were the product of class snobbery in the south; they were, in fact, a nationwide phenomenon.[7] However, it is true to say that electro-plating instruments was an expensive process. In 1927, for example, manufacturer Hawkes & Son charged between £2.3s. and £13.4s. (roughly £128–£835 today) for the process, depending on instrument size, so it was a significant additional expense and would have been the preserve of wealthier bands.[8] In 1928, Heathfield Band purchased a cornet for £5 (about £320 today) and a horn for £12 (roughly £770),[9] but outfitting an entire band with silver-plated instruments would have cost in the region of £200 (about £12,800).[10]

The biggest change to instruments from a tonal perspective was the switch to *low pitch* in the 1960s. *Low pitch* appears to have originated out of a move to reduce the strain on oratorio and opera singers during the late nineteenth century.[11] At the time, instruments would usually be tuned to A_4, defined as 452.5 Hz, but *Low pitch* altered the definition to 440 Hz, resulting in a slightly flatter, duller tone.[12] *Low pitch* was adopted by the UK military in 1929 and became an international standard ten years later.[13] British instrument makers quickly realised that it was inefficient to make two versions of each model, and therefore ceased making *high pitched* ones altogether by the mid-Sixties.[14] Heathfield Band switched to the new standard in 1968 and would, as a result, have to send all its existing instruments away for conversion. Each tuning slide had be fitted with an adapter-collar, which spoiled the instrument's appearance and affected its tone.[15] "Many top bands were dubious of these new-fangled pitch ideas, but it soon caught on," recalls Ben Guile (interviewed in 1981). The total cost to the Band was over £160 (about £2,800 today).

However, one practical upshot of the change to *low pitch* was that cheaper instruments could now be imported from abroad. During the Seventies, the Band began replacing its sturdy old British instruments with Yamaha models from Japan. "Although this is something we regret very much," reports Peter Cornford at the time, "the British handmade instruments are mostly out of our reach."[16] The international instruments also had wide bores which, while capable of great power and a mellower tone, required noticeably more "filling" within a brass band setting.[17] On the positive side, technological advancements, such as the use of modern alloys, would allow for the production of more reliable and hard-wearing instruments.

One area of the brass band which evolved more dramatically was the incorporation of percussion. The early use of drums reflects the military influences on marching bands. The original purpose was solely for keeping time, but their wider musical value would soon be realised and, as composers started writing specifically for brass bands, percussion parts began to appear. As early as the 1930s, Harold C. Hind writes: "Although at present few bands have a complete set of these instruments, yet several, realising that present-day audiences enjoy the additional interest which a good percussion section creates, are gradually paying greater attention to this part of their equipment."[18]

The appearance of percussion in the published repertoire – including parts for cymbals, temple blocks, triangles, timpani, and even bongos – was thus a crucial, if relatively slow, process. "I think one of the biggest things that's helped brass bands develop their repertoire is the introduction of the drum kit, because you can play all sorts of rock styles and things," says the Band's musical director Sarah Leeves. "The exposure of all the brass bands in the charts that you see through the Seventies had some impact. There were some more adventurous arrangers and composers out there writing popular pieces of music for the brass band and everything started changing."

It is difficult to pinpoint the precise date at which Heathfield Band adopted percussion for non-marching gigs. The use of drums at concerts was suggested as early as 1951, but the then bandmaster Bert Wise was not in favour of them; they were still considered unconventional by many brass aficionados and were not generally permitted at contests until the late 1960s.[19] It is another decade before we begin to see evidence of their use at Heathfield Band engagements. However, the tide has now well and truly turned. In recent times, the Band has explored the gamut of potential percussion has to offer, adding timpani and glockenspiel parts, and even special effects, such as duck calls in *The Ugly Duckling* and whip-cracks in *The Magnificent Seven*.

In the early Nineties, the Band experienced a significant drop in membership and would embrace wind instruments as a way to cover gaps in the instrumentation. Given the historic roots of the brass band movement, the idea was not a particularly outlandish one; it is perhaps more surprising that other bands have not been as flexible with their instrumentation. As Harold C. Hind observes: "There is nothing to hinder a go-ahead band from using additional or alternative instruments for concert purposes, some bands making a practice of so doing."[20] Frank Francis, bandmaster from 1990–1992, recalls: "Recruiting was very difficult round the Heathfield area, round the whole of the south coast in fact. So I decided to bring in some other players, like a couple of clarinet players who could play the soprano cornet parts and things like that. In the Sussex area there are far more reed players looking for somewhere to play than there are brass players. Brass players can adapt to concert band styles, but reed players have nowhere to express themselves."

The Band returned to all-brass in 1995, when Richard Sherlock took over as bandmaster. Shortly afterwards, a substantial National Lottery grant would enable it to purchase a brand new set of Boosey & Hawkes and Besson brass instruments. The Lottery application interestingly specifies a desire to return to high-quality British-made instruments, "to raise the playing standards at public performances and increase audience enjoyment."[21] The Lottery-funded instruments remain the core instrumentation used by the Band today, on occasion augmented by a lone French horn.

For a detailed study examining the development of brass instrumentation, see Myers, A., "Instruments and Instrumentation of British Brass Bands" in *The British Brass Band: A Musical and Social History* by Trevor Herbert (2000), pages 155–86.

---

[1] Myers, A., 2000. Instruments and Instrumentation of British Brass Bands. In: T. Herbert, ed., *The British Brass Band: A Musical and Social History*. Oxford: Oxford University Press: 169

[2] Hind, H., 1934. *The Brass Band*. London: Hawkes & Son: 1

[3] Myers, A., 2000: 155

[4] ibid: 156

[5] BBP, 2019. The National Rules of the National Brass Band Championships of Great Britain & The BBP Registry Rules: 2

[6] Hind, H., 1934: 1

[7] Myers, A., 2000: 177

[8] Herbert, T., 2000. Appendix 1. Prices of Brass Band Instruments Extracted from Manufacturers' Advertising Material. In: T. Herbert, ed., *The British Brass Band: A Musical and Social History*. Oxford: Oxford University Press: 311

[9] ibid

[10] Holman, G., 2018a. Brass Bands of the British Isles: a historical directory [online]. Available at: <https://gavinholman.academia.edu>; Cornford, P., 1981. Personal Archive and Interviews

[11] Myers, A., 2000: 183

[12] ibid

[13] ibid

[14] ibid

[15] ibid

[16] Cornford, P., 1981

[17] Myers, A., 2000: 185

[18] Hind, H., 1934: 22

[19] Minutes, 5th December 1951; Horne, n.d. The Past and Future of Brass Bands [online]. Available at: <www.bandsman.co.uk/downloads/history.pdf>

[20] Hind, H., 1934: 26

[21] HSB Lottery Application, June 1997

MEMBERS of NOTE...

George Mepham Jnr.

euphonium, 1919–65.

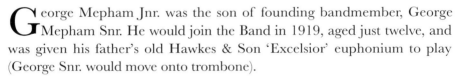

The next to show their paces
were the Euphonium and Baritone,
Trix, Ted and young George Mepham,
a splendid trio by gum,
They blew their notes so awful, they all seemed out of tone,
That the whole band started crying, and murmured "Let's go home!"
– from *Our Village Band* by Len Thorne, ca. 1938.

George Mepham Jnr. was the son of founding bandmember, George Mepham Snr. He would join the Band in 1919, aged just twelve, and was given his father's old Hawkes & Son 'Excelsior' euphonium to play (George Snr. would move onto trombone).

Like his father, George Jnr. would be keen to turn his hand to a variety of instruments. "Years ago," he recalls (speaking in 1981), "Tottingworth Park [at Broad Oak] used to have a little band for the estate. They had brass instruments as black as yer 'at, and a sousaphone. The band died out, so the instruments all went for sale. I bought a cornet and I could kick myself for not buying the sousaphone, but I couldn't get a note out of it!"

George was one of the core of younger members who would go on to form the *new* Heathfield Silver Band in 1928, and he and his father were also to become a part of its first elected committee. He would also serve for a time as the Band's librarian: "[It was] the worst job I ever did. I hated it, but I did it," he was later to confess. George's favourite Band activity was contesting, but he would also enjoy playing at conservative fêtes and garden parties: "They were well paid jobs. Gentry like bands, they used to pay almost what we asked."

George was also a keen footballer, and would play as goalkeeper for Heathfield United Football Club. In 1930, he would memorably win two cups in one day, helping the Band to triumph at the Tunbridge Wells Contest, before heading to play in the Cross-in-Hand cup tie, where his team would also be victorious.

In 1931, George was to marry his fiancée, Emily Irene Dann, at St. Richard's Church in Heathfield, and the pair would settle in Uckfield. However, he was to remain loyal to the town band, making regular trips to Heathfield by bus for rehearsals and engagements.

George and his father were also to play with other local bands, including Warbleton and Mayfield. One particularly memorable gig for the latter would be an annual garden fête at Pennybridge College in Wadhurst, which the musicians would travel to by horse and van: "They were good dos. The brethren monks used to brew their own beer; got the Band drunk once or twice and we couldn't play!"

In 1965, after forty-six years of music-making, George Jnr. would hang up his Band uniform for the final time.

1920s Like a Phoenix: Recovery, Collapse and Rebirth

Heathfield Prize Band, 1924.

(Back Row, L–R) Arthur Frost, Fred Mitchell, Eric Ford, Jessie Oliver Jnr.,
Kay Newnham, Charlie Woodgate, Harold Burchett, Arch Knapp.
(Middle Row, L–R) Bob Roberts George Mepham Snr., Jessie Oliver, Jack Mitchell,
Charles Pettitt, Nelson Harriett, Edward Bean, Bert Thompson, Frank Upfield.
(Front Row, L–R) Horace Mepham, George Upfield.

Photograph by Bray of Heathfield.

The Heathfield Band had returned from war only to face yet more turbulence. But during the 1920s its fortunes were to reverse and it would enjoy a miraculous recovery and growth, and even success on the contesting scene. The new town of *Heathfield Tower* (or *The Station District*) would rapidly grow in tandem with its Band: there was soon a cinema, several banks, a fire station and a bus garage, and it was to appropriate the name Heathfield from the area we now know as Old Heathfield.[1]

Following the public appeal in December 1919, a plethora of jobs had poured in, and the Band would experience one of its busiest years to date. The first engagement, in January 1920, was a fundraising dance at the Hadlow Down School. The Band would next return to the limelight at Easter, staging two evening dances at the Recreation Hall, as hordes of holidaymakers descended upon the town. "The Heathfield Brass Band has made a welcome re-appearance before the public," exhorts the Sussex Express. "This Band always in pre-war days made a special feature of dance music, and they appear to be keeping up their reputation by playing some of the latest dances."[2]

Bandmember Bert Thompson (interviewed in 1981) remembers the community dances with fondness: "We had some good evenings over there, they were proper social evenings. The Band used to sit up on the stage there, and keep the whole evening a-going, there wasn't no other music. The dancing was different then, we used to play quadrilles, foxtrots, the old-fashioned waltzes, and for a quickstep we played marches. We used to stay until about 12 o'clock at night, and then walk home."

The Summer of 1920 was a particularly busy time for the Band, though a drumhead service for St. Dunstan's (a home for blinded sailors and soldiers) and several evening dances were marred by heavy rain.[3] However, the first Heathfield Flower Show since 1916 was "well patronised, whatever the weather," the Band carrying out "an excellent programme of music."[4] Hospital parades were revived in Heathfield, Hadlow Down and Mayfield, and the Band played at evening dances for Heathfield United Football Club and the Heathfield Equitables Juvenile Treat. In addition, it attended the children's treat at Hadlow Down, where a particularly humorous event was to take place: as the company paraded to *The Grange* to enjoy a programme of sports, the driveway divided and, not knowing which fork to take, the Band was split in two, with some members taking one path and some taking the other!

Rehearsals had now recommenced at the practice room in Cade Street, where bandmembers had to make do with long trestle tables in lieu of music stands. It was a space big enough for a dance hall, but cold and dark, lit only by oil lamps. Jack Mitchell (interviewed ca. 1981) remembered standing in as conductor one evening. Impressed by what he had heard, a man entered the room, took three coins from his pocket, and left them as a donation for the Band. No sooner had rehearsals resumed than the man returned, asking to see the coins and, observing that one was a florin (two shillings), he said, "I thought I'd given you three ha'pennies," retrieved the florin and left! Following each rehearsal, players took it in turns to return the practice room key to the *Jack Cade* pub, where complimentary beers awaited them. The task could often require the efforts of several bandmembers!

If mentions in the local press are representative of the Band's activity, the following two years were to be much quieter. In the Summer of 1921, it appeared at engagements such as Heathfield Junior Equitables' Treat, Heathfield Flower Show, and an anarchic fancy-dress football match on the Recreation Ground, where players from Heathfield Comrades and Punnetts Town Football Team dressed as anything from flappers, Pierrots, and an old woman, to Farmer Giles, a Zulu, and a Romish Girl; a Scotchman on a bicycle even served as the Comrades' goalie and the game was refereed by Charlie Chaplin![5]

In November, the Heathfield and Warbleton bands led separate parades of British Legion ex-servicemen to converge at the new War Memorial in Cade Street, for the laying of its foundation stone.[6] After a dedication prayer, hymns were jointly performed by the Parish Church Choir and Heathfield Band. Although the memorial was officially unveiled in early 1922, it would take some time, and several public appeals, before it was fully paid-for.[7] In September 1922, there was still a shortfall of £45 (equivalent to about £2,600 today), and an open letter from the Memorial committee to *non-subscribers* states: "Contributions at this juncture would be most opportune, so that all charges may be cleared and the war memorial be indeed erected by the 'Parish of Heathfield,' and not by a portion of the community."[8]

In 1922, the Band played at Hadlow Down Show and Sports, which had been revived after a nine-year absence. It also appeared at Mayfield Hospital Parade. "My favourites were garden parties or sports days," recalls Bert Thompson. "At a garden party, you sat down and played what you liked, when you liked. We went rampin' ahead, then we'd go and get a cuppa tea, then come back and play a couple of tunes. If we went to sports days, we had to play for the horse jumping, then we had time off while something else was taking place. You had to work in with them."

The government's attempts at quantitative easing had led to an economic slump and mass inflation after the war, and public spending was significantly reduced, as profits declined and prices rose.[9] This would have a significant effect on fundraising and Heathfield Hospital Parade was just one charity which suffered: "A Union Jack in the procession was wrong side up and so indicating a sign of distress," reports the Sussex Express. "Perhaps this was 'according to plan' and really calling attention to the great need of financial help by the hospitals to enable them to continue to carry out their work."[10]

But it was not all bad news. The Sussex poultry industry made a significant recovery, and extra carriages were soon being added to the evening freight trains bound for London.[11] "Sussex before the war [...] was well-known for its table-poultry industry, and in recent years, it has also made big strides in egg production," says an article in the West Sussex Gazette, which goes on to observe that between thirty-six and forty-two tons of chicken were being dispatched from the town each week.[12] The industry was convoluted, involving a *cotter* (who would rear the birds), *higglers* (itinerant poultry dealers),

Heathfield Band, ca. 1925.

a dealer in Kilkenny, and a Heathfield agent, who sold them on to local chicken fatteners. After being force-fed (or crammed) for about two weeks, the birds were then sold on to other interested parties, both locally and further afield. With so many livelihoods at stake, one can appreciate why the industry was vital to the people of Heathfield.

It was also a period of rapid growth for the town band, which now had eighteen playing members. The newest, Bert Thompson, would remain, on and off, for over sixty years. Players often regarded themselves as semi-professional, and although they would lose employment to attend weekday engagements, they usually received a generous share of the proceeds – typically about 10 shillings each (roughly half a week's pay for an average farm labourer, equivalent to £30 today). In addition, they were often fed at such engagements. George Mepham Jnr. (interviewed in 1981) recalls: "Some foremen use to get a bit nardy, but sometimes it worked out more profitable to go to parades rather than to work. Not many used to go, only about ten perhaps, as it was hard work." However, fewer players also meant that each attendee would receive a greater share of the profits!

Constant fundraising was required to provide the Band with new uniforms and music, and to meet other expenses, such as the hire of a rehearsal room. Many of its instruments effectively belonged to the public, as they were originally funded by street collections. Travel to and from engagements was another expense and, by the Twenties, this had evolved from horse-pulled vans: "We used to use the *Sturdy Firm* from Punnets Town, [who] hired out charabancs," remembers George Mepham Jnr. "We used them to go to Goudhurst once or twice."

By now, it was clear that the Band needed help to properly manage its affairs. One gentleman who would be especially supportive was F. Howard Martin, something of a local philanthropist with an interest in a variety of local institutions, from Benefit Societies to sports clubs and amateur dramatics. He was the main driving force who encouraged the Band on its post-war path to recovery, helping to establish a committee and becoming its first chairman and, later, its president. At fêtes, he would sit collecting donations in a pudding bowl. He also supplied bandmembers with cigarettes, and threw open his grounds at *Spring Lodge* to host teas and evening concerts. During this time, the Band became an integral part of the Waldron British Legion Armistice Parade,[13] and Howard Martin would organise Sunday afternoon fundraising concerts on the village green.[14]

In 1924, with the encouragement of its new committee, the Band entered and won its first contest, topping the fourth section of the Tunbridge Wells Band Festival with its performance of *Amorette*, taking away second prize in the march category, and winning two medals for solo performances. Howard Martin's hand in this new found success was acknowledged during a celebratory social at the *Star Inn*: "[He] had been 'a brick right through the piece.' Through no fault of its own, the Band got into rather a bad way, [but

CROSS-IN-HAND
HORSE SHOW
WEDNESDAY, AUGUST 11th,
1926.

Entries Close FRIDAY, AUGUST 6th.

OVER £200 IN PRIZES.

Schedules and Entry Forms to be obtained
of the Secretary, Mr. E. E. HAYWARD,
Cross-in-Hand.

HEATHFIELD PRIZE BAND.

*OLDE ENGLYSHE PLEASURE
FAYRE.*

**Some typical 1920s
advertisements from
Sussex Express and
Kent & Sussex Courier**

DANCE
IN AID OF THE
HEATHFIELD UNITED FOOTBALL CLUB.
at the
RECREATION HALL, HEATHFIELD.
WEDNESDAY, AUGUST 18th, 1920.
Dancing from 7.30 to 1. Admission 2s.
Music by the HEATHFIELD BRASS BAND.

LOOK OUT! FOR A BIG TREAT WHEN
THE HEATHFIELD BRASS BAND
Visits Your District This Christmas.
The Committee hope to raise money in
this way to have some of the instruments
repaired, many of which have been in use
for nearly thirty years.
A. Frost, Hon. Sec., Fairfield Cottage,
Cross-in-Hand.

he] stuck to his guns and the Band had got up to the pitch it was at the present time."[15]

Fêtes and garden parties would become central to the Band's work, offering both generous fees and valuable exposure: "Gentry like bands and they used to pay almost what[ever] we asked," recalls George Mepham Jnr. During one typical fête at Heathfield Park, which attracted about a thousand attendees in the Summer of 1924, it would play throughout the day and for dancing on the lawn in the evening. There were traditional side-shows such as an Aunt Sally (in which battens would be thrown at the model of an old woman's head), coconut shies, a treasure hunt, and even a mixed doubles tennis tournament![16] Such events were often highly patriotic affairs, riding high on the air of nationalism generated by the Great War. The aforementioned fête featured an address by a Colonel Courthope, who would warn of the growing threat to Crown and Empire posed by the Socialist International Movement, a concern which in some ways mirrors current debate concerning British autonomy and Brexit.[17] "The Socialists wanted to see a commonwealth of International Socialists, and to gain that end they were ready to make class warfare," cautions the Colonel.[18]

The fledgling committee would turn the Band's fortunes around in record time. The first AGM took place in November 1924, and one of the committee's earliest tasks was to establish some guiding principles for members. "They made the rules there, that's when they made a start," recalls

Bert Thompson. "They had rules printed in the form of a little book." With the recent spate of well-paid jobs, receipts for the year were in excess of £107 (an outstanding sum, equivalent to over £6,650 today). In addition, the Band's property, such as instruments and uniforms, were valued at almost £250 (£15,500 today). It was decided to drive this successful streak forwards with a season of festive carolling: "Look Out! For a big treat when the Heathfield Brass Band visits your district this Christmas," proclaims the Sussex Express. "The committee hope to raise money in this way to have some of the instruments repaired, many of which have been in use for nearly thirty years."[19]

Heathfield Band, ca. 1928.
Photograph supplied by Mr. Cheeseman.

Howard Martin was extremely keen to bring arts and entertainment to the community and, in Spring 1925 the Band applied, unsuccessfully, for permission to perform Summer evening Sunday concerts on the village green. The chairman of the Parish Council would subsequently admit: "A great deal of unpleasant feeling had been aroused by that discussion," adding that they "had nothing against the Band or against any particular bandsman."[20] "I think the Band is a credit to the Parish," one councillor countered, with another adding: "I am sure we who dissented were not against them."[21] Although Heathfield Parish Council was not quite ready to encourage Sunday concerts, they were relatively progressive when compared to others; one councillor in Bath felt that "the inordinate love of pleasure had been the principal reason for the break-up of the empires of the past!"[22] Some of the Band's committee were concerned about getting on the wrong side of the Church, but Howard Martin was to argue: "The people must have a certain amount of recreation, and there was no reason why they should not get it by listening to decent music. Music had always been connected with religion and the sacred side of life."[23] With an immutable can-do attitude, Howard Martin would neatly side-step the issue by opening the grounds of his home, *Spring Lodge,* for Sunday evening concerts, attracting hundreds of visitors and many donations to the Band.[24]

Other triumphs for the Band during 1925 included a community social at the Heathfield Recreation Hall in February, *not* coming last in the third section of the Tunbridge Wells Contest in June (despite having only fifteen musicians), and several sports events, including a celebrity county cricket dance in July (which it co-hosted with the Heathfield Merrymakers Jazz Orchestra) for a crowd of over two hundred spectators.[25] The year would end with a New Year's Eve dance at the Recreation Hall, organised by the Heathfield Friendly Societies Hospital Committee, featuring music by Heathfield Band and a dance orchestra led by the wife of bandmember Frank Upfield.[26]

1926 began with a another social at the Recreation Hall, this time in aid of Heathfield Football Club, with music again provided by Heathfield Band and by Mr. and Mrs. Upfield, and activities including a tug-of-war, in which bandmembers would thrash the first eleven team.[27] In May, the Band came third in the third section of the Tunbridge Wells Contest, with founder Edward Bean also winning a medal for his trombone solo. It also played at the Warbleton Hospital Parade, during which the Rector presciently spoke of globalisation. "To-day the world was one," he pronounced. "Whatever happened in England affected the whole world because of the cable and wireless."[28] In August, hundreds braved a thunderstorm to attend the Cross-in-Hand Horse Show, with music by the town band and an *Olde Englyshe Pleasure Fayre.*[29] At Christmas, the Band played a series of open-air Sunday evening concerts, at *Spring Lodge* and *Heathfield House,*[30] and appeared at a carol service for the Brotherhood and Sisterhood at the Recreation Hall (an event which would be repeated at the Old Drill Hall in Cade Street, in the new year).[31] There was also carolling which, according to Jack King (interviewed ca.1981), had by now become "a big thing" for the Band. "It was a very popular event. Everyone turned out and walked for miles."

The Band's phenomenal success was beginning to attract an influx of new blood. However, with hindsight, it was possibly the radical reinvention and regeneration which would ultimately lead to its collapse.

Things began to sour in May 1927, when the Band went unplaced at the Tunbridge Wells Contest. Shortly afterwards, attendance at the first-ever Heathfield Sports Day, taking place at the Tilsmore Recreation Ground on Whitsun Monday, was badly affected by poor weather. However, the Band would nevertheless join forces with St. Barnabas (Kensington) Choral and Operatic Society for community singing, and also played selections during the afternoon and for dancing in the evening.[32] Heathfield Hospital Parade also suffered due to poor weather and, to add insult to injury, it was forbidden from collecting donations because another charity had done so the day before.[33]

One of the Band's more successful 1927 engagements was a fundraising concert at the Old Drill Hall in Cade Street, at which it performed selections, Heathfield Brotherhood and Sisterhood Choir sang glees, and there were comic songs and a quartet.[34] On Remembrance Sunday, the Band played hymns at the Waldron War Memorial in Whitehouse Lane, where Jack Mitchell also performed the *Last Post* and *Carry On*. In December, there was a long overdue return to the theatrical world, supporting Howard Martin and the Heathfield Amateurs' production of *Our Flat*, a three-act comedy by H. Musgrave, in aid of the Heathfield and Waldron Ambulance Fund.[35] However, despite public appearances, all was not well with the town band.

The Heathfield Silver Band that is loved and admired today is technically an offshoot from the original, though popular lore accepts it as a reformed continuation. In reality, after several years of relative stability, 1927 would herald the beginning of the end for the original Heathfield Band. During the Autumn, a disagreement occured – "a niggly situation," as newcomer Cyril Leeves puts it – which left the Band divided. The precise details are now lost to us, but Gordon Neve, who also joined that year, tells us: "The old

Band broke up because some members were getting too old." Quite what he means by this is unclear, though it implies that the fresh ideas brought about by the committee and a new generation of players had been difficult for some of the veteran members to adjust to.

A *new* Band was eventually formed by six or seven of the younger players, who were joined by George Mepham Jnr. and Jack Mitchell. Local piano teacher (and plumber by trade) Arthur Rodgers became the bandmaster/conductor, and the group initially rehearsed at his home. "He was a Londoner, [but] he used to talk very high class," recalls Bert Thompson. Arthur led the Band for a couple of years, and then a Mr. Wheale, about whom we know little, briefly took the baton. Rehearsals would switch between the Brotherhood Hall, the Agricultural Hall (outside which members could rehearse in fair weather), and finally Alexandra Road.

Meanwhile, the original Band limped on, reduced to perhaps seven players. By June 1928, there was even a rumour that it might join forces with Waldron British Legion: "The branch has 126 members, among whom there should be a few young men who could play an instrument or soon learn to do so," reports the Sussex Express. "If these young men could be induced to take up music and the Heathfield Band members could be enrolled as members of the branch, the business of forming a British Legion Band should be quite easy."[36] It seems unlikely that this proposal ever came to fruition, as Heathfield Silver Band continued to support numerous branches of the Legion in the future. According to George Mepham Jnr., the original Band could no longer afford its rehearsal room, and was reduced to playing in various members' homes until conductor Charles Pettitt finally decided to call it a day. "The Band sort of collapsed," says George.

Summer 1928 would be a sad time for the formerly glorious Heathfield Band. Neither of the factions had the strength to contest, nor could they represent the town at its own hospital parade (the void instead being filled by the Warbleton Prize Band).[37] In July, the Band's original co-founder Fred Adams passed away at the age of 69.[38] Before the war, Fred had migrated to Canada to run a farm with his brother. There he married a woman from Heathfield before eventually returning to Sussex.[39] No bandmembers were present at his funeral, perhaps due to the pressures of work, though some of their wives may instead have represented them.[40]

It is telling that the *new* Band's committee comprised all the key personnel of the original. Although the chairman was now bandmember Edwin Axell, Howard Martin remained present as its president, Arthur Frost acted as secretary, and Harry Dinnage, as treasurer. Continuity was also maintained through the presence of both George Mephams Snr. and Jnr., and Jack Mitchell. The driving personalities behind the old Band would thus remain. The new committee worked hard to rehearse and rebuild it with novice players, and they also invested in some new instruments.

The inaugural appearance of the *new* Heathfield Silver Band took place at the Recreation Hall on 10th October 1928, at a fundraising concert in aid of the St. Richard's Church Building Fund. It would herald the welcome return of a beloved institution. "A pleasing feature of Wednesday's event was the first public appearance of the new Heathfield Silver Band, which has risen Phoenix-like out of the 40 years old brass band, which collapsed last year," reports the Sussex Express. "The new Band, under the conductorship of Mr. Rodgers, acquitted themselves splendidly, and their playing was favourably commented upon by many during the evening."[41] The Band next appeared at a service of remembrance at the Cade Street War Memorial, where it provided musical accompaniment to the hymns.[42]

By December 1928, the *new* Band was on a roll, carolling throughout the town and firmly re-establishing itself in the public eye. This initiative would net an impressive £41 (ca. £2,600 today).[43] "Heathfield Silver Band […] is making steady but real progress under the tuition of Mr. A. Rodgers, and it is gratifying to know that the public are appreciating its efforts," reports the Sussex Express.[44] Band secretary, Arthur Frost, adds: "It is very encouraging to the various members of the committee, and also to the members of the Band, who are nearly all young players of less than twelve months' experience, to feel they are so well appreciated by the public […]. We trust that in the near future we shall be a real credit to the district."[45]

In March 1929, the Band played outside All Saints Church and accompanied hymns for the dedication of the British Legion's new standard, before parading to the Old Drill Hall at Cade Street.[46] In April, the committee made arrangements to recover the uniforms of former bandmembers, and began planning a return to the contesting scene for the Summer. This was a moderate success, the Band coming third in the fourth section at the Tunbridge Wells Contest. The committee also asked Charles Pettit to return to the Band as its solo cornet player. Interestingly, he must have maintained some prior contact, as he is already recorded as a trustee at this time, alongside George Mepham Snr., F. Howard Martin and Arthur Frost.

As the Summer of 1929 approached, the Band began playing open-air concerts at some of the grander local residences, including *Hurst* in Burwash Weald, *Spring Lodge*, and *Tanners Manor*. In July, it played alongside the Eastbourne Scottish Pipers at the Cade Street War Memorial, and at Heathfield Park Cricket Ground in support of the Heathfield Hospital Parade, after which community singing was held at the Old Drill Hall in Cade Street. This was supposed to have been led by celebrity conductor Arthur Caiger, but he was diverted at the eleventh hour by Royal Command![47] In August, the Band paraded the High Street for the Heathfield Brotherhood and Sisterhood,[48] and found itself in the company of a host of celebrity Olympic, international and county runners at the inaugural Heathfield Hospital Sports Carnival (which, disappointingly, would suffer from poor public interest).[49]

In the Autumn, the Band returned to *Hurst* for a Sunday afternoon concert in aid of Burwash Nursing Association and, in late October, it supplied dance music for a juvenile treat at the Recreation Hall.[50] In November, it combined with the Southdown Drum and Fife Band to lead the Waldron British Legion Remembrance Parade. Later that month it staged a fundraising concert at the Agricultural Hall, held jointly in aid of itself and the Brotherhood Orchestra; this time, it would perform duets and quintets in-between pieces given by the orchestra.[51]

Howard Martin, architect of the Band's two miraculous recoveries, was re-elected as president at the 1929 AGM. The Christmas season again beckoned and full advantage of the townsfolks' seasonal generosity would of course be taken. "Heathfield Silver Band are commencing their usual perambulation of the district this week," writes Sussex Express. "Last year they collected the fairly substantial sum of £41.12.1 [about £2,700 today], and this enabled them to purchase new instruments and have others repaired."[52]

As the Heathfield Band prepared to enter a new decade, it now comprised a healthy line-up of 25 musicians, finances were "very satisfactory,"[53] it was organised by a capable committee, and its services were in high demand. The next quest would be to replace the aging uniforms, to give the Band an appearance more in keeping with its abilities. As the turbulent Twenties drew to a close, the town band and its community could finally look forward with a renewed sense of optimism.

[1] Pryce, R., 1996. *Heathfield Park: A Private Estate and a Wealden Town*. Heathfield: Roy Pryce: 122, 133

[2] Sussex Express, 9th April 1920

[3] Sussex Express, 9th July 1920 & 30th July 1920

[4] Sussex Express, 6th August 1920

[5] Sussex Express, 13th May 1921

[6] Sussex Express, 13th January 1922

[7] Sussex Express, 1st September 1922

[8] ibid

[9] Nationalarchives.gov.uk. 2020. *The Cabinet Papers | Economic Slump* [online]. Available at: <www.nationalarchives.gov.uk/cabinetpapers/themes/economic-slump.htm>

[10] Sussex Express, 1st September 1922

[11] Sussex Express, 23rd September 1921

[12] West Sussex Gazette, 24th August 1924

[13] Sussex Express, 12th October 1923

[14] Sussex Express, 19th October 1923

[15] Sussex Express, 25th July 1924

[16] Sussex Express, 11th July 1924

[17] ibid

[18] ibid

[19] Sussex Express, 5th December 1924

[20] Sussex Express, 24th July 1925

[21] ibid

[22] Hailstone, A., 1987. *The British Bandsman Centenary Book*. Baldock: Egon: 153

[23] Sussex Express, 25th July 1924

[24] Sussex Express, 26th June 1925 & 17th July 1925

[25] Sussex Express, 20th February 1925, 12th June 1925 & 24th July 1925

[26] Kent & Sussex Courier, 8th January 1926

[27] Sussex Express, 5th March 1926

[28] Sussex Express, 7th May 1926

[29] Kent & Sussex Courier, 13th August 1926

[30] Sussex Express, 10th December 1926

[31] Kent & Sussex Courier, 24th December 1926; Sussex Express, 10th December 1926

[32] Sussex Express, 10th June 1927

[33] Sussex Express, 29th July 1927

[34] Sussex Express, 23rd Sept 1927

[35] Sussex Express, 18th November 1927 & 16th December 1927

[36] Sussex Express, 15th June 1928

[37] Sussex Express, 27th July 1928

[38] Sussex Express, 6th July 1928

[39] ibid

[40] ibid

[41] Sussex Express, 12th October 1928

[42] Sussex Express, 16th November 1928

[43] Sussex Express, 28th December 1928

[44] ibid

[45] ibid

[46] Sussex Express, 29th March 1929

[47] Sussex Express, 5th July 1929 & 2nd August 1929

[48] Sussex Express, 16th August 1929

[49] Sussex Express, 6th September 1929

[50] Sussex Express, 1st November 1929

[51] Sussex Express, 29th November 1929

[52] Sussex Express, 13th December 1929

[53] ibid

MEMBERS of NOTE...

Jack King

cornet, euphonium & bass trombone,
1926–32, 1939, 1970–83.

Jack King was an on-off member of the Band for fifty-seven years, having originally joined in 1926 at the age of fourteen. His long association would begin when he saw the Band play in Chiddingly and decided to take himself to the bandroom in Alexandra Road to become a member. He was informally mentored and taught by George Mepham Snr., and with the exception of horn, would go on to play every instrument in the Band. He would also conduct on occasion.

"I first became aware of Jack in the early 1970s when he would bring Julia Seymour (Coggles/Crompton) to play with the Band," recalls Wendy Holloway. "They both lived in Hailsham and he was a friend of Julia's parents. He would play cornet and sat in the back row alongside Julia and I, being very patient as we were always chatting and giggling when we should have been listening. He would quietly but firmly tell us to be quiet and listen, then he'd tell us what we'd missed! He was a very kind man who always helped me, pointing out where we were on the music when once again I'd got lost. He was an ex-military band player, but unfortunately I don't know with which service. He was always smartly dressed and very disciplined."

By this time, Steve Holloway was also a member and, having played bass for a while, he would move to 2nd euphonium alongside Jack. "I also received the same gentle help and encouragement," says Steve. "Jack was a friendly and calming influence and he taught me a great deal. He still had great technical ability and his fingering was still fast, but he was sensible and realistic to accept that his tone wasn't so good anymore. We formed the perfect partnership, with Jack taking the lead but always handing the slower more melodic solos over to me."

Jack was one of the older players who would feel compelled to leave the Band in the late Seventies when a handful of bandmembers were pushing to make it more modern and fashionable. "After the 1979 Extraordinary General Meeting whereupon the aforementioned members were themselves expelled, Jack was encouraged to return. He was assured that not only would he be welcome but the Band desperately needed someone of his ability. He would return as lead euphonium," says Wendy, whilst Steve adds: "We were both fond of Jack. He was a gentleman in the true sense of the word."

Interlude Contesting Times

Contesting is to the brass band world what marmite is to food lovers. Those who love it will expound the benefits, such as encouraging musicality, team spirit and a sense of achievement. Those who don't will tell you it's boring, or that it requires too much commitment. The truth probably lies somewhere in-between. Not every brass band has the capability or temperament to contest, so the decision will normally be determined by a combination of rational assessment and the personal preferences of its musical director.

The popularity of band contests would reach the south of England early in the twentieth century, where they were enjoyed as both as a team activity and a spectator sport. In addition to offering players a shared objective, they "engendered feelings of pride, not just among the members of the bands, but among the people of the communities in which the bands resided."[1] The prospect of recognition and financial reward would also have been an incentive. The Brass Band Nationals, held annually at the Crystal Palace, offered a one thousand guinea first prize. About 60,000 spectators were attracted to the first post-war event in 1919, and the contests would continue to generate a healthy profit, even during the Great Depression.[2]

Although Heathfield Band never took part in the Nationals during its own contesting career, the event would become a highly-anticipated social occasion for its members "At paid jobs, a shilling a member was kept out and at end of year we had a day out to Crystal Palace, by coach or rail, to hear some good bands and championship bands," recalls George Mepham Jnr. (interviewed in 1981). The bands came from all over Britain to compete. "They were mainly colliery bands," explains Bert Thompson (also interviewed in 1981). "There was St. Hilda's, they were top-notchers, used to win something pri'near [pretty near] every year. Then there was Black Dyke and Wyngate Temperance and all them…" The popularity of the Nationals would endure, even after the fiery destruction of the Crystal Palace in 1936. "Pity that place burnt down," reflects George. "We saw it burning from Heathfield!" The contest would relocate to Alexandra Palace, remaining hugely popular until the 1950s, when other forms of entertainment began competing for the public's attention.[3]

More locally, the Tunbridge Wells Amateur Band Federation, an offshoot of the Southern Counties Amateur Bands Association (SCABA), would begin to organise its own band festivals in 1922, which attracted hundreds of bandsmen and thousands of spectators each year.[4] The first of these was held at the Rangers' Ground in Tunbridge Wells. In an attempt to make the contest as appealing as possible, the organisers offered cash prizes and musical variety by means of an "own choice" march category, allowing bands to play to their personal strengths. Competitors in the lower sections were offered extra encouragement, with special recognition being given to conductors who achieved impressive results under "special difficulties." Indeed, the first prize would be trebled if it was reinvested in professional tuition or further contesting.[5]

Heathfield Band's first foray into the contesting world seems to have taken place at the Tunbridge Wells Festival (now held at the Calverley Grounds), in July 1924. This was undoubtedly the initiative of its first committee, who seized every opportunity to publicise and rebuild the Band after the Great War. The event would promise a full day of musical entertainment, with thirty brass bands competing against one another. "Everyone seemed to be out to give the other fellow a good time," reports Brass Band News.[6] As part of the contest, bands were even required to march through the town. "We used to march from the *Hand and Sceptre* (that's the pub down near the Pantiles) to the Calverley Grounds," remembers Bert Thompson. "There was a racket in the town those days, with three or four bands marching up. We played, not in the bandstand room, but outside, standing. We had the contest all day and a concert in the evening – a massed band."

The 18 shillings entrance fee (about £55 today) would prove a sound investment, as Heathfield Band won first place in the fourth section with a performance of *Amorette*, and second place in the "own choice" march category (though sadly the identity of this piece is not recorded). At a celebratory dinner, its chairman Howard Martin offered his congratulations to the players and urged them to go further.[7] Presenting bandmaster Charles Pettitt with a silver-mounted baton, he was to remark that they had done "their first step wonderfully well, and if they only put their backs into it, they would get to the top."[8]

Riding high on its victory, the Band renamed itself *Heathfield Prize Band*, and moved into the third section the following year. Up against stiffer competition, and fielding a band of only fifteen musicians, it nevertheless achieved fifth place, with a rendition of Michael Laurent's *Hiawatha*.[9] It would fare better in 1926, this time reaching third place in the third section and bagging a medal for Edward Bean's trombone solo. The following year, as hundreds of musicians again invaded Tunbridge Wells, the Band were unplaced against six others in the third section, performing Arthur Sullivan's selection *Pirates of Penzance*.[10] But whatever the outcome, the event was always a firm favourite with many bandmembers, in part because they never left for home until after the pubs had closed! Jack King, who joined the Band in 1926 at the age of just fourteen, remembers the contest as "the best job of the year."

In 1928, the Band was in a state of collapse and would be unable to compete. However, by the following Spring, the reformed Heathfield Silver Band busied itself making plans for a return to the contesting scene. At Tunbridge Wells in May 1929, under new conductor Arthur Rodgers, it came third in the fourth section with Greenwood's *The Spirit of Youth*. Considering that a significant portion of its players were complete beginners, this was a remarkable achievement. The following year, the Band would be first in its section, winning the Christie Challenge Trophy with its performance of Greenwood's *Hampton Court*.[11] However, it is implausible that it had improved so rapidly in such a short space of time: the Band's score of 67% suggests that it was more likely the competition who were lacking. A report in the

Courier seems to corroborate this, with its devastating summation: "Some of the bands did not display dazzling brilliance and incomparable fleetness and delicacy of playing."[12]

Nevertheless, the victory elevated the Band back to the third section, where it would remain for the next three years, before dropping out of the contest altogether. In 1932, it lost out on third prize (to Mayfield Band) by only one point. However, this was a respectable achievement considering that four of its players had been unable to take part that day.[13] The test pieces for 1931 and 1932 would respectively be Greenwood's *The Golden Age* and Laurent's *Beautiful Britain*, though the identity of the 1933 piece is unknown. The departure of bandmaster Charles Pettitt appears to have put a hold on further contesting for several years, but by 1937 the Band was rebuilding itself under Frank Upfield's leadership. Although it was not yet "efficient enough" for the Tunbridge Wells Festival, it would participate in the Wadhurst Contest (an

Heathfield Silver Prize Band, 1930.
(Back Row, L–R) Sid Hollands, Jack King, George Mepham Snr.,
Jack Mitchell, Fred Hunt, Alec Piper.
(Middle Row, L–R) Mervin Hemsley, Eric Mockford, Trix Wheale, Gordon Neve,
Charlie Ralph, Edward Bean, Sid Lock, Eric Wheale.
(Front Row, L–R) Edwin Axell, Stan Nye, Ern Axell, Charles Pettitt, Arthur Frost,
George Mepham Jnr., Bert Thompson.
Photograph by A.D. Hellier & Co., Heathfield.

annual march and hymn tune event promoted by Wadhurst Brass Band), where it was to come fourth in the third section.[14]

After a decade of unspectacular results, the Band, now under the direction of Bert Wise, was again ready to pursue victory. In 1939 it entered the SCABA Whit Monday Contest at Copthorne Recreation Ground near Crawley. Although the Band only achieved fourth place in the third section (performing Le Duc's *The Forest Chief*), George Mepham Jnr. would win a prize for his euphonium solo and cadenza. The advent of the Second World War brought a sudden hiatus to the Band's contesting activities, and it was another nine years before it could try again. However, under bandmaster Bert Wise it was about to enter a contesting golden age.

The Christie Challenge Trophy, won by Heathfield Silver Band in 1930 & 1949.

Between 1948 and Spring 1949 the Band would tentatively return to the contesting scene, although it did not win any prizes.[15] It was at the Tunbridge Wells Festival in May 1949 when the Band's fortunes were to change. Its fourth section performance of Le Duc's *Dawn of Spring* was a triumph, the Band carrying away the Christie Challenge Trophy and a £4 cash prize (about £144 today).[16] "It was nice to discover that so many people still possessed the ability to play a musical instrument in spite of the influence of gramophone and radio," the town mayor observed.[17] However, there was no financial gain to be made, as competing required federation membership, the payment of entrance fees, the purchase of test piece sheet music, and transport to the venue by hired coach.

In 1950 the Band moved back into, and won, the third section, with its performance of Greenwood's *The Viking*. Its principal cornet at the time, Ken Russell, remembers: "It was very easy to how it is today, but we won it two years running. Heathfield was quite a nice little band when old Bert Wise took it." The Band secured yet another cup at the SCABA Spring Contest in Lewes, playing Safroni's *Imperial Echoes* and Round's *Gems of Evergreen Memory*.[18] It entered three contests in 1951; however, promoted to the second section it was up against tougher competition. It was unplaced at both

Tunbridge Wells and Eastbourne that Spring, but would fare better in the Autumn, earning third place with Greenwood's *Song of Wales* at Dorking.[19]

Remaining in the second section in 1952, the Band would achieve second place at Tunbridge Wells, beaten only by Monotype Works (Redhill).[20] The test piece was Eric Ball's *The English Maiden* and the evening concert was conducted by Ball himself. "When Bert Wise was there it was a very, very good band," recalls Sue Sutton. "They used to go marching through Tunbridge Wells, like they do in the north, and that was in the contest as well. It was a big band then." At the Dorking Contest in November, the Band again came second, tackling Greenwood's *Recollections of Beethoven*.[21]

Over the next few years, the Band would enter several second section contests a year. In May 1953, it came third at Tunbridge Wells with Ball's *A Holiday Suite* (which it had premiered to the public at St. Richard's Hall in Heathfield the previous week), and second at Dorking in November, this time with its "own choice" test piece, *Songs of Wales*.[22] In 1954 it was unplaced at the Spring contest in Lewes, but this is perhaps unsurprising: the open-air performance of Round's *Gems of Evergreen* would go haywire mid-performance, as a strong gust of wind wreaked havoc with the music stands.[23] The adjudicator, enclosed in his box and unaware of the situation, is said to have observed: "The Band plays extremely well until bar x when it suddenly falls to pieces!"[24] Things were smoother at Tunbridge Wells that year, when the Band achieved second place with Wright's *Glastonbury*, a mere two points behind Crowborough Silver Band.[25] At Dorking it won first prize with Ball's test piece, *Call of the Sea*, and the hymn tune *Deep Harmony*.[26] The Band would top the second section again at Tunbridge Wells in 1955, playing Beethoven's *Mignonne*.[27]

However, now promoted to the first section, it was clear that the Band was beginning to reach beyond its comfort zone. It came fourth at the SCABA Autumn Contest (now held at Godalming) with Wright's *Overture to an Epic Occasion*.[28] "Gordon Neve said at the time when the Band entered the first section, 'We shall never play this damn stuff!' Wise said, 'We'll see,' " remembers George Mepham Jnr. "We played it, but it was a little hard really." The Band returned to Tunbridge Wells in 1956, though the fact that the result goes unrecorded suggests it was not a good one.

Heathfield Silver Band, outside the Assembly Hall, Tunbridge Wells, ca. 1953–57.
(Back Row, L–R) ?, ?, Ken Russell, ?, ?, Dick Turner, ?, Bob Lee, ?, Graham Barton.
(Middle Row, L–R) ?, Cyril Leeves, Bert Wise (bandmaster), ?, ?, Roy Elphick, ?.
(Front Row, L–R) Lloyd Bland, Jack Mitchell, Masters Brown & Brown,
Jeff Hobden, ?, George Mepham Jnr.
Photograph supplied by Mrs. Elphick.

From the Summer of 1956, the Band would instead focus on the Daily Herald Festival, held at the Dome and *Corn Exchange* in Brighton. The advantage of this was that all bar the championship section encouraged "own choice" test pieces, allowing the Band to capitalise on its personal strengths. Information is patchy for this period, but the Band was to move back and forth between the lower sections, distracted by poor player turnout and tardiness at rehearsals, and bandmaster Bert Wise's declining health.[29] In 1956, it tackled Rimmer's arrangement of *Romeo and Juliet* and in 1957, Beethoven's *Mignonne*. Principal cornet Lloyd Bland would take the baton for entries at Tunbridge Wells and Brighton in 1958. On both occasions, the Band performed Handel's *Water Music*, but was repeatedly unplaced.[30] In 1959 Bert Wise made a brief recovery to conduct one final contest at Brighton, though again it went unplaced.[31] As the Sixties dawned, the Band's contesting career would be mothballed. Its overall playing standard had deteriorated and attendance remained poor.

In 1961, Lloyd Bland took over permanently as bandmaster and positivity was to slowly return.[32] In 1966, the Tunbridge Wells Festival relocated to the White Rock Pavilion in Hastings, as part of the Battle of Hastings' 900th anniversary celebrations. "More than twenty bands – some well-known, others little heard of outside their own districts – went by coach with instruments, wives and families to the new venue," reports the Courier.[33] "Their uniforms, often of Ruritanian splendour, sometimes of a more 'mod' cut, added an extra splash of colour to the seafront scene as they mingled with holiday makers between taking their turn on the platform." Having attracted an influx of new players, Heathfield Band embraced the opportunity to return to the contesting scene, entering the third section of the "entertainment contest" with Greenwood's *Pride of the Forest*. Although it came last in the section, its score was in fact only six points below the top band, an astounding achievement considering many members had never previously contested, and five had been playing for a matter of mere months.

The official Tunbridge Wells Contest would be moved to November and, remaining in the third section, the Band reached second place, just two points behind Mayfield Silver Band.[34] The name of the test piece is unrecorded,

Hastings Contest, May 1970.
(Back Row, L–R) Susan Whiting, Dave Wenham, Jim Hall, Ben Guile, Freddie Stanford,
Graham Bland, Sue Sutton, Graham Beeney.
(Middle Row, L–R) Peter Jarvis, Dave Dunk, Dennis Guile, Ted Lee, Lloyd Bland,
Dave Sutton, Gerald Funnell, Jackie Bland, Janice Bland, John Collier.
(Front Row, L–R) Gerald Dann, Bert Thompson, Laurie Knapp, Roy Elphick,
Cyril Leeves, Trevor Rood, Stan Ambuchi, Bob Lee.
Photograph supplied by Peter Cornford.

though it is plausible that the Band revisited the Greenwood arrangement it had previously performed at Hastings. In 1967, there was again a Summer festival in Hastings, and again the Band was unplaced, this time playing Le Duc's *Country Life*. Its strategy at this time seems to have been to use the Summer Festival as a dry-run for the Winter Festival, which was now held at Chatham.[35]

For the 1968 Hastings Festival, the "own choice" category was redefined, with third section bands now given a choice from just three set pieces.[36] Heathfield came second playing Ball's *The Young in Heart*, but at the Winter Festival in Chatham it would win its section with Ball's *Three Songs Without Words*.[37] The prize was £10 (about £177 today) and the Arthur Jarvis Memorial Trophy, from which members would later share a celebratory drink.[38] At Hastings in May, the difficulties of promotion once again became apparent: up against stiffer competition in the second section, the Band came eighth (performing Ball's *Rhapsody on Negro Spirituals*).[39] It could not attend the Winter Festival in 1969, due to a prior engagement with Newick Bonfire Society.[40]

Now relegated to the third section, the Band returned to the Hastings Festival in the Summer of 1970, triumphing with *Three Songs without Words*, and carrying away the Wimshurst Trophy and £10 first prize (about £158 today). "On the coach journey back to Heathfield a short stop was made during which, in an atmosphere of 'We won the cup,' the trophy was suitably filled and passed among members," reports one newspaper.[41] Once again, the Band would not enter the Winter Contest at Chatham, and the Hastings Summer Festival became defunct after 1970. However, it seems likely that the Band returned to Chatham in 1971, as November's accounts record payments to the Tunbridge Wells Federation and the hire of a coach.

To celebrate its golden jubilee in 1972, the Tunbridge Wells Festival was to return home, now restyled as an "entertainment contest" whereby each band would perform a fifteen minute "own choice" programme.[42] Über confident of its entertainment abilities, Heathfield Band entered the first section that year, but unfortunately came away unplaced.[43] It next competed in the third section of the Chatham Winter Festival, against bands from Mayfield,

Cranbrook and Copthorne. This time, the chosen piece was Ball's *A Devon Fantasy*, and again the Band would leave unplaced. Undeterred, it returned to Tunbridge Wells in May 1973, but somehow managed to come last in its section, despite only eleven bands taking part due to competition from the FA Cup Final![44] Thankfully, the Band redeemed itself at Chatham in December, winning the second section with its "own choice" test piece.[45]

In 1974 there was no contesting due to the resignation of bandmaster Lloyd Bland. However his replacement, Tom Kelly, who came from a traditional northern brass banding background, had strong feelings on the matter.[46] "I think it was part of Tom's being that you *had* to contest," says Peter Cornford. "There wasn't a discussion about it." The Band would thus return to Tunbridge Wells in the Spring of 1975. However, the contest was one of the last of its kind, as the festival had become a loss-maker for the Federation.[47] The Band was unplaced on that occasion, but went on to win second prize in the second section at Chatham that year, with its rendition of *A Devon Fantasy*.[48] Hoping to take the Band further, Tom Kelly would increase rehearsals to twice weekly in the run-up to future contests.[49] "He achieved a reasonable result," adds Peter. "We were fourth section but we *were* contesting to a reasonable standard, like we hadn't done since the Fifties."

But how did bandmembers feel about contesting? "I suspect at least half the Band could've done without it, were quite happy to do the fêtes and the marches and the bonfires," reflects Peter. "One of the first contest pieces I played was *Divertimento*. I must've been about eleven and I remember one evening in the bandroom actually bursting into tears because I just couldn't cope with this piece, I was absolutely terrified by the thing. I was playing third cornet and coming in all over the place!" Anna Farley (née Lee) recalls her first contest: "I can remember going with a friend of mine. The bandmaster said to us, 'You can come, you'll be fine, but if you feel you can't do a bit, leave it out!' We just used to be quiet and pretend that we were playing, but it was nice because we were still included."

The Band's contesting history is opaque for the remainder of the Seventies. It did remain a member of the Federation, and we know that it appeared at the East Grinstead Music Festival in the Spring of 1976. It would also come

Heathfield Silver Band Slow Melody Contest, ca. 1977.
Photograph supplied by Kent & Sussex Courier/Tunbridge Wells Advertiser.

second in the second section at Chatham that December, winning the Aylesham Challenge Cup with its take on Vaughan Williams' *English Folk Songs Suite*.[50] This latter event was Peter Cornford's first contesting experience: "It was a great exciting day for me because I was an eleven year-old getting on a coach to Chatham for a full day. That was very frightening and this was suddenly a whole new world. We'd been practicing this damn piece for weeks and weeks and we went and played it on a stage!" In 1978, the Band entered a quartet in the Spring Festival at East Grinstead, for which it was awarded a certificate of merit. However, tensions and disagreements would lead to the resignation of Lloyd Bland, and several other players were expelled from the Band. Under these circumstances contesting became impractical, although an unsuccessful return to Tunbridge Wells was attempted in 1980.

David Threlfall, who also had a northern brass banding background, would find himself becoming the new bandmaster. He wanted to introduce an event that was inclusive of all bandmembers, so an internal Slow Melody Contest was suggested, the idea being that it would not give an unfair advantage to "flash" solo players. "Dave was a great believer in trying to get the best out of everybody. It was an event that everybody could take part in at whatever level," explains Peter Cornford. "Heathfield Band was an average community

band and there were plenty of senior bandmembers who frankly weren't a lot better than beginners or intermediate. But people were worried that if they had to play a solo they would just make a complete fool of themselves and everybody would know what they were really like. And of course that was true, they did!" At the first Slow

> **SOUTHERN COUNTIES**
> **AMATEUR BANDS ASSOCIATION**
> ## AUTUMN CONTEST
> **LEAS CLIFF HALL FOLKESTONE**
> **12-13th OCTOBER 2002**
> **COMPETITOR**

Melody Contest in 1978, Peter's eleven year-old sister Alison won the junior section, David Threlfall won the senior section with his euphonium solo, and Peter won the open section with a performance of *Air on a G-String*.[51] Over the next few years, the contest grew to become a popular Band event; the final one, held in 1982, would attract twenty-three competitors.[52]

There was no contesting during the Eighties or Nineties, as a succession of relatively short-lived bandmasters attempted to reimagine and rebuild the town band. Frank Francis, bandmaster from 1990 to 1992, felt that contesting was not appropriate for the Band at that time. "None of them would have been at an ability to go contesting," he explains. "It's time-consuming and they wouldn't spend the time to rehearse that one number. The more you go through something, the worse it gets. Some of these contest pieces are so complex they give up, especially if they go to a contest and they're listening to a band that's really shit-hot. Suddenly it's their turn and the people who lack the ability and the confidence just fall apart." Current musical director Sarah Leeves adds: "In the run up to a contest, most brass bands have two or three rehearsals a week, and sectionals as well, and by the contest day you're just sick of the sound of the piece. You just think, *Is it really gonna get any better? Let's just do it!*"

In 2001, music teacher and bandmember Frankie Lulham began to take an active role in the Band's direction and entered a quartet in the Eastbourne Music Festival, a relaxed "own choice" contest. Becoming musical director in early 2002, she would give the full Band a taste of contesting the following year. "We will be performing on a stage to an adjudicator who will listen to us and make comments on our playing," she explained to members prior to the contest. "Practise your parts until they are perfect, thinking of the dynamics and your tone. Don't overblow."[53]

The contest was a success, the Band being awarded the Gilbert Foyle Trophy for its performance of Holst's *2nd Suite in F Major* and the hymn tune *Carlisle*. "It was a shame the other band dropped out," writes Frankie afterwards. "We can only assume they were frightened of us!"[54] A few days later, Frankie entered a quartet and an ensemble into the Spring Contest at Ringmer, the quartet coming second in its section with Youngman's *Dragon's Green Suite*.

These initial successes prompted the Band to attend a day-long masterclass with composer Tony Cresswell, to prepare it for the 2003 Autumn Contest at Folkstone. After auditioning three pieces, the Band then chose to focus on Alan Fernie's *St. Andrew's Variations*. "It was well within our capabilities and it was a good tune," recalls Anna Farley. "This left us with five weeks to rehearse it in, not really very long for a band that hadn't contested for well over thirty years, and only a handful of the players had actually contested before."[55] Nevertheless, the Band was to enter the third section at Folkstone with *St. Andrew's Variations* and the hymn tune *Blaenwern*. Of the former, the

GF1702046/24

Silver band celebrates double win

THE SWEET sound of success filled the home of Heathfield silver band on Tuesday when it celebrated its latest competition wins.

The band, which was established in the 1880s, organised a get-together to mark its success at Eastbourne music and arts festival last week and also to present a special trophy to the junior players.

From the competition on Thursday last week, the band took home a rosebowl for best quartet and cup for best band performance, which it won for the second year running.

At Tuesday's event, musical director Frankie Lulham presented the juniors, aged between 11 and 14, with a new home-grown club trophy after they just missed out on the Eastbourne cup by two points. Mrs Lulham said: "I was so disappointed for them I said I would find them a trophy."

Best Quartet: Doug Blackford, Alan Jones, Anna Farley, Sarah Leeves; Junior team: Josh Broadway, David Pursglove, Natahe Sherlock, Abigail de Bruin, Alex de Bruin, Debbie Bailey.

Kent & Sussex Courier, 20th February 2004.

adjudicator notes: "An uncertain start but the music flows well […]. The march is well played and you play the *Romanza* with feeling." Of the latter, he observes: "Not together, open but good sound. Good attempt at dynamics."[56] Frankie would be pleased with the results, saying: "We didn't win and we didn't come last. We played our very best and took part, which is the most important thing."[57]

In February 2004, the Band repeated the initiative, this time entering the Ringmer Contest with several quartets and an ensemble. A euphonium quartet of the traditional melody *David of the White Rock*, and the ensemble's performance of Praetorius' *Dances from Terpsichore*, both came second in their classes and the musicians would leave clutching two shields.[58] The Band entered several more quartets at Eastbourne the following week (one of which won the Alderman Fred Taylor Bowl) and a youngsters' ensemble playing *Pop Rock!* "They didn't win, but I thought they were brilliant and so I bought this trophy and presented it to them at the bandroom," recalls Frankie.[59] Meanwhile, the main Band was to revisit the *St. Andrew's Variations*, for which it retained the Gilbert Foyle Challenge Bowl, (despite one player forgetting to bring his mouthpiece).[60]

In the Autumn of 2004, the Band again entered the third section of the Folkestone Contest, performing *Fanfare and Hymn Repton* and Malcolm Arnold's *Little Suite For Brass*. It achieved a disappointing tenth place.[61] Despite a "good precise opening," the adjudicator criticises *Little Suite* for having insecure rhythm, balance and intonation.[62] Bandmember Stephen Walkley would afterwards offer some words of consolation: "If being the 'worst' band means having more young and inexperienced players than any of the other bands, probably the widest range of individual playing ability and experience of all the bands there, and perhaps rather less ambition (contest-wise) than the other bands, then the cold, clinical (cynical) view might be that Heathfield Band were indeed the 'worst' band there," he writes in an email to Frankie.[63] "What the record book will not show is that Heathfield Band probably benefitted more, and achieved more, from preparing for and performing in the contest than most of the other bands there."

With its confidence knocked, the Band did not enter any contests in 2005, and underlying tensions between members soon made future entries untenable. A handful of disgruntled players would in fact enter themselves in the Ringmer Contest in February 2006, and leave the Band immediately afterwards. How well they fared is unknown, but the Band also fielded an 'A' quartet for the event, playing Kenneth Cook's arrangement *Two Folk Songs: Avenging and Bright and Early One Morning*, and winning second prize in the third section.[64] The adjudicator writes: "Good, stylish opening, with balanced and well-moving parts," and, "Musical in style, very convincing. An excellent finish."[65] Some youngsters were also entered in the Eastbourne Festival that year: "What a wealth of talent we have in the Band. They came away with trophies and medals galore," enthuses Frankie in a subsequent press release.[66]

With the departure of the dissenting members the Band was left short of key players and could no longer consider contesting. However, its youth band did enter various categories at Ringmer and Eastbourne in 2007, winning yet more trophies to proudly display in the bandroom.[67] In November, Frankie would step down as musical director, to be replaced once more by Richard Sherlock. Although he intended for the Band to continue contesting this ultimately did not happen, whether due to a lack of strong or of sufficiently interested players. "One of the problems," says Richard (speaking in 2012), "is that there is a certain musical director who teaches at the school and nicks all the best school-people to go and help them out at contest! Under the SCABA rules you can have a few helpers but you can't be associated with two bands."

There are currently no plans to return to the contesting scene, as the Band's musical director Sarah Leeves does not feel it sits well with the ethos of a community band. "Contesting does tend to split bands," she says. "If you've got a band that's not an established, regularly-contesting band, it has to go through this phase where you lose people that aren't gonna be brought along with the whole concept of doing loads of extra practice. It can also be quite daunting to a lot of people. That's where you end up making people feel isolated." There is another problem, too, continues Sarah: "A lot of contesting bands have a senior band and a youth band, but you've got people working their way up who might never get a shot unless they go to a different band. It's that sort of thing that I just find a little bit problematic with the whole contesting situation." So for now, despite its many past successes, Heathfield Band's contesting years are just another part of its glorious history.

1 Herbert, T., 2000. Nineteenth-Century Bands: Making a Movement. In: T. Herbert, ed., *The British Brass Band: A Musical and Social History*. Oxford: Oxford University Press: 53

2 Hailstone, A., 1987. *The British Bandsman Centenary Book*. Baldock: Egon: 25, 149, 187

3 ibid: 212; Russell, D., 2000. 'What's Wrong with Brass Bands?': Cultural Change and the Band Movement, 1918–c.1964. In: T. Herbert, ed., *The British Brass Band: A Musical and Social History*. Oxford: Oxford University Press: 93

4 Bourke, J., 1996. *The History of a Village Band 1896-1996*. Heathfield: Warbleton and Buxted Band: 21

5 Brass Band News, August 1924

6 ibid

7 Sussex Express, 25th July 1924

8 ibid

9 Sussex Express, 12th June 1925

10 Sussex Express, 13th May 1927

11 Sussex Express, 9th May 1930

12 Kent & Sussex Courier, 9th May 1930

13 Sussex Express, 13th May 1932

14 Minutes, 14 April 1937; Brass Band News, October 1937; www.BrassBandResults.co.uk, 2021

15 Minutes, 30th August 1948

16 Sussex Express, 13th May 1949

17 ibid

18 Bourke, J., 1996: 42

19 www.BrassBandResults.co.uk, 2021

20 Sussex Express, 9th May 1952

21 www.BrassBandResults.co.uk, 2021

22 ibid; Cornford, P., 1981. Personal Archive and Interviews

23 ibid

24 ibid

25 www.BrassBandResults.co.uk, 2021

26 ibid; Kent & Sussex Courier, 19th November 1954

27 Sussex Express, 20th May 1955; BrassBandResults.co.uk 2021

28 ibid

29 Minutes, 4th October 1957

30 Sussex Express, 13th June 1958; Cornford, P., 1981

31 www.BrassBandResults.co.uk, 2021

32 Minutes, 13th October 1960 & 5th August 1961

33 Kent & Sussex Courier, 13th May 1966

34 www.BrassBandResults.co.uk, 2021

35 Kent & Sussex Courier, 1st December 1967; www.BrassBandResults.co.uk, 2021

36 Kent & Sussex Courier, 11th May 1968

37 ibid

38 Kent & Sussex Courier, 30th November 1968; Minutes, 7th January 1969

39 Kent & Sussex Courier, 10th May 1969; www.BrassBandResults.co.uk, 2021

40 Heathfield Silver Band Newsletter, 1970

41 Cutting, source unknown

42 Kent & Sussex Courier, 19th May 1972

43 ibid; www.BrassBandResults.co.uk, 2021

44 Kent & Sussex Courier, 11th May 1973

45 www.BrassBandResults.co.uk, 2021

46 Minutes, 21st February 1975 & 18th April 1975

47 Minutes, 18th April 1975

48 www.BrassBandResults.co.uk, 2021

49 Minutes, 27th January 1976

50 Minutes, 28th July 1976; Cornford, P., 1981

51 Cutting, source unknown

52 Kent & Sussex Courier, May 1982

53 Correspondence, Frankie Lulham to Bandmembers, ca. February 2003

54 MD Report, Frankie Lulham, 12th February 2003

55 SCABA Bugle, December 2003

56 SCABA Adjudicator Notes, 11th October 2003

57 MD Report, Frankie Lulham, 11th October 2003

58 Press Release, Frankie Lulham, ca.9th February 2004

59 Press Release, Frankie Lulham, ca.13th February 2004

60 ibid

61 www.BrassBandResults.co.uk, 2021

62 SCABA Adjudicator Notes, 9th October 2004

63 Correspondence, Stephen Walkley to Frankie Lulham, 11th October 2004

64 Press Release, Frankie Lulham, 14th February 2006

65 SCABA Adjudicator Notes, 12th February 2006

66 Press Release, Frankie Lulham, 14th February 2006

67 MD Report, Frankie Lulham, 27th February 2007

MEMBERS of NOTE...

Cyril Leeves
bass drummer, 1927–1981,
librarian, 1946–9,
assisstant librarian, 1949–57.

by Peter Cornford

"Now Cyril Leeves, he beats the drum, an old one I believe,
They say this drum it first saw light in 1863"
– from *Our Village Band*, a poem by Len Thorne.

Cyril Leeves joined the Band in 1927, at the age of twenty-four. He worked as a gardener for much of his life, and on the railway from 1930–49. He would always be easily recognisable around the town, cycling leisurely on his ancient iron-framed pre-war bicycle, with some long-handled tool or other fastened lengthways to it.

Cyril was absolutely dedicated to the Band. I cannot remember him missing a rehearsal, let alone an engagement; indeed, he was renowned for cutting his holidays short to attend. However, he would never play a brass instrument, remaining the Band's bass drummer for over fifty years. The only break Cyril would take from playing "his" drum was at Christmas, when he was to walk door to door collecting while the others played carols beneath lampposts. When the Band had finished a carol, he would shout "Right-o!" and off everybody would move.

I used to think of Cyril as the Band's most prolific drinker, smoker and swearer. His sense of fun and his laugh were legendary and he would have a permanent mischievous twinkle in his eye. One of my enduring memories is of Cyril, standing at the back of the Band banging that drum, whilst periodically coming out with humorous one-liners or a well-intentioned put down. He would constantly have us in stitches.

Cyril was the epitome of the local Sussex man, with the wry, dry humour for which we in the county are famed; humour and wit trip effortlessly and relentlessly out of the mouth. One Sussex characteristic, at which he was a past master, is to talk quietly with the mouth barely open whilst maintaining an expressionless face, which can have a devastating effect. So many in the Band would do this naturally, but Cyril was possibly the best of all at it. With so many bandmembers behaving like this, laughter would be endemic.

I can also not recall Cyril completing a sentence without inserting "bloody" in it somewhere. This was not to use the word aggressively or unkindly, but simply in the same way that anyone might use other filler words such as "like" or "y'know". It was just a part of how Cyril would speak to everyone, whoever they were.

Cyril would not profess to be an accomplished musician, but he did know exactly how to hit the bass drum to keep a steady beat, particularly when marching. He was very defensive of his drum and would not let anyone else touch it. He was such a permanent fixture of the Band that it would take everyone by surprise when, upon completing 50 years, he was to announce: "Right. That's a bloody 'nuff. I'm gonna stop drumming!"

Cyril would officially retire in 1977, as marching was becoming a challenge. He was featured in the Daily Mirror on 1st July 1977, under the headline "Boomtime," and the Band would present him with a silver tankard to honour his long service. He would continue to play, albeit less frequently, until 1981.

1930s Changing Times and Financial Struggles

Heathfield Silver Band, ca. 1931–4
Photograph supplied by Peter Cornford.

As Heathfield Band entered the 1930s, there was every reason to be hopeful. It had weathered the threat of total collapse and emerged stronger than ever. But the departure of bandmaster Arthur Rodgers, followed by a flurry of short-lived caretaker conductors, would bring a certain instability for much of the decade. The Band also had to cope with the financial pressures of the Great Depression, and the onslaught of another world war. In addition, it was to lose two players in the deaths of founding member George Roberts in early 1931 and Sidney Lock, who was just 39 years-old, in October 1935.

The Wall Street Crash, which began in the Autumn of 1929, was to have far-reaching effects on the brass band movement. Although the Heathfield Band's finances were in good order, raising funds for major projects such as the purchase of new uniforms proved remarkably difficult. When it won the fourth section of the Tunbridge Wells Contest in 1930, the Band would do so attired in a ragtag mixture of lounge suits and ties. Money became so tight that each bandmember was required to contribute weekly subs towards the rent of the rehearsal room. These started out at 3d., rose to 4d. for a time, and then dropped back to 3d. (between approximately 65p and £1.30 today).[1] "We paid and played," says George Mepham Jnr. (speaking in 1981). Other bands resorted to touring or busking. Bandsmen from hard-hit mills and collieries in the north were forced to head south in search of new work.[2] This was to have a disastrous effect on northern brass bands, but would serve to inject new talent into southern ones.[3] At a public meeting to plan the forthcoming Coronation celebrations, Heathfield's temporary bandmaster Frank Upfield gently berated those who expected the town band to perform for free: "If there is any lady or gentleman in this room that has subscribed to the Heathfield Band in the last two years I would like to shake hands with them," he commented, wryly.[4]

The rise of *mechanical music*, such as radios and gramophones, also had significant consequences for the Band. Dedicated dance bands were growing in popularity as musical genres such as jazz and swing became more popular. These, combined with the cheapness of recorded music, eroded a sizable slice of the engagement market.[5] "Village bands are just now feeling the competition of mechanical music," writes the Sussex Express. "More than one flower show and fête in the district this Summer displaced the village band with a radiogram. In one instance this was used for the fête and dance, and was cheaper than a band."[6] To enable it to compete more effectively, the Band's repertoire would be rapidly forced to evolve. Its role in the community also shifted slightly, as it focused on informal events such as charity fundraisers, carnivals, flower shows and fêtes.

In 1932, Heathfield Parish Council reignited the debate surrounding Sunday evening concerts, as it considered allowing the Band to play on Heathfield Tower Recreation Ground.[7] It had, in fact, already voted in favour of such concerts the previous year, but the Band had ultimately declined its offer (which required it to relinquish 50% of any donations towards the upkeep of the grounds).[8] Fortunately, the Band had an ally on the Council in the form of F. Howard Martin, who continued to argue that the best place for worship was in the open air, "in the temple that God Himself has made."[9] But opposition to Sunday entertainment remained strong. One councillor even declared that he would rather have his head cut off than vote in favour of them, adding: "If they really loved God they would be doing something else on a Sunday evening instead of just listening to a band for their own amusement."[10] The Vicar, Reverend Clark, would shrewdly make his position known, quoting Jesus from the gospel of Mark: "The Sabbath was made for man and not man for the Sabbath."[11]

The Parish Council eventually voted in favour of Sunday concerts, though the debate continued into the Summer.[12] "We may expect sooner or later that the example of many towns in attempting to establish Sunday games, Sunday dances, Sunday cinemas, and the like, will be thrust upon us, unless the community rise up and stem the tide of Sunday pleasure-seeking which threatens our beloved and once Bible-loving land," writes the Superintendent of the Welcome Mission, Frank Collins, to the Sussex Express.[13] Other views were more liberal. "Those old-fashioned cranks and faddists, who are opposed to this kind of thing, should remember that the poor ratepayer wants something more than a 'dry' sermon nowadays to cheer him up," writes R.C. James, while H.G. Burtson wonders if the protestors would allow the fire brigade to save a burning house on a Sunday.[14] When it was announced that Heathfield Hospital Sunday would feature an evening concert on the village green, objectors now claimed that it coincided with their hours of worship.[15] However, the Parish Council continued to support such entertainment and by 1938 the Band was giving regular Sunday afternoon concerts on the recreation grounds at Heathfield Tower and Cross-in-Hand.[16]

Annual events such as juvenile treats, Friendly Society socials, carnivals, fêtes and Heathfield Agricultural Show, were to keep the Band busy throughout the Thirties. It frequently undertook charity fundraisers and carnivals for free, whilst paid events such as the Heathfield Flower Show would earn it a fee of £5 (about £350 today) and tea for the players.

In the wake of a global economic slump, the work of Friendly Societies became even more vital to the community, and fundraising initiatives such as hospital parades remained popular. In 1934, the Ancient Order of Foresters at Cross-in-Hand celebrated their centenary with a special church parade and thanksgiving service. Headed by Heathfield Band, the entourage marched in full regalia from the *Cross-in-Hand Hotel* to St. Bartholomew's Church, and thence along Sheepsetting Lane to Heathfield High Street.[17]

The majority of bandmembers were working men who could not afford the luxury of a vacation. Instead, they took part in Bank Holiday festivities, such as those held at *Satinstown Farm* in Broad Oak every August, and the St. Richards Church Whit Monday Fête at Sandy Cross. And, although sports events appear to have dwindled in popularity, the Band would nevertheless support them whenever the opportunity arose. In 1931, it played at the Humble-Crofts Cup Final in Cross-in-Hand, and in 1935 it helped to celebrate the opening of a new pavilion at Punnetts Town, and also appeared at Waldron British Legion's Sports Day and Fair at Cross-in-Hand (which attracted about two thousand visitors).[18] Bandmaster Charles Pettitt, who had returned to the role in 1930, conducted fewer and fewer engagements, and retired altogether by the end of 1933. In the absence of an elected leader, Jack Mitchell and Arthur Frost would share conducting duties, with Frank Upfield returning to the baton in 1935. But one thing was certain: "If the secretary got a job, everyone had to be there," says Gordon Neve. "There was no humming and hawing!"

A close friendship was maintained with local branches of the British Legion, who seemingly never established a band of their own. Heathfield Band therefore played a particularly important part in the Armistice commemorations each November. In Waldron, on the Sunday before Remembrance Day, it would form up with members of the Waldron and Mayfield branches and parade to the War Memorial to participate in an open-air service. After the names of the fallen were read, the *Last Post* and *Reveille* was jointly performed by bandmembers George Mepham Snr. and Jack Mitchell. The company then returned to the Legion Hut for tea.[19] The following week, the Band led a procession from Rushlake Green to Warbleton Parish Church on behalf of the Heathfield and Warbleton branches. This was supported by Scouts and Guides, and members of the women's section of the Legion. At the church, the Band provided accompaniment to the hymn tunes and George and Jack would again perform the *Last Post* and *Reveille*.[20] In 1935, the Band led a Remembrance Parade from the Cade Street Drill Hall to All Saints Church in Old Heathfield, returning by way of the War Memorial where a wreath was placed, prayers offered, and the National Anthem played.[21] The following year, *Last Post* and *Reveille* duties were taken on by Jack Mitchell and Gordon Neve, as George was now beginning to take a step back from the more demanding duties.

The Band also supported many other Legion events and, in return, the various branches would generally make an annual donation or provide the loan of their hut for fundraising socials. In February 1930, the Band headed a memorial parade for the Warbleton and Heathfield branches in honour of the Legion's founder, Earl Haig.[22] Haig had fought in the Second South African Anglo-Boer War, helped to form the Territorial Army, and had been Commander-in-Chief of the British Forces in France during the Great War.[23] The company marched to All Saints Church where a service, with the theme of "Peace on earth, and good will towards men," attracted around 200 parishioners.[24] In February 1932, the Band attended a similar event for the Waldron Legion, marching through the village and making a stop at the War Memorial *en route* to its Parish Church.[25] The British Legion also organised other social events in which the Band took part. In the Summer of 1934, for example, the Heathfield and Warbleton branches held "a great day of thanksgiving for the consolidation and unity of the British Empire."[26] This began with a rendition of *Land of Hope and Glory*, sung by "St. George" from atop his horse, and was followed by a parade through the gaily-decorated High Street to *Satinstown Farm*, where a fête and sports were then held.[27]

Celebrations of the Empire were popular in the Thirties, and Heathfield Band was to perform at many such events. These were in part stimulated by the rise in patriotism following the Great War, but were also a useful way of promoting British and Empire-sourced produce. Indeed, this protectionist economic model was well-respected by Brits, many of whom believed it would safe-guard local agriculture and lead to better living conditions by providing increased opportunities for trade. In addition to the traditional Conservative fêtes there was also Empire Shopping Week, during which shopkeepers and tradespeople worked hard to decorate their windows and engage the community. There would be competitions, schoolchildren competed to write the best Empire-themed essays, films by the Empire Marketing Board played at the cinema, and patriotic concerts were given.[28] The first major Empire event took place in 1931 at the Recreation Hall in Station Road, where prizes were presented, sketches and choruses performed, and "Heathfield Silver Band, resplendent in their new uniforms, played popular airs for community singing."[29] The celebrations transformed the town: "Never has Heathfield looked so gay with flags and bunting as it has this week," writes the Sussex Express.[30]

The growth of nationalism across Europe was rather less innocuous. In Germany, the rise of Adolf Hitler represented a threat to almost every aspect of western liberty; Salvation Army bands were even banned from performing their music in public.[31] The people of Sussex would strongly denounce his accession to power, at carnivals and bonfire parades which were now resuming across the county. Heathfield Band were naturally on hand to complete the atmosphere, but these events were to become more political than ever before. Following the burning of the German Reichstag (parliament) in February 1933, the people of Waldron immediately responded by replacing Guy Fawkes with an effigy of Herr Hitler, and fancy-dress costumes at Uckfield Hospital Carnival would also highlight the rise of the Nazis.[32]

Frank Upfield resumed the role of bandmaster in March 1935. The Band had been floundering since the departure of Pettitt and was not heard in public for about six months.[33] In the early Twenties, the Upfields had been its first large family of musicians, bringing controversy to the bandroom when

HSB: Winners of the Christie Challenge Trophy, Tunbridge Wells Contest, May 1930.
Photograph supplied by Peter Cornford.

Frank's daughter Sylvia had become its first female player. Although this may seem bewildering today, almost the entire brass band movement comprised working-class men, mainly due to its ties with grass-roots industries. From the men's perspective, banding provided some well-earned escapism from the daily grind of work and family affairs. Wives were presumably expected to stay at home on rehearsal nights to babysit the children. A newspaper report of one Tunbridge Wells Contest provides a fascinating window on the prevailing attitudes of the time: "[Most] striking of all was the appearance in the Mayfield Band of one young bands-woman. It was not the first occasion upon which a woman had taken part in the contest, but, smart and debonair, she was the centre of much admiration and interest."[34] Today, nobody would give a second thought to the gender of a musician.

Times were changing, but not all members were happy about women joining the Band. Bert Thompson and a couple of others so strongly disapproved that they were to resign in protest. "We didn't think that was right. We couldn't swear or spin a yarn or nothing, so we left," says Bert. One objection was that they would no longer be able to "use trees" when out on long marches! In the event, the experiment at Heathfield Band was short-lived: Sylvia Upfield soon left to enrol in the Land Army. The Second World War would in fact be the main catalyst for change within many town bands: as male players were called up to serve, they left behind them vacancies that needed filling, and many female musicians were to take full advantage of this situation.[35] It was several more decades before Heathfield Band became fully unisex. However, as females' function in society evolved, a new generation of women and girls, often belonging to brass banding families, would find themselves almost organically becoming members of the Band.[36]

One of Frank Upfield's first responsibilities as bandmaster was to lead the Band for the Jubilee of King George V, in May 1935. Community celebrations were naturally held across the county and, as each parish sought to outdo its neighbour, the Band again found itself torn between Cross-in-Hand (in the parish of Waldron) and Heathfield. The former was the first to offer a paid engagement, which the Band would gladly accept, leading a parade of schoolchildren from Heathfield to Cross-in-Hand for a celebratory sports day. In the evening, it opened a dance for the British Legion at Cross-in-Hand (though the music for dancing was provided by the Legion's own band).[37] Heathfield Band earned a very healthy £13 (about £945 today) for an honest day's work. Heathfield's celebrations at the Recreation Hall would disappointingly have to make do with pre-recorded "tin music." This led to ill-feeling between the parishes and make for some heated debates at planning meetings for King Edward VIII's Coronation the following year.[38]

By November 1936 things had become further complicated: "There appears to be a general move-about by local bands for the forthcoming Coronation celebrations," writes the Sussex Express. "The Heathfield Silver Band will attend the Cross-in-Hand celebrations, and the Warbleton Brass & Reed Band will play in connection with the Heathfield festivities. The question is – What band will Warbleton have?"[39] As the majority of Heathfield Band's players lived in the Waldron parish, it was a fairly natural choice for them to support the Cross-in-Hand event, for which they would earn £7.7s. (over £500 today). The celebrations were similar to those for the Jubilee, the Band again leading a procession of schoolchildren to the sports field for a community sports day.[40] The children were each presented with a souvenir medal or a brooch, a special tea was laid on, the King's speech was broadcast to the company, and the Band played heartily for community singing.[41] The occasion would conclude with a fancy-dress carnival dance, with music by the *Scarlet Serenaders*, and a display of fireworks.[42]

A new era for the Band began in 1938 when deputy bandmaster Bert Wise took over the baton permanently. Bert was a true bandsman who never thought of anything else. According to his contemporaries, he was the best conductor the Band has ever known. During his tenure, it quickly progressed from an average fourth section band to the first contesting section. "That's when it was doing its best at contests and was really disciplined, really regimented and respected by other bands," says Peter Cornford.

Throughout the decade, the Band continued its tradition of carolling, and would go *toffing* (touring the manor houses of wealthy residents – the "toffs") in search of donations.[43] A 1931 appeal reads: "Heathfield Silver Band, who have had another successful year, will soon be reminding the residents that the festive season is approaching, and incidentally that a band of over twenty performers cannot exist without funds."[44] The Band's secretary, Arthur Frost, would write to residents to give advance notice of the tour. Consequently, house parties were often organised to coincide with its visit, from which the Band did very well financially.[45] As it moved from house to house, donations were recorded in a small book, which some residents would ask to see (in order to better their neighbours), in a social game of one-upmanship.[46] Thus, the astute Band would organise its tour in descending order of the residents' relative wealth![47]

"In the heydays we used to do nearly three weeks," remembers George Mepham Jnr. "We used to go all over the damn show. We'd make out a list where we would go for each bandsman. Most people biked. I used to use my bike often, strap my euphonium to my back and pedal off. You used to chuck your bike somewhere and blow!" Bert Thompson recalls one evening with particular amusement: "One night we were out *Christmassin'*, and a lady called Charlie [Pettitt] up to her front door to give him a bit o' money or so, and when he took the money, Arch [Knapp, cornet player and comedian of the Band] said, 'Do a curtsey Charlie!' He had always something funny to say!" There was often nobody available to hold a lamp for the musicians, so they would have to grasp it in one hand whilst playing their instrument with the other. It was cold, too: "Bitter cold. Froze many a time out Cade Street," remembers Gordon Neve. "Jack Mitchell was taking us, there was eight or nine of us, he brought his baton down and… nothing." The instruments were completely frozen up!

Bert Thompson describes the tail end of one such evening: "We'd been carolling, you see, me and Arthur Ralph. We finished at Old Heathfield and everyone else but us went home. We went in *The Star*, and they give us a drink. We'd got two or three pots of beer on the counter and Arthur had got his tenor under his arm there. I picked up the quart pot of beer and said to Arthur, 'What shall I do with this?' He answered, pointing to his horn and laughing, 'Shoot it down there.' So I did, quick, and off we went. Then in the morning, Arthur's mother came round to see the wife. She said, 'Was Bert drunk last night?' Mrs. Bert said, 'No, not that I know of.' 'Well,' said Mrs. Ralph, 'Arthur was. He sicked all over the sofa and it stinks of beer!' But what it was, he used to hang his tenor on the wall over the sofa, and the beer had run down on to the sofa from his horn!" George Mepham Jnr. also recalls some boozy nights out carolling: "Some of us used to get tiddly, 'specially on the home-made stuff. We couldn't play after drinking sometimes!"

Carolling was one of the Band's biggest money-spinners, and was usually well worth the effort. As an incentive for taking part, bandmembers were each paid a shilling (about £3.50) for every evening spent carolling. Proceeds would rise and fall quite significantly from year to year, providing a useful barometer for the state of the local economy at any given time. In 1931, for example, the Band collected over £40 (about £2,780 today) whilst in 1938 it achieved a more modest £20 (about £1,380). Sometimes it would encounter stiff competition: "Heathfield had rather more than its full share of seasonable music and carols," writes Sussex Express in December 1937. "A Salvation Army band played in the vicinity of the High Street […] and the Heathfield Silver Band, about half-a-mile away, in Hailsham Road, could be heard playing the same tune![48] Nevertheless, Christmas was by far the best time to capitalise on the giving spirit of the community. "It is reported that the Heathfield Band are doing well in their collections and are laying a foundation for the £300 [about £20,000 today] they are seeking to purchase new instruments," continues the report.[49]

At Christmas in 1935, the germ of an annual social event came into being when the Band held a variety dance fundraiser at the British Legion Hall in Cross-in-Hand.[50] Similar events were staged in 1936 and 1937, and a concert in 1939. The accounts also show profits from a lucrative Christmas draw, which raised a healthy £17 (about £1,180 today) and £14 (about £960) for the Band, in 1937 and 1938 respectively.

The following year, everything was to change. On 1st September 1939 Hitler invaded Poland and, as a consequence, Britain and France declared war on Germany. Just days later, the reality of a new war hit home, as ten bandmembers returned home from an engagement to find their call-up papers awaiting them. Across the country, veteran brass banders remembered the devastation to the movement caused by the previous war, and urged bands to continue playing at all costs. But the challenge was almost insurmountable. The National Brass Band Finals would be cancelled, restrictions on travel effectively put an end to concert tours, the manufacture of instruments was curtailed, and supplies of sheet music were significantly limited.[51]

In Heathfield, bandmembers called an extraordinary meeting to discuss the future of their beloved institution. It was decided that they would continue having two rehearsals a week for as long as was possible; after all, the 9pm bus was still running to transport out-of-town players home afterwards. It was also agreed to pay bandmaster Bert Wise's travelling expenses, and to gift the families of members serving in the forces a share of Band funds (which would amount to 5 shillings each per week, about £16.50 today).[52] The Band's first

Heathfield Band: One week before the War, September 1939.

(Back Row, L–R) Alec Haffenden, Alan Neve, Bert Baker, Jack Mitchell, ?, ?.
(Middle Row, L–R) ?, Eric Latter, ?, ?, Sid Bunce, Ken Latter.
(Front Row, L–R) Cyril Leeves, Jeff Hobden, Charlie Woodgate, Bert Wise,
George Mepham Jnr., Sam Baker, Gordon Neve.
(Sitting, L–R) George Mepham Snr., Arthur Frost.

Photograph supplied by Sussex Newspapers.

contribution to the war effort was a fundraising Radio Stars Variety Show in aid of the British Red Cross Soldiers' Comforts Fund, held at the Heathfield Recreation Hall in December 1939.[53] It would open the show, to be followed by piano recitals, conjurors, an impersonator, a tap dancer, and a contralto. The evening concluded with a community dance, with music by the *Harmony Aces Dance Band*.

The 1920s had been an eventful decade. The Band had weathered the Great Depression, the growth of mechanical music, and the retirement of its long-standing bandmaster Charles Pettitt. It had raised a substantial sum through engagements and collections, enabling the purchase of new instruments and uniforms, and had admirably performed its function as the town band, supporting community celebrations of national and regional import, and providing the backbone for countless other social events. It had also found a sturdy new conductor in Bert Wise. But just how would it survive the hardships brought about by another world war?

[1] Minutes, 14th April 1937

[2] Hailstone, A., 1987. *The British Bandsman Centenary Book*. Baldock: Egon: 180–7

[3] ibid: 189

[4] Sussex Express, 30th October 1930

[5] Russell, D., 2000. 'What's Wrong with Brass Bands?': Cultural Change and the Band Movement, 1918–c.1964. In: T. Herbert, ed., *The British Brass Band: A Musical and Social History*. Oxford: Oxford University Press: 86

[6] Sussex Express, 2nd September 1932

[7] Sussex Express, 15th January 1932

[8] ibid

[9] ibid

[10] ibid

[11] ibid

[12] ibid

[13] Sussex Express, 22nd January 1932

[14] Sussex Express, 29th January 1932

[15] Sussex Express, 15th July 1932

[16] Sussex Express, 10th June 1938 & 15th July 1938; Accounts, 1938

[17] Sussex Express, 8th June 1934

[18] Sussex Express, 16th August 1935

[19] e.g. Sussex Express, 13th November 1931, etc

[20] Sussex Express, 20th November 1931

[21] Sussex Express, 15th November 1935

[22] Sussex Express, 7th February 1930

[23] Encyclopedia Britannica. 2021. *Douglas Haig, 1st Earl Haig | British military leader* [online]. Available at: <www.britannica.com/biography/Douglas-Haig-1st-Earl-Haig>

[24] Sussex Express, 7th February 1930

[25] Sussex Express, 12th February 1932

[26] Sussex Express, 1st June 1934

[27] ibid

[28] e.g. Sussex Express, 1st May 1931

[29] ibid

[30] ibid

[31] Hailstone, A., 1987: 194

[32] Sussex Express, 15th September 1933 & 10th November 1933

[33] Sussex Express, 22nd March 1935

[34] Kent & Sussex Courier, 9th May 1930

[35] Russell, D., 2000: 80–82

[36] ibid

[37] Sussex Express, 10th May 1935

[38] Sussex Express, 16th October 1936 & 30th October 1936

[39] Sussex Express, 27th November 1936

[40] Sussex Express, 14th May 1937

[41] ibid

[42] ibid

[43] Cornford, P., 1981. Personal Archive and Interviews

[44] Sussex Express, 4th December 1931

[45] ibid

[46] ibid

[47] ibid

[48] Sussex Express, 17th December 1937

[49] ibid

[50] Sussex Express, 6th December 1935

[51] Cornford, P., 1981

[52] Minutes, 27th September 1939

[53] Sussex Express, 29th December 1939

MEMBERS of NOTE...

Jeff Hobden (The Whistling Bandsman)
BBb bass,
ca. 1930–1969.

Jeff joined Heathfield Band around 1930, purchasing his own instrument and becoming its first BBb bass player.[1] He would make a significant contribution to its revival after the Second World War, although he was never to become a committee member. He was well-known in the community for his cheerful demeanour and habit of whistling wherever he went, a habit which was to earn him the nickname *The Whistling Bandsman*![2] "He used to whistle the whole time, you used to always hear him coming down to practice and he used to whistle from the pub right down the road to Sandy Cross where he lived," remembers Sue Sutton. It was even said that he would compose original tunes as he walked! For good measure, he would also be sure to carry a mouthorgan in his pocket.

Although he could not read or write (indeed, fellow bandmembers would have to find his music for him), Jeff was a very practical person. In addition to being one of the country's last surviving wood-carvers,[3] he would also make repairs to the Band's brass instruments. "He has through the years saved the Band pounds with his skill at doing minor repairs [...] and he saved the day many times with his solder and blow-lamp [...]. Nothing seemed too much trouble for him," says former bandmaster Lloyd Bland (in 1969).[4]

Bandmember Bert Thompson (interviewed in 1981) remembers Jeff's particularly lovable way of innocently muddling words: "I remember walking along the straight by *The Crown* once, and Jeff came sailing by, shouting, 'Bert, there's a miticom meeting tonight!' He got his words all muddled, see. Then when we were going on a Band outing once, there wasn't enough seats on the bus, so Jeff said, 'I don't mind sitting on the old regulator.' He meant 'radiator,' you see, poor old Jeff!"

Jeff was one of the most reliable and best-natured players the Band has ever seen, and he would often carry sweets or chocolate to give to junior members. "He was a really keen bandsman, loved by all," says Lloyd Bland. "His double bass was his pride and joy and he always insisted that he carried it and looked after it himself."[5] Jeff could often be spotted around town on his way to gigs, walking or sometimes biking with his instrument strapped to his back.[6] A true bandsman at heart, Jeff was an enthusiastic attendee of the annual contests at the Crystal Palace, and would also play with the Mayfield and Warbleton bands.[7]

Despite practising every day, Jeff was never destined to become a superb musician. He would never get to the end of a piece first, but was more than likely to blow in the wrong place! Later in life, his abilities were to decline further and a special effort would have to be made to help him feel included at contests. "The conductor would cross through the notes on Jeff's part one by one as the rehearsals went by," recalls Peter Cornford. "By the time the big day came, he had only a handful left which would do no damage. Yet he was still bursting with pride to be playing his few notes with the Band on stage!"

Jeff died in early 1969. "We shall all miss him greatly and his death leaves a big gap which will be very hard to fill," comments Lloyd Bland in one obituary.[8] The Band would play at Jeff's funeral, members would act as coffin bearers, and the *Last Post* was performed at his graveside.[9] With Jeff's passing, Heathfield Band would never be quite the same again.

---

[1] Cutting, source unknown, 24th January 1969

[2] ibid

[3] ibid

[4] ibid

[5] ibid

[6] ibid

[7] ibid

[8] ibid

[9] ibid

Interlude It's the Music That Matters: The Repertoire of Heathfield Silver Band

It is difficult to imagine the state of popular music at the end of the nineteenth century. Although Heathfield now boasted its own sheet music lending library and some people had a piano or harmonium in their homes, many of the townsfolk would have extremely limited opportunities to experience live music. For some, the only regular opportunity was through the Church, or via occasional visiting ensembles to the town. The growing brass band movement (which evolved from city waits, and church and military bands) therefore proved an important influence on contemporary musical tastes.

However, brass bands were a fairly new phenomenon; there was no body of specially-composed music available to them. Consequently, early bands had to rely on transcriptions of existing sacred pieces, popular melodies, dances, and marches, whilst Christmas carols were performed from the same Salvation Army hymn books which are still in common use today.

There is no record of the repertoire from Heathfield Band's formative years, but the type of engagement would generally have dictated the flavour of music performed. At bonfire parades, the Band would have relied on well-known marches; at fêtes, popular selections and medleys; and at dances, quadrilles, polkas, schottisches and waltzes. For military occasions, it would primarily have performed marches and the *Reveille*. To obtain further insights, we may look to the British Bandsman's suggested format for park concerts: an opening march followed by a heavier selection, a solo, an overture, a novelty piece, a lighter selection, a suite (usually a themed compilation of three short dances), and a concluding national fantasia.[1] This structure remained popular for the majority of formal concerts until very recently, as the latest generation of conductors have become more fluid in their approach.

Although the identities of early pieces are mostly lost to us, there are occasional mentions in the press of the time. For example, we know that patriotic tunes such as *Rule Britannia* and the *National Anthem* were performed at many engagements, and *Auld Lang Syne* was sometimes played at the close of community events, in addition to New Year's Eve celebrations. At the conclusion of the 1902 Heathfield Hospital Parade, the Band combined with Warbleton Brass Band for a massed finale of *The Young Brigade*,[2] and at a 1903 fundraising concert it would play *Crown of Victory* and *My Colleen*.

However, the first concert for which we can get a true feel is a fundraiser held at Cade Street in January 1906, where the Band's performances included the selection *La Cenerentola*, overtures *Latona* and *La Reine*, quartets *The Soldier's Tale* and *The Village Chimes*, quintets *Majestical* and the grand march *Cambridge*, and an intermezzo entitled *Ye Merry Monarch*.[3] Quartet and quintet arrangements were a popular part of the Band's repertoire at the time, and would prove useful in that they allowed a small ensemble to appear where a full brass band might not have been economical, or even desirable.

For the Artillery Volunteers' Prize Distribution Concert, held at Heathfield's Drill Hall in December 1907, the Band contributed "good musical entertainment, which was undoubtedly the best of its kind held in the hall in recent years."[4] In addition to a valse entitled *My Guiding Star*, it played selections such as *Gems of Song*, *Songs of Other Days*, and *Jubilation*. The latter appears to have been well-liked by bandmembers and would be repeated at a concert in early 1908, alongside contemporary favourites *Eton Boating Song*, *Old Memories* and *Rose Bloom*.[5] At a 1909 concert in aid of the Heathfield Rat and Sparrow Club (whose aim was to assist farmers with pest control), the Band performed *Anchored* and *Go To Sea*.[6]

We have some other insights, too. From 1910 and 1912, there are full programmes from the Framfield Flower Show, which give a fascinating taste of the pre-war repertoire, and suggest that the Band's stock in trade was largely nostalgic and nationalistic pieces. The programmes reveal a special regard for the works of eminent conductor, cornet virtuoso and composer of more than 100 marches, William Rimmer, whose works are still enjoyed by both the Band and the listening public today.[7] In addition, there were valses by the likes of Percorini and P. Fitzgerald, fantasias by S. Cope, A. Calvers and J.A. Greenwood, and selections by Arthur Sullivan and William Wallace, some of whom were now composing pieces specifically for brass bands.[8]

We are fortunate to have a surviving, if well-worn, solo cornet book from the period, retained for posterity by bandmember Jack Mitchell. It contains forty pieces, mostly taken from the Wright & Round Music Journal, which are almost certainly what the Band would have been playing at the outbreak of Great War (the first twenty-nine date from the early twentieth century whilst the remainder were published in 1914). The book contains a wide variety of dances, marches, overtures, selections, transcriptions of orchestral works, and light music written specially for brass band. However, the sole surviving pre-war book cannot represent the Band's entire contemporary repertoire. At the very least, a selection of hymns and Christmas carols would also

The surviving solo cornet book from 1912.

have been required. We know with more certainty that between 1910 and the late 1920s the Band's core repertoire comprised three selection books and five march books. "Covers were bought and music stuck in, and we also had march cards besides the books. Lyres were too small to carry everything," recalls George Mepham Jnr. (interviewed in 1981).

The fact that only the solo cornet book survives suggests that the early repertoire was discarded during, or soon after, the war. Publishers were undoubtedly happy for bands to do this, for whatever reason, as it would guarantee sales of new sheet music. In fact, they actively encouraged the practise: "The pleasure of banding is in rehearsing good, new music, and after you have sucked the orange dry, what matter if you throw it away?" exclaims one advertisement for the Wright and Round Music Journal. "If you have had your pleasure out of the music, burn it like you would an old newspaper that has served its turn. Music at subscription rates is cheap enough. And new music is the life of banding."[9]

Following the Great War, there was a redefining of the Band's social purpose, and it would begin taking part in numerous remembrance services to commemorate the fallen. It accompanied church congregations as they sang, and the choice of music was very reflective of the times, popular hymns including: *O God, Our Help In Ages Past, Abide With Me, Jesu Lover of My Soul, All People that on Earth do Dwell, Fight the Good Fight,* and *Onward Christian Soldiers.* Memorial services in the style of military funerals began taking place at local cenotaphs, and would usually include *The Dead March from Saul, Last Post and Reveille,* and *Carry On.* On occasions when the British Legion had to dedicate a new standard, *O God, Our Help In Ages Past* was again popular, in addition to *O, Valiant Hearts.*

Another insight into the Band's post-war repertoire can be found in an advertisement for the 1925 Wright and Round Liverpool Journal (editor and principal arranger, one William Rimmer), which lists "Heathfield Band (Sussex)" among the many subscribers.[10] The Band's oldest surviving music appears to have been purchased during this time, much of which retains its practical value, such as the marches performed each year at Sussex Bonfire Parades.

Bert Thompson (interviewed in 1981), who joined the Band in 1922, recalls: "When we went on church parades, or anything like that, they'd tell you what marches to take. The marches, we always kept them at home, every march we'd got. We didn't have a librarian then. Everyone had a white bag, you got your mother to make one – a white bag and a white band. They hung down behind. We carried just the music that we wanted on that day. The music we didn't play, we used to keep in the bandroom in a tin box." Asked about the repertoire, Bert adds: "The selections and that were good. Once piece was *La Traviata*, a nice piece of music." Jack Mitchell (also interviewed in 1981) fondly recalls playing pieces such as *Queen of Angels* and *How Lovely it Was* outside Mayfield's Railway Hotel at a Hospital Parade in the early Twenties.

Fundraising concerts continued to be popular with the Band, giving it a chance to perform a good mixture of short, popular pieces and more meaty arrangements. The programme for a 1927 fundraiser includes the marches *London Pride* and *The Thin Red Line*, the overture *Modegiska*, and fantasias such as *Songs of Gallant Wales*, *The Village Gala* and *Rustic Festival*.[11] At another in 1929, held in aid of Heathfield Band and the Brotherhood Orchestra, Jack Mitchell and George Mepham would perform a cornet duet entitled *Down the Vale*, and also join Arthur Rodgers, Horace Mepham and Edward Bean for two quintets, *Silver Moonlit Winds are Blowing* and *Goodnight, Beloved*.[12] By now, community singing had become a fashionable way to boost morale and foster a sense of togetherness, and the Band appeared at one such event in the Summer of 1929, performing pieces including: *Pack up you Troubles, John Brown's Body, Tipperary, Keep the Home Fires Burning, Marching Through Georgia*, and *Land of Hope and Glory*.[13]

During the Twenties, the Band also began contesting, winning the fourth section at the Tunbridge Wells Contest in 1924 with a Rimmer piece entitled *Waltz Amorette*. In subsequent years, test-pieces included Coleridge-Taylor's *Hiawatha*, Sullivan's *Pirates of Penzance*, Greenwood's *The Spirit of Youth, The Golden Age* and *Hampton Court*, Le Duc's *The Forest Chief*, and Laurent's *Beautiful Britain*. At a national level, the contest scene saw notable orchestral composers beginning to take an interest in brass bands for the first time. Gustav Holst would write *A Moorside Suite* for the 1928 contest at Crystal Palace, Edward Elgar would follow in 1930 with *Severn Suite*, and John Ireland was to contribute *Downland Suite* in 1932. As far as we know, Heathfield Band never attempted these pieces at a contest, but they endure today as fine examples of original brass band music. The Band would cease contesting for most of the Forties, but returned to the scene in the 1950s, tackling pieces such as Greenwood's *The Call of Youth, Recollections of Beethoven* and *Song of Wales*, Ball's *Rhapsody on Negro Spirituals, The English Maiden, Call of the Sea* and *Holiday Suite*, Wright's *Glastonbury*, and arrangements of Tchaikovsky's *Romeo and Juliet*, and Beethoven's *Mignonne.*

The Fifties and Sixties are sometimes regarded as years of stagnation for the brass band movement, as the wider population focused its energies and attentions on rebuilding a broken nation. However, as early as Christmas 1950, Heathfield Band began to bring music back to the community, staging a series of open-air concerts around the town.[14] Throughout this decade, the brass band repertoire was to evolve quickly: perhaps there was an economic need to widen the appeal of the genre, or perhaps the general public's musical tastes had simply expanded alongside the growth of broadcast and recorded music. The formation of the National Schools' Brass Band Association in 1952 led to a further injection of new music, by acclaimed composers such as Malcolm Arnold, Gordon Jacob, Gilbert Vintner and Edward Gregson. These works remain staples of the brass band repertoire today. In addition, the movement's ability to adapt to a range of musical influences would lead to a further widening of its arsenal, as it embraced everything from popular stage shows to contemporary pop music. In 1956, Heathfield Band's "library" comprised just 280 titles, but by 1978 the overburdened lone filing cabinet would collapse and break!

Brass bands are sometimes criticised for being behind the times, but this argument wilfully ignores the versatility of the art-form. Many older pieces become classics simply because they constitute great music. Heathfield Band did not simply abandon its past but, by the 1950s, village and town bands were beginning to attempt works by talented modern arrangers such as Edrich Siebert (whose works are still enjoyed today). Therefore, in 1959 the committee felt that it might attract more younger players if the focus was shifted towards newer music.[15] This was a stylistic turning point. Whilst older favourites such as *Amparito Roca, All In The April Evening, Tancredi*, and *Bandology* would remain, they were now complemented by more contemporary fare.

"The Band I remember was a pretty eclectic mix of old and new," recalls Peter Cornford. "Every piece was exciting and different, from contesting music like *Divertimento* and *English Folk Songs Suite*, *Nabucodonosor*, *Lustspiel*, and *Mood Indigo* – really good solid brass band stuff – through to *Last of the Summer Wine*, *Save all Your Kisses for Me*, and *Una Paloma Blanca*, which we did at the fêtes." At a thanksgiving service in 1977, the hymns were accompanied by the selection *Rachmaninov's Prelude*, and bandmember George Miller even contributed a trombone solo entitled *Silent Worship*. However, the Band would also continue to give traditional evening concerts and old-time dances, whilst bonfire parades, services of remembrance, and many other community events remain essentially unchanged to this day. "It was very varied," adds Wendy Holloway (née Guile). "We played marches, hymns, and classical. *Modern* meant Beatles music. Anything newer was slightly frowned upon, but we did do *The Floral Dance* once radio DJ Terry Wogan made it cool. *Hootenanny* was our star piece as whichever section was taking the lead stood up to play. It was a huge hit with the younger players, and an annoyance to the older ones who did not want to keep standing up. In fact, some refused to do so! We also had the music to *Star Wars*, but it sounded like a bunch of cats being tortured! If the librarian, Ted Lee, didn't like a piece of music, it disappeared into his house, never to be seen again. Anyone querying this was told he was 'sorting it…' "

David Threlfall took over as bandmaster towards the end of the Seventies. "We did play some of what had gone before," says Peter, "but there's four I can remember him introducing: *Elvira Madigan* (a Mozart horn feature taken from the 1967 film of the same name), *Chanson d'Amour* (I can see Dave now getting tangled up trying to conduct that one), and we did *Match Stalk Men* (I guess you'd understand that being Dave and [painter] Lowry and Manchester and all that), and a march, *Pendine*, which I'm certain we did at a friendly competition at Tunbridge Wells."

The winning blend of traditional and modern would be retained into the Eighties and Nineties. "There was, I must admit, a fair bit of [Belgian arranger] Frank Bernaerts' music," says former bandmaster Jeff Collins. "But it was still quite popular then, to the players and to the audience, to do selections from musicals: *Sound of Music*, *Mary Poppins*, *King and I* we used to play quite often because you'd get a lot of elderly audiences. If I had my way choosing what a band programme would be, I'd still have at least one musical piece during that time. I prefer the good old traditional brass band."

During this time, the most significant additions to the repertoire were from a new generation of arrangers, such as Gordon Langford, Alan Fernie, Alan Catherall, *et al.* Where once popular stage musicals were adapted for brass bands, now film scores became the fashion, thanks to the efforts of populist radio stations such as *Classic FM*, and the growing affordability of pre-recorded music. These new arrangers would more fully address the range

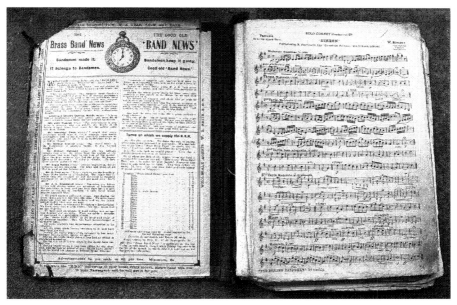

Opening page of the surviving 1912 solo cornet book.

and capabilities of the average town band, attempting to give each section something of interest to play. Music also became more percussion-led. "A piece that is absolutely brilliant to play is *The Final Countdown*. The brass band arrangement of that is brilliant," enthuses Jeff Collins.

The modern repertoire brought with it new challenges, not least that of working up a wide range of material to a high enough performance standard, often with limited rehearsal time. "If you're gonna go out on a concert, you always have to have everything for a public audience," explains former bandmaster Frank Francis. "I believed in doing a concert march to start, an overture of some sort after, a show piece like *My Fair Lady* or something like that, and then you start to be a little bit more flirtatious with the style, like a Latin-American. Then maybe another specific concert piece to start to close the show off with, like the *1812 Overture* or a regal type of piece that would stir and stimulate your audience, and then another light-hearted piece and a closer… And *Sussex By The Sea*."

When Frankie Lulham took over as musical director in 2002, her solution was to introduce simpler arrangements to encourage players and build their confidence, steadily raising the standard over time. The Band was soon able to tackle more solid brass music, such as *2nd Suite in F Major, Aces High, Myfanwy, St. Andrew's Variations*, and sectional features such as *Grandfather's Clock, The Lazy Trumpeter, Solitaire*, and even Eb Bass solo *Forty Fathoms*. Occasionally, bandmembers demanded an even greater challenge, and old test pieces such as *Malvern Suite* or *Moorside Suite* would be dug out of the library for re-evaluation. An enormous quantity of music was brought up to scratch extremely quickly, starting with a clean slate at the beginning of each year. The repertoire for 2005, for example, comprised a staggering fifty-five pieces, all of which would be performed in public during the Summer season!

Wherever an opportunity arose, the Band staged themed concerts. In 2002, there would be a Jubilee concert at Heathfield Fire Station, which emphasised quintessentially British music such as *Rule Britannia, Land of Hope and Glory, English Country Garden*, and *Hootenanny*. An over-fifties concert in Brighton showcased traditional pieces such as *All in the April Evening, Farmer's Boy*, and *Slaidburn*, and at Le Marché, Heathfield's annual French market, the Band played popular French melodies such as *Orpheus, The Bold Gendarmes*, and *Bouquet de Paris*. For an Old Time Music Hall Concert at the Heathfield Community Centre, the Band performed pieces such as *Community Land, The Holy City*, and *Old Comrades*, and it even had the audience singing along to *Down at the Old Bull and Bush, I'm 21 Today*, and *I Do Like to be Beside the Seaside*. For a concert at the *Half Moon Inn* at Cade Street, entitled *Heathfield Silver Band Plays Pop*, it played pieces such as *Amarillo, One Moment in Time, Mamma Mia, and American Pie*. But the pinnacle of these gigs would be the Band's annual Christmas Concerts, with themes such as *Ding Dong Christmas* (2003), *Tartan Crackers* (2004), *Around the World in Eighty Minutes* (2005), and *Christmas at the Movies* (2010).

One unique aspect of Heathfield Silver Band is the various pieces specially written or arranged for it over the years. One early example resulted from a challenge to Peter Cornford by fellow bandmember Jack King, who had received composition instruction whilst playing in the army. "I was complaining about some march that we were playing," remembers Peter, "and Jack replied, 'See if you can write something better!' " The result was Peter's first ever composition for brass band, entitled *The HSB March* (1979), which was performed at several engagements. "There was also my *Cuckoo Line Calypso*, which was a bit better," admits Peter. "One of my first attempts at arranging was *The Wombling Song* and *We Wish You A Wombling Merry Christmas*. I actually wrote to [Wombles composer] Mike Batt's publishing company and received a letter granting permission for the Band to play them, so we did!"

Jack King himself also wrote for the Band, and Peter remembers one especially good march entitled *Warrior Square*. "He was very encouraging towards me as a youngster having a go at composing. He would take home my manuscript scores and make comments and suggestions. I learned a lot from him. He gave me his army composition notebooks just before he retired from the Band, which I still consult." In addition, euphonium player Dick Turner composed easy-to-play pieces such as *Jogalong* and *Isn't it a Lovely Day?*, and bandmaster Frank Francis adapted Territorial Army fanfares with which to introduce formal concerts. His successor John Barratt approached the Band of the Royal Corps of Signals for scores to *Banditenstreiche* and *French Comedy*, with a view to arranging them for the Band.

For the new millennium, a National Lottery grant would enable the Heathfield Choral Society to commission a new piece, from composer Peter Monk, to be performed jointly by the Society and the Band. *Sussex in Silver* took several years to complete, the composer missing several deadlines along the way, including one for a joint concert in May 2000 at which it had been intended to premiere the work. The logistics of rehearsing the piece were to prove challenging, and by the time it was finally completed in early 2001, the

Band was no longer strong enough to perform it.[16] The available evidence suggests that it was sadly never performed as originally intended.[17]

In the Autumn of 2002, the Band's principal cornet player Danielle Lulham, then in the second year of her music degree, would study in America for several months. "Whilst in California I composed this piece for the Band, *Proud Hearts*, and it helped me to feel closer to home," she recalls. "When we performed it, on a sunny day at Charleston Manor, it was a special day because my Grandad was there to listen." A recording would later be played at his funeral. Bass trombonist, Richard Ayres (speaking in 2018), remembers the piece fondly: "It was a simple, unaffected piece which worked really well; easy to play but with nice rich, open harmonies. The bass trombone part was a repeated rolling refrain which was easy, effective, and a pleasure to play."

In 2005, euphonium player Sarah Leeves would write *Fanfare for the Common Band*, a glorious, lively fanfare, for the grand reopening of the bandroom. "Rather than *Fanfare for a Common Man*, it was *Fanfare for the Common Band*," recalls former musical director Frankie Lulham. "It was a good fanfare. I thought it was a great take on it." The piece was dedicated to the Band's eldest member, 92 year-old Fred Richardson. Two other Band originals are mentioned, in documents from ca. 2010: Jasper Darvill's *The H.S.B.* and Dave Mildren's *HSB March*. Unfortunately, little is known about either. Most recently, Sarah has arranged a version of Daft Punk's *Get Lucky*, which was performed as part of a flash-mob at Le Marché in 2018.

Today, the Band's library contains over one thousand pieces, including a few dozen published before the Great War. Most, however, were purchased within the past few decades. Generally speaking, Christmas carols and hymns continue to be performed from the traditional Salvation Army books, and the Sussex Bonfire repertoire changes little from one year to the next. The latter still includes tried and tested favourites from the late nineteenth and early twentieth centuries, such as *Death or Glory*, *Colonel Bogey*, *Sons of the Brave*, *Voice of the Guns*, and, of course, *Sussex by the Sea* (which was first published in 1907). In fact, the latest addition to the bonfire march books is *The Great Escape*, which was written in 1963!

The repertoire continues to evolve, thanks in part to a stream of talented new brass band composers, but the popularity of traditional pieces shows no sign of abating. Indeed, from time to time the Band still enjoys raiding its library for *yellow music* (ancient pieces of manuscript held together with bits of peeling Sellotape). So, when next you hear Heathfield Silver Band play, one thing is certain: its programme will undoubtedly comprise a wide variety of traditional and modern arrangements; anything from Ball to Bacharach, the Beatles to Bublé!

---

[1] Hailstone, A., 1987. *The British Bandsman Centenary Book*. Baldock: Egon: 38

[2] Kent & Sussex Courier, 19th September 1902

[3] Sussex Express, 3rd February 1906

[4] Sussex Express, 28th December 1907

[5] Sussex Express, 8th February 1908 & 11th April 1908

[6] Sussex Express, 16th April 1909

[7] Hindmarsh, P., 2000. Building a Repertoire: Original Compositions for the Brass Band, 1913–1998. In: T. Herbert, ed., *The British Brass Band: A Musical and Social History*. Oxford: Oxford University Press: 258

[8] Sussex Express, 19th August 1910 & 23rd August 1912

[9] Brass Band News, November 1911

[10] Brass Band News, February 1925

[11] Sussex Express, 23rd September 1927

[12] Sussex Express, 29th November 1929

[13] Sussex Express, 19th July 1929 & 2nd August 1929

[14] Sussex Express, 22 December 1950

[15] Minutes, 29th April 1959

[16] Correspondence, Hilary Lane to Richard Sherlock, 10th January 2001

[17] Correspondence, Frankie Lulham to Hilary Lane, 24th February 2002

Poem *Our Village Band*

No doubt you will agree with me this is the very night,
That one and all should praise the Band that plays so very bright.
It does not matter when or where you ask our Band to play,
They just take up their instruments and blow your blues away.

Now a word of thanks to the bandmaster whose name is Mr. Wise,
Who now and then will tap his stick and take them by surprise,
He will scratch his head and murmur in a soft quiet undertone,
"Now George and Arthur let them hear you blow your old trombones."

The other night to Band practice an invitation I received,
To see the Band in action, it filled me with great glee,
For Jeff, Old Sam and Gordon they were playing on the bass,
The way they heaved and puffed and blew, I thought they'd bust their face.

Then the bandmaster tapped up and said: "I'll take the cornets please,"
Now Jack and Sid and Francis they fairly hit the breeze.
The notes came from their cornets, quite clear and very strong,
It sounded like the nightingale, just bursting into song.

The next of these bold Bandsmen on their instruments to perform,
Were Charlie, Ern and another lad, upon their tenor horns.
The way those notes came from those horns filled the bandmaster with glee,
It even brought tears to my eyes when they played *Tennessee*.

The next to show their paces were the euphonium and baritone,
Trix, Ted and young George Mepham, a splendid trio by gum,
They blew their notes so awful they all seemed out of tone,
That the whole Band started crying, and murmured: "Let's go home."

Now in this little poem the drums must have a place,
It is the beat and roll of these that makes the Band keep pace.
Now Cyril Leeves he beats the drum an old one I believe,
They say this drum it first saw light in 1863.

And now to end this poem about our Village Band,
There's one more thing I'd like to say, I think it's *really* grand.
When anyone wants music, at concerts, or at shows,
Just give the local Band a chance for they know how to blow.

by Len Thorne (Lorry Driver) (Poet), ca. 1938/39.

Mr. Thorne was a keen follower and supporter of the Band who occasionally wrote humourouss lines about it. He was a lorry driver for Heathfield Poultry Keepers (where Scats is now situated).

With grateful thanks to Myra & Ken Keeley who supplied the text.

Albert Edward "Bert" Wise

bandmember, 1937–1961,

bandmaster, 1938–40 & 1946–57.

"Now a word of thanks to the bandmaster,
whose name is Mr. Wise,
Who now and then will tap his stick and take them by surprise…"
– from *Our Village Band*, by Len Thorne, ca.1938.

Born in 1904, Bert Wise was to begin brass banding in his Sussex hometown, Newhaven, at the age of eight. By the mid-Twenties, he was playing with and conducting the Rhyl Band in North Wales, as would even work with acclaimed composer and conductor Harry Mortimer. He was to marry Eunice Funnell in 1926 and, returning to Sussex, would become a member of the Mayfield Band, before joining Heathfield Band in 1937. He was elected bandmaster the following year, having "inspired confidence in the men" as its deputy conductor.[1]

Aside from a break for the Second World War, Bert was to conduct the Band for nearly two decades, guiding it expertly from strength to strength. In preparation for contests, he would figuratively tear arrangements to pieces, and this attention to detail meant that the Band would progress all the way to the top section of SCABA.[2] "Bert was honest, well-liked, and sometimes fiery… but for the Band's benefit," says Peter Cornford. "He was the contest king, the guy who was in charge when the Band was at its peak of contesting."

"Mr. Wise was a bandmaster in a class of his own," adds Gordon Neve (speaking in 1981). "He took the Band to a standard that hadn't been known before. There was a difference when he was there… discipline and bite." Ted Lee (interviewed in 2013) says: "I found him very good, he was like a friend," whilst Sue Sutton, whose father, Lloyd Bland, played under Bert during the Fifties, recalls: "He was the old-fashioned type; he was very, very strict. When Bert Wise was there it was a very, very good band."

However, like any perfectionist, Bert could also be temperamental. "I played under Bert for a long time but he was a very difficult man," remembers Ken Russell. "He used to get all upset and then walk off and leave us! Yeah, he did! I can remember we was playing on the rec at Heathfield and something upset him and then he put the baton down and walked off and old Jack Mitchell took us over." Bert was also strongly opposed to having female members in the Band: "Mr. Wise wouldn't have them, they didn't come till after he left," says Gordon Neve.

Bert's confidence seems to have waxed and waned, and several times he was to consider resigning. He would have concerns over poor attendance and firmly believed that everybody could, and should, do better. By 1957, his health had taken a turn for the worse and Lloyd Bland was to caretake the Band for him. Bert would be unable to undertake marches and was adamant that the Band was no longer fit to contest. He was fiercely backed by loyal bandmembers, who said they "would rather give up contesting than lose Mr. Wise as bandmaster."[3]

Bert would resign as bandmaster in January 1958 but, having recuperated by the Summer, was to return in the capacity of deputy bandmaster.[4] He would lead Monday night rehearsals to prepare the Band for contests, whilst Lloyd Bland was to conduct the Band on Thursday evenings.[5] He would continue in this capacity until 1961, before taking his conducting talents to Warbleton Band. "A lot of 'em didn't like to see Mr. Wise go," recalls Ted Lee (in 2012). "I don't really know the circumstances why he left, 'cause we were still friendly. I 'spose [someone] must've upset him!"

Bert Wise was to retire from conducting in 1974 and would sadly pass away in 1985.

---

[1] Minutes, 11th February 1938

[2] Minutes, 2nd January 1958

[3] Minutes, 4th October 1957

[4] Minutes, 2nd January 1958 & 12th August 1958

[5] Minutes, 29th April 1959

1940s World War II: The Boys from the ATC

Heathfield Silver Band, ca. 1948.
Bandmaster Bert Wise.
Photograph supplied by Frankie Lulham.

By 1940, the Second World War was in full swing and, whilst the Band was keen not to cease playing altogether (as it had done for two years during the Great War), keeping it going would prove an uphill challenge. The British government had now passed the *National Service (Armed Forces) Act*, meaning that all men aged eighteen to forty-one were liable to be called-up for military service. As a result, the Band halved in size in just one day. Departing members agreed to return after the war, though many never did: one would perish in battle whilst others would begin new lives away from Heathfield, or simply gave up banding as their priorities changed. The Band which emerged into the Fifties was thus very different from its pre-war counterpart.

Across the nation, the disruption of war brought many bands to a standstill, but the music could not be silenced altogether. Brass bands were to provide a great morale boost, to both soldiers and civilians alike, during the difficult times.[1] In the Spring of 1940, as things began to hot up following the relative quiet of the "Phoney War," the 20th Sussex Battalion Home Guard was formed at Hailsham. This covered a 150 mile swathe of countryside,

148

including Heathfield and the surrounding area, and its part-time soldiers hailed from a variety of backgrounds. Amongst them, musicians from bands including Heathfield and Warbleton would soon establish a Home Guard Band, to cater for military events and church parades, and provide social entertainment in the form of dances and concerts.[2] On occasion, the Band could be seen parading through Hailsham High Street on its way to church. For rehearsals, players were picked up by army lorries and transported to the nearby Green Brothers Factory. The Home Guard Band would play an important part in the war effort, until the Battalion was disbanded at the end of 1944.

But how did Heathfield's town band survive at a time when others were forced to shut down? The answer surely lies in its status within the community. It was a revered institution that had played a key part in the lives of two generations of townsfolk, and keeping it alive had become a continuous pastime for the people of Heathfield. Together, they had seen off severe financial hardships and the devastation of the Great War; they had even weathered a disastrous break-up and phoenix-like reformation. Nobody was about to let the Nazis threaten it now. However, by May 1940, the war on the Western Front was going badly for the Allies, and their forces would have to be evacuated across the Channel. "After Dunkirk a few more of us were called up," remembers Gordon Neve (interviewed in 1981). "There was two or three of us gone overnight."

The Band now comprised a mere handful of players, including Gordon Neve (who was in the Territorial Army), Jack Mitchell and George Mepham Snr. (now members of the Home Guard), and Arthur Frost. Rehearsals were mostly held at the bandroom in Alexandra Road, though the half-yearly rent was not paid in January 1941, suggesting the Band may temporarily have moved elsewhere in a bid to cut its expenditure. This is borne out by the only surviving wartime minutes, dated December 1940, which concern the need to find a cheaper practice room and put instruments into storage in the event of it folding. Several bandmembers recollect cycling to Cade Street for some rehearsals (including Cyril Leeves, who did so with a bass drum strapped to his back), and it seems likely that these memories relate to this period. Arthur Frost would store disused instruments at his home whilst the bass drum purchased by Cyril Leeves at the 1939 Horsham Contest was relegated to his loft.

From early in the war, former bandmaster Charles Pettitt was busy with bomb disposal duties, and the Band's new conductor Bert Wise was away on military business. However, a new hope presented itself in the form of Sergeant-Bandmaster J.W. Durrant, who had a long military service behind him, and boys from the local branch of the Air Training Corps (ATC). Durrant served in France during the Great War and had since retired to Eastbourne, where he became a well-recognised military band conductor. Most recently he had fronted the Band of the Territorial Army Unit, the 58th Sussex Field Brigade, Royal Artillery, who put on popular concerts and led military parades and remembrance events in the town. In June 1940 his 21 year-old son James was killed in action in France, and Durrant and his wife would be evacuated to Alexandra Road in Heathfield.

Durrant soon made contact with the Heathfield Band, with a proposal to help them recruit young Air Cadets into the brass banding world. "They was sixteen or seventeen years of age, 'cause, you see, then you had to join the forces at eighteen, that's what you had to do," recalls principal cornet Ken Russell, one of the youngsters who joined the Band during the war. "I think I was thirteen when I joined. I started to play the cornet, but I couldn't get on with it so I packed it up. I think that's when Mr. Durrant come about. Jack Mitchell called on my place at Maynards Green and wanted me to go back and learn with the others. It was right at the end of the war, when the doodlebugs was coming over." Ken vividly remembers learning to play: "You know the [tutor] book where you learn to do the scales? It'd got the fingering for going up and then went down the scale without the fingering. When he was teaching me, old George thought I was doing well, but I said, 'Well, I'm reading it going backwards!' "

For a time, the Band was known as the *Heathfield ATC Band*, though it would also recruit and train members of the local Fire Services and the Home Guard. "There was about five of us learning," continues Ken. "Peter Greenfield and me used to go down in the wood and practise. He was a good player at the time, but when he got married he joined the police and he never kept it up. There was George Miller; me and George used to walk to Maynards Green from Heathfield after practice, and sometimes we used to catch the bus from the *Prince of Wales*. People used to get on the bus and old

Jeff Hobden – he had a double B [Bb bass] but he couldn't read music very well – he used to sit there and twiddle the valves like he was good! There was two George Mephams: George Mepham Snr. was a trombone player when I was playing in the Band, and the young George, he was a bit older than me, was their euphonium." Durrant himself would conduct and play euphonium with the Band. Jack Mitchell describes him as "a good man," whilst Ken Russell says: "He was a jolly nice old boy. He had a waxed moustache which he twiddled on the ends!"

Sheer determination kept the Band going through the war, from the blitz of 1940–41 to the final days when doodlebugs fell around the bandroom during practices. Blackout blinds on the windows made reading music almost impossible, and the musicians would not dare to use any lighting. During this period official records were not kept, so the available information is scarce. There were very few public engagements, though the Band occasionally played at fêtes and for church parades, and would sometimes be assisted by personnel from other local bands such as Warbleton, who were not active during the war.[3] In 1943, the Band appeared at the Cross-in-Hand Show, which that year was held in aid of the British Red Cross.[4] In addition, it led the Waldron Remembrance Day Parade from the War Memorial to the Parish Church. The Waldron British Legion made annual donations to the Band – of £2 (roughly £100 today) – throughout the war. The Band also played at a secret service on Tilsmore Common, held for locally-stationed Canadian soldiers (who, at the time, were responsible for defending the whole of the Sussex coast[5]), prior to their departure for Normandy in June 1944.

Whilst the Second World War was kinder to the Band than the previous one had been, it would nevertheless lose three musicians, including two of its original members. Seventy-six year-old side drummer Ben Haffenden, a carpenter from Sandy Cross, died early in 1941, whilst eighty-two year-old founder (and trombonist) Edward Bean passed away in June 1942. Yet more tragic was the loss of twenty-two year-old flugelhorn player Sid Bunce/Bunch, who was serving in Africa with the Royal Sussex Regiment. Sid died in October 1942, leaving behind his widow Lilian whom he had married just the previous year. He is commemorated at the Alamein Memorial in Egypt.[6]

Following the Allied victories in Europe and Japan, engagements would slowly begin returning to the town band. One of its first post-war engagements was the 1945 Waldron Carnival. It also provided dance music for three community socials, which collectively raised over £48 (around £2,100 today). "We used to play on the Rec at Heathfield," remembers Ken Russell. "We played there out in the open air, and the cricket ground out at Old Heathfield Church [All Saints]." In September 1945 the Band was invited to participate in Heathfield's Peace Celebrations, accompanying a celebratory tea and sports events. In November, it took part in the usual Waldron Remembrance Day Parade, marching from the Cross-in-Hand Legion Hut to the War Memorial and back. In June 1946, it played at the Cross-in-Hand Victory Show, and in October it held its first AGM since 1940.

As a result of community bands such as Heathfield actively fostering young talent during the war, the aging brass banding scene had been effectively rejuvenated. Some of the ATC boys remained with the Band after the war, so the committee waited until all former members had been contacted before recruiting any new players.[7] "Several of the old boys came back but not all of them. We was more or less all youngsters, all of us," recalls Ken Russell. "We had a good band after the war," adds George Mepham Jnr. (speaking in 1981). "The band of young boys, who weren't old enough to go in the army, were ready-made players." Youth bands began to prosper and by the 1950s the National Youth Band was rising to prominence.[8] In the case of Heathfield Band, the large-scale injection of young players would permanently change its outlook and make-up. It would now be necessary to think in terms of a more structured approach to training and recruitment (see *The New Recruits: Training Future Bandmembers*). As an added benefit, younger players often introduced their friends and relatives to the Band, contributing to the inter-generational, family-like blend which remains at its core today.

Weekly subscriptions were reintroduced (at 4d. per member or about 50p today), the Band would welcome the return of Bert Wise as its bandmaster, and a £3 donation (roughly £128 today) was made to Mr. Durrant in recognition of the part he had played in keeping the Band alive.[9] "About 1946–7 it wasn't a very good band, it never had a very good name for itself," says Ken. "It was just an old band struggling after the war. And then a bloke by the name of Bert Wise took over…" Bert would conceive a masterplan to rebuild and strengthen the Band, which included reinstating twice-weekly rehearsals to allow more rapid progress to be made. "We wasn't a band like they are now," adds Ken. "We was only learning, but it was quite good. We used to have a lot of people come and listen; mostly parents, as always!" Tom Brown joined the Band around this time, as his son Ant describes: "He came from a family of brass banders in the Cotswold town of Wooten Under Edge. After WW2 my parents lived for some years with my mother's parents at No.2 Harding Villas in Alexandra Road, Heathfield. The practice room is at the bottom of the garden, so it wasn't far to go or have any excuses not to go."

Receipts for 1947 show donations from both the Heathfield and Waldron branches of the British Legion, whilst other funds were raised by putting on concerts and community dances. The Band was also able to recommence its annual carolling around town, and performed for a carol service at St. Richard's Church. By July 1948, it had banked £42 (around £1,560 today), and in August this sum would be further boosted by collections at Heathfield Tower Recreation Ground. In addition, the Band made an overdue return to the contesting scene and would go on to triumph at the Tunbridge Wells Contest in both 1949 and 1950, demonstrating significant progress in its performance abilities. "While still young I was taken to many brass band competitions in Tunbridge Wells or Hastings," recalls Ant Brown, "and would ask the same questions every time: 'Why are they playing the same tune again?' 'Why are the judges in a box?' 'Can we go home soon>?' "

The most urgent task now was to begin a concerted fundraising effort, as the Band was in need of two new tenor horns, a complete set of uniforms, and an up-to-date repertoire.[10] Suggestions for generating income included holding jumble sales, whist drives, benefit concerts, old time dances, and a Christmas draw (the latter would net the Band almost £50, a phenomenal £1,800 in today's money).[11] Friends and family of bandmembers assisted with the running of such initiatives, and their involvement would eventually lead to the establishment of a successful Supporters' Club[12] (see *With a Little Help from Our Friends: The Band Supporters*). At Christmas, an almost industrial approach to carolling was taken; the Band toured for a full three weeks that year, raising about £53 (roughly £1,900 today). Finally, weekly subscriptions became a discretionary donation rather than a set amount, not only to encourage wealthier members to give generously, but also so as not to discourage poorer ones from attending. The Band also made a welcome return to the Sussex Bonfire scene, marching for societies at Commercial Square (Lewes) and Barcombe, and raising a further £47 (about £1,700). Collectively, these fundraising initiatives enabled the Band to enter the Fifties from a position of financial strength.

A full ten years after war had been declared, life was finally returning to normal for both the town of Heathfield and its Band, who could again boast an almost complete line-up of musicians. Popular social events, such as flower shows, carnivals and bonfire parades, were all making a comeback and the community was beginning to feel like its old self again. With the return of bandmaster Bert Wise, a successful future was practically guaranteed.

---

[1] Bourke, J., 1996. *The History of a Village Band 1896-1996*. Heathfield: Warbleton and Buxted Band: 36–7

[2] ibid

[3] ibid

[4] Sussex Express, 13th August 1943

[5] c.f. Pryce, R., 1996. *Heathfield Park: A Private Estate and a Wealden Town*. Heathfield: Roy Pryce: 146

[6] Roll of Honour, 2021. *Sussex* [online]. Available at: <www.roll-of-honour.com/Sussex/Heathfield.html>

[7] Minutes, 10th October 1946

[8] Russell, D., 2000. 'What's Wrong with Brass Bands?': Cultural Change and the Band Movement, 1918–c.1964. In: T. Herbert, ed., *The British Brass Band: A Musical and Social History*. Oxford: Oxford University Press: 77

[9] ibid

[10] Minutes, 12th June 1949

[11] ibid

[12] ibid

MEMBERS of NOTE...

Roy Elphick
bass & horn,
1949–1980.

by Peter Cornford

Roy was one of those people liked by everybody, and someone no-one would have a bad word to say about. He had joined the Band in 1949 and would taught by Bert Wise. He was to become a good, reliable player, progressing from horn and baritone and settling on Eb bass where I knew him. He was a fatherly figure, who nevertheless deplored talking in the bandroom while the bandmaster was speaking.

Roy lived with his mother in a railway cottage next to the twitten just off the High Street. He worked at Seeboard as an electrician, his father having been a signalman at the station. Roy was quite rotund and drove an orange three-wheeled Robin Reliant, the smallest car around, yet he would manage to squeeze his Eb bass into the back. As a teenager, he would often to drive me to engagements and we'd chat all the way there and all the way back. He was very genuine and sincere.

Soon after Roy was fifty, he contracted bone cancer and died tragically, aged just fifty-two. The Band was devastated. "The whole Band attended his funeral," remembers Wendy Guile, one of the Band's cornet players. "He was so well-liked. The first job after this was Bexhill and the bandmaster announced we would play *Amazing Grace* in his memory. We all played our hearts out to do him justice, but it was so difficult as we were heartbroken."

Shortly before he died, Roy had been visited by Wendy, then an attractive teenager, in Tunbridge Wells Hospital. As she walked towards him, the other men on the ward had begun calling out to her and Roy spoke up mischievously: "Calm down fellas – she's mine!" He was so good to the youngsters, and he loved the children in the Band, perhaps because he himself had never married.

Roy served as treasurer, librarian, and then chairman, between 1958 and 1980; at the time, he was regarded as the best chairman the Band had ever known. He was always very proud to have been associated with the purchase of the bandroom and to act as a trustee. If there had been a position on the committee of "Father of the Band," Roy would undoubtedly have been elected to that unopposed.

Interlude Blaze Away: Celebrating Sussex Bonfires

Sussex Bonfire celebrations are one of the county's longest-running traditions, and the Band's connection with them can be traced to the earliest days of its existence. Every year (with rare exceptions such as during wartime or during the covid-19 epidemic), a network of bonfire societies organises a series of county-wide celebrations, beginning in the Autumn and culminating in November with the "Glorious Fifth" at Lewes, where they become "a key part of the town's identity."[1] The celebrations typically comprise a torchlit procession with topical tableaux, marching bands and colourfully-dressed society members. There are also fireworks and a central bonfire, upon which the effigy of a controversial public figure is usually burned.

Strictly speaking, bonfire celebrations are not carnivals, for that is to fundamentally misunderstand the gravity of their purpose. They commemorate – and offer thanks to – those who fought for our freedoms, and embody the rebellious "We wunt be druv" (we won't be driven) spirit of Sussex folk. They are an annual protest against the historic attempts of the Roman Catholic Church to regain its power over England and Wales: in

Lewes in the mid-sixteenth century, the Church executed seventeen Protestant martyrs and, in 1605, Catholic activist Guido Fawkes conspired to blow up the Houses of Parliament in London. It is no coincidence, then, that the Sussex Bonfire tradition was formalised during the mid-1800s, at a time when the Catholic Church again sought dominance over the country.

The annual celebrations at Lewes are by far the grandest, and have the longest pedigree of any in the county, as befits the administrative capital of Sussex. "Lewes is ordinarily still and leisurely, with no bustle in her steep streets save on market days: an abode of rest and unhastening feet. But on one night of the year she lays aside her grey mantle and her quiet tones and emerges a Bacchante robed in flame. Lewes on the 5th of November is an incredible sight; probably no other town in the United Kingdom offers such a contrast to its ordinary life."[2] This description, published by E.V. Lucas in 1904, could almost have been written yesterday.

Sussex Bonfire societies have always been proud of their music and many, at least in the past, ran their own musical ensembles. Town bands therefore tended to be engaged for celebrations on an *ad hoc* basis. The earliest recorded Sussex Bonfire appearance of a brass band was at Lewes in 1848. However, the county's unofficial anthem, *Sussex By The Sea* – now a staple part of the celebrations alongside *There'll Always Be An England* – would not be heard at such an event until 1924.[3] Heathfield Band's most enduring connection was with Fletching Bonfire Society, for whom it paraded just about every year between 1955 and the early 1980s. Here it would be accompanied by celebrity guest players Jimmy and Alan Edwards, who ran a farm in the village.[4]

The Band's earliest foray into the fiery, smoky, rowdy world of Sussex Bonfires was in November 1892, when it led two processions in just three days. The first was at Mayfield, as fancy-dressed revellers in "grotesque and indescribable costumes" paraded from the bonfire society's headquarters at the *Rose and Crown* to a bonfire at Court Meadow (as is still done today). The company was jointly led by Heathfield Band and Mayfield Drum and Fife Band, and proceedings would be relatively sedate: "No effigies were burnt, nor any other indications of party spirit or intolerance were to be seen, much to the credit of the village," reports the Sussex Express.[5] Attendees did, however, enjoy several displays of fireworks.[6] The Band's second appearance was at Hailsham, where "No Popery" tableaux were carried high, tar barrels dragged through the streets, and effigies of Guy Fawkes and the Pope burnt on a giant pyre. Even local firefighters would enter into the spirit, burning coloured flames from atop the town's fire engine![7] The Band returned to Hailsham the following year, but it was some time before it would venture back to Mayfield: the town launched its very own brass band in time for the next bonfire season.[8]

Following its association with the Artillery Volunteers in 1894, Heathfield Band was no longer permitted to attend bonfire celebrations. These rules would still apply a century later, as former bandmaster Frank Francis explains: "No army band was allowed to be involved with it because it's political. They put the effigy of a Prime Minister on top [of the bonfire], don't they? Legally, until I left the Territorial Army, I was not allowed to do it. I'd be *drummed out*, so to speak, or on a court martial. So they made up a special band out of all the brass bands in the area." Thus, for several decades from the mid 1890s, the only bonfire event the Band could take part in was the Coronation celebrations for King George V in June 1911. The Great War soon followed and the tradition was to become side-lined for some years.

During the 1930s, Sussex Bonfires enjoyed something of a revival, as organisers began combining them with hospital parades. This was a shrewd move, as it allowed charities to capitalise on the generous carnival spirit of attendees. It was good for the Band's finances, too, though income would be variable (typically between £2–£5 per event, or about £150–£350 today). This suggests it was taking street collections rather than playing for a set fee. Players were initially also paid a shilling per attendance (about £3.50 today), though this practice was soon abandoned. The Band's first bonfire carnival was at Uckfield in September 1933, performing alongside Uckfield Town Band and Crowborough Silver Prize Band and surrounded by penny farthing riders, a Punch and Judy show, trained dogs, decorated floats, and a fancy-dressed entourage wielding colourful tableaux and blazing torches![9]

The success of bonfire carnivals goes some way towards explaining the decline of dedicated hospital parades, and also provides an insight into the origins of the charitable focus which continues today. In November 1933, Waldron's very own celebrations were held, in aid of local hospitals and the motor ambulance. Heathfield Band was accompanied by the Warbleton

Band on the six mile-long torchlit procession to the Recreation Ground, where a "monster bonfire" lay in wait. There was also fancy dress, a decorated model aeroplane and a large pirate boat, and, most conspicuously of all, an effigy of Adolf Hitler![10] In true Heathfield style, the evening concluded with a display of fireworks and a well-attended dance (with music by the Waldron Merrymakers Dance Band).[11]

Other revivals came thick and fast, and the town band was usually on hand to lead the proceedings. 1935 saw the first Five Ashes Carnival since before the Great War, a colourful six mile-long torch-lit parade showcasing antique horse-drawn vehicles, Mayfield's new fire engine and the Heathfield and Waldron Ambulance.[12] Not to be outdone, Ringmer Bonfire Society returned with a six-hour long extravaganza of processions, fancy dress competitions, and an impressive bonfire.[13] Ringmer highlighted the importance of remembrance, the parade's first port of call being the War Memorial, where a cross of poppies was laid and the *Last Post* and *Reveille* were sounded. Fears of Roman tyranny would also be aired, as Benito Mussolini had recently invaded Ethiopia.[14]

Bonfire celebrations were once not as popular with bandmembers as they are today. George Mepham Jnr. (interviewed in 1981), recalls: "I was scared stiff. We relied on torches for lights and hand torches were sometimes fixed on instruments. I got singed up the back of my hair once…" Bert Thompson (also interviewed in 1981) adds: "I didn't care much for bonfires. We used to stink of gunpowder. I never went to Lewes, but I did all the others – East Hoathly, Herstmonceux and Punnetts Town. They did it for about two seasons, then packed it up."

The Band continued to support the Five Ashes and Waldron celebrations for the next few years. At Waldron in 1938, bandmembers Bert Wise, George Mepham Snr. and Jack Mitchell heralded the crowning of the Carnival Queen with a brass fanfare, and the torchlit procession featured the additional services of Buxted Brass Band (who were, incidentally, defeated by Heathfield Band in a novelty push-ball match). The evening culminated with a dance on z, though this unfortunately relied on pre-recorded, rather than live, music.[15] 1938 turned out to be the final season of this bonfire revival, as proceedings came to a rude halt following the outbreak of the Second World War.

i) **Cliffe Bonfire Society, Lewes Bonfire, 2012.**

ii) **Lewes Bonfire, 2013.** *Photograph supplied by Esther Brooks-Ells.*

iii) **Lewes Bonfire, 2009.** *Photograph supplied by Keith Pursglove.*

iv) **Lewes Bonfire, 2013.** *Photograph supplied by Keith Pursglove.*

v) **Uckfield Bonfire Carnival, 2005.** *Photograph supplied by Kent and Sussex Courier.*

vi) **Uckfield Bonfire Carnival, 2019.** *Photograph supplied by UckfieldNews.com*

vii) **Crowborough Bonfire, 2007.** *Photograph supplied by Keith Pursglove.*

viii) **?Mayfield Bonfire, 2015.** *Photograph supplied by Heidi Watkins.*

As the somewhat depleted Heathfield Band struggled to rebuild itself following the war, its appearances at bonfire celebrations were understandably sporadic. It played at Waldron Carnival in 1945 and Cross-in-Hand in 1946, but undertook none in 1947 or 1948. "Heathfield Band never really had any after the war, only one or two, but it didn't come to much," recalls George Mepham Jnr. The situation improved in 1949 when the Band was engaged to play at Barcombe and Commercial Square, the latter representing its first foray to the world-famous celebrations at Lewes. These engagements were extremely lucrative, earning the Band £20 and £27 respectively (about £722 and £975 today). It also earned a further £15 (about £540) for attending Horam Carnival. There was undoubtedly a healthy profit to be made, even after expenses such as coach hire and the cost of wear and tear to players' shoes! It returned to Barcombe and Lewes the following year.

The Band was engaged by over a dozen bonfire societies during the Fifties and Sixties. In July 1954, the end of rationing was celebrated with a special parade to Heathfield Tower Recreation Ground, where a bonfire waited to engulf the ration books of jubilant townsfolk.[16] As children danced and the pyre was lit, the Band struck up with *Land of Hope and Glory*, *On the Quarter Deck*, and *Sussex by the Sea*.[17] The event would be heard on the radio by ex-pats living as far afield as Africa, and was filmed by both the BBC and CBS Television.[18]

One event which the Band has always been sure to support is Heathfield Bonfire, which appears to have originated as an initiative of the *Prince of Wales* pub. Indeed, its own bonfire society donated £5 (about £160 today) to the Band in November 1951, suggesting that this was the bonfire's inaugural year.[19] An identical donation was made a year later, this time by the more formalised *Heathfield Bonfire Association*.[20] The parade commenced from the *Prince of Wales* (which, at the time, had a large beer garden), from where the Bonfire Queen was presented, accompanied by the Band's fanfare, to the enthusiastic crowd.

There would be annual celebrations at Heathfield until 1957, when the Association was forced to wind up due to a lack of support.[21] This is surprising, as the occasion was hugely popular, typically attracting around a thousand torchbearers each year. Its demise was undoubtedly a loss to the charities it supported, which included the British Red Cross, the Old Folks' Fund, the Lord Mayor's Hungarian Appeal Fund, and Heathfield Silver Band.[22] After several unsuccessful attempts, Heathfield Bonfire Society was finally reformed, and the celebrations revived, in 2019, when it was once more supported by the town band. However, after just one season it was forced into another hiatus, this time by the covid-19 epidemic.

In 1967, the Band made a return to Lewes for Borough Bonfire Society, and every penny of its £50 fee (roughly £900 today) would undoubtedly be earned: processions are physically demanding and generally run from 6pm until midnight. Lesley Dann remembers one Lewes bonfire with particular amusement: "One lad kept throwing bangers into the Band when we were playing, that used to happen a lot. Cyril Leeves, the drummer, told him to stop because it was dangerous. He told him twice and the lad didn't stop. The next time he did it, Cyril hit him on the head with the bass drum stick and knocked him out! A policeman saw what happened and just said, 'Don't worry mate, I saw what was going on!' " Peter Cornford adds: "Lewes was a law unto itself, really. There are always twits in the crowd who'll come along and try and singe you. I remember the odd occasion where people would try and throw bangers into the upright instruments."

There would be other challenges, too. "It was hard work doing a parade for the bonfire nights when they had all these old torches near your face and you were sweating. Didn't like doing them but we used to do 'em," recalls Ken Russell. Former musical director Frankie Lulham adds: "It's all very well being able to play your instrument sitting down in the bandroom, but when you have to march, play, keep in step and in line, it all becomes much harder. Not to mention the fact that it's dark and if your torch batteries run out you're in trouble!"[23] Wendy Holloway remembers: "There were the *Heath Robinson* lights, made from a bulldog clip and a bulb attached to a battery carried in my pocket. To turn the light off between playing, we just unscrewed the bulb slightly. Occasionally it was twisted too far, fell out and would be impossible to retrieve, so the call would go up, 'Ted, I need a new bulb!' Poor Ted Lee carried quite a large bag with him to supply bulbs, batteries and other random items."

However, there were rewards for taking part: "In those days, you used to get fed well before you did them," says Sue Sutton. "They used to do piles of sandwiches and drinks and God knows what. And it was quite boozy. I don't think they do that much now." Gordon Neve (interviewed in 1981) recalls: "At Barcombe there was a meat supper – there was a butcher in the Band – and each member had a quart of beer and a quart to take home."

Nothing more perfectly encapsulates the neighbourly camaraderie of community ensembles than a massed band. In 1954, Heathfield Band led a spectacular procession at Rotherfield Bonfire, in the excellent company of the Band of 129 (Tunbridge Wells) Squadron and Mayfield Silver Band. "Finest spectacle of the evening," writes the Courier, "was presented as the procession reached the outskirts of the village, with the two silver bands massed at its head playing *Sussex by the Sea*, and the long, flaming ranks of torches stretching back along the road into the darkness."[24] Today the massed band tradition continues at Uckfield and Lewes, during which Heathfield Band and Uckfield Concert Brass join forces for the final processions, performing such marching classics as *Slaidburn, Sussex By The Sea, and There'll Always Be An England*.

During the Seventies, the Band made annual excursions to Fletching and Newick and, in 1971 and 1972, the *Prince of Wales* and *Runt in Tun* would hold their own bonfires, which it would also attend. It returned to Lewes for Borough Commercial Square Bonfire Society (now amalgamated) between 1976 and 1978, and made occasional appearances at Buxted, Herstmonceux, Crowborough and Edenbridge, often to help other bands in return for reciprocal assistance at a later date.[25] "East Hoathly was always a bit of a funny one, because you started in the middle of town and you marched out into the fields to nobody, to the cows" recalls Peter Cornford. "I don't think we did Uckfield, the Uckfield one was the Christmas carol service in December when all the bonfire societies and bands got together and marched up the hill to the church."

The Band enjoyed a flurry of bonfire celebrations during the first half of the Eighties, including children's events at St. Bede's School and Cross-in-Hand.[26] "The children's procession, with a variety of imaginative costumes, proved a delightful sight, lit by the blazing torches as it wound its way to the field on a warm Autumn evening," reports the Courier of the latter.[27] In 1984, the Band appeared at a staggering eight bonfire parades: Rotherfield, Hailsham, Mayfield, Cross-in-Hand, East Hoathly, Rusthall, Crowborough, and its debut performance for Cliffe Bonfire Society at Lewes. This is a record yet to be surpassed. After the 1986 season, the frequency would drop off significantly, as membership was going through a lean period. To encourage attendance, players were offered £1 (about £3 today) for each appearance, but this initiative met with only limited success: the Band performed at only seven bonfire celebrations over the next thirteen years.

The modern Band owes much of its involvement with the bonfire tradition to the enthusiasm of Frankie Lulham, who became musical director in 2002. One of her first tasks was to raise funds to extend the bandroom, and bonfire celebrations, some of the highest-paid gigs available to local brass bands, seemed ripe for exploitation. Since 1997 the Band had played only occasionally, at Uckfield and Mayfield, but for the 2003 season it would bravely accept five bonfire engagements, and also commit to the Uckfield Bonfire Carol Service in December. This was a serious undertaking, and the first thing Frankie did was to train members properly in the art of marching. "This did cause some amusement amongst the ranks, especially when attempting to countermarch," writes Frankie. "Mike Smith [trombone] seemed to always end up being left behind... and he's in the front row!"[28] To add a veneer of professionalism, the Band recruited experienced Sussex bander Heidi Watkins as its drum-major.

The bravest decision of all would be its return to Lewes, albeit with assistance from Seaford Silver Band, Mayfield Band and Mid Sussex Brass. "Lewes is a long march and everybody blasts their head off," explains Frank Francis. "If you're blowing hard all the way around, your lip starts to fail and you go flatter and flatter." But the evening is a unique experience: "It's really quite something playing in the Band at Lewes," says Frankie Lulham. "The crowds are magnificent and you feel that you are really giving people pleasure, as well as enjoying yourself, of course. It's hard work but definitely worth it and only for the fittest."[29] As is tradition the 2003 season concluded at East Hoathly, where the Band received a trophy for "Best Band of the Evening." It had been a bold and brave undertaking, but it had firmly re-established itself as an integral part of the Sussex Bonfire scene.

Today's bonfire celebrations are more professionally organised and less dangerous than they once were, and trained stewards are on hand to ensure nobody comes to harm. However, accidents occasionally still happen. At

Newick in 2011, the principal cornet player's hair was singed when a group of torchbearers failed to maintain a safe distance from the Band. "We were left feeling a little disturbed last Saturday and felt very embarrassed at practice on Tuesday," complains the Band's secretary to the organisers.[30] Fortunately, this kind of incident is extremely rare.

Richard Leeves, the Band's former chairman (and father of musical director Sarah Leeves) remembers being recruited to the rhythm section: "Sarah came home one night and said could I take the bass drum? It was for Lewes, it was the big one. She says, 'It's not difficult, all you've gotta do is just sorta give it a tap. You just go *boom… boom… boom boom boom*.' And I said, 'Well, that doesn't sound too difficult.' [But] the problem with the bass drum is it's quite heavy work because I have to keep going, I've gotta keep the step right, you see. We used to share Mayfield: Mostyn would do the High Street and I'd do the low streets, I'd do the lanes, the hill. I really enjoyed it. One time, in Crowborough, my drum stick fell to bits. I was giving it a good hiding because they used to tell me to really leather it, give it a good bashing, and suddenly the whole thing flew to bits, and bits of it were rolling down the road and into a drain!"

Marching at Sussex Bonfires is one of the Band's most enduring traditions. They are a fun and unique experience, and are now more popular than ever with players. "Most of the Band want to do the bonfires, they love doing the bonfires," says Mostyn Cornford. A 2010 ballot of bandmembers would elicit responses such as: "I really enjoy taking part. It's fun and enjoyable and something different for the Band to do"; "Please don't do fewer;" "I like doing the marches best;" and, "The November fifth tradition should be kept going." Richard Ayres (writing in 2019) says: "Especially favoured is the big Lewes Bonfire celebration – the Band becomes considerably augmented by rarely seen past members and an influx of enthusiastic drum banging, brass-blowing refugees from other bands. Members away at university commute miles to be there as a welcome relief from their studies. Over the years I've seen photos of the event showing happy, even euphoric, faces and I'm inclined to wonder whether the proximity of the Harvey's Brewery has anything to do with its popularity?!"[31] Whatever the truth, one thing is certain: as long as there exists a Heathfield Silver Band, it will always be on hand to enhance the spirit of the Sussex Bonfire celebrations.

[1] Roper, J., 2015. The Ad Hoc Calendarized: on the basis of November 5th effigy-burning in southern England). *Western folklore*, [online] 74(2 (Spring 2015), pp.161–183. Available at: <www.jstor.org/stable/24550793>

[2] Lucas, E., 1904. *Highways and Byways in Sussex*. London: Macmillan: 250–1

[3] Munt, B., 1958. Bonfire. In: B. Pugh, ed., *Bonfire Night in Lewes* (2011). London: MX Publishing Ltd: 60; Pugh, B., 2011. *Bonfire Night in Lewes*. London: MX Publishing Ltd: 144

[4] Kent & Sussex Courier, 15th November 1957

[5] Sussex Express, 11th November 1892

[6] ibid

[7] ibid

[8] Kent & Sussex Courier, 10th November 1893

[9] Sussex Express, 15th September 1933

[10] Sussex Express, 10th November 1933

[11] ibid

[12] Kent & Sussex Courier, 1st November 1935; Sussex Express, 1st November 1935

[13] Sussex Express, 15th November 1935

[14] Petruzzello, M. 2020. Benito Mussolini - Rise to power | Britannica. In: *Encyclopædia Britannica* [online]. Available at: <www.britannica.com/biography/Benito-Mussolini/Rise-to-power>

[15] Sussex Express, 16th September 1938

[16] Kent & Sussex Courier, 9th July 1954

[17] ibid

[18] Kent & Sussex Courier, 30th July 1954

[19] Accounts, 1951

[20] Accounts, 1952

[21] Kent & Sussex Courier, 25th October 1957

[22] Heathfield Bonfire Carnival Programme 1957

[23] Press Release, Frankie Lulham, 23rd September 2002

[24] Kent & Sussex Courier, 22th October 1954

[25] Minutes, 13th July 1977

[26] Kent & Sussex Courier, 11th November 1983

[27] ibid

[28] Press Release, Frankie Lulham, 8th September 2003

[29] MD Report, Frankie Lulham, 5th November 2003

[30] Correspondence, Band Secretary to Kingsley Smith, 4th November 2011

[31] Heathfield Magazine, February 2019

MEMBERS of NOTE...

Bob Lee
trombone, 1947–1996,
trustee, 1955–1996,
treasurer, 1954–7 & 1964–8,
secretary, 1957–63.

by Peter Cornford

"Hello mate. I thought you were dead!" That was how Bob would greet anyone and everyone. It brought a smile to your face every time. Bob would do anything for anybody and he was probably the most happy-go-lucky person I have ever come across. He was really jovial extrovert, and you would never see him downcast. He always made you feel good about the world.

Wherever we played, however far from Heathfield, he would always know someone and someone would know him. He worked in a grocers in Broad Oak and was known as a local personality amongst the wider public. If we happened to be marching, he would constantly be shouting out or waving to someone he knew in the crowd, or someone would be calling out to him. He was the epitome of Heathfield Band and the two were synonymous. So many of the public would come to know of the Band through Bob.

Bob would be the first to admit that he was not the greatest of players, but he was a good, middle-of-the-road bloke who had picked up the trombone and had made a half decent noise out of it. He was to play for just about every band around, and was at his best at Christmas when he would become Santa Claus for the Band's Christmas Fayres. He could be seen at every carolling engagement, not least because there was always a fair bit of beer to be had.

Maureen Guile, wife of bandmember Dennis, recalls a typical bonfire parade: "The Band always stopped at pubs for refreshment. On the way back, they had their own torches to read the music, but Bob hadn't got anything, so he kept veering to the right. We had to keep pushing him back or he would have ended up in the hedge I think. He did not follow the music; he 'knew' all the pieces. Sometimes there were a lot of wrong notes, but Bob was happy!"

Bob would always have a pint on the go and he was generally the worse for wear by the end of an evening. I remember once when we had finished carolling around the streets of Heathfield and we ended up in Hailsham Road near the recreation ground. Bob was completely drunk and had no idea which way to walk home to his bungalow at Theobalds Green. "Don't worry Bob, just follow the white line in the middle of the road," someone called after him. And Bob did just that… but going the opposite way, in the direction of Tower Street, singing at the top of his voice and swinging his trombone in all directions.

Bob was famed for finding humour in every situation (and would sometimes write humorous poems about the Band). At the Heathfield Show in about 1980, George Miller, seated next to Bob on trombone, was unfortunately to fall backwards off the bandstand whilst playing. George's legs went up in the air and his trombone was to catapult off in the other direction; thankfully, he was unhurt. Bob's reaction, and as quick as a flash, was to announce: "Thought 'ed 'ave a go at some o' them low notes!"

I used to play sometimes in Bob's Frothblowers group. The playing standard was not great, but it had all the elements of what I imagine a rag tag group of amateurs from any period of history must have been like, whether they were town waits or itinerant minstrels; it was all about making merry. I remember well some of Bob's comical inverted Sussex humour, comments like: "I reckon they woan't hear anything better than us this evening"; "Did you play that wun upside down then, Ted?"; "Was the rest of you all playing the same piece as me?"; "Good job we 'aven't got a conductor… he'd never 'ave kept in time with us!"; and "They clapped that one… cold 'ands, I 'spect!" This was just the kind of chatter that you won't read in regular band histories, but is absolutely a reflection of the non-stop fun we were having.

1950s Rising to Giddy Heights

Daily Herald Contest, Brighton, June 1958.
(Back Row, L–R) Jeff Hobden, ?, Dick Turner, ?, ?, ?.
(Middle Row, L–R) ?, George Mepham Jnr., Roy Elphick, ?, Laurie Knapp,?, Ted Lee.
(Front Row, L–R) Jack Mitchell, Graham Bland, Lloyd Bland, ?, Bob Lee, ?, ?.
Photograph supplied by Sussex Newspapers.

Despite outwardly appearing in good health, by 1950 the Band was struggling to retain members, and was affected by poor discipline at rehearsals. On a sad note, it was to suffer the death of treasurer Harry Dinnage, who had successfully guided the Band's finances since the earliest days of the committee. More positively, its services were in great demand and it continued to expand its social role. It would also rise to giddying heights on the contesting scene, become a familiar part of the Sussex Bonfire traditions, launch an annual Christmas Fayre, form a successful Supporters' Club, and even go on tour to France (see *With a Little Help from Our Friends: The Band Supporters*).

Although the Band's post-war recovery had been steady, membership was not quite back to full strength. A number of former players never returned after the war, and some of the young wartime recruits had now moved on. A concerted effort was made to attract new members, and cornet player

Maurice Collins volunteered to have a go at running a training group.[1] One of the new recruits was Ted Lee, who joined the Band in 1952 after hearing it play at a cinema in Battle. Ted was persuaded along by his best friend, Roy Elphick, who himself belonged to the Band from about 1950 until his death thirty years later. "It was his fault I joined the Band, I just got pulled into it," says Ted (interviewed in 2013). "I come out the Air Force in 1951 and I joined the Band. I wanted something to do I 'spose. I taught myself, mainly, they just give me an instrument and said, 'Learn to play that!' " Ted soon became the Band's librarian, and would go on to become one of its longest-serving members, finally retiring in 2018.

The Band made considerable progress under bandmaster Bert Wise, who held players to a very high standard. However, he was a true perfectionist and could therefore be temperamental to work with. The minutes record a lack of order at rehearsals, suggesting a certain amount of unrest among members,[2] and the solution would be to improve the Band's sense of team spirit. In part, this was achieved by holding occasional team-building socials. "Dinners were had once or twice to celebrate one thing or another, but bands were too poor to have outings," recalls George Mepham Jnr. (speaking in 1981). "We had a job to keep going, had to work hard to keep going."

There was always the worry that members might choose to leave the Band, so extra incentives were offered to encourage loyalty. Subscriptions had recently been made voluntary and in 1950 it was also agreed to pay bus fares for those who lived further afield. "Three of us, in Mr. Wise's time, used to bus up from Uckfield," recalls George Mepham Jnr. "The Band used to pay the fares. I used to keep a record and we were paid once a month." Members' willingness to travel some distance to rehearsals gives us an indication of the Band's status under Bert Wise. "Gone are the days of the turn of the century when all members lived pretty much within walking distance of the bandroom," observes Peter Cornford. "The fact that players were travelling to Heathfield in the days when there were more bands around to choose from is telling. The contest successes presumably played a part in this, and also Bert Wise's renown as a musician." In addition to bus fares, members were also paid one shilling (about £1.75 today) for each night they spent carolling. From 1951, the proceeds of some engagements were shared among them, and they could even claim for lost working time.[3] By 1955, membership had increased to a new high of twenty-nine players, more than the standard requirement for a brass band.

Finances now became a priority, firstly to purchase the bandroom and then to replace the Band's aging uniforms. As a result, the secretary suggested that monies due to members from engagements should be temporarily held back, to be paid at a later date; however, this proposal would not be approved and members continued to pocket their share of expenses (Bert Wise was eventually to put a stop to the practice, arguing that Band's income belonged in its bank account).[4]

Engagements remained as varied as ever. There were Spring and Summer concerts at St. Richard's Hall, where the Band would sometimes premiere its test-piece ahead of the Tunbridge Wells Contest.[5] It also took advantage of fair weather to play at venues where collections could be taken, such as Heathfield Park, Waldron Thorns, the playing fields at Cross-in-Hand, and in local beer gardens. In addition, it entertained the public at cricket matches and sports events, and at the All Saints Church Fête. The first Heathfield Carnival was also held, a joint initiative between the Band and the *Prince of Wales Pub*,[6] and players would enter into the spirit by dressing as tramps one year and clowns the next.[7] It even made several excursions to France, and would take the opportunity to entertain fellow passengers during the ferry trips across the Channel.[8]

One of the Band's most successful initiatives was the formation of its Supporters' Club, which grew out of the need to secure funding and practical assistance at engagements (see *With a Little Help from Our Friends: The Band Supporters*). In addition to organising social events for the Band, the club was instrumental in establishing an annual Christmas Fayre, the first of which was held in December 1952. By 1955 the initiative had expanded in scope, and now included the highly-anticipated spectacle of Santa Claus arriving into town on a decorated van. The Band then escorted him to the Fayre at the State Hall, and later a dance would be held.[9] In subsequent years, Santa arrived in a chimney mounted upon a horse-drawn cart, a six metre-long sledge, and even by train to Heathfield Station, where the whole of Heathfield seemed to be waiting to greet him.[10] The Fayres would pause in 1960 after Bert Wise disbanded the Supporters' Club; however, they were to recommence a few years later.

The Band's wider programme of festive gigs included, in 1950, a series of "open-air concerts of seasonable music in the Parish," an experience which must have tested the mettle of even the hardiest of players, annual appearances at the town's Christmas light switching-on ceremonies, and regular concerts at St. Richard's Hall.[11] In December 1954, the Band also staged a joint carol concert with the Cross-in-Hand Choir, to raise funds to hold a party for the elderly.[12] The concert, which took place at the Cross-in-Hand Legion Hut, included a cornet solo by future bandmaster Lloyd Bland and culminated with a massed performance of *O Come all ye Faithful*.[13]

The Band also braved the Winter weather to continue its tradition of carolling, performing around town every night for two or three weeks straight. "When we used to go carol-playing along Hailsham Road in Heathfield, the valves of the cornet I was playing, they used to freeze, you couldn't move 'em," remembers Ken Russell. In 1956, uproar swept through the community when a rumour circulated that the Band had spent its collections on a slap-up Christmas dinner, prompting bandmember Jack Mitchell to own up to,

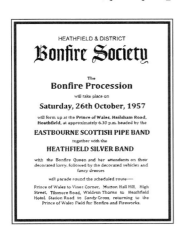

Programme from Heathfield Bonfire Parade, 1957.

A 1957 advertisement for Heathfield Church Summer Fair which appeared in Sussex Express.

and apologise for, the leakage of misinformation![14] In reality, the Band regularly made donations to other charities. In 1952, half its *Christmassing* proceeds went to the East Sussex Association for the Blind, and in 1953 half were given to an "Old Folks Committee." In 1954, the Band shared half among its carolling players, with one quarter going to Band funds and the remaining share to an unspecified charity. In years when it did not donate to other charities, the proceeds were spent entirely on new uniforms, instruments or music, or the greatest fundraising challenge of its existence, the purchase of the Alexandra Road bandroom.

Throughout the decade, the Band appeared at many events for ex-servicemen's organisations. In June 1950, it led a parade for the Association of the Royal Army Service Corps (RASC), from the *Heathfield Hotel* to the Heathfield Tower Recreation Ground, where it accompanied hymns for the dedication of a new standard.[15] It also provided a programme of light music for attendees of Cross-in-Hand Legion's AGM in October 1953.[16] In June 1954, it helped the Goudhurst Legion to celebrate its silver jubilee, leading a procession to St. Mary's Church in Goudhurst, and thence to a garden fête at *Maypole* and a fun fair on the village green.[17] In August, the Band provided music for an open-air service on the Hurst Green Recreation Ground,[18] whilst in July 1955 it performed for the Blackboys Legion, before staging an evening concert at the *Blackboys Inn*.[19] In Heathfield in September 1957, it led a parade of ex-servicemen, cadets, Scouts and Guides to a Battle of Britain Day Service.[20] Naturally, it also appeared at annual Remembrance Day events.

The 1950s engagement calendar would also contain two events of national significance. The Festival of Britain was staged in the Summer of 1951, to coincide with the centenary of the Great Exhibition, and was intended to celebrate the achievements of the British people and signal an end to wartime austerity. To this end, arts events and exhibitions were installed in cities across the country, whilst more modest festivals were held at smaller locations. In Heathfield, the town band entertained jubilant crowds at the Tower Recreation Ground.

A second national celebration took place in the Summer of 1953, for the Coronation of Queen Elizabeth II. The Tunbridge Wells Amateur Band

Heathfield Band leading a British Legion Parade, details unknown.

Federation marked the occasion at its festival in early May, at which Heathfield Band achieved third place in the second section.[21] There were further celebrations on 31st May, when Heathfield's "biggest-ever drumhead service" was held, the Band leading a large procession of service organisations from *The Crown Hotel* to the Heathfield County Secondary School.[22] Here, a service was given and a wreath laid at the War Memorial. The offertory, in aid of Heathfield Band, raised about £14 (about £400 today).[23] The Band was also busy on the morning of the Coronation, 2nd June 1953, as members paraded to the Polegate Recreation Ground for a commemorative service. After lunch, they took a coach to Cross-in-Hand to appear at a Coronation sports day, before decamping to the Heathfield County Secondary School for a celebratory tea and more sports.[24] The occasion concluded with an evening concert by the Heathfield Band, an old-time dance, and a display of fireworks.[25]

Contesting again became a popular activity and the Band participated in several contests each year (see *Contesting Times*). "We used to do a lot of contesting then," remembers Ted Lee. "We used to do quite well." The Band worked extremely hard, making its way to the top section of the Southern

Counties Amateur Bands Association (SCABA) league by the Summer of 1955. It was even invited to perform at a demonstration and lecture for the National Association of Brass Band Conductors in Tunbridge Wells, whose guest speakers were the legendary conductors, Cyril Yorath and Edrich Siebert.[26] However, had it opted to pursue a career in the first section, it would have become a small fish in a big pond, and the necessary level of commitment would have been difficult for many bandmembers to sustain. In the Summer of 1956, it instead chose to compete in a more relaxed manner, in the fourth section of the Daily Herald Festival in Brighton. This festival was to become its contest of choice going forwards.

Bert Wise often felt that members were not being fully supportive of him and in 1956 he suggested that it was perhaps time that they found a new conductor.[27] "Mr. Wise was so valuable that we couldn't let him go," recalls George Mepham Jnr. "We had to let him have his own way, so I went and got him back. I remember my father calling me all sorts of a fool for being and going on me knees. Still, Wise was a good musician and precise conductor." But Bert's confidence and health were becoming fragile and he would soon be unable to manage the more demanding engagements. Attendance at rehearsals was once again suffering and, as a result, he declared that it was impossible to prepare the Band adequately for contests. According to the minutes, the general feeling among members was that they "would rather give up contesting than lose Mr. Wise as bandmaster."[28] Nevertheless, he was to pass more and more conducting responsibilities to principal cornet player Lloyd Bland, and resign altogether in early 1958.

An Extraordinary General Meeting was called to "discuss the future of the Band owing to the illness of Mr. Wise,"[29] and Lloyd Bland narrowly beat Jack Mitchell in a vote to decide on a temporary bandleader. Jack was somewhat hurt by this outcome (he was, after all, the duly elected deputy bandmaster), but he was admirably magnanimous, conceding that a younger person might be better suited to the role.[30] "Maybe they didn't like losing him from cornet," suggests Ted Lee. Bert Wise's health improved by August and he continued to offer Lloyd his support. Lloyd was appointed bandmaster in October and rehearsals would return to twice-weekly, alternating between the conductorship of Lloyd and Bert every Monday and Thursday evening respectively.

By 1959, however, membership had fallen considerably, and new players were proving difficult to recruit. The apparent lack of interest in brass banding may reflect the many social changes that were occurring at the time. The growing town now boasted a population in excess of 3,000, and traditional rural ways were beginning to die out.[31] The Heathfield Band Supporters' Club, which once organised successful community dances and boasted hundreds of subscribing members, was wound up in September, partly due to political wranglings amongst its committee, but one wonders if it, too, was succumbing to obsolescence. Social interests, traditions and vocations were all evolving. The town's chicken-fattening industry was vanishing as more effective rearing methods were introduced, and the ancient Cuckoo Fair had completely lapsed. The phenomenally successful dances at the Recreation Hall were becoming less popular (the venue would be sold off altogether in the early Sixties), and the Plaza Cinema had now closed.[32] With greater disposable income and a choice of affordable transportation, the younger generation now had access to a far wider suite of pastimes than their parents had once done, and could more easily travel further afield to pursue them.

Despite constant worries over recruitment, the decade had proven one of the Band's most successful to date. It had climbed to giddying heights under the baton of Bert Wise, and its rise to the top contesting section was something that previous bandmembers could only have dreamed of. It had for a time become a driven, focussed Band, attracting strong support from willing subscribers, putting on well-attended dances (for which folk from neighbouring towns were literally bussed in), appearing at prestigious local venues, proudly supporting community celebrations, and even introducing a Christmas Fayre to the town. But change was inexorable and the Band would once again be forced to adapt. As the Swinging Sixties beckoned, the time was right to explore a bold new direction.

---

[1] Minutes, 31st October 1949

[2] Minutes, 5th December 1951

[3] Minutes, 5th December 1951

[4] Minutes, 31st October 1955; Cornford, P., 1981. Personal Archive and Interviews

[5] e.g. Kent & Sussex Courier, 1st May 1953

[6] Cornford, P., 1981

[7] ibid

[8] ibid

[9] Kent & Sussex Courier, 9th December 1955

[10] Sussex Express, 14th December 1956; Kent & Sussex Courier, 13th December 1957; Cornford, P., 1981

[11] e.g. Sussex Express, 22nd December 1950; Kent & Sussex Courier, 24th December 1954

[12] Kent & Sussex Courier, 17th December 1954

[13] ibid

[14] Minutes, 24th January 1957

[15] Kent & Sussex Courier, 23rd June 1950

[16] Sussex Express, 23rd October 1953

[17] Kent & Sussex Courier, 11th June 1954

[18] Kent & Sussex Courier, 20th August 1954

[19] Minutes, 1st June 1955 & 19th July 1955

[20] Kent & Sussex Courier, 20th September 1957; Sussex Express, 20th September 1957

[21] www.BrassBandResults.co.uk, 2021; Sussex Express, 8th May 1953

[22] Sussex Express, 5th June 1953

[23] ibid

[24] ibid

[25] ibid

[26] Brass Band News, 1st November 1955

[27] Minutes, 4th October 1956

[28] Minutes, 4th October 1957

[29] Minutes, 8th April 1957

[30] ibid

[31] Pryce, R., 1996. *Heathfield Park: A Private Estate and a Wealden Town*. Heathfield: Roy Pryce: 161–3

[32] ibid

MEMBERS of NOTE...

Lloyd Bland
bandmaster & cornet,
ca.1953–1978.

"We are all interested in music in our family. There is always a practice session-going on at home" – Lloyd Bland.[1]

Lloyd Bland, a master shoemaker and talented brass musician from Uckfield, joined the Band around 1953, whilst in his early thirties. He was a much-admired solo cornet player who would serve on the committee (and briefly as treasurer). In July 1955, he was to become one of the Band's four original trustees.

In 1957 Lloyd would find himself covering for the ailing bandmaster, Bert Wise, and was formally elected to the position in 1958. "Little bands like Heathfield never advertised for conductors," says his eldest daughter, Sue Sutton. "It was always that they came out of the Band. Normally the top cornet player took over, and then of course you're losing a player; he was a brilliant cornet player, my dad. My family came from the north – Northamptonshire – and they were in brass bands up there. We were quite a musical family."

Lloyd was also to occupy the position of secretary from 1963–1974, which would allow him greater control over the nature of engagements. However, he would eventually be forced to vacate this role due to growing work commitments.

Lloyd was a good sort of chap who rarely upset anyone. He was small in stature and quiet in nature, but nevertheless would make a significant impact on the Band, boosting morale and guiding its transition to the modern institution we recognise today. In addition to updating the repertoire, he was to pave the way for female bandmembers, introducing his three daughters (and son) and recruiting and training many other youngsters. "Lloyd was really lovely, a real Sussex man who would tell us to 'play as rit,' " recalls Lesley Dann.

Lloyd resigned as bandmaster in January 1975, ostensibly because his health was no longer tip-top, though the true story may have been more complex: his daughter, Sue, says he was voted out of the role at AGM, to be replaced by Tom Kelly. By June 1975, he would severe his ties with the Band (though he was to briefly return to coach junior bandmembers the following year). He appears to have begrudged being side-lined: "When Tom Kelly took over, Lloyd wouldn't wear a normal red jacket," remembers Wendy Holloway. Instead, he would continue to wear his old bandmaster's jacket, with its special inverted red and black colour scheme!

After a quarter of a century's service to the Band, Lloyd would permanently retire around 1977/78. He sadly passed away in 1985, but his modernising legacy to the Band lives on.

---

[1] Evening Standard, ca. November 1960

Interlude With a Little Help from Our Friends: The Band Supporters

From its earliest beginnings, Heathfield Band has enjoyed overwhelming support from the community. Running a brass band is a huge undertaking in terms of time and expense, and none could manage without some assistance from time to time. The Band's founders, Edward Bean and Fred Adams, put tremendous effort into attracting the interest and funding required to launch the Band, and the former continued to offer support until his death half a century later. F. Howard Martin, the Band's first president, helped it to rebuild after the Great War by establishing a committee, raising its profile, and attracting new sources of finance (see *1920s Like a Phoenix: Recovery, Collapse and Rebirth*). In the Seventies, Sir Edward Caffyn proved invaluable as a vice-president, gifting the Band financial assistance and advice during turbulent times. But it was during the 1950s that support was to reach a high point in the wider community, with the founding of the Heathfield Band Supporters' Club.

The club was inspired by a lengthy discussion, in July 1952, at which the committee agreed that a separate entity for "all kinds of women and townsfolk" might be a practical way to increase support for the Band.[1] The bandsmen – for members were indeed all men at the time – thus resolved to ask their "women folk" if they would be interested in forming a separate committee to oversee such a club. The initiative was championed by bandmaster Bert Wise and his wife Maureen, who became the club's first secretary.

The idea would prove a masterstroke, capitalising as it did on the Band's cachet within the community. The club solicited patronage from the wealthier local residents, many of whom would provide regular assistance to the cause, and introduced a penny-a-week minimum subscription, allowing the wider townsfolk to express their support.[2] "This club has been formed just a year and its object is to help and support the Band," writes the club's secretary in 1954. "In the past year we have bought a reconditioned euphonium and a new cornet, and have given a donation to the Band" (a not inconsiderable £100, equivalent to over £2,600 today).[3]

Within just a few years, the club had attracted over 400 members and would generate a significant annual income. "Heathfield Silver Band, with twenty-six or so musicians, is one of the best to be found in any Sussex village, and the Parish is justly proud of it," writes Sussex Express in 1956. "This has been expressed, in the most practical way, by the Supporters' Club, founded in 1952 to raise funds to help the Band. [This is] a signal example of what can be done, even in a small village, to further interest in local bands."[4]

The club would greatly contribute to the town's community life, organising dances, Fayres, and other social events, many of which took place at the State Hall in Station Road. Within months of its founding, the club staged its first Christmas Fayre, an occasion which was to become a highly-anticipated annual fixture with a popular Christmas dance. Bandmaster Bert Wise would even don the famous red Santa outfit on one such occasion. The club's dances were ambitious affairs, employing professional dance bands and even providing late-night buses to transport guests home afterwards, to locations as far afield as Eastbourne, Hailsham and Warbleton.

"It worked wonderful," says George Mepham Jnr. (interviewed in 1981). "It got money for instruments and the bandroom. They held dances with groups, and many outsiders joined in. The club used to have sales of work, they bought stuff from shopkeepers and wives knitted stuff to sell. We also used to have huge Christmas Draws, sold hundreds of tickets."

Though the club was essentially autonomous, its members, many of whom were friends and family of bandmembers, would take a close interest in the activities of the Band. They marched side-by-side at bonfire parades, were welcomed at Band socials, provided with free transportation to attend contests, and organised initiatives such as joint concerts with the Callenders Band.[5] The members also took part in eccentric fund-raisers from time to time: "No-one knows for certain who won, but it was evident that players and spectators at this comic cricket match between Heathfield Stoolball Team and Heathfield Band Supporters, played on the Recreation Ground on Friday, all enjoyed themselves," reports the Courier in 1957.[6]

In 1955, the club would play a crucial role in the purchase of the bandroom, contributing £100 to the venture (approximately £2,600 today).[7] "They used to give these concerts and had jumble sales and different things to get money to buy the bandroom," remembers Ken Russell. "It was quite a big occasion when we bought that." As soon as the bandroom was paid for, the club immediately began another fundraiser, this time to purchase a new set of uniforms for the Band.[8] "It was quite nice, the challenge," remembers Ted Lee (interviewed in 2013). "We used to have jumbles and different things to raise money for the red uniforms that took over from the blue. We did a sponsored walk from Heathfield to Hellingly, we had different draws, lotteries, lots of things to raise money for them. Some companies in Heathfield even sponsored us."

(COPY of Audited A/cs.)

HEATHFIELD SILVER BAND SUPPORTERS' CLUB

Balance Sheet for Year ending July 1959

INCOME	£	s.	d.	EXPENDITURE	£	s.	d.
Balance brought forward ...	324	9	0½	Hire of Dance Bands ...	21	0	0
Xmas Fayre and Dance ...	105	2	9½	Hire of State Hall ...	29	8	0
Dance ...	39	4	1	Hire of St. Richards Hall ...	1	0	0
Jumble Sale ...	12	19	2	Printing Ed. Errey (4 a/cs.)	8	0	10
Members' Subs. (Penny-a-Week Fund-1219)	5	1	7	Hosbens Stores	3	1	9
Vice-Presidents' Donations ...	5	14	6	T. H. Screen (2 a/cs.)	4	7	9
Mile of Pennies (12 envelopes) ...	12	1	1½	G. Baker (fruit 2 a/cs.) ...	1	6	0
Cheque from Band towards Uniforms	34	0	0	Proctors (Chemist)		5	0
Sale of Pencils ...	1	0	6	Refreshments (Pucks Parlour) ...		6	8
				Northern Counties Rubber Co. ...	6	3	0
				Neve Bros.		1	9
				Mrs. Russell (for Jumble Sale) ...	1	0	0
				Mr. Coles (Sherry)		6	6
				Postage, etc. (for Secretary)	1	0	0
				Ambrose H. Allcorn, Ltd. ...	66	18	3
				Band Uniforms ...	250	0	0
					£394	5	6
				Cash in Bank (as per Statement) ..	132	2	8
				Cash in Hand ...	1	15	7½
	£528	3	9½		£528	3	9½

Given to Heathfield Silver Band in Cash and Kind July 1952 to July 1959   £733 11s. 6d.

Balance in Hand   £133 18s. 3½d.

The final Supporters' Club Balance Sheet, dated 1959.

The following year, the Band faced a large bill for repairs to the bandroom, and the Supporters' Club once again came to the rescue.[9] The Band gratefully accepted their assistance, but its committee was somewhat reluctant to do so, as the club had been taking a greater and greater interest in the running of its affairs. The Supporters now expected a say over how their donations were spent and the Band's new chairman, Roy Elphick, began to feel that it was a case of the tail wagging the dog. In August 1958 a row erupted after the club's committee took it upon themselves to alter arrangements for some bandroom repairs.[10] In October, the style of the new Band uniform was chosen, not between bandmembers and their committee as one might expect, but through a lengthy joint discussion with the club's committee.[11]

The conflicts continued and by May 1959 the two committees decided to merge the Supporters' Club into a joint finance committee within the Band.[12] But not all bandmembers approved, and members of the Supporters' Club refused to stand on the new committee. Negotiations had reached an impasse and Bert Wise was at the end of his tether. In September 1959 he chose to close down the club completely. "No one understood why it folded," recalls George Mepham Jnr. "Wise got it going and finished it. Suddenly he said he didn't need the club, so he broke it up. Mr. Wise said, 'We've got plenty of money now, so we don't need you!' Everyone was upset. The Supporters were workers, gave up their time and raised a lot of money, [and] there were several

Santa came by 'sledge' to Heathfield bazaar

Santa Claus had a busy time on Saturday at the State Hall, Heathfield, when he presented gifts to all the young visitors to the Silver Band Supporters' Club bazaar, including three young people who came in fancy dress

NEARLY 500 children queued at Heathfield State Hall on Saturday to receive gifts from Father Christmas.

It was the main attraction at the fifth annual Christmas fair organised by Heathfield Silver Band Supporters' Club. The event was staged to raise money to buy new uniforms for the bandsmen.

Father Christmas—beneath the disguise was Mr. M. A. Noakes—made a ceremonial entry at the State Hall, after riding round Heathfield on a "sledge" towed by a Land-Rover. He was accompanied by six children from the London County Council school at Tutting-worth.

The sledge, which was 17ft. long and 1ft. wide, was made by members of the supporters' club.

The fair was followed by a dance, attended by about 200 people. Mr. C. Wise was M.C.

STALLS AND HOLDERS

Toffee apples: Mr. F. Woods; balloons: Mr. A. Shelley; Christmas decorations: Mrs. Cooper; confectionery: Mrs. C. Wise and Miss B. Dann; cakes: Mrs. K. Dann and Mrs. B. Knapp; bottles: Mrs. Russell; needlework and knitting:

Miss Lawrence, Mrs. B. Lee and Mrs. Bland; arts and crafts: Mr. G. Dann and Mr. Asell; honeycomb: Mr. C. Wise

White elephant: Mr. R. Thompson and Mrs. F. Leeves, toys and novelties: Mrs. E. Driver and Miss n. Cooper; refreshments: Mrs. A. Frost, Mrs. A. Elphick and Mrs. Scrace; competitions: Mr. K. Lee and Mr. B. Odies; produce: Mr. Russell, Other helpers included Mr. B. Standen, Mr. Pink, Mr. Cooper, Mr. C. Dann, Mr. and Mrs. R. Leeves, Mrs. C. Hook Mrs. M. Leeves, Mr. R. Thompson, Mr. Bridger, Mr. Frost and Mr. Elphick.

Kent & Sussex Courier, December 1957.

business people in the club." The final audited accounts, dated July 1959, record that the club had gifted the Band an impressive £733 in cash and kind during its brief lifetime (over £17,000 today). Despite the club's indisputable success, the Band's committee resolved never again to hand away so much control.

However, as the new bandmaster Lloyd Bland became established, it was suggested that a new Ladies' Committee be formed, similar in function to the defunct Supporters' Club. This was formed during early 1967, and would again comprise wives and friends of the Band, with the stated aim of "organising money-raising schemes for the Band funds."[13] One of their first tasks was to arrange the annual Christmas Fayre, now relocated to St. Richard's Hall in Heathfield, which had been run by the lady supporters of Heathfield United Football Club since the collapse of the Band Supporters' Club. The revitalised Fayre would commence with a procession through the town, headed by a decorated float upon which was Father Christmas (in reality trombonist Bob Lee), and Heathfield Silver Band.[14] In its first year the Fayre raised £53 (about £980 today) towards the Band's instrument fund.[15] The committee would follow it up with frequent coffee mornings and jumble sales.

"The women just sat at home, knitted and made things," recalls Maureen Guile, wife of bandmember Dennis. "[It's different now], there's quite a lot of young ones and some are just not interested." Ted Lee's wife, Clarice (interviewed in 2013), adds: "I can remember the first jumble sale I got up was with my neighbour at Vines Cross, who said we could have it in her drive. We did a small tombola and we sold cakes and we had all this jumble. After that we got braver and my daughter Anna and I used to do it between us. We booked St. Richard's Church Hall and had jumble sales regularly there. At one time we had a table-top sale in the field at Vines Cross pub [*The Brewers Arms*]. We was always having Christmas bazaars, but we don't do them anymore." Asked how she got involved, Maureen replies: "You were just included. I don't suppose my husband said, 'Come and help?' He just presumed I would!"

The Ladies' Committee also had a hand in organising social events for bandmembers. "In the Autumn the Band will hold another of its social evenings," reports a Heathfield Band Newsletter.[16] "Organised by bandmembers, this was originally a means of saying 'thank you' to the Ladies' Committee; but now it has been found that a social evening is an ideal way to give an enjoyable evening to members' wives and children, and friends of the Band of all ages." Maureen Guile remembers: "We used to put on quite a few parties and dances and things. We had one dance at Broad Oak when all the lights went out. The band who were doing the dance, they couldn't use their guitars and things because there was no electricity, not like *The Band*!" As the social role of the Ladies' Committee grew, they began to organise excursions such as annual trips to the pantomime. The first of these was *Sleeping Beauty*, at Hastings' White Rock Theatre in January 1976.

By 1977 the Band was a registered charity, and it was felt that the time was right to form a new Supporters' Club, based around the core of the existing Ladies' Committee. Weary of his experience with the original Supporters' Club, Roy Elphick would assume the role of the new club's president and encourage close collaboration with the Band's committee.[17] Despite this, politics soon resurfaced and things would quickly sour. Wendy Holloway, baritone player and daughter of Dennis and Maureen Guile, recalls: "Some of the women felt they should have a say in how the money was spent. One of the wives in particular was very forceful. On one occasion she kept on about 'in case of precipitation,' and dad would immediately mutter 'or in case it rains!' " Peter Cornford believes: "The need for influence is surely a reflection that this banding thing is all pervasive in band families' lives. My Mum [Esme Cornford] was often bemoaning the fact that the ladies were not appreciated enough for all the time and effort they put into raising money. They thought that entitled them to some input on how things should be done at the Band. [They] certainly had firm ideas about how the Band should be, how it should behave, where it should and should not play, and what the Supporters' money should be spent on."

Disagreements would erupt over the most trivial things and the final straw was very silly indeed. "There was an argument over 50p," remembers Esme Cornford. "I think there was somebody trying to rule the roost as usual and we weren't gonna have any of it. We had a stall up Heathfield Park, somebody bought a cake and she didn't come back for it. We all wanted to get home and so we left the cake there and someone took it, and we was 50p out over this cake." A heated argument soon ensued. "I said, 'Well, if that's

i) Esme Cornford and friends, ca. 1993.
Photograph supplied by Kent and Sussex Courier.

ii) Esme, Jean and Alison, 2011.
Photograph supplied by Mostyn Cornford.

iii) Esme Cornford & Maureen Guile prepare HSB banner for Wiesbaden trip, 1991.
Photograph supplied by Mostyn Cornford.

iv) HSB Christmas Bazaar, ca. 1992.

v) Lady Supporters, ca. mid-1990s.

how you're gonna be, you can stick your treasurer's job!' That was the end of that. It was so petty. I think the Band dismantled it after that, don't think it lasted more than about twelve months." Fundraising reverted to the former Ladies' Committee, under scrutiny of the Band's committee, and this arrangement endured until the new millennium.[18]

Stalls and jumble sales, usually held at fêtes and carnivals, would remain the stock in trade of the Ladies' Committee. "Jumble sales! I had a childhood of them, sorting the stuff in the morning and selling it in the afternoon," recalls Wendy Holloway. The men would generally bag the *White Elephant* stall, selling *bric-a-brac* to children, whilst the women were lumbered with the muckier jobs, such as sorting and selling second-hand clothing. "Later," adds Wendy, "the women would make items to sell wherever and whenever the Band played (how sexist that sounds now)." In the 1980s, Christmas carolling was augmented by the arrival of the Dickensian Market to Heathfield High Street. "That was always the beginning of December," says Esme. "[The Band] used to play outside *Errey's* [a large furnishing shop, now *Trading4U*], and if I'd got a lot of bits and pieces left I'd even have a stall out there. That used to be cold sometimes!"

Fundraising has undergone a radical transformation in recent times, as traditional methods have become less profitable and collections on public land an administrative headache. "Society was changing, Heathfield was growing," observes Peter Cornford. "Things have moved on step-by-step to the fragmented social state in which we now find ourselves. The community of Heathfield was becoming more diverse and difficult to marshal into behaviour of times past." Esme adds: "The Christmas Fayre was so much work and it didn't pay in the end. Jumble sales are out of fashion; you can't get rid of the rubbish at the end, so we tend to do quiz nights instead now."

Today, even the concept of a Ladies' Committee is completely outdated. Where once the women would chaperone members' children at bonfire parades, carnivals and other gigs, or provide refreshments at engagements, today's assistants are more diverse. Bandmembers are now more involved in every aspect of brass banding and everyone – young or old, female or male – is encouraged to muck in. The "magnificent band of ladies who always take charge of this kind of event" has metamorphosed into "the many behind the scenes supporters [who] help at Band concerts, etc, running the raffles, making the tea and refreshments and generally helping events to run smoothly."[19]

A new Supporters' Club – *Friends of Heathfield Silver Band* – was briefly mooted in 2011, though public interest was lukewarm.[20] In some respects, this highlights just how the Band's relationship with the community has changed. A century ago, Heathfield Silver Band was a vital social enabler; today it plays a different, more specialised role in the public eye. Indeed, the notion of hundreds of rural townsfolk voluntarily subscribing to support their town band is now unimaginable, and this only serves to highlight the unique and special nature of the original Supporters' Club.

---

[1] Minutes, 4th July 1952

[2] Sussex Express, 24th February 1956

[3] Correspondence, Maureen Wise to Prospective Subscribers, ca. Summer 1955

[4] Sussex Express, 24th February 1956

[5] Minutes, 21st July 1953

[6] Kent & Sussex Courier, 5th July 1957

[7] Minutes, 1st June 1955

[8] Minutes, 4th October 1957

[9] Minutes, 1st April 1958

[10] Minutes, 12th August 1958

[11] Minutes, 2nd October 1958

[12] Minutes, 26th May 1959

[13] Sussex Express, 22nd March 1967

[14] Kent & Sussex Courier, 15th December 1967

[15] ibid

[16] HSB Newsletter, Spring 1970

[17] Minutes, 13th July 1977

[18] Minutes, 18th Oct 1978

[19] Press Release, Frankie Lulham, ca. 23rd Apr 2004; Minutes, 9th February 2010

[20] Minutes, 17th October 2011 & 12th January 2012

Poem *The Band Social Dinner*

My very dear friends, on behalf of the Band,
A welcome I give to you all.
At this dinner of ours, an occasion so grand,
May friendliness spread through this hall.
You could tell it was Bandsmen who sat down to eat
— It's surprising how low they can stoop!
They started the dinner with a prelude to meat,
By making a tune eating soup!

[Chorus]
Bless 'em all! Bless 'em all! –
The long, the short and the tall.
Bless the dear people in Alexandra Road
(The poor souls have got the patience of Jobe!)
Twice a week there's a racket they hear
For fifty-two weeks in the year.
And at Christmas of course, with a bit of a sauce,
We go round with the box for good cheer!

The year has gone by, and events have moved fast.
We've had lots of fun on the quiet.
We entered two contests, and almost came last,
The result almost causing a riot!
The horns blamed the basses; the basses went mad;
They said they'd been playing "so mellow."
But we soon found the reason – the tuning was bad –
Dear old Jack had been playing his Cello!

[Chorus]
Bless him all! Bless him all!
He's not such a bad lad after all.
His musical knowledge and playing is swell,
But the boys in the Band seem to make his life — well!
But last week he scored one right in the middle
In the fine Pantomime, Hey Diddle Diddle.
He got a big hand, with his own little Band,
Playing cornet and dear old bass fiddle!

They say there's a good bunch of lads in the Band
"A good-looking lot," we've heard say.
At a concert a girl took a look on the stand,
Then jumped in the air shouting "–ray!"
She went starry-eyed, as her eyes came to rest –
She had fallen for what she did see.
She rushed on the stage like a woman possessed,
And swooned flat over handsome Ted Lee!

[Chorus]
Bless 'em all! Bless 'em all!
The baritones, basses and all.
Bless all the tenors, the cornets as well,
(I won't bless the drummer; I'll send him to — well!)
I think that their playing is grand
But there's one thing you must understand;
It's a fact that's well-known, that without those trombones
It just wouldn't sound much like a Band!

We give a good concert, (so we have been told),
Large selections of tunes we can play.
We start with an overture brassy and bold,
And carry on with a waltz, come what may.
We play by request – people ask for a tune;
We try to please every good soul,
But we had to give up, just as some crazy buffoon
Shouted out – "Fox and Hounds," "Rock and Roll!"

[Chorus]
Bless 'em all! Bless 'em all!
As into the bandroom they fall.
Some need a haircut, and some need a shave;
Some look as though they just left a cave!
There's Geoff with a fag in his ear,
Brian Leeves with a big lipstick smear,
Not forgetting young Roy, his mum's pride and joy,
With his hair hanging down past each ear!

It's a wonder old Bert doesn't go round the bend,
After two days a week with this shower.
He stands in the middle – arms stretched, knees bent,
Facing 24 goons for two hours.
He's just racking his brain, for he just can't explain
Why *Finlandia* sounds out of tune.
As he stops once again, poor Roy gets the blame
He had been playing *I See the Moon!*

[Chorus]

Bless 'em all! Bless 'em all!

As home from this dinner they crawl.

It's been a good evening, you all must agree;

A real get together; a jolly good spree.

Here's a toast, one and all, to make here,

That we hold this affair once a year.

It's a darned good excuse to get out on the loose

And fill yourself right up with beer!

by Bob Lee

With grateful thanks to Bob's family for supplying the text.

MEMBERS of NOTE...

Dennis Guile
baritone, 1966–1996,
secretary, 1979–1996.

"Dennis was an average musician but a superb bandsman"
– Peter Cornford.

Dennis Guile was already middle-aged when he joined the Band in 1966. He had left school in 1940, at the age of fourteen, and gotten a job at the GPO (later to become British Telecom), with help from his father and grandfather who also worked there. He was to steadily climb his way up to an executive position, and would become known for his role in rebuilding the Mayfield telephone exchange after it (and also the bandroom of Mayfield Silver Band) was levelled by a devastating gas leak and explosion in 1978.[1]

It was whilst at the GPO that Dennis and several colleagues would be encouraged to join Heathfield Band. "It really started as a joke," explains Dennis in an article for the GPO staff magazine. "Susan [Bland, daughter of bandmaster Lloyd] could already play and she brought along an instrument, the flugel horn, for me to try. I couldn't get used to it so I passed it on to my brother who soon learned to play. Then Susan brought along a baritone horn and I soon took to it."[2]

"Dad absolutely loved Band, he took it extremely seriously," recalls Dennis' daughter, Wendy. "It was the most important thing to him after his family. Band practice couldn't be missed, and days out were organised around Band jobs." However, fully aware of his limitations as a player, Dennis would always gladly move down his section to make way for a better musician. "He said,

'I'm not terribly good. I don't mind where I go, I just wanna play,' " explains his wife, Maureen. "Some [players] are so dedicated, but he joined because it was just an evening out of fun."

Dennis would always be immaculately dressed in a tweed jacket and straight tie, and he couldn't stand it when others bandmembers turned up looking scruffy. He was slight in build and wiry, and it was perhaps his constant smoking which would help to keep him so thin. "I used to think that band practice for Dennis was about being able to have a good smoke, interrupted by playing occasionally," jokes Peter Cornford.

"Dennis had a rigid sense of right and wrong, and an often unshakeable belief that he was right, that his way was right, and that the rest of the world was wrong, but not in an unpleasant way. He was quite a gentle-mannered man really," adds Peter. "He was an absolute admirer of Margaret Thatcher, and he had the occasional good-natured political exchange with Dave Threlfall, the Band's socialist bandmaster."

"Dad was steadfast, loyal, highly intelligent, stubborn, and pragmatic," says Wendy. "He had a sharp, dry wit and he loved to mess around and be silly. He and I were avid readers and he would regularly move my bookmark and quietly watch my confusion when I began to read! In the woods one evening we discovered a load of arrows attached to the trees and spent a happy hour turning them all around… I have no idea what poor soul's activity was ruined!"

Having left school so young, Dennis had never achieved any academic qualifications; this would be rectified in the 1970s when he decided to take up evening classes. "He took O levels, A levels and art classes… just for the fun of it," recalls Wendy. "It was mortifying, because I was doing my exams at the same time and he got better results than me!"

When Dennis retired in 1984, he and Maureen would move to Burwash to run the *Daisy Tearooms*. "To call him bloody-minded would be an understatement," says Peter. "He believed that customers should be grateful for the privilege of being in his tea shop, and if they asked for something not on his menu, then they were just not going to get it!" According to Wendy: "Saturday and Sunday afternoons, dad went to play in the Band somewhere, leaving mum to serve the cream teas!" The venture was to last about two years before Maureen had had enough.

After the Band's infamous 1979 split which Dennis had in part orchestrated, he would feel obligated to become its new secretary. In 1991, he was to take on the role of Band manager, to assist with bookings and publicity.[3] Dennis would sadly succumb to cancer in March 1996.

[1] Mayfield and Five Ashes Community Website (2018). *The Day a Telephone Exchange Died – Part One*. [online] Available at: https://mayfieldfiveashes.org.uk/the-day-a-telephone-exchange-died-part-one/

[2] GPO Magazine, November 1966

[3] Minutes, ca. March 1991 & April 1995

1960s Creating a Modern Band

Parade to Christmas Fayre at St. Richard's Church Hall, Dec 1964.
(Clockwise from Back Left) Ben Guile, Dave Wenham, Ted Lee, Father Christmas, Cyril Leeves, Roy Elphick, Bob Lee, ?, Dennis Guile, ?, ?, Stan Ambuchi, Laurie Knapp, Sue Bland, ?, Christine Ambuchi, Tina Harris, Janice Bland, ?, Jackie Bland, Lesley Dann.
Photograph supplied by Sue Sutton.

The Sixties would undoubtedly be one of the most varied – perhaps even revolutionary – decades for Heathfield Band. Times were changing and popular music had undergone a radical shift in the wake of rock'n'roll, jazz and other emerging genres. Although it was struggling to attract players, the new era under bandleader Lloyd Bland was a mostly happy one. A sense of musicality was encouraged and tape recordings of concerts were made and listened to with a critical ear (if these tapes were ever rediscovered they would be an invaluable document for future generations to revisit).[1] A more structured training band was soon introduced, and female musicians were welcomed for the first time since Sylvia Upfield had caused uproar in the 1930s. Meanwhile, the main practice would move to Tuesday evenings, where it has remained ever since. The changes made during this decade reflect a clear point of transition, from a traditional town band to the modern, forward-thinking one that we recognise today.

The primary catalyst for change was Lloyd Bland. "He was principal cornet player under Bert Wise and, when Wise left, he took the stick," says Lloyd's eldest daughter Sue Sutton. His son Graham played soprano cornet with the Band, and Sue was soon encouraged to take up the side drum. However, aged just twelve at the time, she not only had to deal with criticism of "children" playing in the Band, but was also to face age-old the prejudices against female bandmembers. "Quite a few left because I joined,' says Sue. "They thought that was all wrong, that you shouldn't have females in the Band. And that was in the 1960s. Can you imagine that these days?! There was only about two or three females in different [local] bands then. It was a very male-dominated thing." Even after women were finally admitted, the uniform would remain distinct for each gender, only recently becoming truly unisex. "Female members were not allowed to wear trousers at that time. How dated that is now?" says Wendy Guile. Towards the end of the decade, the committee even considered adopting air hostess-type hats "for the girls."[2] Dave Sutton, Sue's husband and also a contemporary bandmember, recalls: "They were those long hats, but they wouldn't wear them. By the time they made their mind up to get them it was too old to start." Ben Guile (interviewed in 1981) adds: "They wore them for a while, but the interest faded with the new uniform."

Membership had fallen dramatically by the early Sixties. At the 1961 , "the old, old story of bad Thursday practices was again brought up" – a reference to the continuing poor attendance at rehearsals.[3] "Sometimes they pick the wrong days for their rehearsals," explains former bandmaster Frank Francis. "Heathfield Band have got their own space to rehearse, so they shouldn't have any problems with two to three rehearsals a week when necessary, but they go home and their wife says, 'No, you're not going out again this week, you've gotta take me out!' People don't mind being sociable for one day, that's their social event and they go round the pub afterwards because that's what they do, that's their day. It's brass band syndrome." In a bid to avoid clashes with other bands, and perhaps even encourage other players to join Heathfield as their "second band," the main practice night would switch to Tuesdays.[4] Other initiatives included the discontinuance of weekly subs and paying travel expenses for members. Nevertheless, by 1963 attendance had plummeted to a record low of just nine members.[5] The Warbleton & Buxted and Hooe bands were both approached regarding the possibility of an amalgamation; however, this ultimately came to nothing.[6]

Low attendance would also have the knock-on effect of further discouraging the remaining players. "There was a bloke from Horam Road – Hunt, his name was – he always used to come on the bus and he'd look through the window to see how many there was. If there wasn't many in there he wouldn't come in, he'd go back to Horam," remembers Ken Russell! "He was a cornet player named Fred," adds Sue Sutton. "About quarter of an hour, twenty minutes, after rehearsal started he used to come down and peer in the window. We used to see him and think, *Is he gonna come in or not?* It was so silly. He wasn't a bad cornet player [but] I think he felt too exposed if there was only one or two there." Perhaps this was the reason that it was suddenly deemed necessary to purchase a set of curtains for the bandroom.[7]

In November 1964 a new recruitment drive was begun,[8] but a major reversal of the Band's fortunes would be initiated by Sue Bland, who persuaded several Post Office engineers with whom she worked – her fiancé David, James Hall and brothers Ben and Dennis Guile – to have a go at banding. Dave recalls: "I was on construction, Ben was on construction, Jim and Dennis were on maintenance, and we were all working in Heathfield at the

Heathfield Band marching at Waldron, ca. 1960s.

204

time and Sue collared us all. The other one joined about that time, that year, was Lesley [Bray]." A contemporary issue of the GPO Staff Magazine takes up the story: "None of them could read a note of music or play an instrument. But they were keen to learn, so the bandmaster formed a junior section. Susan also brought in her younger sisters [Jackie and Janice Bland] and they began regular practice."[9] The Band was now on its way to a full recovery, with a healthy compliment of twenty-five playing members.

Several long-standing innovations would occur during the Sixties. Firstly, coaches were phased out as a means of transportation to engagements. "They used to always have coaches 'cause there wasn't enough cars," remembers Anna Farley. "It used to have a stop at the bandroom, where the heavy painted trunks for all the music, and then all the instruments, used to go on. When I watched the film *Brassed Off*, the Band was very like that at that time." However, by 1966 enough players now owned a car so that transportation could be arranged between them; this was considered more cost-effective than hiring a coach for every job. The decade also saw the formation of a Ladies' Committee which would support the Band, essentially unchanged, until the new millennium (see *With a Little Help from Our Friends: The Band Supporters*). The final innovation was the introduction of a weekly fundraising raffle in 1969, which would initially cost sixpence to enter (about 30p today). This replaced weekly subscriptions and would endure until 2018, when it was finally declared unprofitable.

Heathfield Band continued to attract a wide range of engagements and one especially valuable client was the Bexhill Corporation, who organised Summer concerts at the De La Warr Pavilion. From 1960 the Band would become a regular attraction at the venue, undertaking several concerts there each year. "There was an old bandstand at the back and we used to pile in the coach and go there," recalls Sue Sutton. The Summer of 1963 brought with it a major coup, as the Band was booked for an impressive ten dates at the Pavilion. These collectively earned it £120 (about £2,500 today), though deputy players would have to be sought, refreshments purchased, and coaches from Heathfield to Bexhill hired.[10] Nevertheless, these seaside excursions remained a profitable and social venture and the Band could regularly be seen at the venue throughout the Sixties and Seventies.[11]

Egerton Park, Bexhill, ca. early 1960s.
(L–R) Ben Guile, Dennis Guile, Sue Bland, Dave Sutton, ?James Hall.
Photograph supplied by Maureen Guile.

Bonfire marches remained a staple part of the Band's calendar, village and school fêtes and garden parties would once again become popular, and it continued to support ex-servicemen, performing at Battle of Britain Day commemorations, Remembrance Day services, and other events, for branches of the RAF Association and the British Legion. "In them days we didn't have many jobs," says Sue Sutton. "We did a few carnivals and we used to go to Bexhill, and then we did Alexandra Park in Hastings. But that was all the big jobs we did, there wasn't many." Roger Meyer, Captain of Bands for Cliffe Bonfire Society from 1993 to 2015, remembers the Band playing at the Brighton & Hove Albion football grounds: "As I recall, the Band played from the centre circle before kick-off and had a march around the pitch at half-time," says Roger. "On one occasion the bass drummer caused much merriment by beating too forcefully and putting his left stick straight through the drumskin!"

The repertoire under Lloyd Bland was varied and borrowed heavily from popular stage shows of the day. "We used to play a lot of popular musicals, like *Carousel*, *Around the World in Eighty Days*, *Pirates of Penzance*, *Chitty Chitty Bang Bang*, *Mary Poppins*, and other pieces like *Cavalleria Rusticana*," recalls Lesley Dann. "We would start concerts with marches, to get people going, and always finish with *Sussex By the Sea*." As membership increased and the Band's overall ability improved, it was once again able to tackle more ambitious music.

By the Summer of 1966, membership had recovered sufficiently for the Band to contribute to the 900th anniversary commemoration of the Battle of Hastings. Celebrations began in May with the Tunbridge Wells Contest, which was held at Hastings' White Rock Theatre as part of the festivities.[12]

Broad Oak School Fête, July 1966.
(Back Row, L–R) ?, Ben Guile, James Hall, Dennis Guile, ?, Trevor Rood,
Stan Ambuchi (in brown suit).
(Middle Row, L–R) Graham Bland, ?Doug, Lloyd Bland, ?.
(Front Row, L–R) Sue Bland, Jackie Bland, Janice Bland, ?.
(Girl at Front) ?Karin/Karen Bland.
Photograph supplied by Christine Ambuchi.

Although it went unplaced, the Band nevertheless obtained an admirable score and would thus resolve to contest again as soon as possible. It also appeared at the 1066 Commemoration Fair in Battle, where it massed with Burwash and Warbleton & Buxted bands.[13] "Bands played each night for a week," recalls Ben Guile (speaking in 1981). "A massed band played in the Abbey and in the church for a service. The massed band was conducted by a local bandmaster and Major Jaeger came along and took the Washington Grays [the Band of a volunteer light infantry corps from Philadelphia, USA]. It was quite an experience to play under him. There was a parade, too." Over the following few years, the Band delivered solid performances in third section contests at Chatham, Hastings and Tunbridge Wells.[14] At Chatham in November 1968 it won first prize in its section, and members would later share a celebratory toast from the Arthur Jarvis Memorial Trophy![15]

Several decades before Heathfield's Le Marché made its debut, the local branch of the Round Table (a non-political, non-sectarian organisation for young men) experimented with bringing themed markets to the town. The first, a Caledonian Market, was held during the 1966 Whitsun Bank Holiday. The town band naturally gave their support, and are pictured "hard at work entertaining their fellow villagers," in the Courier. "Whether the event be happy or sad, these enthusiasts contribute so much to the atmosphere of the occasion."[16] The following year an Arabian Fair was held and its parade, headed by the Band, included Scouts, Guides, Ms. Heathfield, and a group of "very British Arabs," complete with a live camel![17] The event attracted over two thousand attendees, and the profits would be used to send schoolchildren to the Holy Land.[18]

Throughout the decade the Band continued its Christmas tradition of carolling from house-to-house. As a result, it would form a particularly close friendship with Sir Edward Caffyn and his wife. "It started when the Band played carols without warning outside their sitting room," explains Anna Farley. "It frightened the life out of them, but then they asked us to come every year. So every Christmas we used to go down and play at his house – *Norman Norris* – at Vines Cross." The Caffyn family would thus organise an annual house party for their friends, ensuring it coincided with the Band's visit. "It was a huge part of Christmas," says Wendy Holloway.

"The first time I had too much to drink was at Sir Caffyn's annual Christmas party. The Band would play some carols for the guests to sing to, then we were free to help ourselves to the buffet, which included some very strong punch!" Anna adds: "After that we used to do carol playing round Vines Cross, house to house collections. We used to go round the village and then finish up at the pub, *The Brewers Arms*, and play carols in there." Sir Edward became a much valued life-long patron and vice-president of the Band.

An unusual, and somewhat unplanned, performance took place in June 1968. As the Band arrived at Polegate Gala expecting to spend a relaxing afternoon playing some light music, members were surprised to hear an announcement over the Tannoy: "Heathfield Silver Band will now give a display of marching…"[19] By all accounts the unrehearsed demonstration was carried off without calamity, and the musicians even managed to remain more or less in step with one another![20] A further surprise presented itself when one of the *It's A Knockout* teams failed to arrive; players suddenly found themselves competing as substitutes in bonkers challenges such as piano-smashing and a beer-drinking boat race.[21] "Heathfield Band's euphonium player, Dave Wenham, proved himself in a class of his own," writes the Evening Argus. "Eight big 'bangers' and a plate full of mashed potato disappeared, as well as a pint of beer, and Dave was soon ready for his tea!"[22] Ever the professionals, bandmembers gamely carried off these extra duties in addition to performing the scheduled programme of music.

HSB having a smashing time!, June 1968.
Photograph supplied by Newsquest.

Early in 1969 tragedy struck as the Band suffered the death of sixty-seven year-old Jeff Hobden – "the Whistling Bandsman" – who had been a key member for almost forty years.[23] Things would never be the same again. "He was a really keen bandsman, loved by all," said Lloyd Bland at the time. "We shall all miss him greatly and his death leaves a big gap which will be very hard to fill."[24] The Band played at Jeff's funeral and performed *The Last Post* at his graveside, whilst several members also acted as coffin bearers.[25]

The sheer range of 1969's engagements was indeed impressive. "We played in a variety of conditions, from a garden party on the lawn of a country house in the heat of a Summer afternoon, to caroling in the dark and windy side roads of Heathfield on cold December nights," reports a Band newsletter. "During the Guy Fawkes celebrations the Band marches enclosed in a circle of fiery torches; at church parades we think ourselves lucky if the rain does not quite soak through to the skin; and when we parade Santa Claus through the streets to our Christmas Fayre – it snows!"[26] Indeed, the Band faced such heavy snow that year that one member was to slip on the ice and damage his cornet.[27] "Those North Country bands playing their fancy *appoggiaturas* certainly have the edge on Heathfield Silver, but can they match our stamina in facing the English weather?" asks the newsletter.[28]

As humankind set its sights on reaching the moon, Heathfield Band was harbouring high hopes of its own. Its hard work under the leadership of Lloyd Bland was beginning to pay off: membership was high (with twenty-seven musicians by the decade's end), the Band's musical ability had improved significantly, and contesting was yielding considerable results. It had once again proven incredibly resilient to adversity, and had taken every opportunity to rebuild itself in a more modern image. The Band would thus emerge from the Sixties triumphant, approaching its future from a position of strength, relative prosperity, and optimism.

---

[1] Minutes, 8th May 1961

[2] Minutes, 8th December 1969

[3] Minutes, 12th October 1961

[4] Minutes, 11th October 1962

[5] Minutes, 15th October 1963

[6] Minutes, 26th November 1963

[7] Minutes, 17th November 1964

[8] ibid

[9] GPO Magazine, November 1966

[10] Accounts, 1962–1963

[11] see Accounts, 1963–1964, etc

[12] Kent & Sussex Courier, 13th May 1966

[13] Cornford, P., 1981. Personal Archive and Interviews

[14] www.BrassBandResults.co.uk, 2021

[15] Minutes, 7th January 1969

[16] Kent & Sussex Courier, 3rd June 1966

[17] Kent & Sussex Courier, 2nd June 1967

[18] ibid

[19] Kent & Sussex Courier, 15th June 1968

[20] ibid

[21] Evening Argus, 17th June 1968)

[22] ibid

[23] Cutting, source unknown, 24th January 1969

[24] ibid

[25] ibid

[26] HSB Newsletter, Spring 1970

[27] Kent & Sussex Courier, 29th November 1969

[28] HSB Newsletter, Spring 1970

MEMBERS of NOTE...

Ben (Bernard) Guile
cornet & flugel horn,
chairman,
1966–86.

"What the Band lacks in finesse is more than made up
for in enthusiasm" – Ben Guile.

by Peter Cornford

Ben was one of the best friends I have ever had. He was someone I really looked up to. He was self-effacing and self-deprecating, a man of great wit and wisdom, someone who in a different environment could have gone on to be in a position of great influence. Yet despite having studied art at Goldsmith's College, he was to pack it all in to work locally for the GPO, mending wires in telephone junction boxes. He had a rare artistic talent for drawing and was a prolific reader, particularly of history books.

Ben was a first-class amateur local historian, renowned in Heathfield for researching its history. He was a pillar of the Heathfield Local History Society, and would frequently speak at meetings. He was a great encouragement to me when, in the 1970s and '80s, I was researching the history of the Band. One Summer, we were to spend long periods of time together researching various aspects of mediaeval Heathfield, going out on field trips around the parish and undertaking hedge dating, surveying field patterns and poking about in woods for lost relics of the iron industry. Later, when we were to present our findings at a talk to the Local History Society, every slide was to have printed in Gothic capitals down its side the acronym of the name Ben had chosen for us: *Old Heathfield Settlement History Investigation Team*! It was typical of Ben's mischief and he would take great delight in the fact that no-one in the audience seemed to have worked it out!

Ben had taken up playing the flugel horn at the age of twenty-nine, joining the Band at the same time as his older brother, Dennis. He would become treasurer in 1979, and subsequently chairman, two positions which he was to carry out very professionally. He had a wicked sense of humour and would regard one of his objectives at rehearsals as amusing those sitting either side of him, particularly the youngsters. He would sit straight-faced, making quiet, devastatingly funny remarks about the other players and the conductor, in an attempt to make us giggle.

Everyone liked Ben. He had a constant supply of humorous stories. I always found it remarkable (because he was colour blind) that he mended wires in GPO junction boxes. He once dropped a piece of red wire on the grass and, because to him the wire looked indistinguishable from the grass, he had to stop a pedestrian and ask her to point it out for him; he subsequently would have to reassure her that his intentions were not dishonourable!

Interlude The New Recruits: Training Future Bandmembers

Community bands normally recruit people from a diverse range of musical backgrounds and new players are often tutored from scratch. As such, most bands will run a training group from time to time. Such an initiative, when carefully managed, can provide a stream of new talent and the opportunity for existing bandmembers to progress in a meritocratic way. During its earliest years, Heathfield Band had no organised recruitment strategy. Local labourers would essentially have assembled to have a blow, with the laudable aim of putting together a functioning community band. Today, recruitment and tuition is integral to the Band's activities. On a fundamental level, such efforts exist to help it sustain and grow but the underlying ethos, which is today enshrined in a constitution, is more nuanced. Its objective has always been to bring musical appreciation to the wider community, whether that be through public performances, or through the tuition of new players and the shared rehearsal of music.

All of Heathfield Band's original members had little or no musical experience, and certainly no formal training; however, they did receive tuition. Stephen Saunders, an experienced musician and talented local cornet player, coached the original drum and fife band, whilst Mr. G. Cuthbert, the bandmaster of the old 2nd Sussex Artillery Band at Eastbourne, was the tutor during its early years as a brass band.[1] By the late 1920s when the offshoot

Stan Nye and Jack King, who both joined in the late Twenties, pictured May 1931.
Photograph supplied by Peter Cornford.

Heathfield Silver Band was formed, new players were tutored by piano teacher Arthur Rodgers. During the Forties its wartime bandmaster Mr. Durrant introduced young ATC members to the art of brass banding. However, the latter two initiatives were essentially rapid responses, designed to keep the Band afloat during troubled times. It was not until after the Second World War that bandmaster Bert Wise would contemplate a more structured approach to recruitment and tuition, and in 1957 a dedicated learners' rehearsal was trialled.[2]

In the early Sixties, under bandmaster Lloyd Bland, the committee proactively began to recruit and train new players.[3] "I was playing piano at school and dad said, 'Would you like to play drum?' " remembers Lloyd's eldest daughter, Sue. "I thought, *Ooh, that sounds good!*" At the time, there was no training band or formal tuition for learners. Instead, more experienced members would simply help them along as best as possible. "There was a chap called Cyril Leeves on the bass drum," continues Sue. "He was a very patient chap, really lovely, he nurtured me through the side drum. In them days you didn't have brass playing at school, only pianos and things like that." Sue soon progressed onto brass instruments and began playing tenor horn: "I remember a chap, Ted Lee, used to play solo tenor horn. He sat with me, so I just learned off

Drummer girl Sue Bland, ca. late 1960. *Photograph supplied by Sue Sutton.*

him." A major boost to the Band came when Sue persuaded four work colleagues and her two younger sisters to join. As a result, a new junior band would have to be established.[4] Soon, the Band's fortunes were beginning to reverse. "We went and practised on Monday evenings separately, then eventually we went into the Band," remembers Ben Guile (interviewed in 1981). "On the first night we played *Ballerina*. [Afterwards], we all asked one another where we'd all got to in the piece. I'd got to the end of the second bar!" However, within just three months, the hard-working new recruits were ready to participate in the Band's main rehearsals.

Nevertheless, the training band was still not a permanent fixture. Instead, it was dropped and resurrected with each new influx of learners, a by-product of successive recruitment drives. Peter Cornford recalls joining the Band sometime around 1974: "I was on a Remembrance Parade with the Cub Scouts and we marched behind Heathfield Band and I was ambling along thinking, *I wouldn't mind actually being in that band.* And that coincided with Dave Sutton coming to Cross-in-Hand Primary School [on the outskirts of Heathfield], which was very enterprising, and talking to our class and saying,

Alison Cornford and Sarah Threlfall, ca. 1979.
Photograph supplied by Mostyn Cornford.

216

'Is anybody interested in joining the Band?' So I went along to the learner band with a friend. There were probably half a dozen of us there. I was given the oldest instrument they could find, a flugel horn, a really battered old thing, and about a year after they actually bought me a new instrument. Dave Sutton just turned up at my house one day with a brand new flugel horn, a Boosey Sovereign." As a result of this drive, the Band's demographics became much younger, a characteristic which endures to this day. "There were quite a few of us who were teenagers, which is what you're looking for, really, for the future," adds Peter.

In the mid-Eighties, the training group became a more structured and permanent part of the Band, and in 1987 a minimum age for learners would be set – at eight years old.[5] Sarah Leeves, who joined at the age of ten, recounts the typically eccentric recruitment process: "I walked in and Frank Francis was conducting. He was very jolly, very friendly, so I was not fazed by any of it. He looked at me and said, 'Ah, you look like a euphonium player,' and so they gave me a euphonium straight away (it happened to be the only empty seat in the bandroom)! I sat down next to Sid [Forward]. He showed me how to play a note, and I did it, and he said, 'Now every time I nod, I want you to play that note.' So I just sat there watching Sid and waiting for my cue. Sid was lovely. He used to sit and tell me all sorts of stories, and he used to try and teach me to do little technical things, which were quite possibly a bit too tricky for me, but I'd have a go anyway. They sent me home with a tatty old book, to try and learn a few tunes from, and the battered old euphonium that smelt funny (which I quite liked)! I did *Twinkle Twinkle, Little Star* in assembly the next week and that was it. I didn't think about it, I just tried to do it. So it was straight in at the deep end. I look back and think, *Did they really do it like that?*"

There was now a regular Friday night training band, which had been run on and off since 1976 by veteran bandmember, Ted Lee. "We used to have such a laugh," remembers Sarah. "Every single Friday night we'd go up to the bandroom, that was officially *junior band night*. However many of us there was – two of us, twelve of us, sixteen of us – Ted was there. He gave up all his time for that without a thought. He tolerated so much, bless him, he was just so sweet. He'd let us play the drum kit, we'd play some duets, he'd let us nip off to Heathfield Wines Stores to buy some sweets, and then we'd come back

i) Uckfield Bonfire, September 2009.
Photograph supplied by Keith Pursglove.

ii) Training Band, ca. 1995–97.

iii) Cuckoo Fair, April 2008.
Photograph supplied by Kent & Sussex Courier.

iv) Oldest and Youngest, December 2009.
Photograph supplied by Kent & Sussex Courier.

v) Charleston Manor, August 2006.
Photograph supplied by Frankie Lulham.

vi) Hailsham Bonfire, October 2007.
Photograph supplied by Sussex Newspapers.

vii) **Training Band, December 2013.**

viii) **Christmas Lights Switch On, Heathfield High Street, December 2003.**
Photograph supplied by Kent & Sussex Courier.

ix) **Sussex Day at Chapel Green, Crowborough, June 2011.**
Photograph supplied by Kent & Sussex Courier.

x) **Christmas Concert at State Hall, Heathfield, December 2009.**
Photograph supplied by Kent & Sussex Courier.

xi) **Heathfield Agricultural Show, May 2013.**
Photograph supplied by Sarah Tate Photography.

up and we'd play some more music, play some quartets. It was good fun. I loved that, actually."

By the early 1990s, the junior band had developed into a more distinct entity within Heathfield Silver Band. There was a feeling that learners should be given more opportunities to play in public before progressing to the main Band. Jeff Collins, who played Eb bass and whose daughter Sara had recently begun to learn cornet, became involved in the running of the junior band around 1991. "Conductor Frank Francis used to do hour-long sessions for the junior section of the Band," recalls Jeff. "I helped him out and then took over running the junior band practice sessions before the main practice. I used to thoroughly enjoy getting them practising bits. During the interval of the annual Christmas concert, the deputy bandmaster or junior section bandmaster would get the children to play a piece to entertain the audience. I found a really good ten-piece younger persons' version of the *Star Wars theme* and that sounded absolutely brilliant when they played that."

Keith Pursglove (speaking in 2012) recalls the experience of his son David, who also joined the Band aged about ten: "Being part of this Band allowed David to grow and develop his personality, it boosted his confidence. He absolutely loved the fact that he could talk to people on a level par, as a member of the Band. I'm sure that has helped him be the person he is. They lent David a cornet and every week he used to go along the bandroom – sometimes there were two or three and sometimes it was just David – and Ted Lee would just give him basic instruction. I don't think Ted's a teacher, I think he's just a guy that loves music and likes to encourage the kids."

In 1997, the Band applied for a National Lottery Grant, and the application documents contain some fascinating information about the training group: "Our aim is to teach novice players the fundamentals of music and bring them up to a level of experience to enable them to join the main Band. There are currently fifteen beginners: eleven children and four adults. Tuition is free and, as well as one group session per week, each beginner has a one to one and a half hour lesson."[6] The benefits to the community were clear. The Band was awarded a large grant towards the purchase of new instruments, whilst older ones were transferred to the junior band.[7] Spare instruments would also be loaned to local schools, creating further learning opportunities for youngsters.[8]

From the outset of her leadership, musical director Frankie Lulham recognised the importance of recruiting young players. "Men, women, boys and girls are all welcome," says Mostyn Cornford in a contemporary press release. "We have a good mixture, including a good junior section that are now referred to as *The Improvers*. [...] It isn't always the youngsters who are the beginners either."[9] Frankie made a point of showcasing the training band and worked hard to make its members feel included. She would also ensure that troubled individuals were given a chance to prove themselves: "X was a bit of a troublemaker, always in trouble. He had lots of problems at primary school," recalls Frankie. "Basically, people didn't understand him and he desperately wanted to join the Band. I presented him with a jacket and he was overwhelmed that I was trusting him in inviting him to join the Band. He became a lovely member, from nothing to grade eight!"

**Grand Bandroom Reopening,
September 2005.**

Photograph supplied by Frankie Lulham.

In an attempt to avoid the problems of the past, there was now a clear plan for incorporating learners into the main Band. "We want the training band members to feel proud of their own band and aspire to the main Band," wrote Frankie at the time. "I don't want too many beginners in the Band at one time again. [...] I have a plan whereby they are allowed up to the main Band a couple at a time, when they reach a standard and are able to cope."[10] The strategy would provide a graduated path to integration, avoiding new players becoming overwhelmed by the experience. In a memo to the committee, Frankie explains: "It is quite true that a number of members of the main Band started playing in the Band when they were very young and not a good standard. They had no tuition in the art of marching and were expected to just

221

come along and learn as they went along […]. They took up a lot of time and effort which could have been better spent on other players in the Band."[11] Learners were now required to attain the equivalent of grade three to progress to the main Band. They were also encouraged to take part in contesting, and to learn how to march. "We wanted to train them properly, so that they didn't come to a Band engagement thinking, *Gosh, what do I do?*" adds Frankie.[12]

The training band required a dedicated music teacher, a role which Frankie's daughter Danielle was to briefly occupy, prior to undertaking her final year at university. Fortunately, Sarah Leeves had now re-joined the Band and would fill the void until Danielle could return, filled with renewed enthusiasm and fresh ideas. "Danielle decided to try to train people properly," explains Frankie. "She'd learned through the school and had belonged to a number of concert bands and orchestras. She'd had a wonderful time being trained properly, you know, how to sit, not talking in-between, being ready to play, how to hold your instrument and this sort of thing, and she really tried to do that. She was teaching brass and brought a lot of the youngsters to the Band. They learned to play how we thought they should learn to play." Danielle adds: "We tried to make it more inclusive and appealing. I had a lot of brass pupils starting and progressing after I came back from uni and so this was a great way of getting youngsters and new players into the main Band. It really needed it after all. We were trying to stop it from dying out and becoming something only a certain age group did."

In July 2004, Danielle set out her ethos to the committee: "Along with keeping traditions, which are very important to the Band's history, it is important to move with the times. We have to remember that the youngsters are the future of the Band and it is important to keep them interested, make the youngsters feel that the Band is as important to them as is it to the more mature members of the Band." Danielle would make further suggestions, such as painting a mural in the bandroom ("It would be an exciting opportunity for the young members of the Band to help come up with ideas and designs, and also to help paint the mural […] and give them a sense of ownership"), and organising a Band tour to Germany ("The younger generation would benefit from experiencing festivities in another culture as well as travelling to see another part of the world").[13] Meanwhile, a questionnaire was circulated to gauge the feelings of existing learners. The responses suggest that the training sessions were considered helpful, the repertoire was broadly suitable, and that players were happy with their position in the Band.[14] In early 2006, *The Improvers Group* was divided into a junior band and a training band, to allow for a more bespoke path of progression for players of varying abilities.[15]

The training band would arguably reach its zenith at this time, as a stream of new players filtered quickly into the main Band. In July 2007, Danielle suggested making the training band a more self-contained youth ensemble, to be named *Heathfield Silver Youth Band*. However, the committee had several caveats. Firstly, no additional costs beyond the "agreed annual allowance" were to be incurred. Secondly, "The youth band is for contesting, quartets etc. No other engagements without the full agreement of the committee."[16] This suggests that the committee wanted to exert control over the youth band whilst simultaneously showing not the "slightest bit of interest in it," as Frankie puts it.[17] "They weren't really prepared to invest any Band money into it," she explains, "so we applied for a donation from the Uckfield Lions [which] bought all the training band members smart waistcoats and ties. We held a Coffee Morning to raise more money, but the committee members didn't come along and support it."[18] A contemporary of Frankie and Danielle's, Keith Pursglove, adds: "Danielle was young, enthusiastic, she'd just gone through university studying music and of course she'd obviously picked up on all the new [ideas]. She probably saw a band that needed modifying. I think she realised that changing a very, very entrenched organisation is not easy."

Following the departure of Frankie and Danielle, Richard Sherlock took over as the main Band's musical director, and Cheryl Goodsell would initially run the training band. Recruitment and integration now returned to a more *ad hoc* approach and the leader of the training band was to change fairly often. To help with recruitment the local newspaper made it known that new players were welcome. An open day was also organised, at the Union Church in Heathfield, and showcasing the training band at school fêtes was also considered.[19] "We suddenly started to get a few youngsters that were interested in the Band and things just started to improve. I think schools were starting to teach brass again, and a lot of the youngsters have lessons at the Community College," explains Richard.

One of the youngsters who joined at this time was eight year-old Charlotte Butcher. "I first became a part of the Heathfield Silver Band community in 2008. I had recently moved to Heathfield and decided that I wanted to take up learning a musical instrument. Brass instruments had always interested me so one day we turned up to the bandroom and I had a go! I tried out playing both the cornet and the tenor horn and, immediately, the tenor horn felt more comfortable to play, so I began having lessons. After a while of learning how to read music, I finally felt ready to progress and joined the Heathfield Silver Band's training band, which was where I had my first performance in front of the general public, playing during Heathfield Silver Band's annual Christmas Concert. I eventually joined the main Band as Heathfield Silver Band's youngest member. Initially, I began playing the 2nd horn part in our tenor horn group, which is slightly lower in pitch, and this really helped me to acclimatise to the slightly harder pieces of music they played in comparison to the training band."[20]

As more youngsters were to join, tutoring was distributed amongst willing senior bandmembers.[21] However, this had its disadvantages: "There's nobody competent enough to really teach," explains former bandmaster Frank Francis. "Anybody that wants to teach wants money for it, and when you're let down by a pupil it's really soul-destroying, so people give up on that. Now what's happening is you're getting bad players passing on bad information because they don't have the proper knowledge. Once upon a time you'd learn a brass instrument at school, and you'd join the local brass band when you left school. That was the social system." Foreshadowing the direction of things to come, Richard Sherlock believed that what the Band really needed was: "a music teacher who could be part of the Band, someone who's got a good knowledge of how to play an instrument, how to form the notes and how to move people along. That would make a huge difference. I think our biggest challenge, really, is how to get people started in brass bands."

Another of the junior members promoted to the main Band during this time was Lucy Clements, grand-daughter of Mostyn Cornford. Lucy worked hard to attain her grades and would eventually become its principal cornet player. "In Heathfield Silver Band some have had no formal musical training and some cannot sight read," she says, noting that the Band sometimes attempted music that was too difficult for everyone to cope with. "It should be easy so that people can play well and have confidence." Lucy is a firm believer in the advantages of proper tuition and suggests that some members would significantly benefit from having private lessons, as she had done. "Most of them haven't got any qualifications at all," adds Mostyn. "It's mainly the younger ones who have got qualifications because they're taught at school and so on."

During the past decade, the training band has had a variety of short-lived leaders, all of whom would bring their own unique insights to the teaching of music and musicality. In the Summer of 2011, Mark Welch (then vicar of Heathfield's Union Church), would try an ambitious approach. "So far I have

Half Moon Inn, July 2019.
Photograph by Tony Withers.

concentrated on the following things: controlled playing, attention to dynamics and markings, recognising and celebrating achievements to build confidence," he writes in one report.[22] In another, he says: "I was delighted by their first attempt [at *Grieg's Last Spring*]. On the whole the junior band managed to play with real musicality and interpreted quite well. We have also continued looking at marches for syncopation and hymn tunes for balance and intonation, and I have selected tunes with verses and choruses in differing styles to give experience of interpreting and playing musically and expressively. By having high expectations, but encouraging and building confidence, I have found that the junior band have delighted me with their achievements."[23]

However, regardless of who is at the helm of the training band, the core aim has always been to provide everyone with the opportunity to learn and play a brass instrument.[24] "We take anyone with any ability, and any age, and there were never any charges, that was part of what was said in the Lottery Statement," says the Band's former chairman Richard Leeves. The solution has hitherto been to make clear that any paid-for lessons must not be undertaken in the Band's name or on its property. "The Band acknowledges that 'private' lessons would benefit new members of the Band, but those wishing to learn an instrument must be made aware that the Band can provide lessons free of charge," affirms the secretary.[25] However, in November 2018 the committee began to ask for "contributions" from training band members, at a rate of £30 per year.[26] According to Peter Cornford, this underlines "changing perceptions of the value of music-making to society, and even a prevailing (Thatcherite?) view of the modern committee that 'everything has a cost.' " For some, this change represents a real threat to the inclusive ethos of the Band. In particular, it could affect those from less-privileged backgrounds, precisely the people who were once the life-blood of the brass banding movement.

The Band's musical director Sarah Leeves is nevertheless optimistic for the training band's future, and has taken a close personal interest in its direction. "With new members joining our *Start Out* lesson group and the training band beginning to feel like a really well-established group, we are pushing ahead with recruitment of new youngsters from local primary schools, in particular ones where brass tuition is not currently offered," she reports. "We may well find ourselves needing to acquire more instruments appropriate for these new learners, maybe new music, and who knows, maybe even a bandroom extension!"[27]

---

[1] Sussex Express, 28th June 1935

[2] Minutes, 31st October 1949 & 5th December 1950

[3] Minutes, 14th January 1953, 24th January 1957 & 17th November 1964

[4] GPO Magazine, November 1966

[5] Minutes, 27th January 1987

[6] Lottery Application, June 1997

[7] Press Release, 28th October 1997

[8] Cutting, source unknown, April 1997

[9] Press Release, Mostyn Cornford, ca. June 2002

[10] Minutes, 6th February 2007

[11] Memo to Band Committee, ca. Autumn 2006

[12] ibid

[13] Minutes, 1st July 2004

[14] HSB Questionnaire, June 2004

[15] Minutes, 20th February 2006 & 10th April 2006

[16] Minutes, 12th July 2007

[17] Memo to Band Committee, ca. Autumn 2006

[18] Correspondence, Frankie Lulham to Isla Sitwell, 17th October 2007

[19] Minutes, 10th January 2008 & 6th April 2009; Heathfield First, January 2009

[20] Heathfield Magazine, November 2018

[21] Minutes, 7th December 2009

[22] Minutes, 5th September 2011

[23] Minutes, 17th October 2011

[24] Sussex Express, 15th March 2013; www.heathfieldsilverband.com, 2019

[25] Correspondence, Band Secretary to Cheryl Goodsell, 1st February 2010

[26] Correspondence, Band Secretary to Bandmembers, 6th November 2018

[27] Minutes, 26th February 2019

Poem *The Bandsman*

I am a true-bred bandsman, boys,
Me father comes from Fareham.
Me mother ain't got no more like I
'Cause she wouldn't know how to rear 'em.
I can play a comb, or a slide Trombone –
I can beat the drums as well,
And when I'm practicing hard at home,
It really sounds like — well!

Like all good bandsmen, I believe
To keep my Trombone clean.
And so to work with string and rag,
I really make it gleam.
But, alas, one day (it's sad to say,)
My cleaning, it did end –
The string, it broke, as I tugged away,
And the rag got stuck round the bend!

With my Trombone going once more again,
To practice I did go.
I sat on a chair, with my head in the air
Intent on a jolly good blow.
We opened with 'Finlandia,'
I thought "It's in the bag."
But when I hit the first note, It came through the air,
Like tearing a bit of old rag!

Way down Lewes I did go,
Upon a bonfire night,
Me and my Trombone right up the front,
We looked a lovely sight.

The drummer, he set a steady pace,
Up the High Street we did wend.
Then my music flew all over the place,
And me slide dropped off the end!

One day in May, on a Saturday,
To a contest we did go.
We had practised hard, and did intend
To put up a really good show.
I sat on the stage, feeling just about swell –
(I was playing 'lead Trombone'.)
Then I 'mucked up' my solo, I'm sorry to tell.
I then wished that I'd stayed back at home!

Mr. Wise did say, on the very next day:
"I've got news for you!
Your playing was bad, and what's more my lad,
You lost us the contest, too!"
I went pretty red, "and what's more" he said,
"You'll never play a slide Trombone."
So my heart went like a great lump of lead,
And I crept out the door to go home.

I was a true-bred bandsman, boys,
But now my hopes have gone.
My thoughts of being a Trombone star
Just didn't last very long.
But a ray of hope from my old friend Phil
Has made me feel so grand —
I'm bashing away with my Trombone still,
With the boys of the 'Southdown Band!' [a dance band]

by Bob Lee

With grateful thanks to Bob's family for supplying the text.

MEMBERS of NOTE...

Tom Kelly
trombone, 1972–74,
conductor & musical director, 1974–82,
honorary life member.

by Peter Cornford

A retired council official, Tom Kelly would join the Band in 1972, playing trombone and occasionally assisting with the baton for the next two years before taking over as its permanent bandmaster.[1] He would also be instrumental in its move to become a registered charity in 1976.[2]

I think Tom was a Lancashire man, I'm pretty sure he played with Fairies, and in his day he would have been a fairly good player. He was fairly strict and he set the tone with all this background and heritage of good banding. By the time he took Heathfield Band he was in his late sixties/early seventies, but he'd got that hinterland of experience and knowledge. The late Seventies was a high-water mark in terms of the Band's ability and what it was achieving. I think it was a given that it would contest and Tom was to guide it to a reasonable level of success in the fourth section.

Tom was to have a bit of a bad press with some people. With the benefit of hindsight, he deserves a bit more credit than people were giving him at the time. It wasn't the case that he was stuck in the past; the repertoire really was a good mix of traditional and contemporary, which is why it rankled a little bit when some in the Band were saying: "The old codger's music needs to go!" Tom was, I think, across all of it and was doing quite well.

However, by the end of Tom's tenure, I think he'd lost touch a little bit of the Band's ability. He was beginning to get out things from his past that the Band of the early Eighties wasn't managing. They were all good average players, but there was no good soloist and there was no good section that could really carry something off.

In September 1978, Tom announced that he would resign as bandmaster as he didn't wish to let the Band down.[3] His health was beginning to fail and he was losing the ability to conduct effectively. It would be a gentle retirement and my memory is that he sort of faded away. In 1979, he was made an honorary life member, and would transition to a more advisory role within the Band.[4] He would retire completely in October 1982.

You could say, from a musical perspective, that the Band was to decline after Tom left. It would be a watershed moment which felt like a real change.

---

[1] Courier, 29th September 1978
[2] Minutes, 14th April 1976
[3] Minutes, 17th September 1978
[4] Minutes, 6th February 1979

1970s Activity & Achievement, Friendliness & Fun

Heathfield Silver Band, ca. 1976.

The Band's activities during the Seventies give a sense of ongoing achievement and evolution. Membership was to grow under bandmaster Lloyd Bland and a typical year would see the Band undertaking between thirty and forty engagements. There was a happier, optimistic and more ambitious outlook. During the decade, the Band would upgrade most of its instruments and embrace a completely new public image with its transition to the now-characteristic red uniform. Two half century-long connections would end with the death of long-time supporter, and vice-president, Nelson Harriett, and the retirement of bass drummer Cyril Leeves. There were also three different bandmasters, each bringing their own approach and style to the running of the Band. But the continuing push for modernisation would not be fully realised until a satisfactory balance between current and traditional was reached. This tension was to result in a major bust-up and loss of membership before the decade was over.

The decade began with the promise of a host of interesting and varied engagements, including a charity concert in aid of the Leukaemia Research

Fund. Lloyd Bland enjoyed considerable control over the Band's direction, mainly to his dual role as bandmaster and secretary. Under Lloyd, it continued to be prominent at community events, including fêtes and carnivals, the Heathfield Show, St. George's Day parades, Remembrance Day commemorations, and Christmas events. It would also expand into new territory, such as giving Sunday evening performances outside local pubs and, in 1975, playing at Warrior Square in St Leonards.

There was a triumphant return to the Sussex Bonfire scene, during which the Band would foster a long-standing relationship with Newick Bonfire Society. It also made its first foray to Lewes Bonfire, initially on behalf of the Commercial Square Society. In November 1977 it took to the streets of Eastbourne, as part of the annual Royal Engineers' Parade. Clarice Lee, wife of Ted and mother to horn player Anna (speaking in 2012), remembers an amusing incident at one such parade: "Anna was marching with the soldiers' barracks along Seaside Road. Being young she was wearing high-heel shoes, and she got her foot stuck in a drain and had to go off without her shoe! The chaps playing behind got it out for her, but it taught her a lesson… to wear flat shoes."

The Band continuously sought ways to raise its profile within the community and one such initiative was a sponsored walk, which was held in September 1976.[1] The walk led participants from Heathfield to Hellingly and back, by way of the disused railway line now known as the Cuckoo Trail. It raised about £150 for the Band's instrument fund (ca. £1,100 today).[2] "Most of the bandmembers walked, whilst some of the older members were officials," recalls Ben Guile (speaking in 1981). "Everyone finished, including old Lloyd, who took it at a steady pace and with his walking stick. He was determined to do it and he did!" That evening, as the Band celebrated Bert Thompson's golden wedding anniversary, the exertion of the day would lead Lloyd to pass out at the reception.

Perhaps the most exciting venture of the time was the Band's long overdue return to France, in July 1970, to take part in the annual band festival at Calais. Here it played alongside several dozen bands from across Europe, including its High Weald friends and neighbours Warbleton & Buxted Band, now led by Heathfield's previous conductor Bert Wise.[3] It was an overwhelming event: "The French were very enthusiastic about Heathfield Silver Band," remembers Ben Guile. "There were crowds of people. We were in with German and Dutch bands, all playing different kinds of instruments, [each] with up to a hundred bandsmen and around fifty majorettes in front." The initiative would prove such a success that the Band returned twice more in subsequent years.

Heathfield Carnival, 1977.
Photograph supplied by Peter Cornford.

The Band dominated the third section of the Hastings Festival in May 1970, earning the headline: "Heathfield Band: Best in its Class," in the local press.[4] It also performed well at contests in Tunbridge Wells, Chatham, East Grinstead and Folkestone. At its peak, in 1975, it secured 2nd place in the second section. However, Peter Cornford believes that the Band was really a third section band that would rather not be contesting at all. "It did it because it's like eating cabbage, it thought it was good for you," he says. "There were people like Ted Lee, Bob Lee, Jack Mitchell, Jack King, the *elders* of the Band who, if not directly in charge, were certainly influential. They had been players when it was at its peak in the Fifties and had that background and experience of what contesting can do for a band."

In 1970, Heathfield's RAF Association staged the first of what was to become a popular annual town carnival. Heathfield and Warbleton & Buxted bands massed together to lead the parade from Mill Road to the Recreation Ground, accompanied by the Heathfield Nautical Training Corps Band.[5] In addition, Ms. RAFA rode a vintage 1906 Cadillac and one float depicted a ghost town and questioned the future of Heathfield.[6] "It was always a struggle to get a decent band to march and it was hard work," says Peter Cornford. "The only thing that carried us off was the fact that the Band was used to doing the bonfire marches and so we could march. There was a first class drummer in those days, Cyril Leeves, he just kept the thing working." Wendy Holloway adds: "Cyril controlled the speed. If we were marching and it began to rain, he'd speed us up to finish sooner!" In subsequent years, the carnival would grow to include a donkey derby, a chariot race, and other amusements.[7]

In 1973, the town's new tradition was taken over by the Heathfield Round Table.[8] By now the carnival was attracting thousands of spectators, who would gather on the streets to enjoy the colourful spectacle.[9] "It was fun. I always enjoyed playing in the carnival," remembers Wendy Holloway. "It was my first ever Band job, I was roped in to swell the numbers as the older players couldn't march. I was about eight and struggled to take big enough steps. I'm not sure I played a single note. The double-taps came for the end of the march and I was just finishing the first line of my music!" In 1976, it was suggested that bandmembers should appear in fancy dress, but the idea was not well-received: marching and playing in public is difficult enough without added complications.[10] "Marching was hilarious," says Wendy. "Half the Band were too old and couldn't keep up, and some seemed unable to march in step. Music would regularly be dropped and picking it back up would cause members to trip!" Support for the carnival dwindled during the 1980s and the event would lapse for some years; however, it has since been successfully resurrected.

Heathfield Fire Station, December 1976.
Photograph supplied by Kent & Sussex Courier.

In April 1973, the Band was present for the reopening of Heathfield Park, which had been redeveloped into *Heathfield Wildlife Park* by its new owner Dr. Gerald Moore. The park now housed an eccentric array of exotic birds and animals, of which there would be the occasional escapee: Moses the camel once went for a wander around Cade Street and wallabies were sometimes seen making a break for freedom across the cricket ground![11] "We used to go up to Heathfield Park and play concerts, about a couple a year, and people used to wander around," recalls Sue Sutton. Rather than taking collections as it had done at other parks, the Band would play for a fixed fee. This was because its committee considered the very notion of collecting at such an upmarket venue "unsavoury."[12] The park was now the final destination for Heathfield Carnival, where it would play host to a fun fair and fête. The Band also played for its cricket club, who made a generous donation to the new uniform fund in January 1974.[13] It is through these engagements that it became closely connected with Dr. Moore.

Moore, a retired oral surgeon, was the brother of the famous sculptor Henry Moore, and was himself something of an artist. Creativity was in his blood: he had been a prominent child actor and would later become a published poet, sculptor and painter.[14] He was therefore eminently suited to become a patron of the Band and in early 1975 he would become a vice-president. The Band was soon a popular fixture at the park, performing Summer concerts beneath the Gibraltar Tower.[15] Dr. Moore continued to expand the park's attractions and by 1977 it is said to have received around 150,000 visitors a year.[16] However, the increased traffic to the town earned criticism from some residents and the park would fall foul of changes to planning regulations. By the Autumn of 1979, it was sadly forced to close.[17]

1975 was a year of significant change for the Band, most notably due to the introduction of its trademark red uniform. "I suspect it was an attempt to take it away from the more traditional, braided and hatted brass bands that were around," says Peter Cornford. "They were a very 1970s jacket, the sort of thing that a lot of bands of that era were wearing. Heathfield was thought to be a bit more go-ahead because there were more youngsters in it. It had these outsiders – the northerners – who'd come in, and it had a modern-looking uniform, so that marked us out a bit."

Lloyd Bland, whose health was now declining, would officially step down as bandmaster in January 1975.[18] "It took about eighteen months to actually get around to replacing Lloyd," explains Ben Guile. "It was more a question of: Do we let the Band fade under Lloyd, being kind to him and letting him stay, or do we risk him being upset and vote Tom in?" Lloyd was understandably hurt by the decision and by June had cut his ties with the Band.[19] However, he was to briefly return the following Summer to conduct the training band, before retiring permanently.

The new bandmaster, Tom Kelly, had been a trombonist with the Band for the past two years and had actually been conducting it on and off for some time. He is described as: "Very good, a very nice man," by Ted Lee and "Strict but fair," by Wendy Holloway. "The Band was very much directed by Tom to be the best it could and it was quite a dedicated band," adds Peter Cornford. "He was imposing a more traditional northern brass band structure on a group of local Sussex people who'd not ever had that tradition, and trying to achieve discipline." The main rehearsals, which Tom would conduct, took place on Tuesday evenings whilst Fridays became a secondary practice night.

One of Tom's earliest ideas was to persuade the Band to become a registered charity.[20] As a result, it would become necessary to develop guiding rules for members and a written constitution setting out its charitable aims and objectives.[21] The move offered financial benefits, such as tax exemptions, and simplified the collection of donations, and it could also raise the Band's cachet as a local institution. It became a registered charity in early 1977 and this status has governed and guided its ethos ever since.[22]

By 1976, bass drummer Cyril Leeves was beginning to struggle. He was now having problems with his eyesight and it was perhaps inevitable that old age would eventually catch up with him. He had, after all, been performing drumming duties with the Band for almost half a century. "I think it's fantastic," says Sarah Leeves. "I don't know of any other brass band that still has specifically a bass drummer, it just doesn't happen anywhere else. Heathfield has its own rulebook!" Cyril officially retired in 1977 after completing fifty years with the Band, but he continued to play, albeit less frequently, until 1981. It would prove difficult to replace him, so Peter

Cornford's father Mostyn was persuaded to, literally, have a bash.[23] Mostyn initially agreed to help the Band for just one march; he would eventually retire some forty years later, having expanded his performance talents to percussion and glockenspiel. He also acted as treasurer for most of the duration. The combined length of service from Cyril and Mostyn means the Band had just two bass drummers across a span of ninety years!

One novelty for the Band would be playing and providing a guard of honour at the wedding of member Lesley Bray (née Dann). This took place in March 1975 at All Saints Church in Old Heathfield, and was one of Tom Kelly's first appearances as the new bandmaster. "We couldn't afford to pay for the bells and the organ, so I asked the Band if they'd play; this meant we could afford the bells," says Lesley. "They played *The Wedding March* from Cavalleria Rusticana for my entry and, of course, they also played all the hymns. We didn't know about the guard of honour, which was a lovely surprise."

Scouts and guides on parade

OVER 300 Scouts, Guides, Cubs and Brownies from the Hailsham and Heathfield area took part in the annual St George's Day parade at Hailsham on Sunday.

Led by the Heathfield Silver Band, the procession toured the town centre before joining up with parents and friends at Battle Road Comprehensive School for a dedication service.

Picture shows the band leading the procession up North Street.

St. George's Day Parade, Hailsham, April 1977.

Despite the generally uneconomic nature of brass banding, the Band nevertheless enjoyed some of its most prosperous years during the Seventies. Until his death in 1969, bandmember Jeff Hobden had helped to keep the instruments serviceable, but they were in desperate need of replacement. A gradual programme of part-exchanging them for reconditioned ones was now undertaken.[24] By the early Eighties, no member would be playing an instrument that was purchased before 1970.[25] Further funds were spent on repairs and upgrades to the bandroom, and this was something of a long-running joke: if a job was identified, it would generally be a great surprise to see it completed the same year![26]

By the late Seventies, discipline in the Band appears to have declined. In September 1976 a strong reminder was given that "talking while the bandmaster is speaking was deplored by the committee."[27] In March 1978, trombonist Bob Lee was reprimanded for unsatisfactory behaviour at one engagement[28] and, considering his reputation for enjoying a drink or two, it is fairly safe to speculate that alcohol would have been the cause. Indeed, a telling edict was soon issued: "All members will be in a fit condition before and during a performance where drink is available!"[29]

1977 was the year of the Queen's Silver Jubilee and there would be commemorative events taking place nationwide. In June, the Band appeared at a thanksgiving service on Heathfield Tower Recreation Ground, played in Hailsham and Crowborough and at a celebratory fête in Hellingly, and provided evening music for a Jubilee event at Heathfield's *Prince of Wales* pub.[30] Local celebrations culminated with a street party in Alexandra Road, at which the children of bandmembers were each presented with a Jubilee Crown.[31] There were further celebrations throughout the year, including a

Royal Engineers' Parade, Eastbourne, November 1978.
Photograph supplied by Peter Cornford.

thanksgiving service at Greenway Fruit Farm in Herstmonceux that October, given in aid of the Chailey Heritage Foundation. "It is a Jubilee; it shall be holy to you," proclaims the order of service, with a footnote proudly declaring: "Singing to be led by the Heathfield Silver Band."[32]

In the Autumn of 1978 the Band appeared at a garden party in aid of the Heathfield & District Talking Newspaper (now Wealden Talking News). The charity, which produces spoken word editions of newspapers for the visually impaired, operated at the time from a caravan at the home of its founder Ted Davis.[33] The garden parties would prove a good way to raise awareness – and funding – for the Heathfield-based charity and were hugely successful, the Band making regular appearances at these until the late 1980s.

Since the end of the Second World War the Band had traditionally gone *Christmassing* around town, and this practice continued into the Seventies. "We used to walk around, knocking on doors, the Band playing," says Maureen Guile, wife of bandmember Dennis. "We ended up at the *Prince of Wales* and they played there. Mostyn had to get his drum through the window because there were so many people! They collected quite a lot of money there 'cause most of the people had had quite a lot to drink, so they were emptying their pockets. Some of the bandmembers went over to Hadlow Down, ended up in a pub over there." Peter Cornford adds: "You would go from door to door, and there was a lot of drink involved. By the evening, several people had had so much that they had a job to play!"

Anna Farley, daughter of Ted Lee, remembers one carol evening which did not end well: "We went down to my father-in-law's [Graham Farley] for a hot drink, some alcohol, mince pies and sausage rolls. It was bitterly cold, snowing. We come out of his place and we were all walking along together, but our trombone player, Bob Lee, had rather too much whisky. We heard this clatter and we all looked round: he'd slipped and fell on his instrument. We picked him up but when we picked his trombone up it had doubled over itself and so he couldn't play it at all!"

Wendy Holloway remembers another unprofessional incident: "I recall one well-lit bungalow in the days before there were any street lights," she says. "We really struggled to open the gate but we finally got through and it slammed shut behind us. As we walked up the path we *admired* a very ornate fish pond and its ghastly gnomes. We pressed the doorbell – no answer. Tried again, and knocked loudly – no answer and all the lights were turned off! We got the hint and, as we tried to find our way out of the now very dark garden, I found myself by the pond. With great delight I *helped* the gnomes into the water with my foot. Stephen Lester may have helped. Or not. I suspect some bandmembers tutted…"

From the mid-1970s door-to-door carolling became increasingly challenging. Firstly, there were changes to licensing laws to take into consideration. "The police had a go at us and said, 'You don't have a licence, you're in trouble,' " recalls Ted Lee (interviewed in 2013)! New residents, unfamiliar with the town's festive traditions, would sometimes shout at the Band to shut up. "People used to like it years ago but it's changed now," explains Anna Farley. "They used to wait for the Band and they said it used to be very Christmassy. But as time went on they were nervous to open the door and we felt that it wasn't fair to do it anymore." Instead, the Band would tour the local pubs and do more High Street carolling. It also continued to put on an annual Christmas Fayre (which usually featured trombonist Bob Lee in character as Father Christmas), and a good mixture of carol services for the Rotary Club and charity concerts at St. Richard's Hall in Heathfield.

In September 1978, aging bandmaster Tom Kelly announced that he would retire as he did not wish to let the players down.[34] An advertisement for his replacement was placed in the Kent & Sussex Courier, but it failed to attract any suitable candidates. One was auditioned but would prove unsatisfactory, another required an honorarium of £500 per year (almost £3,000 today), and a third had no transport of his own.[35] In addition, deputy bandmaster Jack King would resign, leaving us to speculate as to why he was not considered for the role. Fortunately for the Band, euphonium player David Threlfall (although a relative newcomer), quickly took an interest in its development.

In January 1979 an extraordinary general meeting was called to discuss the present and future of the Band. There were two points of concern. The first was the need to appoint a new bandmaster, a role which David Threlfall immediately volunteered for, despite possessing almost no conducting experience.[36] "Dave was very different from Tom," explains Peter Cornford. "He didn't have really the first idea about what to do with this stick in his hand. He was all over the place and there was a lot of thrashing around with it. The Band didn't know how to follow him. A lot of the time he ended up following the Band, and getting lost because he couldn't read the scores. He would just collapse in a fit of laughter and say, 'I'm sorry, I don't know where we are!' "

The second and more pressing issue was to address an undercurrent which had been simmering for some time: finding a balance between the traditional and modern aspects of the Band and its repertoire. This was not a problem unique to Heathfield. There was in fact comparable tension in the professional banding world, championed by Versatile Brass, Black Dyke Mills and Grimethorpe, who would epitomise the diversity of thought on the matter. A handful of Heathfield's bandmembers (primarily Graham Bland, Sue and Dave Sutton, and Trevor Rood) favoured the more progressive approach and proposed that the Band split into two groups, one concentrating on traditional repertoire and the other playing up to date music. "[They] wanted the Band to play more modern music and move away from sitting on a bandstand to play at more interesting venues. They thought they could form an off-shoot to do this, using the Band's instruments and money," explains Wendy Holloway, whilst Anna Farley adds: "They wanted different little jobs. They picked players that they liked and they called that the 'crème of the Band.' "

"It was a sad and unhappy time," says Peter Cornford. "The issue was actually about who should control the Band. What Tom was trying to achieve was a fusion of heritage and modern to please all audiences and members. They actively wanted to remove those of pensionable age because their removal would surely be the way to break free from the 'heritage' and move to concentrate on the modern." The "persecution" of less useful players would undoubtedly lead to a drop in membership at this time. "It was a bit of a witch-hunt really," recalls Wendy. "A lot of oldies were 'encouraged' to leave; also some younger members who weren't great players but just enjoyed it. They made these players feel very uncomfortable. This caused an outrage which led to the infamous Extraordinary General Meeting. That's when dad

[Dennis Guile] decided drastic action was called for. He was the instigator and he certainly didn't do it lightly." Accordingly, a members' vote was held and the majority opted to eject the dissenting players from the Band.

The immediate aftermath of the General Meeting would see the Band reduced to nine or ten players. "We had to cut our jobs right down," remembers Anna. "Sir Edward Caffyn stepped in and gave us advice. He helped fund us as well. We kept practising, we got learners going again and gradually the Band came back up." Peter says: "As is so often the case when an organisation is faced with adversity, those left to manage rise to the challenge. We certainly had a very capable chairman and secretary in brothers Ben and Dennis Guile, and Dad [Mostyn Cornford] began his almost 40 years stint as treasurer." Wendy adds: "It was a very difficult period for the Band as it struggled without most of the soloists and its [experienced] secretary. Players were rounded up to fill holes in the Band, anybody who could string a few notes together. Any older members who had been forced out were welcomed back. The Band was pretty rubbish, but it was the best time to be a member, everyone pulled together. It was a great place to be."

As the decade drew to a close, the Band was in a bit of a mess. It had gone from great success on the contesting scene and a plethora of well-paid engagements to near-collapse in the wake of divisive internal politics. It was now led by an inexperienced bandmaster and membership was low, but the spirit of friendliness and fun had returned to the fore and would become the dominant driving force behind the now fully-modernised Band. "I think one very positive effect of the split was that everyone left was of one mind and voice," concludes Peter. "I think that new atmosphere of relief and determination was what ensured that the Band emerged a better organisation." As the Eighties beckoned, the only way was up for the Heathfield Band.

---

[1] Minutes, 2nd June 1976

[2] Accounts, 1976

[3] Bourke, J., 1996. *The History of a Village Band 1896-1996*. Heathfield: Warbleton and Buxted Band: 74

[4] Cutting, source unknown, ca. May 1970

[5] Kent & Sussex Courier, 25th September 1970

[6] ibid

[7] e.g. Kent & Sussex Courier, 22nd September 1972

[8] Kent & Sussex Courier, 16th July 1976

[9] ibid

[10] Minutes, 12th November 1975

[11] e.g. Heathfield Community Group on Facebook, 1st February 2021; Sussex Express, 12th June 2018

[12] Minutes, 15th August 1973

[13] Accounts, 1974

[14] Sussex Express, 12th June 2018

[15] Minutes, 21st January 1975, 21st February 1975, 18th March 1975 & 28th July 1976

[16] Pryce, R., 1996. *Heathfield Park: A Private Estate and a Wealden Town*. Heathfield: Roy Pryce: 170

[17] ibid

[18] Minutes, 21st January 1975

[19] Minutes, 11th June 1975

[20] Minutes, 14th April 1976

[21] Minutes, 2nd June 1976; HSB Constitution and Rules, April 1977

[22] Minutes, 10th January 1977, 19th January 1977 & 30th March 1977

[23] Minutes, 25th February 1976 & 14th April 1976

[24] HSB Newsletter, Spring 1970; Minutes, 31st January 1975, 21st February 1975, 18th April 1975, 12th November 1975, etc

[25] Cornford, P., 1981. Personal Archive and Interviews

[26] ibid

[27] Minutes, 24th September 1976

[28] Minutes, 22nd March 1978

[29] Minutes, 17th May 1978

[30] Minutes, 25th January 1977 & 9th February 1977; Cornford, P., 1981

[31] Minutes, 30th March 1977; Cornford, P., 1981

[32] Thanksgiving Service Programme, 20th October 1977

[33] https://wealdentalkingnews.org.uk/about-us/

[34] Minutes, 17th September 1978

[35] Minutes, 18th October 1978

[36] Minutes, 16th January 1979

MEMBERS of NOTE...

Mostyn Cornford

bass drum & percussion, 1978-2018,
treasurer, 1979–2018.

Mostyn joined the Band as its bass-drummer in 1978 and would go on to become one of its longest-serving committee members, acting as treasurer for almost forty years. "My children, Peter and Alison, were both in the Band at that time," recalls Mostyn. "My son suggested I could take over the bass drum from Cyril Leeves, who had retired after many years. I had been in the army [as a Corporal] and was good at marching and keeping time. My first march was Heathfield Carnival… the Band said I was the fastest drummer they had ever had and I was to slow down a bit. They had never marched so fast before!"

During his time with the Band, Mostyn would expand his role to more closely emulate the rhythm sections of other modern brass bands, learning to play glockenspiel and all manner of percussion. "I first met Mostyn when I took my son to his first practice seventeen years ago," recalls Keith Pursglove. "He was settled in a corner with his bass drum, glockenspiel and a large bag of assorted tools of his trade. There seemed to be everything in that bag from castanets to homemade devices created to embellish a specific piece of music. He attended all the bonfire marches, carrying the bass drum and if required a side drum." However, during the 2010s Mostyn would begin to struggle with marches, and was instead to concentrate solely on formal concerts.

A builder by trade, Mostyn would also find himself taking responsibility for the upkeep of the bandroom, which had gotten into a poor state of repair by the time he joined the Band. The crowning glory was the project to extend the space, which would be completed in 2005. "As the Band's membership increased, the bandroom was not large enough," explains Mostyn. "I suggested I could enlarge the bandroom to accommodate the extra players. I drew up plans and got permission to proceed. I constructed the extension, including a small kitchen and toilet, and I connected the mains water and drainage to the highway." Keith adds: "Mostyn carried out most of the work himself, free of charge, and not once did he seek the deference he probably deserved."

The Cornford family are descended from the Band's co-founder, Edward Bean, and there have been multigenerational links over the years. Mostyn's children, Peter and Alison, would be bandmembers during the Seventies and early Eighties and more recently, during the 2010s, Mostyn's granddaughter, Lucy, would become the Band's solo cornet. Her younger sister, Katy, was also briefly a member.

"Mostyn was more than a percussionist; he was clearly a well-respected member of the Band. He was a member of the Band's committee, a position he took very seriously, and was treasurer and a trustee for many years," says Keith. During his stint as treasurer, Mostyn would guide the Band's finances from strength to strength and, indeed, was to leave it in an enviably good state, with savings of almost £20,000. "I retired from the Band after it was suggested another person take on the treasury," says Mostyn. "I felt I was not needed any longer. However, my forty years in the Band was enjoyable."

Interlude Continental Adventures: The Band Tour

The post-war peace and economic recovery which took hold during the 1950s would lead to an increase in leisure time, especially among the working classes, and foster a growing desire for cultural exchanges across Europe. In the brass banding world, this manifested as transcontinental music festivals and concert tours, to which Heathfield Band soon began receiving invites. Although the movement originated in Britain, it has now become popular globally, with bands competing in both European and World Championships. It has even been suggested that international audiences think more highly of brass bands, because they are less "class-conscious" than the British.[1] The growing popularity of brass bands abroad would thus lead Heathfield Band to undertake numerous cross-Channel trips over the years, firstly to France and, more recently, Germany. This chapter explores its continental adventures.

The French Connection

The Band's earliest trips to Europe are said to have been to France during the 1950s. The evidence for these is rather sketchy, but we do have two grainy black and white photos from an unidentified French music festival which appear to be of the correct vintage (see opposite). The details are difficult to distinguish, but the photos depict a brass band – supposedly Heathfield Silver Band – performing on a stage in a town square, surrounded by hundreds of enthusiastic spectators. Research by Peter Cornford shows that the Band did

HSB French Trip, ca. 1950s.

Photographs supplied by Jack Mitchell.

make several visits to Calais and Paris at this time,[2] though further details have proven difficult to trace.

The Band would next venture across the Channel in the 1970s, by invitation of the town of Calais, to take part in its annual music festival.[3] The international initiative began when representatives of Calais made contact with the Tunbridge Wells Amateur Band Federation, of which Heathfield Band was a member, with a proposal for British bands to become involved. Heathfield Band jumped at the chance, making its first appearance at the event on Sunday, 5th July 1970, and returning the following two years (accompanied by several other Sussex brass bands). The festival typically attracted about thirty bands from across Europe, each of whom comprised roughly fifty musicians. Therefore, for subsequent trips, Heathfield Band would boost its complement by massing with another Sussex ensemble, such as Edenbridge Town Band in 1971.[4] That year, in the spirit of friendship, the Mayor of Calais presented the Band with a commemorative plaque bearing the French town's coat of arms.[5] The following year, the Band reciprocated with a specially-commissioned plaque depicting the Cuckoo Lady of Heffle Fair.[6]

249

"The French were very interested, and asked Heathfield Silver Band to come," explains Ben Guile (interviewed in 1981). "It's all done in a day. We have an early start and arrive back late at night. All the bands that go from this country – three or four – bundle onto buses and meet at Dover at 8am. In Calais, there's a very large transport café where we stop for a meal, with vinegary, oily wine. Of course, any unopened bottled wine was pocketed!" The bands would then disperse to the far reaches of the suburbs, from whence they led four or five separate processions back to the town square.[7] Each then performed an own-choice musical arrangement before the Mayor of Calais.[8] "At the first Calais trip, we played a popular French march which had an upbeat and the Band was all over the place," recalls Ben. "Another time, we played *Margie* whilst countermarching. The two didn't mix somehow…"

The occasion is described by one Sussex newspaper thus: "*Sussex by the Sea*, played by two Sussex bands, proved a great favourite with the French on Sunday. It was rendered at different times, by Heathfield Silver Band and Warbleton & Buxted Band, two of five English bands taking part in an international musical parade at Calais."[9] A reception and luncheon was then held at the Town Hall, after which the bands joined together in an impressive procession which continued for two hours.[10] "The bands played continuously throughout the parade, stopping at intervals along the two and a half mile route to allow the large crowds a better opportunity of appreciating the music, and at the finale in a large arena each band played a farewell item."[11] Other British bands in attendance included Eastbourne Silver Band, brass bands from Margate and Birchington, military bands from Horsham and Bexhill, and Whitstable Scout Band.[12]

Aside from a day trip to Dieppe in 1981, Heathfield Band would not undertake any further visits to France for several decades.[13] It did, however, participate in a twinning celebration in August 1986 for Rotherfield and St. Cheron, whereupon residents of the latter were invited to attend a traditional Sussex Bonfire parade.[14] "There was much to enchant the guests as the pageantry […] paraded through the village," writes the Courier. "The familiar strains of *Colonel Bogey* from Heathfield Silver Band gave a lift to dragging feet and there was also stirring stuff from the youngsters of the Band of TS Spartan and Wadhurst Drum & Fife. Crowborough Town Band

and Tunbridge Wells Marching Band played in the village during the procession's absence."[15] It had been hoped that a joint excursion to France could be arranged with Crowborough Town Band for the Summer of 1995, but the challenge of finding accommodation for everyone (an ongoing issue for brass bands due to the large numbers of people involved) unfortunately thwarted these plans.[16]

Heathfield hosted its first Anglo-French venture, *Le Marché*, during the 1997 August Bank Holiday, and the town band graciously supported the event for free. "The old boys would always say it was 'Le Marsh!' I think they wound me up on purpose, really, but it drove me mad," says former musical director Frankie Lulham. "I would say, '*Marsh* means to march. *Le Marché* is the market!' " The occasion was such a success that it would soon lead to the town's twinning with Forges Les Eaux in Normandy. Le Marché is now a firm annual fixture and typically attracts about 20,000 visitors to Heathfield each year. The initiative is an invaluable one, both strengthening cross-Channel relations and returning its proceeds to the community. In 2004, for example, the organisers were able to donate £1000 towards the refurbishment of the Band's Alexandra Road rehearsal room.[17]

Heathfield Band has appeared at *Le Marché* almost every year since its launch, on the cosy bandstand in Station Road and sometimes also in the High Street.[18] In 2007, it experimented with marching through the town: "We marched up and down the street and it was ridiculous because there were so many people there," recalls Frankie. The Band's *Le Marché* repertoire is normally a mixture of brass band classics, modern pop, and a sprinkling of stereotypically "French" tunes, such as *The Bold Gendarmes*, *Orpheus*, *Bouquet de Paris* and *Plaisir d'Amour*. However, in 2011 the organisers would make a special plea against "durgy" [*sic*] slow pieces.[19] The Band has since taken this request to heart, shifting the emphasis towards more mainstream popular music. In 2018 it even staged its first flash mob, as musicians dispersed amongst the crowds "spontaneously" struck up with a rendition of Daft Punk's *Get Lucky* and casually sauntered onstage.

Heathfield's twinning with Forges Les Eaux would lead the French town to invite the Band to its own market in 2001. "We went on a coach and had a job finding the place: we stopped at a Police Station to ask directions," recalls Frankie Lulham. "I remember being on drum kit and setting up in the market with Jeff Collins conducting." Jeff adds: "I don't know who it was arranged by, but when we got over there it was almost as though they weren't expecting us. Nobody took any notice of us while we were playing. I'd chosen pieces of music with a French flavour, like *Bouquet de Paris* and *Can Can*, and you'd expect them to think, *Ooh, they're playing French music*. But it didn't make any difference, everybody was just meandering past, not taking the slightest bit of notice of us. It seemed a complete non-event!" Despite the occasional invitation, the Band has yet to make a return visit to France.

German Encounters

In 1991, the Band broadened its horizons with the first of several trips to Wiesbaden in central-western Germany where, Ted Lee chuckles: "We all behaved ourselves!" The tours were by invitation of the Wiesbaden branch of the Karneval Club Rheingauviertel, which is in many ways analogous to a typical Sussex Bonfire society. Wiesbaden is actually twinned with Tunbridge Wells, but that town has no brass band of its own so bandmember and chairman George Patterson (who had connections with the latter's town council) proposed that Heathfield Band take part instead. On 7th February 1991, the Band would thus sail by overnight ferry from Sheerness, naturally entertaining fellow travellers *en route* with an impromptu late-night concert that continued until 2am! "You could book a *couchette* or just stay in the cheap seats drinking… and we did," recalls Janet Baker! The trip coincided with the traditional German carnival known as *Fasching*, but there was such a snowstorm that the main parade had to be cancelled. Instead, bandmembers paid a visit to Heidelberg Castle. "We still did indoor parties, receptions and other gigs that they could find for us, but no public parades," says Janet.

The Band returned to Wiesbaden in 1992, with Frank Francis now officially its bandmaster. This time the parades went ahead as planned: the town staged a children's procession on the Saturday and held its main parade the following day. "The Wiesbaden one was always memorable," says Frank. "We did an *oom-pah* group and we marched through the towns, through Wiesbaden." For the Germans, the real charm of Heathfield Band lay in its uniqueness as a traditional British brass band. Most groups in attendance were German-style ensembles, drumming or playing fanfares; by contrast, Heathfield Band could offer a more interesting range and a wider repertoire. "We were welcomed with open arms, fed and watered well everywhere," recalls Janet. "The parades were really crowded, with every float in the parade throwing confetti and sweets all over the roads. The local kids would take a carrier bag and pick up as much as they could. Not just sweets either; all sorts of stuff. One of the Band picked up some brightly coloured 'bubble gum' and redistributed them to some children… until it was pointed out that they were condoms!" Anna Farley adds: "Their carnivals are so different. Over here we'll sort of lead the procession, but over there our number was like three hundred and something. That's how big the procession is!"

In addition to the Wiesbaden Fasching Parade, which covers a distance of about four miles, the Band also marched at smaller events in the surrounding areas: "I liked the small village parades best, Freudenberg for instance," says Janet. "They cover a shorter distance but are slower and more intimate. Every street corner had a couple of people with trays of schnapps ready to offer the Band a drink." Maureen Guile remembers the schnapps fondly: "There was these tables out there and you'd just help yourself," she says. "[Trombonist] Bob Lee's wife helped herself quite often, and I think she had to be put on one of the floats to get her back to where we'd started from!"

Despite its generally warm welcome, the Band would not be popular everywhere it played. It was verbally abused by young Nazis during one village parade, presumably for performing music with offensive undertones. "We did a concert at an old people's home," says Janet Baker, "a mixture of German and English music to keep them entertained, and finished with both national anthems. Those that could stood up to ours but promptly sat down for their own. One old boy, in broken English, tried to explain that they were ashamed of theirs." Other pieces which did not go down well were those considered to be Nazi marching songs, and German music written during the Second World War. "I used to feel a little bit like, *I hope we're not gonna play Colonel Bogey*, because it just didn't feel quite right," admits Sarah Leeves.

It was barely two years since the fall of the Berlin Wall when the Band travelled to Erfurt in East Germany. "We stood on the steps of the Cathedral and played," recalls Frank Francis. "The walls should've been white and yet it was filthy, it was black, and you could still see the bullet holes from the war days. It was a huge square but nobody came out, they were reluctant to come and listen to us. We did get a small crowd eventually, but they were still a bit fearful of the West's intrusion."

i) **Wiesbaden, February 1999.** *Photograph supplied by Heidi Watkins.*

ii) **Wiesbaden Carnival, February 1992.** *Photograph supplied by Maureen Guile.*

iii) **Drum-major Heidi Watkins leads the Band, Wiesbaden, ca. February 1997.** *Photograph supplied by Heidi Watkins.*

iv) **Brewery Gig, March 1992.** *Photograph supplied by Maureen Guile.*

v) **Wiesbaden, February 1992.** *Photograph supplied by Maureen Guile.*

vi) **Mike Smith as the "dead" Carnival Prince, Wiesbaden, ca. February 1997.** *Photograph supplied by Heidi Watkins*

vii) **Wiesbaden Carnival, February 1997.** *Photograph supplied by Mostyn Cornford.*

viii) **Freudenburg, February 1992.** *Photograph supplied by Maureen Guile.*

ix) **Erfurt, East Germany, February 1992.** *Photograph supplied by Mostyn Cornford.*

x) **Heidelburg Castle, February 1991.** *Photograph supplied by Maureen Guile.*

xi) **Rüdesheim am Rhein, April 2010.** *Photograph supplied by Keith Pursglove.*

Frank remembers with amusement how the Band would self-segregate when travelling: "The coach was always divided up into two. The *Librarians* (they were the snobby end) would get on first and sit down the front because they didn't want to be at the back with the *Rowdies*. The ones with the sense of humour (we thought) were at the back of the bus singing rugby songs, and we got the driver to put on things like Roy Chubby Brown which was absolute filth. We were always reprimanded by *The Librarians* for having such smut going on. As the bandmaster I should've known better…"

Subsequent trips were made to Wiesbaden in 1993, 1997 and 1999, and although no other parades would have to be cancelled, the weather could sometimes be extreme. "The Wiesbaden parade was very testing indeed," recalls Janet Baker. "[One year] the street thermometers were varying from -17° to -21°C, depending on which way the wind was blowing. I recall the icicles from the water keys hanging from my coat. The basses were the first to freeze up, followed by the trombones, euph and horns. Gradually the Band became quieter, only the drum beat and a few notes from the cornets could be heard. Finally the valves froze on the cornets, and the hands were frozen too. It was so cold you couldn't even talk properly, let alone manage to get more than three different notes. It was like trying to play after a dentist visit, a stark contrast to the year when our necks and faces got sunburnt!"

Band tours usually involve plenty of alcohol, and this was especially true at the Wiesbaden parades. "You stopped, played a march, moved onto the next one, drank another, someone would rush out with another tray and we got nowhere fast," recalls Janet Baker. "There's a couple of bars in *Colonel Bogey* I used to judge my alcohol content by. If my tongue couldn't play it fast enough, I'd miss out the next drink. We were also given a ticket for a beer and bratwurst at the end, in a barnyard with straw all over the floor and livestock in pens." Trombonist Dave Imray would be a guest player on the 1997 and 1999 trips: "I seem to recall girls walking behind the Band in the procession handing miniature bottles of schnapps forwards," he says. "By the end, us poor trombones at the front were still nearly sober whilst the back of the Band was substantially the worse for wear!!"

One especially memorable occasion was the evening of Ash Wednesday in 1997, as carnival organisers sought a volunteer from the Band to represent their dead carnival prince. Trombonist Mike Smith would rise to the challenge, covering his face with white makeup in order to appear more corpse-like. "At the end of the carnival there's a sort of mock funeral. The carnival prince dies and they have to carry him through the crowds," explains Sarah Leeves, recalling with amusement how the "dead" prince would keep waking up! "Michael Smith's acting was astounding, he was playing up and being very silly. It was absolutely hilarious."

Unfortunately, connections with Wiesbaden would eventually break down. The instigator of the first trip, George Patterson, had now retired from the Band and Graham Farley, who had organised the subsequent tours, would be forced to step away due to ill health. At the same time, the Band was experiencing a lull in membership, and support for the carnival society was dwindling. Further trips to Wiesbaden therefore became unfeasible.

However, in April 2010 the Band would make a return to Germany, under musical director Richard Sherlock. This time it would make a five-day excursion to the winemaking area of Rüdesheim am Rhein. Former Band president, Geoff Pickering (interviewed in 2013), had fond memories of the trip: "I thought the place itself was just like a bus stop on the Rhine. It was all the front street mostly, and then the ferries, the boats, came in." The Band played concerts at the bathhouse in Bad Ems, in the Rüdesheim market

Rüdesheim am Rhein, April 2010.
Photograph supplied by Keith Pursglove.

square, and at the Loreley Visitor Centre (which celebrates the local folklore). "They played in fairly grand places sometimes," recalls Geoff. "It had been advertised beforehand, with little A4 posters, but we thought, *Well, who's gonna watch?* But, immediately the Band started, people would come and just sit down and listen."

The trip also included a sightseeing tour of Rüdesheim, cable car and chairlift rides, visits to Marksburg Castle and the Roman settlement at Boppard, and a river cruise on the Rhine. There was other fun, too. "The youngsters had gone off ten-pin bowling or something, and there was about a dozen of us went to this wine tasting... and it wasn't strictly just wine *tasting*," remembers Geoff Pickering. The owner, who was celebrating his birthday, challenged bandmembers to sing songs such as *Molly Malone*, and then "produced this ancient-looking instrument, they dragged it out from somewhere, and they wanted somebody to play it. Sarah got a tune out of it!"

The Band has yet to organise any further overseas excursions, but such ventures should be strongly encouraged in the future. They present players and their families with rewarding cultural exchanges, enable valuable outreach, and often represent young members' first experiences of travelling abroad. They also offer an opportunity to bring the distinctive sound of the British brass band to the wider world. Indeed, the universal language of music makes them ideal for extending the hand of friendship to our European cousins. It is hoped that the Band will soon add some new chapters to the story of its international adventures.

---

[1] Cornford, P., 1981

[2] ibid

[3] HSB Newsletter, Spring 1970

[4] ibid

[5] Cuttings, source unknown, ca. July 1971

[6] ibid

[7] Cuttings, source unknown, ca. July 1971

[8] ibid

[9] ibid

[10] ibid

[11] ibid

[12] ibid

[13] Minutes, 19th January 1977, 7th May 1981, 18th January 1982

[14] Kent & Sussex Courier, 29th August 1986

[15] ibid

[16] Minutes, 5th December 1994 & 24th January 1995

[17] Sussex Express, 24th September 2004

[18] Heathfield First, July 2007; Le Marché Programme, 2007; Correspondence, Frankie Lulham to Phil Marr, 13th May 2006

[19] Correspondence, Jenny Woodhouse to Band Secretary, 8th February 2011

Poem *Bless 'em all! HSB Lyrics*

Now I'll sing you a song all about Heathfield Band,
A Band full of talent and class,
In their red uniform, looking ever so grand,
They won't make the Best in Brass!

There's no class distinction, between females and males,
They all mix together so well.
If he plays his cards right a male never fails,
To get himself fixed with a gal!

CHORUS
Bless 'em all, Bless 'em all,
As into the bandroom they crawl,
Bless the dear people in Alexandra Road,
The pour souls have got all the patience of Jobe,
Twice a week there's a racket they hear,
For fifty-two weeks in the year.
Then at Christmas we knocks, with the old money box,
And wish them a Happy New Year!

Every Tuesday, is practice night for all the Band,
Every body turns up prompt on time.
Conductor Dick Turner looking ever so grand,
Says- "We'll start with the march *Thin Red Line*."

He raises the baton, all ready to go,
It's all quiet, you can't hear a thing.
Then a little voice says- "Hold on half a mo!!"
It's the voice of the sweet Jenny King!

Bless her all, Bless her all,
she nearly creates an uproar,
Dick turns and says- "What's the matter my dear?"
Jenny replies that the music's not clear!
When at last the Band gets under way,
The march, it goes off with a sway,
Mostyn thrashes the drum,
Paula wiggles her bum- The practise is well under way!

The cornets let rip, with a good rasping sound,
Played by Janet and Peter and Steve,
The basses then lift off the roof to the ground,
The leader is young Gordon Neve!

There's many a face that is red as a rose,
As cheeks all puff out like balloons.
The floor it fair rocks with the tapping of toes,
And poor Anna Lee she just swoons!

Bless 'em all, Bless 'em all,
Ben Guile and Susan and all,
Bandings their hobby, they're there all the time,
A musical duo, they're just doing fine,
And it's so very plain to see,
That with children like theirs - one, two, three,
They play other games, we won't mention names,
It's practised in bed, plain to see!!

The trombone are blowing a little off key,
Jim gets the blame in the end.
He gets a real rollicking too, from Bob Lee,
Who says, it drives him round the bend.

Then Roy Crompton joins in with his north country voice,
"If you don't Bloody stop I'll go 'ome!!"
"I'm solo trombone, I've got the choice,
I've got the privalidge to moan!"

Bless ol' Ray, Bless ol' Ray,
He sure is a hell of a boy.
He learnt to play trombone up on Wigan Pier,
Still trains at night, with large glasses of beer.
His wife plays with him in the Band,
She's the opposite side of the stand,
A cornet, she plays, and the eyebrows all raise,
When Julie blows out three pints - canned!!

The Euphos are two handsome blokes you'll agree
And excellent players as well.
There's Taffy from Wales, and Young David T.
They give out a tone that is swell.

Now Dave is a teacher, a J.P. as well,
As a hobby he also keeps bees.
Now Taffy's main hobbies are guzzling beer,
And studying girls legs and knees!

Bless 'em all, Bless 'em all,
Taffy and David Threeefall [*sic*],
The things they enjoy after practice at night,
Is blowing the froth off a pint!
I think that their playing is grand,
And there's one thing you must understand.
As everyone knows, that without the Euphos,
It just wouldn't sound like a Band.

I must give a mention to dear old Ted Lee.
The Band's Tenor player for years.
He's not I point out a relative to me,
For which I give out three big cheers!

He sorts out the music for which the Band play,
A job which he does to a turn.
If there's anything there that he knows he can't play,
He takes it to Vines Cross to burn!!

Dear old Ted, Dear old Ted,
We want the bandroom painted red!
Being a painter he's is in charge of the job
Painting the bandroom - assisted by Bob.

But he can't name the date for a start,
So it's dropped the Band right in the cart.
The walls are all peeling and so is the ceiling
The bandroom is falling apart!

There's Dennis the baritone from Tunbridge Wells,
He's also the Secretary as well.
As well as band business, he chats up the girls,
He has a good story to tell!

He does all the fixing of jobs for the Band,
A job that he works at so hard.
But he'll get no promotion or shake of the hand,
And not many thanks - times are hard!!

Bless 'em all, Bless 'em all,
The Baritones, Basses and all,
Bless all the tenors, the cornets as well,
Also the drummer for banging like hell.
Poor old Dick he sure needs a big cheer,
For starting out front for the year.
Trombones on the right, - cornets blowing with might,
Enough to drive him to the beer!

Carnivals, Bonfires, Church Fêtes, Church Parades,
The Band plays at these every year.
It brings lots of fun to the lads and the maids,
Especially when there is free beer.

The Band looks a treat as it goes down the street,
I must say especially the girls.
With their split shirts and minis, looking so neat
The sight of their legs gives you thrills!

Bless 'em all, Bless 'em all,
They march like they're ready to fall,
Mostyn keeps step with a bang on the drum,
Paula's still out there an' wriggling her bum!
But they're such a good crew one and all,
the long and the short and the tall,
The old Heathfield Band's not the best in the land,
But they're certainly having a ball!!!

by Bob Lee
(for the HSB Social evening at Horam Village Hall, 30th September 1983)

With grateful thanks to Bob's family for supplying the text.

MEMBERS of NOTE...

David Threlfall

euphonium, 1977–8,

bandmaster, 1979–83.

David Threlfall was born in Waterloo, near Liverpool, in April 1943. His family would later move to Nantwich, where he learned to play brass instruments and ring church bells. He was an adventurous school pupil, and would lose his prefect's badge for larking about on the school roof. He was also a talented sprinter, which must have come in handy!

David would meet his wife, Lesley, at Kesteven Teacher Training College, and the pair would eventually relocate to Horam. "Dave joined the Band in 1977 and I became very good friends with him," recalls Peter Cornford. "He burst into the bandroom one day and said, 'Hello, I've just moved into the area. Can I join?' He was an accomplished euphonium player and would quickly become one of the Band's best bandmasters, despite having no previous conducting experience. He was a jovial, cigar-smoking, drinking, dirty laugh sort of guy who had got new ideas by definition – he was a younger generation – and just wanted to make the whole thing fun."

During his time with the Band, Dave worked at St. Mary's School in Horam, which caters for students with special educational needs. "He was a really kind and gentle man with a great deal of empathy and compassion," continues Peter. "He was very much a Labour man. He wanted to be inclusive and was a great believer in trying to get the best out of everybody, which is why he took the idea of conducting at contests with a pinch of salt, he didn't want to be competitive."

Dave was soon to find himself more widely involved with the running of things. In January 1978, bustling with ideas for improving public awareness of the Band, he would be elected its press officer, and in early 1979 he was to become bandmaster, under the expert guidance of his predecessor, Tom Kelly. Musically, Dave was in favour of a good mixture of both old and new repertoire, and would bring with him fresh ideas for features, solos and duets.

The Band suffered a major split in 1979, and membership would be seriously depleted, but Dave took the remaining core and worked it back into a capable, happy and social ensemble. However, despite his successes, Dave would continue to see himself as something of a caretaker, looking after the Band until a more capable contender was to come on the scene. He would willingly hand the reigns to Dick Turner in 1983, and take a smaller role in the organisation of the Band. In the Autumn of 1984, he was to begin studying for a degree, which would occupy much of his time, and would resign from the Band the following year.

Dave was to live a fantastically varied life. After leaving the Band, he would become deputy head at Spring Gardens School in Tunbridge Wells, before returning to St. Mary's School to teach brass. Later in life, he was to decorate the local Indian restaurant and even drive a hearse! He would also find time to travel the world, including visiting Australia and the Arctic. "He was always planning a new adventure and encouraging others to embark on their own," says his eldest son, Nicholas.

"He was a man of many hats: musician, bandsman and conductor, beekeeper, rambler, chairman of the East Grinstead and District Guild of Church Bell Ringers, quiz writer, political activist (who stood for parliament), darts player, Everton season ticket holder, Vines Cross Wheeler, investment club founder, cricketer, umpire, painter and decorator, car enthusiast and builder, path layer, baker of pork pies, boatman, and much more." David sadly passed away in January 2018.

Based on Nicholas Threlfall's eulogy to his father.
Available at: <www.egdg.org.uk/news-about-members/>

1980s Comradeship, Craftsmanship and Showmanship

Fordcombe Fête, August 1983.

(Back Row, L–R) Ben Guile, Ted Lee, Anna Lee, Bob Lee, Roy Crompton,
Jim Dawson, Janet Baker, Peter Cornford, Sue Guile.
(Middle Row, L–R) Mostyn Cornford, Duncan Bachelor, Nicholas Threlfall, Chris Threlfall,
Paul Wells, Sarah Threlfall, Jenny King, Alison Cornford, Gerald Vickers, Gerald Dann.
(Front Row, L–R) Bert Thompson, Gordon Neve, David Threlfall, Dick Turner,
John "Taff" Denison, Dennis Guile, Laurie Knapp.
Photograph supplied by Maureen Guile.

The 1980s would bring new challenges and setbacks, including the deaths of several Heathfield Band veterans: chairman Roy Elphick, vice-president Max Farrow, former bandmasters Bert Wise and Lloyd Bland, along with players Cyril Leeves, Freddie Stanford and Bert Thompson. But despite these losses, the Band would remain a happy and successful one, with members celebrating the high points together as an extended family. In addition to formal concerts there was a wide variety of other engagements, including weddings, fun runs and pancake races, fêtes, parades, military events, football matches, and even an appearance at a wine-tasting event. During this period, its leadership would rarely stand still: "Since I've been in the Band, we've had nine or ten bandmasters," observes Mostyn Cornford. "Either the bandmaster gets fed up with us or we get fed up with the bandmaster!"

As the decade dawned, both the nation and the Heathfield Band were in a sorry state. Whilst British Prime Minister Margaret Thatcher busied herself restructuring the ailing country, bandmaster David Threlfall would perform a similar task for a community band left in tatters. "It was a watershed moment when Tom went and Dave came along," reflects Peter Cornford. "It felt like a real change. Tom was, by the end, the face of the past." David Threlfall worked hard to reinvigorate the Band's sense of community and social ethos, and began thinking more widely in terms of its outreach. "Dave was liked by everybody and he did such a lot for the Band. He was the *new era*," adds Peter.

Under David Threlfall, the Band once again became a very social one, and members would enjoy regular dinners and dances, trips to the pantomime, and outings to see championship brass bands in concert; in September 1981 they would even take a day trip to Dieppe.[1] David also made an attempt to improve relations with the breakaway Hailsham & Vines Cross Band.[2] In addition, a renewed sense of community was instilled in bandmembers: "A brass band is unique. It doesn't matter what your job, in a band everyone is equal," bandmember Ben Guile would once declare. "The three most important things are comradeship, craftsmanship and showmanship."

In early 1981, the health of Tom Kelly had improved sufficiently for him to return to mentor David Threlfall.[3] Now awarded the title of musical director, Tom presided over Tuesday evening rehearsals whilst David would take Friday night practices, the latter aimed primarily at learners. Tom's new appellation was to mark the Band's first use of the term "musical director" (or MD), a role subtly distinct from those of bandmaster or conductor, which had hitherto been used to identify its leader. In principal, the term "bandmaster" should denote the person who maintains discipline, and rehearses and tutors a band, whilst "conductor" generally refers to the person who is its more public face at engagements. However, Heathfield Band would use these titles interchangeably throughout its history. Indeed, the roles were often filled by one and the same person. Therefore, since the turn of the new millennium, the Band has permanently merged them into the role of musical director, with a deputy MD providing assistance as required.

Before the days of the internet, member recruitment and public relations would rely on word of mouth, publicity gained from local newspapers, and exposure at gigs. "If you went out on an engagement, like marching through the town, then someone moving into the area would suddenly turn up at the bandroom and say they were interested [in joining]," explains Anna Farley. But this *ad hoc* approach yielded variable results and so, in the Summer of

Marketing material from the 1981 PR campaign.

1981, a co-ordinated publicity drive began in earnest.[4] "Dave was really the first person who thought about marketing the Band," says Peter Cornford. "At weekends, one or two of us went all around Heathfield with some flyers, and put them through every letterbox, and we had posters everywhere. It was a very buzzy time." The pamphlet, which outlines the Band's ethos and charitable aims, states: "Recently, we felt that we had become complacent about our public relations, so we decided to tell you of the work we do and suggest ways that the people of Heathfield could help its Band."[5] The publicity campaign included a stall at Heathfield Carnival, a display in the window of Heathfield Library, and an illustrated talk (given by bandmember Peter Cornford to the Heathfield and Waldron Community Association.[6]

The effort to rejuvenate the Band would pay dividends, and funds were to reach a record high, assisted in part by an extremely generous donation from Sir Edward Caffyn (£500, equivalent to about £1,800 today).[7] Engagements soon began to pour in, increasing from about eighteen in 1980 to a staggering forty-six by 1984.[8] Membership was also recovering: 1981 was the first time for several years that assistance from other bands was not required.[9] "The Heathfield Silver Band of the 1980s seems set to prosper," writes Peter Cornford in 1981. "Our membership stands at 28, and of these over a third are eighteen or under – a marvellous prospect for the future. There are also about half a dozen young children learning under the guidance of Dave, our bandmaster, and Ted Lee, our valued librarian."[10] By early 1982, there would be over a dozen junior bandmembers.[11]

Throughout the decade the Band celebrated several weddings. The first was that of members Wendy Guile and Steve Holloway who had met through the Band in 1978. The wedding, which took place in April 1981, would be a joyous event, the Band providing music and a guard of honour for the couple.[12] "They

Wedding of Steve Holloway and Wendy Guile, St. Mark's Church in Tunbridge Wells, April 1981.
Photograph supplied by Maureen Guile.

played in St. Mark's at Tunbridge Wells. It was lovely to have the Band play in a big church," recalls Wendy's mother, Maureen Guile, whilst Wendy adds: "When the Band played was an obvious highlight. Dad [member Dennis Guile] thought he'd play me up the aisle, [but] he wasn't allowed to! After the wedding ceremony, the whole Band plus partners were invited to my parents' house, where a buffet was laid out, and then to the evening disco. It shows how close the Band was in 1981." In July, the Band helped the whole of Heathfield to celebrate the wedding of Prince Charles to Lady Diana Spencer. "We played outside the *Prince of Wales* pub," says Wendy. "I remember Bob Lee saying he preferred my wedding dress to Diana's!" In March 1985, the Band turned out for the wedding of another of its members, Anna Lee [daughter of Ted], to Mark Farley, at St. Richard's Church in Heathfield. "The Band played in the church as I walked down the aisle, and they did guard of honour with their instruments," remembers Anna. "Mark was in the Heathfield Fire Service and they parked with the fire engine as we came out the church."

During the Eighties a craze for running swept the nation, with marathons and fun runs becoming extremely popular. In October 1982, bandmember Steve Holloway would brave the torrential rain to undertake a twenty mile sponsored run for the benefit of the Band, from Heathfield's Red Cross Hall

Sponsored run drums up £170 to help band

HEATHFIELD SILVER Band member Mr Steve Holloway's sponsored run on Saturday is expected to have raised about £170 for band funds.

Mr Holloway, a bass player with the band, set off from the Red Cross Hall in Heathfield High Street at 7.45am and ran a total of 20 miles round Heathfield and Uckfield and he finished back at the hall at 11am.

On his return, Mr Holloway, 23, was greeted with a few tunes from the band and cheers from shoppers.

Mr Peter Cornford, band secretary said: "Steven did marvellously well and got back to the hall about two hours earlier than expected. The money will go towards some new music and I expect some instruments will need to be repaired or replaced."

Mr Holloway, of Pebsham Lane, Bexhill, spent two months training for the run which took him through Cross-in-Hand, Blackboys, Halland, Uckfield, Framfield, Hadlow Down and back to Heathfield.

Recently the band held a jumble sale which raised £130 towards the band's running expenses. Another jumble sale is being organised for October 23 at St Richard's Hall although the band's next major fund-raising event will be the annual Christmas Fair at the end of November.

Mr Cornford said: "While Steven was doing his run we held a fete at the hall which raised just over £80. We were very pleased with the sum raised and the money is certainly needed."

STEVE HOLLOWAY sits before his colleagues of the Heathfield Band having just completed a 20-mile sponsored run for band funds.

Article from Kent & Sussex Courier, October 1982.

to Uckfield and back.[13] "Fellow bandsmen Peter Cornford and Nicholas Threlfall cycled ahead of him along the route, followed by the decorated van of bandmaster David Threlfall," reports the Sussex Express.[14] The event raised about £170 (over £600 today). "Steven did marvellously well and got back to the hall about two hours earlier than expected," adds Peter in the Courier. "The money will go towards some new music and I expect some instruments will need to be repaired or replaced."[15] The Band also found itself playing at fun runs and a Roadrunners event for the Heathfield Round Table. From 1988 until 2001, from the campus of St. Bede's School located beside the South Downs in Eastbourne, it would launch the annual Seven Sisters Marathon with a boisterous rendition of *Sussex by the Sea*, before removing to Litlington to continue the musical entertainment.

Many local events became regular fixtures for the Band, the most high-profile being the Heathfield Agricultural Show, which takes place at Broad Oak every late May Bank Holiday. The show is quite spectacular, occupying several fields and attracting thousands of visitors each year. Although the Band could be seen here on an *ad hoc* basis since 1949 (the year after the inaugural show), and earlier still at the pre-war forerunner the Heathfield Horticultural Show, it had now become a permanent part of the proceedings. The show is often a wet affair: in 1984, for example, the venue would be subjected to a nine-hour deluge, but the Band played on regardless. "Heathfield Silver Band which, from the limited shelter of its canvas bandstand, opened its afternoon programme with a lively rendering of *Colonel*

Bogey," writes the Courier. "It was in that spirit of stiff-upper-lip defiance that the show went on."[16] The Band was also now a regular attraction at Horam Flower Show and Fordcombe Fête.

Bonfire parades and carnivals enjoyed something of a resurgence during the 1980s. In 1981, the Band expanded its regular carnival line-up to include the festivities at Hailsham. Also that year, returning to Rotherfield Bonfire after a long absence, the Band became the victim of a practical joke: as it passed underneath the railway bridge, a bucketful of water came pouring down over the musicians' heads![17] However, the Band was mostly adored by the spirited

Hailsham Carnival, September 1981.
Photograph supplied by Peter Cornford.

public and in 1985 there was uproar when it was unable to attend Heathfield Carnival due to a prior engagement. Secretary Ben Guile would feel compelled to issue a public apology: "The members of the Band are worried that [...] people might have come to the conclusion that the Band could not be troubled to take part," he writes in the Sussex Express.[18] "We regret being unable to play at the carnival this year, as it is one of the few opportunities the Band has to show itself on its 'home ground' and to repay in some measure for the support it enjoys. All our members hope that the Band will be booked in time for the carnival next year when, once again, we can look forward to Blowing up the High Street."[19]

Providing ceremonial support for the military has been engrained in the fabric of the Band since its days with the Volunteers. The relationship would endure, Remembrance commemorations in particular changing little from year to year. "We used to do Heathfield in the morning and Waldron in the afternoon," recalls Ted Lee (speaking in 2013). "When the British Legion finished at Waldron, we went to Burwash in the afternoon. Then, when Heathfield stopped, we went to Burwash in the mornings, Goudhurst after that." This pattern continued throughout the decade, as would the annual parades for the Royal Engineers at Eastbourne (the Band even received invites to the latter's Autumn Harvest Suppers).[20] In 1985 it also played in Eastbourne for a celebration of the Allied Victory in Burma, and between 1984 and 1986 it travelled to Crawley to lead Remembrance Parades for the Dunkirk Veterans Association and the Royal Navy Old Comrades.[21]

There was a plethora of bookings for church and school fêtes during the Eighties, at locations such as Maynards Green and Old Heathfield. "We don't do many school fêtes now. See, they got their own players now," reflects Ted Lee, acknowledging the array of bands now in existence as a direct result of brass tuition returning to schools. In addition, there were numerous engagements in support of the Scouts and Guides, including a St. George's Day Parade which rotated annually between locations as far afield as Cade Street, Heathfield, Hailsham and even Hawkhurst in Kent.[22] The Band also assisted the Heathfield Guides with several events, including their 75th anniversary celebrations in 1985, and would take part in a torchlit children's parade, with a bonfire and fireworks, which was jointly organised by the 1st Heathfield Scout Group with the Cross-in-Hand and All Saints & St. Richard's primary schools.[23]

One significant evolution would be to the nature of the Band's Christmas arrangements. "For at least the past forty years your local Band has knocked on your doors during the run-up to Christmas, collecting for some charity or other," writes Peter Cornford in late 1981. "The money collected Christmas Eve is traditionally solely for the Band fund. The 1981 season took a slightly different form, in that we were booked to play at more private parties, so our door-to-door playing was shortened this time. Not that we minded greatly: it's warmer playing inside, with no ice to slip on!"[24] Whilst door-to-door carolling was fast becoming a thing of the past, playing at pubs would

Burwash Fête, August 1986.
Photograph supplied by Kent & Sussex Courier.

continue, and there was a surge of late-night shopping events. From 1983 this meant an annual excursion to Tunbridge Wells, and occasional trips to Hailsham. In 1984 the Band began another tradition: carolling at Vines Cross Post Office.[25] It also appeared at Heathfield's Dickensian Market, and at an annual carol service for the Union Church in Heathfield.

The Band's popular Christmas Fayre would continue into the early Eighties, now taking place at Heathfield's Red Cross Hall. "The Band, followed by Father Christmas, was a marvellous sight," reports bandmaster David Threlfall in one newspaper article.[26] "The Fayre attracted a marvellous turnout, which was very pleasing, and I think Mr. Farley [Graham], a friend of the Band [and soon to become its chairman and a bass player], enjoyed himself as Father Christmas."[27] However, the Christmas Fayre was becoming less profitable than it had once been and would come to an end in 1982. More recently, Christmas Concerts have become the favoured method of seasonal fundraising. The Band performed several in the Eighties, including gigs at Stonegate School in 1985 and Five Ashes in 1986 and 1987.[28] Its first official appearance at the Uckfield Bonfire Carol Concert seems to have taken place in 1983.

999 Emergency Services Weekend, Eastbourne Seafront, ca. July 1990.
Photograph supplied by Mostyn Cornford.

Variety continued to be a watch-word throughout the decade and there was never a dull moment. The Band made regular trips to the De La Warr Pavilion in Bexhill and annual appearances at the Pantiles in Tunbridge Wells.[29] There were also engagements at Eastbourne Football Club, themed events such as an Old Empire Celebration at Batemans in Burwash (the seventeenth century manor, once home to Rudyard Kipling), a Real English Apple Fair on Paddington Green in London (in aid of Barnardo's), Heathfield Pancake Race, anniversary celebrations for the St. Helen's Park Preservation Society in Hastings, and even gigs for the Winemakers' Association and the Association of Cyclists.[30] The Band also returned to Eastbourne for the 999 Emergency Services weekend in 1989, and paraded through Brighton in aid of Brighton Spastics.[31]

Heathfield Band would experience a host of conductors, too. Dick Turner had been a bandmember in the late Fifties and early Sixties, before moving to Warbleton & Buxted Band which he subsequently led for a time.[32] He returned to Heathfield Band in 1982 and, given his previous conducting experience, David Threlfall would gladly surrender the baton to him.[33] "Dick came along, brought some pieces he'd written, and was clearly the guy who should be leading the Band," recalls Peter Cornford. "Dick took the stick and injected a bit more discipline into the Band. He was a local man, a joiner/carpenter I think, self-taught and quite a reasonable musician." However, the improved discipline would not be at the expense of camaraderie. At one rehearsal, as Dick suggested that the Band attempt Grieg's *Spring*, bandmember Gordon Neve (then in his seventies) announced that he could not find his part. "Well," said Dick with a grin, "I expect you lost your Spring years ago, didn't you Gordon?" "Yes," came the reply, "and I shan't be able to get a new one now!" Unfortunately, Dick Turner's time as bandmaster was short-lived, as ill health forced him to retire in the Summer of 1984.[34]

David Threlfall began studying for a degree in the Autumn of 1984, and would consequently have less time to offer the Band. The result was an urgent hunt for a new bandmaster, and an advertising campaign would draw the attention of John "Taff" Denison, who assumed the role in November.[35] "The Band went into a bit of a freefall," explains Peter Cornford. "Taffy came along and was very much a caretaker. He was a northerner, an ex-military man who lived in Hailsham. I think he'd retired, he certainly seemed to live on air, but he wasn't old, probably in his forties. He had army playing experience – he was a really good euphonium player – but no experience of conducting or managing a band or controlling the thing as a unit. He seemed to be a bit of a wastrel, so he wasn't a very positive influence." An ongoing "situation" would arise when John was to borrow some money from the Band, and it was probably this that led to his ousting as bandmaster at the 1987 AGM.[36]

John Denison was briefly replaced by Norman Wragg, a gentleman from Eastbourne who seemed to have limited conducting experience and ultimately proved unsuited to the role. "He wasn't a serious prospect," says Peter Cornford. "I think he might have been there a matter of months. The Band was fishing around for some security and long-term tenure really." John Denison soon returned and would continue to come and go until the mid-Nineties. However, by the final quarter of the 1980s the ongoing air of instability had led to a drop in membership, the number of engagements had fallen significantly, and there were no Band socials or even formal committee meetings for a time.[37]

The Heathfield Band of the Eighties had taken a proactive approach to recruitment and publicity, and was rewarded with a spectacular, if short, recovery. It lost a number of veteran members, but the camaraderie fostered by David Threlfall would, at least for a time, result in a happy and productive Band. However, in the space of a few short years, unstable leadership led it back to shaky ground. By the decade's end, it would be transformed from a successful and co-operative family unit with a blossoming junior contingent, to one with an uncertain future. In order to survive, the Heathfield Band of the Nineties would have to embrace fresh ideas and new innovations.

---

[1] Cutting, source unknown, ca. February 1982

[2] Minutes, 18th January 1982

[3] Minutes, 20th January 1981

[4] Minutes, 2nd July 1981

[5] Support The Band Pamphlet, July 1981

[6] Cutting, source unknown, ca. February 1982

[7] Accounts, 1982

[8] Minutes, 20th January 1981, 19th January 1983, 26th November 1983 & 22nd January 1985

[9] Minutes, 18th January 1982

[10] Cornford, P., 1981. Personal Archive and Interviews

[11] Minutes, 24th February 1982

[12] Cutting, source unknown, 4th April 1981

[13] Sussex Express, 17th September 1982; Kent & Sussex Courier, 8th October 1982

[14] Sussex Express, 10th October 1982

[15] Kent & Sussex Courier, 8th October 1981

[16] Kent & Sussex Courier, 1st June 1984

[17] Cornford, P., 1981

[18] Sussex Express, ca. July 1985

[19] ibid

[20] Accounts, 1980–89

[21] ibid

[22] ibid

[23] ibid; Kent & Sussex Courier, 11th November 1983

[24] Cornford, P., 1981

[25] Cornford, M., Personal Archive, 4th December 1983; Accounts, 1984

[26] Cutting, source unknown, ca. December 1981

[27] ibid

[28] Accounts, 1980–89

[29] ibid

[30] Accounts, 1980–89; Barnardo's Programme, 17th August 1986

[31] Accounts, 1989

[32] c.f. Bourke, J., 1996. *The History of a Village Band 1896-1996*. Heathfield: Warbleton and Buxted Band

[33] Minutes, 19th January 1983

[34] Minutes, 27th July 1984

[35] Minutes, 23rd November 1984

[36] Minutes, 30th August 1985, 14th March 1986 & 27th January 1987

[37] Kent & Sussex Courier, 6th February 1987; Minutes, 27th January 1987 & 26th January 1988

MEMBERS of NOTE...

Cedric "Sid" Forward
baritone, 1980s–2000s.

"We all referred to him as *Hissing Sid*, I don't know why..."
– Frankie Lulham.

Sid learnt to play cornet at the tender age of ten, and would later progress to baritone and euphonium, playing with Salvation Army bands in Crawley, Burgess Hill and Crowborough. He was also involved with Wadhurst Brass Band and Crowborough Town Band, but was to finish his playing career as a vital member of Heathfield Silver Band.

"Sid was a lovely man," remembers Frankie Lulham. "He was a Salvation Armyist, very, very religious, and so gentle. He used to have three spoons of sugar – at least – in his tea and he always had sweets in his pockets. Every now and again when I was conducting, he'd throw me a sweet and he'd always give sweets to children. Sid was the perfect person because he knew when to move aside for a younger player who was better than him; he approved of all the youngsters being taught properly."

Sid was passionate about encouraging the next generation, and would take every opportunity to mentor young bandmembers. "Sid used to sit and tell me all sorts of stories, and he used to try and teach me to do little technical things, which were quite possibly a bit too tricky for me – but I'd have a go anyway," says Sarah Leeves. "He would shout out 'C' and she'd play a C," recalls Frankie. "He encouraged lots of people."

For the latter part of his working life, Sid had been a plumber, and in 2005 he would generously lend his services to help finish the bandroom extension, installing a water heater and a toilet in the new restroom. Sid's previous career had been growing and developing roses, and when Frankie left the Band in 2007, he presented her with two, one called "Lovely Lady" and the other, "In Loving Memory," for her recently-deceased father.

In December 2004, Sid was presented with a SCABA award for more than fifty years' service to the brass band movement. He sadly passed away in 2010, but is remembered in the *Cedric Forward Cup*, which is presented annually to a player who has made a significant contribution to the Band.

Interlude Room for Improvement:
##　　　　　The Story of the Bandroom

Very few brass bands own their rehearsal space, and even fewer have enjoyed the luxury of a permanent base of operations for a continuous span of 85 years. Happily, Heathfield Silver Band is no ordinary case, and can lay claim to both these advantages. This chapter charts the story of the Alexandra Road bandroom.

The Band began its existence rehearsing at the National School in Old Heathfield (now All Saints & St. Richard's Church of England Primary School). Whilst attached to the Artillery Volunteers, it rehearsed at the Drill Hall in Station Road, Heathfield, and it has also been suggested that it practiced briefly in Alexandra Road at the beginning of the twentieth century. It soon relocated to the Drill Hall in Cade Street, which was its primary rehearsal space until the original Band broke apart around 1927–8.

In 1927 a breakaway faction was formed, as things were turning sour at Cade Street. The new Band would rehearse anywhere that it could around town, including in Ghyll Road at the home of its first bandmaster Arthur Rodgers. It also practised at the Brotherhood and Sisterhood Hall, a non-conformist chapel located in the High Street, on the site that is now occupied by the medical surgery. In addition the Band briefly rehearsed in Alexandra Road, but soon "had to get out for a bit," according to bandmember Gordon Neve (speaking in 1981). Gordon does not give the reasons for this but it is worth considering that Edward Bean, founder of the original Band (and one of the forsaken in the wake of the Cade Street bust-up), resided in Alexandra Road at the time, so the venue was not the most tactful choice.

Around 1928–9, the *new* Band would move to the Agricultural Hall in the High Street, which by now was a store room for local business *Errey's* (where *Trading4U* stands today). One benefit from this move was that the growing music library could be kept in a cupboard on-site. The Band must have been relatively content here as it was to remain for a number of years, until it was forced to leave in the Spring of 1936 after falling behind with the rent.

Fortunately, the owners of the rehearsal room at Alexandra Road, Mr. and Mrs. Francis, were willing to accept rent in arrears. So in April 1936 the Band would move into what remains the bandroom to this day. The move was considered something of a homecoming by the Sussex Express: "Heathfield Silver Band has this week returned home! After practising in the parish of Waldron for several years they now practice in a building in Alexandra Road, Heathfield, which was their headquarters many years ago."[1] The rent was initially about £1 a month (roughly £72 today), but it would rise to around £1.4s. by the early 1950s. However, due to the quirks of negative inflation, the rent would seem to have become better value (about £44 today). Nevertheless, in 1940 the Band began hunting for a cheaper rehearsal space, though ultimately it would remain at Alexandra Road, continuing to pay its rent throughout the war.[2]

In July 1953, Mrs. Francis hinted that she might sell the bandroom, perhaps because it was becoming subjectively less profitable year-on-year. The rental agreement allowed either party to give just one month's notice to terminate the arrangement and so, rather than risk becoming homeless, the committee decided to obtain a valuation and request first refusal on any potential sale.[3] By March 1955, the bandroom had been valued at £225 (about £6,000 today), and the Band was invited to make an offer.[4]

The purchase would undoubtedly be a wise investment, but the Band only possessed savings of £46 (about £1,200).[5] There were also other expenses to consider, such as utility bills, insurance, and having the property wired for electricity.[6] It therefore approached the Heathfield Band Supporters' Club for assistance, who were willing to donate £100 to the cause (about £2,600 today).[7] An Extraordinary General Meeting was therefore called to discuss the matter and the proposal was carried unanimously.[8] "The people who was band supporters, they used to give these concerts and had jumble sales and different things to get money to buy the bandroom. It was quite a big occasion when we bought that," recalls Ken Russell.

By July 1955 legal matters were well underway. Four trustees would be required to oversee the property, so bandmembers Lloyd Bland, Roy Elphick, Bob Lee, and Graham Barton were duly appointed. "It is a testament to the first trustees that they each remained in position for twenty-plus years and thereby gave the bandroom ownership stability and competence in its early years," observes Peter Cornford. The Band's crude governing documents would also have to be updated. One amendment to the rules saw the addition of a crucial objective which had hitherto been absent: "The Band shall exist to provide entertainment." On 27th July, a deposit of £22.10s. (about £600 today) was paid towards the purchase of the bandroom and between August and September the building would be wired up and connected to the mains electricity and gas supplies, and insurance purchased. A bank loan of £125 (about £3,300) was obtained and, on 30th September 1955, the Band settled its outstanding rent of £7.10s. (about £200), and paid the remaining £202.10s. of the purchase price (about £5,430). It was now firmly on the property ladder. "This was a real coup and an act of foresight," says Peter. "It has always been a source of pride for the Band and conveys a sense of permanence."

It has been suggested that the Alexandra Road bandroom began life in the late nineteenth century, possibly as an estate office for the Rummary family, before becoming a private school, a reading room or meeting house for a non-conformist church, and the headquarters of the *Band of Hope* (a temperance organisation). It was later used by special-interest groups, such as a sewing club, and for Guide and Scout meetings, amongst other things.[9] "It's a strange place to have a band hut. The ceiling is no height at all and the volume is just tremendous," observes former Band president, Geoff Pickering (speaking in 2013). Ken Russell adds: "Bit deafening in there, wasn't it? It weren't very big." There was no inside toilet, and the two crude outhouses at the rear of the building had long since fallen into disuse. "When we wanted a piddle, we had to go outside and piss down on the wall," remembers Ken! With the evolution into a uni-sex Band, this state of affairs would be completely inappropriate, and so an arrangement was made whereby players could use the neighbours' outside toilet in return for allowing access to the Band's pathway.

While difficult to imagine today, the tiny bandroom of yesteryear would be forever filled with tobacco smoke, a situation which persisted into the early 1980s. This is somewhat perplexing to the modern mind, as the ills of smoking were certainly known about, if not openly discussed, as far back as the nineteenth century. Indeed, one 1890s piece in The British Bandsman entitled *Cleanliness in the Bandroom* directs: "No smoking, as this poisons the air."[10] Peter Cornford recalls: "I can remember not liking it particularly because it's a job to play, you just breathe the smoke in. In the wintertime, when all the windows and doors were shut, it was frankly quite tricky seeing across the fog of a bandroom. There was no sense that you had to go outside to do it."

"The main culprit was chain-smoker Dennis Guile. He would arrive smoking, put his cigarette on his baritone-stand, and it would just smoke away all evening. When that one ended, he'd light another. His brother, Ben, used to sit behind me on flugel and smoke, Dave [Threlfall] smoked his cigars, Roy Crompton on trombone would smoke. We used to have a break in rehearsals and it was called the 'smoke break' – a funny idea really because it was a continuous thing anyway. If you weren't chain-smoking like Dennis, that's when you would have your smoke. Tom Kelly would get his roll-ups out and old Albert [French] did, too." Tempers would sometimes run high over the issue: "We had a bloke from Tunbridge Wells," says Ken Russell. "He only played the side drum (or tried to), and he used to roll his cigarettes and smoke when we was playing. And when we finished, I said, 'Do you have to smoke when we're playing?' And he didn't like it. He said if he wanted to smoke, he was going to. He was gonna punch my 'ead and he was gonna punch ol' Mostyn's 'ead... The trouble with Heathfield is they was always falling out!"

Another on-going challenge was maintenance, such as painting, repointing walls, and fixing the roof (which was finally soundproofed in 1958).[11] Jobs would usually be undertaken by volunteers, with Ted Lee and Mostyn

Cornford (a builder by trade) taking charge of proceedings.[12] "When I joined the Band, the condition of the building was poor," remembers Mostyn. "Amongst other work, I repaired the rusty, corrugated roof sheets and painted them with bitumen paint, and replaced a large section of rotten floor, adding new floor joists and re-boarding it."[13]

However, getting things done was rarely a speedy process. For example, in December 1966 it was observed that the corrugated iron roof needed a coat of paint; this task was finally completed two years later![14] This is perhaps unsurprising, as the job was not an easy one. "I spent a couple of weeks in one of my school Summer holidays doing the whole roof, just off a ladder with no scaffolding," recalls Peter Cornford. "It involved rubbing it all down with a wire brush and then using some sort of sticky black coating." The corrugated iron has since been replaced with tin sheets which slot together and are easier to paint. In 1973 heating the bandroom was finally made a "priority"; this would also take nearly two years to address.[15]

The bandroom in the process of being renovated.
Photograph supplied by Mostyn Cornford.

Major works were occasionally necessary, too. In 1980, a bandroom wall developed a bulge and was in serious danger of collapse.[16] The cost of reconstruction work was estimated at around £900 (nearly £4,000 today) and the Band hurriedly set about raising the necessary funds, receiving some assistance from Heathfield Lions and Wealden District Council.[17] Mostyn would provide the labour, with assistance from "eager" volunteers: "I enlisted the help of my wife, Esme," he recalls, "and two committee members, Ben Guile and [retired brick layer] Jack Mitchell [...]. After forty years the wall is still standing."[18]

The first suggestion of a bandroom extension came in 1985, though the idea would not progress far until some nine years later, by which time there was a pressing need for extensive upgrades.[19] The bandroom's roof and door now also needed replacing, and neighbours had complained that the outhouses to the rear of the building were an eyesore. The latter complaint would in fact be the catalyst which began a decade-long campaign to install internal toilet facilities.[20] The project would continue to expand, even as consideration was being given to organisational challenges such as obtaining planning permission, raising the necessary funds, and building appropriate drainage. The Band's secretary Dennis Guile began an application for Lottery funding, but he was now in ill health and the initiative would have to be abandoned.

Concurrent to the upgrade project was an escalating dispute with some of the Band's neighbours, which seemingly began when a boundary hedge was removed to make way for a new garage.[21] Matters were further complicated because the bandroom was not recorded with Land Registry.[22] Subsequently, this would lead to a series of disagreements over water drainage, the neighbours' fixing of lights and cabling to the bandroom, and a tree which encroached on the Band's property. It would even be discovered that said neighbours were using the disused outhouses for storage, so Mostyn shrewdly bricked-up the entrances, removed the dividing wall, and made the handy space accessible from within the bandroom.

The unavoidable involvement of solicitors would further delay progress to the extension project, but the upgrades were eventually given a fresh boost of motivation by the Band's new conductor Frankie Lulham. In May 2002, a planning application was submitted to Waldron Parish Council, but the plans had again grown in scope.[23] "I drew up plans and got them passed for an extension to include a kitchen and toilet, neither of which we had before then," recalls Mostyn. The cost of the work was now expected to be a not-inconsiderable £16,000 (equivalent to over £26,600 today).[24]

Such was the public enthusiasm for the project that the first donations were received within weeks of its announcement, beginning with a £1,000 grant from Heathfield and Waldron Parish Council.[25] There would be a steady stream of appeals and press releases to promote the initiative, and a huge quantity of engagements were undertaken. "We raised a phenomenal amount of money," remembers Frankie. "It was quite amazing what we did. I badgered them mercilessly and we did so many engagements that it did consume my life... and theirs!" The feverish activity and shared objective was to foster camaraderie unlike anything the Band had witnessed in years.

By the Summer of 2003, planning was complete and agreements were finally reached with the neighbours.[26] In July, construction work could commence. "Most of the credit has to go to Mostyn, he did most of the work," recalls Keith Pursglove. "But the youngest and the oldest members were always willing to lend a hand whenever he asked for help. When a pipe needed to be laid from the bandroom up to the road, you'd get ten bandmembers turn up at the weekend with a shovel and we'd dig the trench." Richard Ayres (speaking in 2018) remembers: "I was the main *large hole digger* outside for drains. I suppose, being small, and in those days fairly strong, I was able to do that sort of stuff."

The fundraising goal had now grown to £18,000 (about £29,000 today) but generous donations would continue to be received, in addition to money raised by the Band's dedicated supporters. It also made a return to Lewes Bonfire in November 2003, primarily to secure a significant contribution from Cliffe Bonfire Society.[27] By early 2004, over £10,000 had been raised, but still more money was required. "Installing a new toilet these days requires all sorts of rules and regulations and people coming and standing around with a clipboard and saying, 'Oh yes, you can do that but it will cost you a lot of money'," explains Frankie.[28] Fortunately, the Co-Op came to the rescue with a Community Dividend Award, as would South East Water, and the sewerage outlet could finally be connected.[29] By May 2004 the brickwork was complete and the new roof installed, made possible by a £3,000 advance from Mostyn's wife, Esme.

Meanwhile, the Band pulled out all the stops to clear its remaining debt.[30] In June 2004, it would stage a sponsored walk around Old Heathfield: "We are putting on our walking boots in an endeavour to raise lots of money for the

Building work underway on the bandroom extension, July 2005.
Photograph supplied by Mostyn Cornford.

bandroom extension," reports Frankie. "The walk is supposed to be six miles long… I hope it's not more than that as we all have to be back and ready to play hymns at an open-air service at St. Bart's Church, Cross-in-Hand, in the evening."[31] Despite the rain the walk was a great success, raising a further £617 towards the extension funds. "I have to say that a very good time was had by all twenty-eight of us who trudged the footpaths around Old Heathfield, Warbleton and Cade Street, finally arriving back at the Star Inn some 3 hours later, only slightly bedraggled," adds Frankie.[32]

In August 2004 Heathfield First Magazine carried an update on the project: "The roof is on and we are just waiting for the new door before knocking a wall down and opening up the room in all its glory. Then we will be installing the toilet and kitchen facilities and slapping a bit of paint on."[33] In September the Band marched at three bonfire parades, and received an unexpected surprise in the form of a £1,000 cheque from the organisers of Le Marché. "I was totally amazed," writes Frankie. "We will be able to pay off our debts and be able to afford some new heaters for the bandroom."[34] In addition, Frankie's father contributed a rather special gift: "My dad, he was very supportive of me being conductor," says Frankie. "I said to him, 'We want to have a cuppa tea, we need to have an urn.' 'Oh?' he says, 'How much does

Grand bandroom reopening, September 2005.

Photograph ii shows Richard Ayres.

Photograph iii depicts the Band's eldest member, Fred Richardson, with Frankie Lulham.

Photographs i, ii, iv, v, vi, viii, ix supplied by Frankie Lulham.

Photograph iii supplied by Danielle Budden.

Photograph vii supplied by Mostyn Cornford.

an urn cost then?' I said, 'I think it's about a hundred quid.' He whipped out a hundred quid and gave it to me, so he bought that."

In March 2005, Anna Farley took the place of the late Bob Lee as the fourth appointed trustee, alongside Ted Lee, Mostyn Cornford, and Graham Barton. In June, Graham would step aside to be replaced by Richard Leeves. The new trustees were immediately embroiled in further legal wranglings as one of the neighbours had complained that the appearance of the bandroom was unsightly; they also had concerns about the drainage of water onto their land and expected an adjoining fence to be replaced.[35] The trustees countered with their own concerns, including the incorrect siting of a fence and garage on Band property. Eventually a series of compromises was reached, leading to a more harmonious relationship in the future.[36]

By the Summer of 2005, all outstanding loans had been cleared and a team of volunteers could move in to complete the remaining jobs. These included plastering, painting and carpeting the bandroom, installing a new heater, toilet and washbasin, and tiling the bathroom floor.[37] Bandmembers Doug Blackford and Cedric "Sid" Forward respectively carried out the electrical and plumbing work. "Whilst the work was being done, I was always conscious of not disrupting our Band practices on a Tuesday evening," recalls Mostyn. "There were some compromises, however, the conductor having to wield her baton between scaffolding poles being one! I think only one Band practice had to be cancelled during the whole project."[38] Frankie would warmly praise the final results: "The bandroom looks stunning and is quite transformed from the 1950s decor to our very clean and modern white walls and fabulous red carpet."[39]

Grand Opening & Coffee Morning

THE HEATHFIELD SILVER BAND
INVITES YOU TO JOIN
DAVID DIMBLEBY
IN CELEBRATING OUR
GRAND OPENING &
COFFEE MORNING

DATE: SATURDAY
3RD SEPTEMBER 2005

TIME: 10.00 - 12.00

PLACE: THE BAND ROOM
ALEXANDRA ROAD
HEATHFIELD

RSVP

Grand reopening invitation.

With work complete, the refurbished and extended bandroom was finally revealed to the public, amidst much tea, cake and (quite literally) fanfare, at an open day on 3rd September 2005. Television personality David Dimbleby would graciously perform the ribbon-cutting ceremony for the occasion, Sarah Leeves composed a special fanfare, and there was a display of the Band's history and heritage on show. Invitations were sent to all the project's donors, friends of the Band, the media, and former bandmembers. "We had about 100 people in our little bandroom over the course of the morning," recalls Frankie.[40]

The final cost of the project was in the region of £22,000 (about £33,600 today), but the bandroom had now doubled in value to around £50,000.[41] The only downside would be the 50% increase in council tax, but that was a small price to pay for the added comfort and convenience of the new amenities.[42] Mostyn would be presented with a special plaque in recognition of his work and Frankie, mainly for her role in driving the project to success, was invited to a garden party at Buckingham Palace (see *Fame and Glory: Celebrity Encounters*).

The bandroom requires ongoing upgrades and maintenance to remain safe, secure and functional. In Spring 2011 a large pillar near the cornet section would be removed and a support beam added, creating additional rehearsal space for the ever-expanding Band.[43] In 2012 the roof required work to rectify a moisture issue. And, in 2017, £4,000 was spent repairing the bandroom's roof and pathway.[44] However, no work has so far compared to the 2005 project in terms of scale and cost. As of 2019, the committee reports: "Our main asset, the bandroom, is in a good state of repair and no major expenditure is expected in the foreseeable future."[45]

Nevertheless, the occasional expenses involved with owning the bandroom are easily outweighed by its benefits. "We've got our own property, which most bands don't have," says Mostyn (speaking in 2013). "We can leave music and everything. We just go there, play and come away. That's a big advantage." So let's raise a toast to the sturdy, dependable Alexandra Road bandroom, which remains a silent witness to the countless music-making memories and happy times made therein. Long may the Band continue to call it home.

[1] Sussex Express, 9th April 1936

[2] Minutes, 1st December 1940; Accounts, 1940–49

[3] Minutes, 21st July 1953

[4] Minutes, 22nd March 1955

[5] ibid

[6] ibid

[7] Accounts, 1954–55

[8] Minutes, 24th March 1955

[9] Cornford, P., 1981. Personal Archive and Interviews

[10] Hailstone, A., 1987. *The British Bandsman Centenary Book*. Baldock: Egon: 18

[11] Minutes, 4th March 1958; Cornford, P., 1981

[12] e.g. Minutes, 13th October 1960 & 25th February 1975

[13] Heathfield Magazine, February 2019

[14] Minutes, 13th December 1966, 2nd January 1968 & April 1969

[15] Minutes, 30th June 1973 & 31st January 1975

[16] Minutes, 3rd September 1980; Heathfield Magazine, February 2019

[17] Cutting, source unknown, 20th June 1981; Leaflet: Support the Band, July 1981; Cutting, source unknown, ca. February 1982

[18] Heathfield Magazine, February 2019

[19] Minutes, 22nd January 1985

[20] Minutes, 6th December 1993 & 7th March 1994

[21] Minutes, 22nd January 1974

[22] Minutes, 10th May 1995

[23] Sussex Express, 24th May 2002

[24] ibid

[25] Press Release, Mostyn Cornford, ca. June 2002

[26] Minutes, 22nd May 2003

[27] MD Report, Frankie Lulham, 5th November 2003

[28] Press Release, Frankie Lulham, ca. March 2004

[29] Minutes, 4th March 2004; Cutting, source unknown, ca. April 2004

[30] MD Report, Frankie Lulham, 3rd June 2004

[31] MD Report, Frankie Lulham, 27th June 2004

[32] Press Release, Frankie Lulham, 5th July 2004

[33] Heathfield First, August 2004

[34] Press Release, Frankie Lulham, 20th September 2004

[35] Correspondence, Richard Rummery, 13th July 2005

[36] ibid

[37] Minutes, 6th June 2005; Heathfield First Magazine, December 2019

[38] Heathfield First Magazine, December 2019

[39] Sussex Express, 16th September 2005

[40] Heathfield and the Weald X-Tra, October 2005

[41] Minutes, 8th February 2005

[42] Minutes, 9th January 2006

[43] Minutes, 7th March 2011 & 9th May 2011

[44] Minutes, 6th March 2018

[45] Minutes, 26th February 2019

Poem *David Threlfall and His Band*

Now the finest people in the land
Are David Threlfall and his Band.
There's Cornet Tommy, Tenor Ted,
Eupho Jack, & Cornet Fred,
Drummer Gerald, Flugel Guile,
And Roy the Bass stands out a mile.

Now to a contest they did go,
Intent on having a smashing blow.
With Cornet Peter, Cornet Sue,
All intent to win it through –
Instruments all sparkling bright,
Hoping for a successful night.

Now David waves his stick to start,
But Tenor Jack has lost his part.
The trombone section – they aren't blowing –
They're watching Julia – her leg's all showing!
But then at last, they set off fine, with a roaring march
That's called *Pendine*.

Next on the programme, what a joy;
A solo played by Trombone Roy.
He stood out front, all stiff and pale,
And said: "I just can't play – I've had no ale!"
But *The Acrobat* came out so well –
How he played it sober, we just can't tell!

by Bob Lee

With grateful thanks to Bob's family for supplying the text.

MEMBERS Of NOTE...

Graham Farley
Eb bass,
chairman,
1993–ca.1999.

Graham was known in Heathfield as the owner of a fencing business, but he would also serve the community as a fireman for twenty-five years. As the father-in-law of bandmember, Anna Farley, he was a long-term friend of the Band, and would even sometimes accompany it, dressed as Father Christmas, to the annual Christmas Fayre. Whilst carolling around the town, the Band would always be sure to call on Graham and his wife, Margaret, at their home in Ghyll Road, where it would treated to plentiful supplies of alcohol and mince pies. When he retired from the fire service, Graham was to become the Band's chairman, and he would also take up playing the Eb bass, while Margaret would play the horn.

Graham was a very down-to-earth, no-nonsense man. "He was quite radical and he would call a spade a spade; he'd say what he thought," says Frankie Lulham. "If there was a problem, Graham would sort it out." However, in ca. 2000, after a long and fruitful connection with the Band, Graham was to arrive at its AGM to find he had been replaced as chairman. "He said rather sadly, 'Oh, you don't want me then?,'" turned round and walked out, and that was the end of his playing career," remembers Richard Ayres. "I think he was quite heartbroken about it, to be honest," adds Frankie Lulham. "I really liked him and I know he approved of me. Graham was a lovely man."

During his time as chairman, Graham organised many engagements and activities, including trips to Wiesbaden in Germany. His lasting legacy was initiating a National Lottery application (subsequently completed by Jennifer Leeves), which would lead to the purchase of a completely new set of instruments for the Band.

When Frankie became the Band's musical director, she would soon invite Graham to return. "I wanted him to come back and I actually gave him his jacket. He said, 'Oh, I'd love to come back.' And then he got very ill…" she recalls. Tragically, he was never able to return, and would sadly pass away in the Spring of 2005. Shortly afterwards, at a concert on Eastbourne Bandstand, the Band would play one of Graham's favourite pieces – *Highland Cathedral* – in his memory. He is fondly remembered by those who knew him.

1990s Serendipity and the reinvention of a Sussex Institution

Heathfield Silver Band, Christmas 1996.

Heathfield Band began the Nineties as a shadow of its former self. Membership was down and bookings had dropped significantly: in 1990 it enjoyed barely a dozen paid engagements. To compound these difficulties, several conductors would pass through the bandroom doors in relatively quick succession. This precarious state was mirrored by nearby Crowborough Town Band and the pair would build a symbiotic friendship, supporting one another at every opportunity. As the decade progressed, there was a renewed interest in overseas tours, and a National Lottery grant would lead to the purchase of a completely new set of instruments for the Band. However, it would also require a radical reinvention to survive into the twenty-first century...

As the decade arrived, recruitment was once again a priority for the ailing Band, and a new champion would present herself in the form of cornet player Janet Baker. Janet worked for British Telecom and played for a Territorial Army Band in Kent, and would make full use of this network to bring necessary aid to the Band. Among the players she recruited were drummer George Patterson and trombonist and future bandmaster Frank Francis. "I found George Patterson because we needed a drummer for Lewes and he worked for BT," recalls Janet. "He came along and enjoyed it so much that he decided to join. Frank was a mate of mine from the TA Band and I talked him and a few others to bolster the Band up for marching." Frank adds: "We managed to boost 'em up a wee bit by bringing in good players from other local bands and some of the TA Band used to go down and help out, especially when we had gigs, because they could read the music sight read. The best players that were there – the corner people – were the ones that were in the TA Band. There were a lot of girls, once the girls started joining the TA Band Janet would bring all them down."

Frank Francis, a recently-retired army band Sergeant Major with extensive musical knowledge, soon found himself guiding the direction of the Band: "I was brought in because I was helpful to the trombone section who were pretty weak at that time," he says. "At the same time I started, they had someone conducting who didn't really want to do it. So I took it on. They were losing players and the standard of musicianship was more enthusiasm than knowledge, there weren't that many that had a good knowledge, and they needed more guidance and encouragement to practise. I was trained at Kneller Hall so I had a good background. I think I managed to stimulate the confidence of a lot of people that were dragging their heels a bit and they got a little bit more of an incentive, that was the idea: every time I conducted it was a workshop, not just a run-through. So that increased the ability of the Band to be able to take on engagements and sound quite good."

Frank was elected bandmaster on a trial basis following a successful tour to Wiesbaden, Germany, in early 1991, and the position was made permanent in July. Of his time with the Band, he fondly remembers the fun of Christmas carolling: "We used to get a small band together and we'd just go around all the village pubs collecting. They were nights to remember. I wouldn't say we got pissed, but it were a fun night out!" Frank also recalls the challenges of the Heathfield Show: "We did a couple of concerts there, but the weather wasn't that great and I think we got rained-off a couple of times. They put us under cover, but it was one of those covers that the rain would come in anyway, whichever way you looked out. So you sat there in a field, you played, you got a little bit wet, you went for a cuppa tea, and then went back and tried to play again. It was a long day and you got filthy shoes!"

Although guest players helped the Band enormously, it was not a strategy for long-term self-sufficiency. New players were required, and several fortuitous events would happily lead to a boost in membership. Euphonium player, Sarah Leeves (who was to become the musical director in 2013), reflects on how, quite by accident, she came to join the Band. "I must've been ten, I was in my final year at primary school," she says. "I was swinging off my climbing frame and a family friend, Will Banfill (quite an eccentric chap) just pulled up in his car and shouted out the window, 'Sarah, what are you up to this evening?' He was obviously on his way to Band and he just saw me there. I'd seen the Band at school fêtes and fairs and Heathfield Show and all sorts of things. I used to sit cross-legged in front of the Band and watch Sid [Cedric Forward] play euphonium as I made daisy chains. So I just shouted up to the garden, 'Mum, I'm going to Heathfield Silver Band with William!' I often think back to that. What would my life have been like, what would I be doing if I hadn't gone to Heathfield Silver Band, if Will hadn't pulled up at the bottom of the lane that day? Would I have ever taken it up? I can honestly say I don't think I would've. It's one of those chance happenings."

By another stroke of luck, the chair of Hellingly School's Parent Teacher Association, Frankie Lulham (also destined for the annals of Heathfield Band musical directors), befriended veteran brass bander Fred Richardson whilst out selling Avon products door-to-door. "I said, 'Ohh, will your band come and play at our Summer fête?' And so they came and played, and that was my first meeting with the Band," remembers Frankie. "My son Geoffrey started to learn to play the trumpet at school, and Fred said, 'Why don't you get your son to come along and play?' So I took him and another boy up, they had a little bit of an audition with Frank Francis, and they started playing in the Band. I used to sit in the bandroom while Geoffrey played, and my youngest daughter Danielle used to come along and we'd just sit there and listen 'cause it was easier than going to and fro. And then, one day, the drummer wasn't there and Frank said to me, 'Can you put a beat in for us?' So I got up and played the bass drum. A couple of weeks later, the trombone player Bob Lee said, 'Frankie, why don't you have a go on the kit?' I'd never played the drum kit in my life 'cause I'm a piano teacher, but I was able to read the music and work it out. Before I knew it, I was a fully-fledged member of the Band, playing the drum kit, and my little daughter played the triangle!"

The recruitment drive would not stop there. Before long, the Band was to become a full wind band for the first time since the 1920s, taking advantage of the plentiful supply of local wind musicians who were in need of an ensemble to play with. Frankie explains: "They were very low on cornets, and I said, 'My daughter plays the clarinet,' and Frank said, 'Bring her along!' Then I said, 'Well, my niece plays the flute…' 'Bring her along!' 'Another niece plays the oboe...' 'Bring her along!' And then a couple of other clarinettists and a saxophone player came along. So we contributed to the members of the Band quite a bit. They had to buy new music!"

Heathfield Agricultural Show, ca. June 1991.
Photograph supplied by Mostyn Cornford.

With this burst of newcomers 1991 would see a dramatic upturn for the Band, which undertook 34 engagements during the year.[1] The switch to a wind band made very little difference to the type of bookings it would attract. In addition to regulars such as Heathfield Agricultural Show, Bexhill's De La Warr Pavilion, and the Seven Sisters Marathon, 999 Emergency Services Weekend and Royal Engineers Parade at Eastbourne, the Band also attracted new and prestigious gigs, such as traditional seaside concerts on Eastbourne Bandstand and performances at Fordcombe Fête and Batemans, the manor house in Burwash.[2]

In 1992, the Band returned to Batemans to take part in an open-air production of Charles Dickens' *Hard Times*: "As part of the play, a band had

Heathfield Agricultural Show, ca. June 1993–5.
(Back Row, L–R) Laurie Hoad, Laurie Knapp, Nelson Russell,
Charlie Funnel, Dennis Guile, Ted Lee.
(Middle Row, L–R) Fred Richardson, Sarah Leeves. Catherine Redknap, Samantha Hart,
Anna Farley, Mostyn Cornford, Jeff Collins.
(Front Row, L–R) Cheryl Goodsell, Geoffrey Lulham, Danielle Lulham,
Frankie Lulham, Nicola Lulham, Mark Laxton.
Photograph supplied by Mostyn Cornford.

to march past," recalls Janet Baker. "Apart from our heads we were unseen, as we were marching up the path with a hedge in-between us and the audience. I can remember having bright red hat bands with big silver paper badges for extra effect." There would also be a trip to Wiesbaden, a return to the Heathfield Pancake Races, and the Band's first Christmas Concert to be held at the Sheepsetting Lane Community Centre.[3] The latter remained the venue of choice throughout the decade, offering reasonable acoustics and a useful, if somewhat cosy, stage… from which veteran bandmember Fred Richardson would actually topple on one occasion: "I was in charge of the curtain that night," recalls Richard Leeves. "It was a big band and it was crammed onto this stage and Fred was on back row cornet. Suddenly, one of the legs of his chair came off the edge of the stage and he went backwards. It happened that I was standing behind him and I cushioned the fall. It was a bit of luck, but it didn't do my shins any good!"

Unfortunately, the Band's good fortunes were marred by the resignation of Frank Francis in the Autumn of 1992 and, without a bandmaster, engagements would have to be scaled back. However, new hope was to present itself in the shape of the Sherlock family, brothers John and Richard and their father Ernie, who had all joined the Band during the 1980s. John Sherlock took the baton for a short period, before relocating to Devon, and then Richard would function as deputy bandmaster until a suitable replacement could be found.

In September 1993 another ex-army conductor, John Barratt, was to become the new bandmaster. "He was a woodwind player with the Royal Corps of Signals Staff Band and then, when he retired, he took over their Royal Corps of Signals Association Band down at Blandford," recalls Jeff Collins. "He lived in Eastbourne and on the run-up to Remembrance Sunday you'd always see him out on the poppy stands selling the poppies. You couldn't mistake him as ex-military, he was ram-rod straight whenever he stood." Unfortunately, Barratt would sometimes be discontented with the poor discipline and lack of commitment from players.[4] "Some of the younger

Heathfield Silver Band Marching, ca. mid-Nineties.

305

members of the Band, those in their teens and that, didn't take to him that well because he was a typical ex-military person. They couldn't get on with the strict way he liked to run a practice," says Jeff. "The older members got on with him quite well, I got on with him absolutely brilliant. I was conducting the junior band when he was bandmaster."

During this time the Band approached local schools and even the County Council in search of new members, but woodwind players in particular would prove difficult to attract, perhaps because its music library often lacked the necessary sheet music.[5] John Barratt used his library contacts at the Royal Corps of Signals in an effort to obtain suitable arrangements, but sourcing music would prove an ongoing problem.[6] He also insisted that no trumpets be played in the Band, due to the brashness that they add to the tonal palette.[7] Plagued with these challenges and a continuing lack of discipline, John resigned after the 1994 Christmas Concert, complaining that "a few members seem to have the wrong attitude."[8] "What he wanted to do wasn't really working out," reflects Richard Sherlock. "He was probably more old-school and, what with the wind instruments and what have you, I don't think we really got on 100% together."

Richard Sherlock would again fill the role of bandmaster on a "temporary" basis, until a replacement could be found. However, the only application of note that the Band received was from one John "Taff" Denison![9] "Oh Taff," says Jeff Collins. "He would come and then go, disappear for a while, and then he'd come back again if we needed a bandmaster. But I never got to the reason as to why he left and come back, and left and come back." Richard Sherlock would eventually offer to take over permanently, and was elected bandmaster in May 1995.[10] "I sort of stepped in and said, 'Well, it'd be nice to follow in my grandfather's footsteps and take a band.' [But] I'd not had any training on how to conduct or anything like that. I'm self-taught," says Richard. "Finding more brass players, I turned it back into a traditional brass band, which from some points of view is probably easier to manage than wind instruments."

During this time, Heathfield Parish Church found itself without a regular organist so the Vicar, Barry Jackson, asked Sarah Leeves if she could provide

Heathfield Silver Brass Quartet, 1995.
(L–R) Sarah Leeves, Cheryl Goodsell, Georgia Brown, Louise Baldwin.

music for the family service. As a result, Sarah and some school-friends – bandmembers Louise Baldwin, Georgia Brown and Cheryl Goodsell – put together a dedicated quartet. "We used to go out and play if someone asked for a small ensemble," recalls Sarah. "Barry Jackson used to give me the hymns to arrange every week, and then we'd go in and we'd play for the service. It was good to help people out and we used to just have such a giggle, the four of us girls together. It was always hilarious!"

Word of the talented quartet quickly spread and in 1997 it was invited to play at a *Fireman Sam* book launch in London. "It was a big parade for the turning-on of the lights on Regent Street, the usual London affair, lots of current celebrities and things," says Sarah. "We hadn't practised it and we hadn't really arranged it, I wrote the music out on the train. We got to London, got ferried to the Grosvenor Hotel, got done up in all these firemen's uniforms (which was very surreal and really funny to a load of teenage girls) and we had to play on the back of an old-style fire engine. I'd just got my brand new euphonium at the time and I was clinging onto it for dear life 'cause this thing was whizzing up the road, and it got scratched to pieces by the buttons on my uniform. But we had a great time. We got to the other end and there was this big champagne reception. Suddenly, we're all there with our instruments, dressed like firemen, and [pop musician and actor] Ross Kemp was there and [Italian jockey] Frankie Dettori, he was nice and he came over and said hello. Louise, who was quite giggly at the time having had quite a few glasses of champagne, dropped her champagne flute on his feet!"

Eastbourne Bandstand, September 1995.
Photograph supplied by Mostyn Cornford.

By the mid-1990s, Heathfield Band was working hard to boost its income. One new engagement, in July 1995, was Sedlescombe Flower Show and Country Fayre, at which it would prove extremely popular. However, when the Band returned the following year, it found itself relegated to the rear of the parade: "I understand some members of the Band were a bit upset about being asked to bung up the rear of the procession rather than lead it," writes the organiser, Sylvia Cook. "The aged horse, which usually takes our Flower Princess and her attendants to the field, died a week or so ago, and the horse which we used was a very unknown quantity for such a job. One year a horse bolted with unhappy effect and I think the ring master of the procession wanted to play absolutely safe. Please forgive us then if we appeared to treat you with less courtesy than we should."[11]

Other notable ventures included a joint gig with Crowborough Town Band to commemorate the fiftieth anniversary of VJ Day, and a birthday party for friend of the Band (and compere of its annual Christmas Concerts) George Saunders, for which it performed an hour of non-stop bonfire marches! There was also a Christmas bazaar in the bandroom, and an appearance at the *Tour de Heathfield* (a local cycle race). In addition, good money would be made from marching at Sussex Bonfires. "I absolutely thoroughly enjoyed marching, specially through bonfire season and Remembrance Parades," recalls Jeff Collins. "I remember, we were booked to play at Rotherfield Bonfire and we'd put our instrument cases and tune up at the village hall. They put a pipe band on the other side of the partition in this hall and you're having a competition as to who could tune up the loudest. It was absolutely horrendous by the time we were ready to go outside on the march!"

In 1996, the Band approached Horam-based business Merrydown Cider in search of sponsorship for its forthcoming trip to Wiesbaden.[12] The chairman of Merrydown suggested a possible association, such as *The Merrydown Heathfield Silver Band* or *The Two Dogs Heathfield Silver Band*, but there was cautiousness from both parties: Merrydown rightly expected a return on their investment and the Band was reluctant to associate itself with alcoholic lemonade ("alcopops" being extremely popular with youngsters at the time).[13] Discussions would continue for several months but the association ultimately did not go ahead.

From the moment the UK's National Lottery was launched the committee had been thinking in terms of grander fundraising projects and in 1996 it applied for a Lottery grant, with the hope of purchasing new instruments for the Band. During this process, the constitution would have to be updated to better represent its charitable aims and ethos. The Band was also required to raise 10% of the total applied for, and therefore resolved to take on as many engagements as possible.

The application, put together by Jennifer Leeves and chairman Graham Farley, gives a fascinating insight into the makeup of Heathfield Band at the time: "Over the past three to four years, the Band has expanded and currently has around 30 regular playing members – nine between the age of twelve to eighteen years. Of these, five are members of the East Sussex County Youth Brass Band, three are also members of the East Sussex Wind Orchestra, and one is a member of the National Youth Wind Orchestra of Great Britain. Each musician started their tuition with Heathfield Silver Band."[14]

Heathfield Agricultural Show, 1998.

(Back Row, L–R) Mostyn Cornford, Graham Farley, Jeff Collins, Cedric "Sid" Forward, Mike Smith, Paul Holmwood, Richard Ayres.
(Third Row, L–R) Fred Richardson, Vicky Lasham, Adam Milward, Sarah Leeves.
(Second Row, L–R) Richard Sherlock, Frankie Lulham, Cheryl Goodsell, Ted Lee, Anna Farley.
(Front Row, L–R) Alan Jones, Sara Collins, Danielle Lulham, Alison, Kirsty, Abigail Lasham, Tim Jones, Georgia Brown.

Photograph supplied by Frankie Lulham.

The timing of the application was perfect, as the Band had recently been approached to appear in a television commercial for Camelot, the company which runs the National Lottery.[15] The advert was filmed on Eastbourne Bandstand, over two evenings in the Autumn of 1996. "It was quite a coup for us and was a big moment for a local band," reports Graham Farley. "I think they chose us because we have bright uniforms and, as we have performed on the bandstand before, they knew we played well."[16] Although the Band can barely be glimpsed in the final broadcast commercial, the gig paid exceedingly well, contributing £1600 to its bank account (roughly £3,000 today).[17]

News of the successful Lottery application arrived in the Autumn of 1997, and would be announced by the Band in a press release in late October.

"Heathfield Silver Band has long been a centre of local musical life, and thanks to a grant from the Arts Council of England's National Lottery Fund, there is a bright future ahead for both young and experienced players. The award of £42,750 [about £79,500 today] will enable the purchase of a new set of brass instruments and will allow those currently in use by the senior band to be transferred to the work of the training group."[18] In March 1998 the Band held a concert at All Saints Church in Old Heathfield, to showcase its new instruments to the public for the first time.[19]

Although the Band experienced many high points during the Nineties, there would inevitably be some sad occasions, too. 1996 was to prove a particularly bad year, with the deaths of two members who were arguably part of its very foundation. The first loss, in March, was Dennis Guile, who had been secretary, publicist, manager and baritone player with the Band for over thirty years.[20] In August, it was dealt a second blow with the passing of trombonist Bob Lee, whose cheerful, optimistic outlook would be sorely missed by bandmembers and the general public alike.[21] In September 1997, the Band found itself performing hymns in the High Street in memory of Princess Diana, who had died in a tragic motor accident just days earlier.[22]

As the Band looked forward to the new millennium, the outlook remained hopeful. True, it had recently lost two of its veteran members, and six of its brightest young players to university, but there was something eternal about its very soul. "It didn't seem to change at all," recalls Jeff Collins. "It was a typical country band, really, the only form of entertainment in the area. You had the good old die-hards of Ted [Lee] and Mostyn [Cornford] and the others who were the glue that held the Band together. It tended to be half a dozen families, you'd have several people from the same family." This traditional yet modern, closely-bonded and family-orientated institution had enjoyed more than a touch of serendipity during the Nineties, and its bold experimentation and reinvention was to ensure that, despite the occasional ups and down, it would survive intact for the benefit of future generations.

---

[1] Minutes, 21st January 1992

[2] Accounts, 1991

[3] Accounts, 1992

[4] e.g. Minutes, 6th December 1993; 11th July 1994

[5] Minutes, 11th June 1993; 8th August 1994; 8th March 1995

[6] Minutes, 6th December 1993

[7] ibid

[8] Minutes, 24th January 1995

[9] Minutes, 8th March 1995

[10] Minutes, 10th May 1995

[11] Correspondence, Sylvia Cook to Band Secretary, 29th July 1996

[12] Correspondence, C.J.R. Purdey to Band Secretary, 21st May 1996

[13] Minutes, 7th August 1996, 21st October 1999 & 25th November 1996

[14] Lottery Application, June 1997

[15] Sussex Express, ca.18th October 1996

[16] ibid

[17] Accounts, 1996

[18] Minutes, 8th September 1997; Press Release, 28th October 1997

[19] Sussex Express, 19th December 1997

[20] Minutes, 24th March 1996

[21] Minutes, 23rd August 1996

[22] Minutes, 8th September 1997

MEMBERS of NOTE...

Fred Richardson

cornet & soprano cornet,

SCABA long service award.

ca.1930s+, 1986–2005.

Fred Richardson began his long brass banding career in 1926, aged just thirteen, learning to play solo and soprano cornet with Mayfield Band. However, when the son of bandmaster Tom Watts began playing, Fred and other youngsters felt that they were being somewhat sidelined. Before long, he would be encouraged to defect to Heathfield Band, under bandmaster Bert Wise.

Fred loved making music and the advent of the Second World War would not stop him from playing; whilst serving his country, he would perform across Europe, in France, Belgium, Holland and Germany. After the war, he was to move back and forth between Mayfield and Heathfield bands, but would finally settle at the latter in 1986.[1]

During his time with the Band, Fred was to encourage and mentor countless new players. "Dear old Fred invited us along, probably about 1990," recalls former musical director, Frankie Lulham. "I met him shortly after his wife had died. He told me about his band he played in and encouraged us to go along to the bandroom one Tuesday evening. If it wasn't for him, I would never have played in a brass band, let alone conduct one." Danielle Budden (née Lulham) adds: "The amazing Fred introduced us to HSB and used to drive us to Band every week. [He was one of] the unsung heroes of the banding community." Frankie continues: "He was amazing, a great friend and a true brass bander. The stories he told of banding in the war..."

At the Band's Easter Concert in 2003, Fred would be presented with a SCABA award for his long service to the brass banding movement. By December, he was stuck at home awaiting a hip operation, but would diligently continue to practice his instrument. "[He] has no intention of relinquishing his lovely red jacket yet," said Frankie Lulham at the time.[2] To cheer him up, the Band was to turn up outside his home to play him some Christmas carols. "I went inside and found him smiling all over his face! He was so pleased," reported Frankie afterwards.[3]

Unfortunately, Fred was not able to return to the Band as a musician, but he would be an honoured guest at the grand bandroom re-opening in September 2005. He would sadly pass away soon afterwards, but the Band was to perform at his memorial service. He is remembered in the *Fred Richardson Cup*, which is awarded to the most improved young player each year.

---

[1] Presentation Notes, Frankie Lulham, 26th April 2003

[2] Press Release, Frankie Lulham, 23rd April 2004

[3] MD Report, Frankie Lulham, 16th December 2003

Interlude Fame and Glory: Celebrity Encounters

Frequent public appearances will inevitably lead any community band to mingle with the stars from time to time and Heathfield Band has met its fair share of celebrities, and even royalty, over the years. It appeared in the fine company of "Favourite Southern Soprano" Madame Edith Welling at Framfield Flower Show in 1905, "whiled away the tedium" as crowds waited to see well-known Sussex cricketers Maurice Tate, "Tich" Cornford and Bowley at a community dance in 1925, and crossed paths with Olympic athletes Herbert Bignall and Stan Tomlin, and Sussex cross-country champion E.W. Bourne, at the Heathfield Hospital Sports Carnival in 1929.[1] At Christmas 1939, at a variety show for the British Red Cross Soldiers' Comforts Fund, it rubbed shoulders with contemporary radio stars Al & Bob Harvey, Big Bill Campbell, and Albert Richardson the Singing Sexton.[2] And, although the Band would have to wait many decades to meet forces sweetheart Dame Vera Lynn, both would eventually appear on the same billing at the Streat and Westmeston Summer Fête in 2005. However, those meetings were all brief and somewhat coincidental. This chapter focuses on some of the Band's more memorable celebrity encounters.

Jimmy Edwards

For almost three decades from the mid 1950s, the Band made annual appearances at Fletching Bonfire Parade. Here, it would be accompanied by resident comedian and experienced brass bander Jimmy Edwards and his brother Alan, who had moved to Fletching to run a farm together.

Jimmy was best known for his comedy roles in *Take It From Here* on BBC Radio and *Whack-o!* on BBC Television, but he was equally well-loved on the silver screen.[3] His involvement with the Band was simply a natural expression of his larger-than-life personality. "It was just accepted that they were there, they did it every year," recalls Peter Cornford. "As we went past his farm, Jimmy used to come out in this very heavy, dark camel-coloured coat and out would come his euphonium and his trombone and they would come into the Band. He was just this really big man, wasn't he? With The Whiskers!" The trademark handlebar moustache had, in fact, been grown to conceal scars obtained when Jimmy's Dakota aircraft was shot down at Arnhem during World War Two.[4]

"He was a nightmare," remembers Sue Sutton. "He used to walk everywhere, a weird bloke. His brother was different altogether, really nice." Peter adds: "He didn't care where he stood in the Band, the fact that he'd got a trombone, he just went in the Band. One year I marched behind him – I must've been perhaps eleven or twelve – and the Band stopped and I careered into him. He turned around and said, 'Who was that?!' " Ken Russell recalls: "When we used to go bonfire-ing in Fletching, Jimmy Edwards always said to us, when we'd finished the first half everybody go in a certain pub and he'd treat us to a drink. Well, of course, we all went in this pub and that bugger went out another one!"

Roger Daltrey

A rather more generous local celebrity is rock legend Roger Daltrey, who runs *Lakedown Trout Fishery* from his 400-acre estate in Burwash, just four miles from Heathfield. The Band encountered the lead singer of *The Who* whilst out carolling one Christmas. "We were playing at *The Kicking Donkey* in Burwash," recalls Wendy Holloway. "I was about twelve but, as usual, I was doing the collecting, as I looked a lot younger than I was. The landlord appeared and said that Roger Daltrey was in a back room asking who was playing, whether we were collecting and would someone go and speak to him. I was rugby-tackled by various members of the Band as they tried to prise the collecting box from my hands to take through to Roger. I hung on and curled around it, refusing to relinquish it. My argument was that I had to constantly ask people for money, which is not much fun, and I was going to see him. I won and went through to where Roger was, sat and had a chat with him for a while, and I remember he put a £10 note in the box – a lot of money in the early 1970s [indeed – roughly £130 today]!"

For more than a decade, Roger has been an ambassador for local charity Wealden Works! (formerly Heathfield Works!), a programme which aims to help young people in isolated rural communities to find vocational training, apprenticeships and work placements.[5] In 2013, the Band donated £250 to the charity, from the proceeds of its anniversary celebrations, and treasurer Mostyn Cornford was fortunate enough to be photographed with Roger and ice-skating legend Jayne Torvill (another of the charity's ambassadors) as he handed over the cheque.[6]

Keane

The Band would also have other encounters with the world of pop music. In May 2012 it appeared in a music video for the internationally-renowned band Keane, which was filmed in their Sussex hometown Bexhill-on-Sea. "There's a café down there called *Sovereign Light Café* and that was the title of their new single," recalls Keith Pursglove. "They were making a promotional video and they wanted a lot of traditional things within that, and one of the things they wanted was a brass band, one that marched. Our name was put forward and they rang up and we said, 'Yeah!' We managed to get a band together and we all went down and were part of it. It seemed odd, seeing the video on the telly and the Band being in it!"

Sussex Express reports: "Sixteen members of the Heathfield Band responded at short notice and the sun came out on the seafront as they were filmed marching with Tom, Keane's lead singer, leading them towards the café."[7] Following the shoot, Keane would place a full-page notice of thanks in the Observer. "This is a place we used to go as kids, and the song talks about a lot of local spots we remember from growing up around here," says the band. "We wanted to say a big thank you to all the people who generously gave up their time to come and be in the video with us, and to the people of Bexhill for the very warm welcome."[8] The video can be found on YouTube, and eagle-eyed viewers may even spot a cameo by veteran Heathfield Band horn player Ted Lee, who is seated outside the café.[9]

Cyril Fletcher

From the late 1970s and throughout the Eighties, the Band made annual appearances at the Heathfield Talking Newspaper Fête, to help raise funds for the charity for the visually-impaired. The fête was regularly opened by local celebrity and national treasure Cyril Fletcher, who was well-known for his comedic appearances on television and radio and who had a regular spot on the BBC television show *That's Life*. "When he arrived to be greeted and escorted down to open the garden party the Band always struck up with the opening bars of his radio show theme, Julius Fucik's *Entry of the Gladiators*," says Peter Cornford. "I recall Cyril a couple of times taking the baton from [bandmaster] Tom Kelly's hand and continuing to conduct the Band while it played the piece. It was not an easy piece to play – at the far edge of the Band's capability – and so we used to have to rehearse it for a few weeks each year before attempting it at the event." At one such practice, bandmaster David Threlfall thought it would be helpful to rehearse the piece at a slower-than-usual tempo. However, unused to this tempo, horn player Ted Lee would somehow get ahead of everyone else and finish the piece early. When David paused and looked over, questioningly, Ted drily announced, "I've won!"[10] For the fête in 1982, Cyril Fletcher would instead conduct the more straightforward *Floral Dance…*[11]

David Dimbleby

A real coup would come in 2005, when the Band secured television journalist and political commentator David Dimbleby for the grand reopening of its bandroom. Frankie Lulham, musical director at the time, recalls how this came about: "I was teaching David's little boy Fred, and I was teaching David piano for a little while. It stopped the day of 9/11. I was there teaching him

i) **Cyril Fletcher at the Talking News Fête, September 1989.**

ii) **Jayne Torvill, Mostyn Cornford and Roger Daltrey at a Heathfield Works! presentation, December 2013.** *Photograph supplied by Mostyn Cornford.*

iii) **David Dimbleby with Mostyn Cornford and Frankie Lulham at the bandroom re-opening, September 2005.** *Photograph supplied by Kent & Sussex Courier.*

iv) **Gordon Ramsay with members of HSB in Brighton, July 2007.** *Photograph supplied by Danielle Budden.*

v) **Members of HSB meet Keane in Bexhill, May 2012.**

that day and we didn't have any more after that, I [just] taught his son." It is through this connection that the Band performed at garden parties at the Dimbleby residence near Polegate in Sussex. In 2005 Frankie asked David to open the newly-refurbished bandroom and, to the Band's delight, he promptly agreed: "I would love to do that on Sept 3, 10–12 (about). Will the Band play?"

The reopening was a great success. "David Dimbleby [...] spoke of his delight that a country band was doing well, to the crowd packed well into the hall," reports the Sussex Express. "Dimbleby told us that he only really knew two bands: The Black Dyke Mills Band and Heathfield Silver Band. Heathfield's conductor told us that Heathfield owned its own bandroom, whereas Black Dyke Mills did not!"[12] In her regular Parish Pump column, Frankie adds: "[David] certainly has quite a fan club in our Band and spent an hour chatting with everyone, signing the odd autograph or two. He even had a go at playing Danielle's flugelhorn, much to everyone's amusement."[13]

Gordon Ramsay

In July 2007 the Band encountered quite a different celebrity – television chef Gordon Ramsay – after the makers of Channel Four programme *Hell's Kitchen* asked whether it might be available for a gig at short notice: "We are looking for a small band, or even just a few key players from a band, to take part in some filming next Friday lunch time in Brighton. [...] It's a very exciting shoot involving a major celebrity and so we would love you to be involved."[14]

A band of ten players was rapidly mobilised and, as the venue was a seafood restaurant, the repertoire was given a seaside theme. "Gordon Ramsay was charm personified," recalls Frankie Lulham. "We were approached as a marching band to play up and down the streets of Old Town, Brighton, outside a café that he was in the process of 'improving.' " Frankie's daughter Danielle adds: "I remember Gordon telling the boys they were 'too cool for school!' " Gordon would even insist that he be allowed to play the bass drum, though the programme's four million viewers were regrettably never able to see the spectacle as the footage was cut from the final edit.

Queen Elizabeth II

By far the most famous person to whom the Band can claim a link must surely be Her Majesty, Queen Elizabeth II. In September 2004, it played at a wedding reception in Waldron and one of the bride's parents, Rosemary Mays-Smith, was to nominate Frankie Lulham to attend a garden party at Buckingham Palace, to be held in honour of those who had made a significant contribution to their organisation or charity. "I was absolutely astonished," remembers Frankie. "I really felt that other people in the Band deserved to go just as much as me. It was exciting but I did feel very humble about it. I was allowed to choose when I would like to go and the 11th July was very auspicious, it leaped out at me because that was my mum's birthday (mum had died when I was 18). This is 2006 and my dad, who I absolutely adored, had taken a turn for the worse that year. I said, 'Dad, I'm going to see the Queen, I've been *commanded* to go to Buckingham Palace!' There were tears in his eyes and he was made up with it. He was so terribly proud of me."

Frankie describes her experience in Sussex Express: "I had a wonderful time at Buckingham Palace. It was very exciting getting in the taxi, especially when my husband said to the driver, 'Take us to the Palace!' Rumour has it there were 8,000 people there, so, as I'm only five feet and half an inch tall, I didn't manage to get to the front to actually speak to Her Majesty. Prince Philip, Prince Charles and Camilla, Duchess of Cornwall, were there, along with Prince and Princess Michael of Kent. [...] There were two military bands playing, one at each end of the lawn: The Royal Engineers and The Welsh Guards. I spoke to the conductor of The Royal Engineers. Not sure he had actually heard of the Heathfield Silver Band... but he has now!"[15]

---

[1] Sussex Express, 19th August 1905, 24th July 1925 & 6th September 1929

[2] Sussex Express, 29th December 1939

[3] Sport & Country, 22nd June 1955

[4] Lee Flying Association, 2021. https://jimmyedwards.wordpress.com/2018/11/23/via-lee-flying-association/

[5] Wealden Works. 2021. *Home*. [online] Available at:

[6] Sussex Express, 13th December 2013

[7] Sussex Express, 18th May 2012

[8] The Observer, 25th May 2012

[9] Youtube.com, 2012. *Keane - Sovereign Light Café (Official Video)*. [online] Available at: <www.youtube.com/watch?v=bH13eUiDhmo>

[10] Cornford, P., 1981. Personal Archive and Interviews

[11] Cutting, source unknown, 11th September 1982

[12] Sussex Express, 9th September 2005

[13] Sussex Express, 16th September 2005

[14] Correspondence, Claire Lloyd-Evans to Band Secretary, 27th June 2007

[15] Sussex Express, 21st July 2006

Story *The Silver Band*

It's a warm sunny Saturday afternoon in June. Marquees and stalls have been erected and the centre of the field roped off to form an arena.

People are scurrying about making last minute preparations because today is the day of the Annual Village Fête and Flower Show. It has taken weeks of planning and argument to reach this stage.

Major Somebody or Other has given his kind permission for it to be held in his field and his Lady will graciously open it at two o'clock.

One of the several attractions on offer is to be "Music throughout the afternoon by the Silver Band."

During the "smoke-break" at the previous Tuesday' s Band Practice Dennis Secretary had stressed the need for the players to get to the field by 1-45pm to be all ready for a 2-0pm start.

In spite of the fact that the job had been listed on the Engagement Board since early February and also had been displayed in large letters on the black-board in front of them for the last month it still came as a surprise to certain band-persons.

"Oh we are not out on Saturday are we?" said one.

"I don't think I can make it" muttered another.

Dennis who was only Secretary because he could do joined-up writing thought, "I've heard this all before."

Some discussion took place regarding the possibility of borrowing from another band. This was thought to be most unlikely at such short notice and anyway it was the peak of the fête season so the majority of the local bands would have their own engagements.

The talk then turned to the best way to travel to the job. Some suggested one way, some another, some just looked blank because anywhere outside a three mile radius of the bandroom was unknown territory.

A buzz of cross-conversation then broke out.

"Can you give me a lift Mostyn?"

"I'll meet you here at a quarter past one Laurie."

By the time the bandroom had filled with smoke everyone had more or less made their arrangements for Saturday.

The Secretary gets to the fête at 1-30pm. He dare not be late himself after exhorting the others to be sharp on time.

Early attendance pays off because, not unusually, the twenty chairs promised by the Fête Organiser are nowhere to be seen.

Enquiries lead him to Mrs. Smith.

"I'm just Cake Stall dear. Try Mrs. Jones."

Mrs. Jones turns out to be Tombola. She points him in the general direction of a Mr. Smith.

Mr. Smith is Entrance Gate but "will see what he can do."

It is now twenty minutes to two o'clock and Laurie Bass roars up in his Reliant Robin.

"Bob's on the way" he calls.

Bob Trombone has to push the slide of his instrument in and out all the afternoon so he needs to fortify himself before-hand with a jar or two of the amber nectar.

Just after a quarter to two it begins to look as if the music for the afternoon will be given by the "Silver Sextet." Then the figure of Ted Solo Tenor and Librarian can be seen staggering across the field a heavy case in each hand. One is packed with metal music stands, the other contains all the music for the afternoon.

He has also brought two more players.

Meanwhile the chairs have been found and have been set out in two horse-shoes, one behind the other. They need to be watched now to prevent old ladies pinching them for their own use.

Gradually the stragglers start to arrive. Janet Principal Cornet who can read her way through fiendish patterns of quavers and semi-quavers has enormous difficulty with sign-posts. Today, her unbroken record of being late remains intact. Mind you she did try hard to make it on time by slinging her Ford Cortina round winding country lanes - mostly in the wrong direction.

Two o'clock has come and gone and Ted is busy setting up the music stands and folders. He tries not to get in the way of the players who are standing about chatting. At any minute now one might open his or her instrument case.

Uniform is standard-red jackets, black trousers or skirts, white shirts, bow ties and black socks or tights with black shoes. However, some seek sartorial individuality by appearing with grey pullovers, green socks or, horrors, brown shoes. Some sport an ordinary tie instead of a bow. Thus the "village band look" is preserved and they are very seldom mistaken for "Black Dyke Mills."

By now the Major's Lady has declared the Fête well and truly open. The Tannoy crackles into life and a hopeful voice announces that the Silver Band will now provide some music.

This falls on deaf ears as the players are now busily occupied in cluttering up the space in front of the Band with their instrument cases. Some are clearing the spit out and tentatively trying a few notes.

Finally everyone is seated and waiting for Taff Conductor to announce the first item. A slight breeze Springs up and plaintive cries of "Have you got any pegs Ted" are heard.

Ted patiently hands round clothes pegs to people who have had their seat arranged for them, their music stand erected, their stand fall hung and their music folder placed in front of them. Don't think for a minute they have been idle though. They have had to arrange their cans of lager carefully under their chair. "What time do we finish?" asks Sue Front Cornet, "only I have got to cut Ben's sandwiches when I get home."

Much to the Band's amazement Taff says:

"Put up Slaidburn." An original start!

"All ready?" he enquires raising his baton.

"Just a minute" cries Bob First Trombone. "What are we playing?"

He has been deep in conversation with some people standing behind his seat. No matter where he goes somebody knows him or knowing them he will call out:

"Wotcher you old sod. I thought you were dead."

Taff tries again. Up goes his stick. The band takes a deep breath, ready, for when it comes down to launch themselves into the first march. At that precise second the Tannoy decides to say a few words. Taff continues to hold up the baton while trying to hear what's being said thus bringing the Band to bursting point.

At long last the opening notes are heard and Taff is happy to note that all the players are playing the same piece of music; unlike the celebrated occasion when, at an Armistice Parade, the front of the Band played 'Colonel Bogey' while the cornets at the rear just as enthusiastically gave their rendering of 'Sussex by the Sea.'

After giving his all in this item some bright spark gasps:

"What time is tea break?"

"We will play until three o'clock" replies Taff. "Then it's dancing in the arena so we will have a twenty minute break." A few people gather round as the Band goes through its repertoire of marches, waltzes and novelty pieces.

Taff winces with pain at the odd wrong note and Janet gets away with some embellishments that the composer had not seen fit to include in his work.

The cornets endeavour to maintain the melody against the blasting accompaniment.

Janet, Charlie and Sue Front Cornets with Gregory Part Time Cornet are supported in this by Fred, Laurie and Peter Back Row Cornets. Mostyn Bass Drum gives a good wallop on the first beat of each bar. Now and then he has a mad moment and gives an almighty crash on the cymbal to ensure that nobody dozes off. His bad back is giving him gyp again but he just grins and keeps whacking away.

A lively number draws quite a crowd, some even recognising the tune. When it reaches a crescendo finish a few go as far as to clap. Perhaps their hands were cold.

The applause inspires the musicians. With an appreciative audience waiting for more it's the right moment to put the instruments down, have the odd conversation, light up a fag, have a swig of beer or shuffle through the music folders until the onlookers drift away. Giving the audience what they want is not part of the deal.

During this interlude Taff has been turning over the contents of his folder.

He comes to the conclusion that perhaps the Band wouldn't be too exhausted if they played one more short piece before the tea-break.

Thoughts of tea galvanises the Band into action. It takes them no longer than five minutes to find their parts. That is except for the Basses.

"We haven't got it Ted" they chorus.

Long suffering, Ted gets up and finds it for them. This happens all the time. Sorting their folders into large sheets at the back and small at the front to halve the searching time has been suggested to them many times but always falls on deaf ears.

The last offering before tea is to be 'Spanish Eyes.'

"I can't get right up there" moans Sue and doesn't.

The band had played this particular piece many times and still had hopes of getting it right the next time. Should this ever happen it will probably be put back into the library and forgotten.

Tea time. "Be back by twenty past three" Taff calls to the fast disappearing backs of the musicians.

At the tea tent refreshments for twenty are set aside.

Plates of sandwiches, cakes and cups of tea are put away in no time at all by the famished throng who have had nothing to eat for all of two hours. Bob, who of course knows the tea lady, wanders back to the counter for a refill.

When all the plates and cups have been emptied the players disperse. Some look round the stalls seeking a bargain, others try their luck on the Tombola and one or two have reserved a minute or two to talk to their wives. These band widows have accompanied their husbands to six fêtes already this year and the novelty is wearing off, but they are stuck with it until the Band packs up at five o'clock.

In the arena there are buxom ladies in black leotards. They are from the local "Keep Fit Club" and are prancing about in time to canned music. Some members of the Band show great interest in this keep fit lark. Puffing away on their cigarettes they closely follow every movement, while making uncalled for comments about the mounds of wobbling flesh inside some of the leotards.

At 3-20pm half a dozen of our heroes have managed to find their way back to their seats ready for the second half.

Scattered across the field red jackets can be observed aimlessly wandering about as if they had all the time in the world. In order to call in these stragglers Mostyn gives the drum a few hearty whacks. This is largely ignored, although Sue hobbles in saying she doesn't know what to do with her bad leg and anyway her lips gone. She doesn't say where to.

Fred Back Cornet and oldest member of the Band reluctantly tears himself away from an "old flame" of fifty years ago he has met again during the break.

By three-thirty only Gregory Part Time Cornet is still missing.

He has mastered 3/4 and 4/4 time but the facts of British Summer Time eludes him. He finally remembers why he is wearing his red jacket and his little face lights up as he notices that the Band has re-assembled. Janet places the plants she has bought under her chair and sits eating her ice-lolly.

Bob is still reminiscing with another old acquaintance he has run across. Arthur Euphonium is rolling a cigarette and telling Dennis how he tracked down a pint or two during the interval. He has a nose for watering holes equally as good as Bob's. Taff is studying his music wondering what to treat the punters to next.

Ken Soprano Cornet calls out "What about doing 'Bandology?' "

"Have we got it with us Ted?" says Taff.

"It's in the case. I'll give it out" replies Ted.

"I know it's here somewhere" Ted mutters, throwing folders in all directions.

"I have been meaning to sort it out."

By 3-45pm all the players have the right piece of music securely pegged up in front of them and after more spit clearing are ready to go.

'Bandology' goes with a swing. George Side Drum gives it some welly. Anna Second Tenor bashes in the off-beats with gusto all the while fighting off a persistent wasp which seems intent on stinging her. A music lover perhaps!

Next comes a chance for the trombones to have a minute or two of glory. They will stand up and dazzle the crowd with their rendering of 'Edelweiss.'

The great moment arrives. Bob gets on his feet but Mike Second Trombone remains firmly fixed to his seat. Ah well that's show business.

The afternoon is now well advanced and it will soon be time for the Grand Draw at four-thirty.

The Tannoy, with the odd screech thrown in, is wittering on that it is the last chance to buy tickets.

Taff riffles through his music. After much deliberation he announces,

"We'll finish with 'Sussex by the Sea.' " This with a fine geographical disregard of the fact that the Band is in Kent.

"Twice through" queries Bob.

"Once" says Taff conscious of the old adage about leaving the listeners wanting more.

Within a second of the last note instruments are being repacked and stands are coming down.

"Don't forget it's 10-30am tomorrow morning for the Church Parade" pleads Dennis.

"Ooh I can't march" cries Sue. "Not with my leg."

Mostyn Bass Drum and Treasurer goes off to collect the fee for the afternoon's work.

When he returns for his drum all that remains of the Band's visit is a few empty lager cans, a large number of cigarette butts and of course Niall Flugel's coat.

All the characters and events depicted in the fore-going are, of course, fictitious. There couldn't be a band like that, could there?

by Dennis H. Guile, August 1990

With grateful thanks to Maureen Guile who supplied the text.

MEMBERS *of* NOTE...

Eric "Animal" Kemp
cornet & drums,
committee member,
2013–20.

Eric was only a member of the Band for about seven years, but he is nevertheless worthy of mention for the significant contribution he would make during that time. He would start out in the cornet section, but was soon to became the "face" of Heathfield Band as its enthusiastic and often amusing drummer, providing a steady and reliable rhythm and seizing every opportunity to bring added entertainment to gigs, wearing themed paraphernalia or encouraging comic turns on stage. As part of the committee, he was to prioritise the well-being of every playing member and would fight passionately to safeguard the Band's legal and moral obligations.

Eric would originally make contact with the Band in the capacity of entertainments organiser for Le Marché. "I had a chat with the MD at the time, Richard Sherlock, about how possible it would be to have all upbeat, popular music at the next Le Marché," explains Eric. "I'm not sure it went down particularly well, but I later had a call from [the] Band secretary, [and] she found out that I had played cornet in Lingfield Silver Band many years ago (I started learning at age seven but guitars became more interesting by the time I left school)! The conversation went along the lines of, 'Join the Band, then you can influence the choice of music from the inside.' "

"So, early 2013 saw me getting my lip back after over forty years! I played 3rd cornet but the young man on the drum kit, Steven Anderson, wasn't always able to attend and so I soon found myself filling in on the drum kit when he was not there." Before long, Steven would leave the Band to pursue his career and Eric was to take control of the rhythm section, hanging up his cornet once more. "I had always been able to play but I certainly hadn't seen drum music in my life so, to coin a phrase, the Band got what it got," he says! "I must have been a bit lively at times, as the then chairman, Richard Leeves, soon related me to Animal from *The Muppet Show*. Well, that stuck like glue and I still get called Animal to this day."

Eric was soon to find himself in great demand, regularly assisting the Mayfield and Warbleton bands. "It got a bit busy some weekends, I can tell you," he says, "sometimes playing for two different bands on the same day!" Away from the brass banding scene, he also plays bass guitar and sings in a choir, enjoys walking and, as a lifelong train enthusiast, has built himself an impressive model railway.

Unfortunately, in 2020 Eric marched away to pastures new.

2000s Music for a new Millennium

Heathfield Silver Band at Christmas, December 2002.
Photograph supplied by Kent & Sussex Courier.

As the Band entered a bright new millennium, the present stood in stark contrast with the past. During this decade, it would welcome its first female conductor, embark upon a major project to enlarge the bandroom, make a return to the contesting scene, and embrace publicity like never before. And, even as new approaches to recruitment and teaching were being developed, several veteran members would be presented with long-service awards. Heathfield Band was about to experience a new golden age.

Richard Sherlock had led the Band for several years, but an increasingly busy work schedule meant he was now struggling to do the bandmaster role justice. He therefore stepped down from the position following the Band's busy Summer 2000 season, which included a joint concert with Heathfield Choral Society, a concert at Bexhill's De La Warr Pavilion, a Songs of Praise service at Cross-in-Hand, a private wedding reception, and its first excursion to Devon, performing with Sidmouth Town Band at Connaught Gardens. Advertisements for a new conductor were to prove unfruitful, so the Band's deputy conductor Jeff Collins would assume the role, allowing Richard to return to euphonium.

Jeff inherited a highly successful Band, with more than thirty playing members and a busy engagement schedule. Regular gigs included the Cuckoo Fair, Le Marché, the Seven Sisters Marathon (which would eventually cease in October 2001), and the annual Christmas Concert (which took place at the Community Centre in Sheepsetting Lane in 2000, and Broad Oak Village Hall in 2001). The Band's appearance at the Heathfield Show had to be cancelled in 2001 due to extremely poor weather conditions, but it would pay a one-off visit to Heathfield's twin town Forges Les Eaux, and make a return visit to Sidmouth. There were also bonfire parades, Remembrance events, and a plethora of Summer fêtes, including one for All Saints Church in Old Heathfield, which had now evolved into a weekend-long flower festival. "The Band did a couple of slots in that," remembers Jeff. "I think we did a quintet or sextet as well." At Christmas there would be carolling in Heathfield High Street and at Lady Caffyn's annual party, alongside gigs at Heathfield House in Old Heathfield and Hawks Farm School in Hailsham.

Jeff would steer the Band for the next eighteen months. His approach as bandmaster was to combine old favourites with contemporary (and sometimes more challenging) music such as *Lord of the Dance* ("That went down an absolute storm, we thoroughly enjoyed it, and it really did motor towards the end," he says). However, Jeff would soon discover that he preferred playing his bass to waving the baton: "With conducting it didn't take long for you to lose your *embouchure* [the state of lips and facial muscles required to play a brass instrument] and it was a real struggle to get a decent tone back if you did have to play. You've got to keep playing and practising all the time." Despite his best efforts to keep players engaged, membership fell drastically by the Autumn of 2001. Jeff was also doing shift work which limited his availability, so he resigned from the position following the Christmas 2001 season.

2002 would thus begin with a conundrum. The Band had no conductor and no obvious contenders for the role, but it had already resolved to recruit someone "who will fit in but can exercise discipline."[1] Within a year, its fortunes were to completely reverse, largely due to the efforts of Frankie Lulham, who had no experience of conducting a brass band but who was nevertheless ready to accept the challenge. "I played the drums for ten years or so, absolutely loved playing the drums," she recalls. "But we were at a bit of a low point and I said, 'Well, I could have a go if you like.' Before I knew it I was the bandmaster!"

The following memo, from January 2002, offers a useful insight into the direction the Band would take under Frankie's leadership:

Where we are at the moment?

Struggling to keep the Band together.

Struggling to play a lot of our music through lack of players.

Unwilling to take on jobs for fear of not having a capable Band.

No clear goals.

No conductor.

In our favour

Plenty of good instruments.

A number of good and committed players.

An unknown number of beginners waiting to join us.

Plenty of good music.

Where we want to be one year from now

A happy, united Band.

Capable of playing a good repertoire suited to our players.

Confident of our abilities when taking on engagements.

A larger, more stable Band.

A large contingent of younger players.

A confident and happy conductor.

These objectives would be achieved by aiming to play easy pieces really well (rather than struggling with difficult music), building a repertoire suited to a smaller band, focussing on performance techniques (such as sight-reading, awareness of tone and tuning), advertising for new members, and making an effort to ensure newcomers felt welcome and supported. "There didn't seem to be a future because everybody was sort of stuck in the past, you've gotta bring it up to date,' reflects former bandmaster Frank Francis. "Frankie was absolutely phenomenal, so motivated. If it wasn't for her, probably the Band would still be in those doldrums, they might never have come out of them."

Sarah Leeves, the Band's current musical director, says: "Frankie was great for the Band, she was spot-on. Her charisma, her way of dealing with the public, the way of enthusing everybody in the bandroom and just having a good time. She had so much energy. She listened to bandmembers. It fitted perfectly with everything that was going on with the Band, with what they wanted."

The initial challenge would be to rehearse the Band properly and develop its repertoire. To encourage players, Frankie organised workshops with guest conductors and entered the Band in contests. She believed strongly in the importance of musical education. "Quite a few of them actually weren't reading the music," admits Frankie. "They were just playing from numbers and knew which valve they had to press down. I'd say, 'How loud are you supposed to be?' 'Oh, it's *p*!' 'Oh yes? So what does that mean?' 'Well… it's *p*!' It was quite interesting but quite tricky. I found that I was trying to educate them, but I think they took it well." On the rare occasions when Frankie was

Frankie Lulham prepares for her first Christmas Concert as musical director, December 2002.
Photograph supplied by Frankie Lulham.

unavailable to conduct, she would conscientiously provide her stand-in with helpful notes on style and musicality. For example, for Le Marché in 2004, the Band was conducted by Dr. Isla Sitwell (musical director of Seaford Silver Band), who would receive such helpful pointers as: *Amparito Roca* – "They LOVE to shout *olé*… Not! But I make them!"; *Ground Force* – "Encourage horns in middle section"; *Pedal Pusher* – "Watch Tom! Make him play quietly at times"; *Can Can* – "Not too fast! Doug gets scared!"; and *Sussex By The Sea* – "Once through. Don't let anyone persuade you to play it twice through… someone will forget!"[2]

Frankie would also reach out to championship musician and conductor Bob Childs for advice: "The problem I have is only one decent cornet player on solo and a very weak 1st cornet player, a jazz maniac on rep [repiano cornet] and a recent repatriate on flugel, an eighty-nine year-old on 2nd, along with one adult improver and four youngsters of nine years of age in the back row. One youngster puffs his cheeks out when he plays […], I think he is blowing rather than tonguing!"[3] Bob Childs (who, incidentally, taught Sarah Leeves at the Royal Northern College of Music) offered several suggestions, such as advising the solo and repiano cornets switch to larger, deeper mouthpieces to improve their tone and curb any blasting. "The young boy puffing his cheeks should be encouraged to 'smile' more when playing and to consciously pucker the corners of his lips in to build a stronger embouchure," writes Bob. "But the most important thing is to get the players breathing deeply in a relaxed way."[4]

Frankie's approach was evidently working. Within a few months of her appointment the Band would grow to twenty-five members. "It was a hoot, there'd be silliness all the time," says Sarah Leeves. "At bonfires we used to have such a laugh. If we were marching along and it came to a halt, the drums would carry on going! Frankie was quite a manic drummer, there'd be more notes in the wrong place than there were in the right at times but she had such a good sense of humour, you could always poke fun at her and she'd take it on the chin. She was a massive character. One time at Eastbourne Bandstand there was this grumpy old man sat in the front row, and Frankie conducted something really slowly and he kicked off. He was booing at the end of it but she just shot him down in flames, made some comment that shut him up instantly. She was über-confident with stuff like that, completely fearless. It was quite often hilarious."

One factor which contributed to the Band's rapid resurgence was a succession of high profile gigs, including appearances on television and radio. In the Summer of 2002, it was filmed at the Heathfield Agricultural Show for BBC South-East, and appeared on the main stage at Heathfield's bustling Le Marché. It also took part in the celebrations of Queen Elizabeth's Golden Jubilee, playing rousing, patriotic music outside Heathfield Fire Station.[5] In January 2004, another high-profile job presented itself, this time at London's Grosvenor House Hotel in Park Lane, for a gathering of comedians and celebrities. "One of our trombone players, Bob Mayston, landed us this rather swish engagement, playing for some very well-dressed people, amongst who were spotted [contemporary pop duo] The Cheeky Girls," explains Frankie.[6] The suitability of the gig for younger bandmembers was perhaps questionable, but a fun time would be had by all.

The Band also performed at Brighton Pavilion for the launch of *Music Works*, a government-funded Experience Corps initiative promoting volunteering among the over-fifties. The event was covered by Meridian TV and BBC Southern Counties Radio, giving the Band some of its widest exposure to date. "Music brings people together who have a shared passion for a hobby or interest. Whatever your age, it becomes irrelevant," Experience Corps chair, Baroness Sally Greengross, would proclaim.[7] In addition to ranging in age from eight to ninety years-old, the gender divide of players – sixteen men to ten women (and, crucially, a female conductor) – is also worthy of note, as it underlines the Band's steady progress towards equality.[8]

Publicity was seized at every opportunity, and one of Frankie's most successful initiatives was to begin writing weekly press releases, which would soon lead to a regular, dedicated column (dubbed *Frankie on Friday*) in the Sussex Express. "Not everybody knows about the Band and I felt that very strongly. You needed to publicise it all the time, keep it in people's minds," explains Frankie. "I used to have people come up to me all the time and say, 'I love your Parish Pump. I go straight to that bit in the paper!' " Further publicity came from local radio: for several years, beginning in December 2003, the Band would bring festive cheer to the residents of Eastbourne, Hailsham, and the surrounding areas, with its Christmas Eve performances on Sovereign Radio. The studio could only accommodate seven players, but the broadcasts were nevertheless a great success, with healthy numbers of Sussex folk listening in specially to hear the Band.

Christmas was once again a major banding event and carolling would enjoy something of a renaissance, the Band playing in Heathfield High Street and at supermarkets in neighbouring towns. It would also make appearances in Old Heathfield at the All Saints and St. Richard's Primary School Christmas Fayre, at *Emjays* (a music store in Herstmonceux), and at festive services at Kings Church in Heathfield. In addition, there was Lady Caffyn's annual Christmas party and *Light A Life* events for St. Wilfred's Hospice. In 2003, the Band even serenaded two of its players, Ted Lee and Mike Smith, at their homes, much to the surprise and delight of the poorly gentlemen.

The Band's annual Christmas Concert, now relocated to the more central Heathfield State Hall, was compered by Sussex Bonfire personality (and friend of the Band) George Saunders. Comic turns would be encouraged, too: at one concert, the principal cornet was playing a somewhat tedious and lengthy piece, and both audience and bandmembers were beginning to get fidgety. Quick as a flash, drummer Mostyn Cornford donned a hat and apron and began "decorating" the hall whilst other musicians threw bits of paper about! For the *Tartan Crackers* concert in 2004, the Band wore fancy dress. "Sarah [Leeves, principal euphonium] was dressed up in a choir boy's outfit," recalls Frankie, "Doug [Blackford, principal cornet] dressed up in a kilt, and

I had on a bright red dress that cost me a fortune, and I had a tartan scarf made." At the 2006 Christmas Concert, principal cornet Adam Kearley would perform the *Post Horn Gallop* – on a real stagecoach post horn!

Christmas Concert at State Hall, Heathfield, December 2004.

Photographs supplied by Frankie Lulham.

A small group would also go carolling for charity. "Just the one night, but we did about three or four pubs," recalled former Band president and Vicar of All Saints Church Geoff Pickering (interviewed in 2013). "Some of the choir would come, probably about a dozen, and then three or four from the Band would supply the music. [Former Band chairman] Richard Leeves would dress up as Father Christmas. At one time I gather they went round on a sort of tractor or a horse and cart." In 2005 the Band appeared at Eastbourne Rotary Club's Christmas Carol Concerts at the Congress Theatre, fulfilling a role which had previously been handled by Eastbourne Silver Band. In December 2006 it played at a party in Nutley for the Uckfield Lions, who had recently purchased waistcoats and ties for members of the training band.[9]

In the early 2000s, the Band had begun attending an annual Carols by Candlelight Service at All Saints Church in Old Heathfield. "It didn't always go down well with the choir because they drowned out any singing," remembers Geoff Pickering. "And then the music… the keys were different for the Band and the organ, so the Band would play something, then the organist would play something, and that seemed to work well. It's not everybody that likes brass bands, but I always thought, *Well, the uniform's red, it's kind of Christmassy*! And people will come because you've then got two followings: you've got the Band followers and then you've got the sort of people who would come to that service in any case. It filled the church up, and it's better to have a sing with the full church than with an empty one."

Bonfire parades would become a major industry, too, accounting for the lion's share of the Band's annual income. During Frankie's first bonfire season, in 2002, it played at Mayfield Carnival and East Hoathly Bonfire. Buoyed with confidence, the Band returned to both the following year and added Crowborough and Rotherfield to the mix. It was also head-hunted by Cliffe Bonfire Society in Lewes, for whom it had officially last appeared in 1990, and although the whole Band was not yet ready to tackle the madness that is Lewes Bonfire, a selection of stronger players would take part. The Band also made a triumphant return to Uckfield Bonfire Society's annual carol service, in which various bonfire societies parade the streets of Uckfield to Holy Cross Church to take part in a festive service of Remembrance. The event is always an eye-opener, with participants taking to the pews dressed as anything from Captain Jack (from *Pirates of the Caribbean*) to Laurel & Hardy or even an ersatz Bishop!

The Band's final Remembrance appearance at Hurst Green took place in 2001, but it would continue to support the British Legion at Burwash. Frankie's daughter Danielle played her first *Last Post & Reveille* at Burwash in 2003, albeit with a slight difference. "After I asked her to play *Last Post*, she researched its history and asked for lots of advice on its performance," recalls Frankie. "She decided to play it on the flugel horn as it has such a warm mellow tone. She played it beautifully and must have achieved her ambition, which was to make the old soldiers proud."[10] Also in 2003 (and again in 2005), the Band took to the streets of Seaford, leading a St. George's Day Parade on behalf of the Seahaven Scouts.

The Heffle Cuckoo Fair is perhaps Heathfield's oldest tradition, dating back to 1315 when a licence to run an annual fair was granted by King Edward II. It started out as a livestock and produce market, centred along the Battle Road at Cade Street and around the site where Heathfield Community College now lies.[11] The last fair of this kind was held in 1931, but the event would be reimagined and resurrected in 1987 as a craft fair with cream teas and a barn dance, by the Heathfield and Waldron Community Association. This iteration took place at the Youth Centre in the High Street, lapsing briefly in 1995 before being taken over by the Girl Guides. It is now managed by the Friends of Demelza Hospice for Children.[12] The fair is always held in April, when local tradition requires the release of a single cuckoo (nowadays a pigeon) to signal the arrival of Spring. The Band's involvement with the fair is difficult to trace, but we do know that by the 2000s it was regularly leading the parade from Heathfield High Street to the Community Centre at Sheepsetting Lane. In 2010 the event returned to Cade Street, from where it continues to enjoy the support of the town band.

Several special engagements are also worthy of mention. In August 2002 the Band played at Horsted Place Hotel, for a rendezvous between some life-long English and Canadian friends. "We played [*O Canada*] with great enthusiasm while the English people presented them with gold medals for Friendship (Commonwealth Games eat your heart out), champagne was poured (not for us) and then we played it again while they sang along," says Frankie.[13] In October, the Band would literally become part of the furniture at William Hill's Interiors, "some people sitting on armchairs, some a sofa, and others dining room chairs," recalls Frankie![14]

The Band shows off its new uniforms at Charleston Manor, August 2006.
Photograph supplied by Frankie Lulham.

In 2003 it unexpectedly landed what was to become a regular Summer fixture at Charleston Manor, the former South Downs home of renowned painter Sir Oswald Birley. "What a wonderful setting to play in, a beautiful garden and a magnificent fourteenth century old Sussex barn to have tea and cakes inside," writes Frankie. "A large audience sat and listened and seemed to be enjoying themselves and Ray Maulkin [one-time head of Lewes Academy of Music] said he was sure we couldn't be a real brass band as we played the hymns at an excellent tempo and with such sensitivity and thoughtful phrasing."[15] Suitably impressed, the organisers invited the Band to return the following year.

Perhaps the quintessential venue for any Sussex ensemble is Eastbourne Bandstand, and Heathfield Band would make a triumphant return there in July 2004. "What a great reception we got from the people who came to listen to us playing on Sunday morning," writes Frankie. "120 people paid to listen to us but there were lots more standing at the top and enjoying the entertainment for free."[16] The following year, as holidaymakers and residents basked in their deckchairs, the Band performed a *Traditional Sunday Afternoon* concert to commemorate the end of the Second World War, playing pieces such as *Arnhem*, *The Dambusters* and *Cockleshell Heroes* alongside such classics as *Highland Cathedral* (in tribute to the Band's late chairman Graham Farley) and *Oklahoma*. Frankie would even charm the audience into singing a chorus of *Oh What A Beautiful Morning*![17] The Band returned in September 2006 to deliver a *Saturday Afternoon on Broadway* concert.

A number of members were presented with SCABA long-service awards during the decade, for their unwavering support and dedication to the brass band movement. Ninety year-old Fred Richardson was the first to receive such an award, at the Band's Easter Concert in 2003.[18] Awards were also presented to Ted Lee and Ernie Sherlock at a Christmas concert later that year. Ted had joined the Band in 1952, and such was his loyalty that he missed only three engagements in fifty years![19] Ernie, whose father was the conductor of Mayfield Band, had begun playing in 1948 after completing his National Service. "He came out of the RAF, was thrust an Eb bass in his hands, and told, 'You've got to play at a contest in three weeks' time,' " says his son Richard. After a spell with Wadhurst Brass Band, Ernie transferred to Heathfield Band in the 1980s.[20] In 2004, the long-service award was presented to Cedric "Sid" Forward, whose musical career had begun at the tender age of ten playing cornet with the Salvation Army.[21]

In 2002 with membership steadily rising, one urgent and long-term concern – major upgrade works to the bandroom – was finally underway. Planning permissions were obtained and the lengthy task of fundraising could now commence (see *Room for Improvement: The Story of the Bandroom*). As a result, the number of engagements would increase significantly, and although the project brought bandmembers closer, it also caused friction at times. "The last couple of months have been extremely busy ones, and quite stressful at times, but on the whole we have all had a lot of fun playing good music and raising a magnificent amount of money for band funds," reports Frankie in January 2003.[22]

Tribalism, politics and sniping undoubtedly became more prevalent as the decade progressed. This in part reflected an underlying resistance to the Band's first female musical director and originated mainly from a few old-school members. "Some of them I don't think ever really thought that I should be there, some gave me a hard time," says Frankie. "When I became musical director nobody told me what I was supposed to do. I didn't know how a committee was supposed to be run, I just did what I thought needed to be doing. I think they thought that was wrong." Things began to unravel with the resignation of bandmembers Alan Jones and Ernie Sherlock in early 2005. In June Richard Sherlock wrote a letter of concern to the committee, questioning their professionalism and dedication, and berating the public behaviour of junior bandmembers. "I feel the Band has changed," he writes. "It is not a happy band, as it used to be, there nearly always seems to be an atmosphere."[23]

There was a disappointing attendance at the Band's 2006 AGM, hinting at a deep unrest among a contingent of players. By the end of February, Janet and Doug Blackford and the entire Sherlock family had all resigned. "Unfortunately, in brass bands you do get a certain amount of politics," explains Richard Sherlock. "I felt I wasn't being listened to [and] there was a certain amount of personality clash. I've been with brass bands ever since I started, I know how they tick. The musical director was a more classical background. I tried to make some suggestions, there were weak areas in the Band (you get people move away and you've got holes and everything else), and nothing ever happened. So I went to Mayfield, as did my father and my family." Others would quickly follow, leaving the Band in a weakened state with holes in several key positions. However, Frankie stayed optimistic: "The Band remains stable with a good corps of players," she reports in April 2006. "Having moved a few players around we have all areas covered."[24] The downside was that the repertoire would have to rely heavily on undemanding arrangements and old favourites.

The Band made a remarkably rapid recovery, in part due to the loyalty and camaraderie among its remaining members, but mainly, perhaps, due to the efforts Danielle Lulham invested in recruiting, training and promoting newcomers. To showcase the junior band, a small group – dubbed *Brill Brass* – would compete at the 2007 Ringmer Contest, and perform a special Easter Concert at St. Mary's Church in Hailsham. Meanwhile, the main Band, whilst accepting fewer engagements, continued to appear at all the major venues, including the All Saints Flower Festival, Heffle Cuckoo Fair, Le Marché, Eastbourne Bandstand, the Heathfield Show, and Charleston Manor, in addition to undertaking six bonfire marches, a St. George's Day parade, and several private parties, coffee mornings and countless community fêtes. It even made a long overdue return to Waldron Fête; so overdue, in fact, that the local press (incorrectly) proclaimed: "The Heathfield Silver Band played a starring role, appearing for the first time in the fête's history."[25] The Band also enjoyed a day trip to Brighton, filming for Gordon Ramsay's hit TV show *Hell's Kitchen* (see *Fame and Glory: Celebrity Encounters*).

However, underlying the successful veneer there was further unrest. Having graduated with a degree in Music and Education, Danielle returned to guide the training band from strength to strength. But a small section of the Band, including some of its committee, would find her forward-thinking and modern methodologies difficult to accept. In addition Frankie, who believed in a hierarchy based on merit, had to contend with members who felt *entitled* to promotion above those who had actually made significant progress. The friction came to a head at the 2007 Crowborough Bonfire Parade, as a very public argument erupted between several players. Following yet another bitter committee meeting, both Frankie and Danielle, and some of their closest friends, would decide to leave the Band.

A general meeting was quickly held to discuss the Band's leadership. Amongst those present was Richard Sherlock, who offered to take back control of the baton.[26] "My heart at the time was still in the Heathfield Band and I just thought they could do with a bit of help," explains Richard. "I think we got down to about fourteen [players]. Some didn't go straight away, some stuck it for a little while. Luckily, I didn't have to do too much for them. Word got around and we got one or two back." In the short term the Band was weakened, but the remaining members would pull together to honour all its forthcoming engagements. "When he came back," says Keith Pursglove, "the guy had a band that was out of tune with each other, there weren't many of us, and he really worked hard and actually got the Band up to a very good standard." Richard tried to introduce some harder music to the repertoire, and this would meet with some success. Soon Heathfield Band could be heard performing renditions of pieces such as *War of the Worlds*, *Adagio from Spartacus*, and *Solitaire*.

Maintaining team spirit was clearly important to Richard, and social events would continue to be a significant part of the Band's calendar. An inter-band quiz was even attempted, to improve relations with other local bands.[27] The committee also planned a trip to Germany for the Spring of 2010. In addition, Richard occasionally brought in guest conductors from Lewes, Glynde & Beddingham Band (for whom he played euphonium), to give players a chance to experience different techniques and styles from his own. Richard was also a strong advocate for raising the Band's profile by generating goodwill in the community,[28] and this was achieved by making healthy donations to local charities, including Shoreham Lifeboat Appeal, Sussex Air Ambulance, and the Royal National Lifeboat Institution, the latter receiving the proceeds of a joint concert held with Wealden Consort (a Sussex-based choral society) in 2009.

Membership subscriptions were introduced around 2005, to comply with a clause in the Band's constitution which was under a general review at the time.[29] As a result, £1 membership fees were introduced for senior players, with subscriptions for junior members being introduced a year or so later. The constitution would be scrutinised and updated in 2007, and further refined in 2011, and the membership fee for adults would double in 2008

Burwash Remembrance Parade, November 2009.
Photograph supplied by Kent & Sussex Courier.

**Cuckoo Fair,
April 2008.**

*Photographs supplied by
Kent & Sussex Courier.*

and increase to £5 in 2009. A members' code of conduct was also considered (though ultimately not adopted) following complaints from a bonfire society regarding the *attitude* of the Band's drum-major Heidi Watkins. The responsible and safe behaviour of society members and the public is of paramount importance at all bonfire events, and Heidi would sometimes be forced to give urgent, blunt and stern words to thoughtless revellers, irrespective of their feelings!

During Richard Sherlock's second stint as musical director, there were few changes to the engagement calendar. However, there was a marked reduction of Summer fêtes, in part due to a revival of music education in schools, who were now able to produce their own bands for such occasions. In 2008 there was some surprise when the Band was informed that it would no longer be required at Le Marché. However, it would be reinstated the following year after the organisers received a stream of complaints. December 2008 would be the end of an era as the Band attended Lady Caffyn's final Christmas party; her age was advancing and she now felt unable to host such grand events personally. Finally, the Band was unable to take part in band contests

Heathfield Band at Barcombe, August 2009.
Photograph supplied by Mostyn Cornford.

as its size and overall ability was no longer up to the task. Disappointed players were instead encouraged to compete with other local bands.

There is no doubt that the Noughties would be one of the high points of the Band's colourful history. Its past was honoured and the future embraced, and while the innovations, landmarks and growth were met with mixed feelings by bandmembers, there is no question that it would end the decade in a much-improved state from where it began, fit for purpose in the new millennium. Meanwhile, the digital age had arrived. The growth of the world-wide web would do much to promote a broader diversity of music, bringing brass band culture back into the wider consciousness. Mainstream music would cross over into the brass repertoire faster than ever, and the Heathfield Band would find itself evolving at break-neck speed. The 2010s were about to commence, and the Band would never look back.

[1] Minutes, 18th December 2001

[2] MD's Notes and Running Order, 30th August 2004

[3] Correspondence, Frankie Lulham to Bob Childs, 3rd November 2002

[4] Correspondence, Bob Childs to Frankie Lulham, 3rd November 2002

[5] MD Report, Frankie Lulham, 3rd June 2002

[6] Press Release, Frankie Lulham, ca. February 2004

[7] Experiencecorps.co.uk. 2002. *The Experience Corps.* [online] <www.experiencecorps.co.uk/xq/ASP/id_Content.320/id_Page_Parent.4/qx/article> [Accessed 26th June 2002 – No Longer Active]

[8] Correspondence, Frankie Lulham to Sonya Wratton, 9th June 2002

[9] MD Report, Frankie Lulham, 27th February 2007

[10] Correspondence, Frankie Lulham to Susan King, 11th November 2003

[11] Correspondence, Heffle Cuckoo Fair to the Author, April 2021; Heathfield and Waldron Community Association Magazine, ca. April 1987

[12] ibid; Correspondence, Roger Ferry to the Author, May 2021

[13] MD Report, Frankie Lulham, 8th August 2002

[14] MD Report, Frankie Lulham, 24th October 2002

[15] MD Report, Frankie Lulham, 3rd August 2003

[16] Press Release, Frankie Lulham, 12th July 2004

[17] Press Release, Frankie Lulham, 11th July 2005

[18] MD Report, Frankie Lulham, 26th April 2003

[19] SCABA Bugle, December 2003

[20] ibid

[21] Presentation, Frankie Lulham, 11th December 2004

[22] MD Report, Frankie Lulham, 15th January 2003

[23] Correspondence, Richard Sherlock to Band President, 25th June 2005

[24] MD Report, Frankie Lulham, 10th April 2006

[25] Kent & Sussex Courier, 8th June 2007

[26] Minutes, 8th October 2007

[27] Minutes, 6th April 2009

[28] Minutes, 15th November 2007

[29] Correspondence, Band Secretary to Bandmembers, 31st March 2005

Story *The Silver Band Committee Meeting*

It was a quarter to eight by the bandroom clock on this Friday evening. During the break at last Tuesday's band practice the Secretary had announced that the Committee Meeting would start at 7-30pm. The date and time had also been shown on the blackboard for the last three weeks. Oh well, thought the Secretary, the members may not have heard him above their own private conversations, the tootling of one of the cornet players demonstrating his lack of ability and the crash as the odd music-stand got knocked over. He felt though that they should have noticed it on the blackboard which was behind the Conductor. He realised of course that when concentrating on the notes the last thing the musicians would look at was the man with the baton.

The Treasurer, the only other arrival, had helped the Secretary to erect the old table for their respective files and papers. A little rickety, its proper use was to paste wall-paper. The stands had been moved into a corner and the chairs placed in a semi-circle facing the table. On each chair the Secretary had placed an Agenda.

Committee Member 1 strolled in.

"It is tonight then" he said to no-one in particular as he brushed the Agenda off one of the chairs and sat down. Next to come was the Chairman. He would have been earlier but had met "Old George" on the way and been held up. It seemed that Committee Member 1 knew George and a long discussion began. At eight o'clock the Librarian and Assistant Secretary arrived together and took their places. This was followed by a flurry of arrivals including the Bandmaster, Committee Members 3 and 4 and the Assistant Librarian.

"I think we'll make a start" announced the Chairman who was now sitting at the table flanked by the Secretary and Treasurer.

He picked up the Agenda, turned it the right way up, and spoke. "Item 1. Apologies for Absence."

No one could work out if anyone was missing and no apologies having been received the Chairman solemnly ticked Item 1 on his Agenda and called for

Item 2 - Minutes of last Meeting. The lady Assistant Secretary read them out at a fair old rate and passed the book to the Chairman.

"Is it your wish that I sign this as a true record." he asked. As most couldn't remember what had been discussed at the last meeting and some were not sure if they had even attended it was agreed that it was a true record. The Chairman appended his signature with a flourish.

"What's the date?" he enquired ignoring the fact that it was printed at the top of the Agenda. He chose one from the selection offered him and entered it alongside his signature. At that moment the door flew open allowing a blast of cold air and Committee Member 2 to enter.

"Sorry I'm late" she said plonking herself down and lighting a fag.

Matters Arising was the next item on the Agenda. Painting the outside of the bandroom was a permanent feature in the Minutes and had been for several years. During the Spring and Summer the Committee agreed to leave it until later in the year when the Band's engagements would be completed. It wasn't really convenient then because of Armistice Parades and then Christmas carolling and the Committee postponed the idea until the New Year. By then the bad weather had started so the Committee after much discussion thought it best to wait for Spring. The interior of the bandroom was a similar matter. It was still going to be difficult to find the time and volunteers to do it but there was the added complication of what colour it should be painted and who would get the paint.

After allowing some discussion on the matter the Chairman made a decision.

"I suggest we all give it some thought and come up with some suggestions at the next meeting. Meanwhile are there any other matters arising?"

Committee Member 1, who had been deep in conversation about gardening with Committee Member 3, broke off his chat long enough to make his contribution.

"I always think beige would be a nice colour for the walls."

This was largely ignored as the Chairman had decided it was time for the Treasurer's Report.

He gave the current state of the Band's finances to the nearest penny but added that one or two outstanding bills needed to be settled. The Band wasn't in the red but was not very flush.

This statement led to talk of ways to raise funds.

"We could have another Jumble Sale," suggested the Assistant Secretary. As this didn't involve much effort by the Members, a few of the wives of the Band Members doing most of the work, this was passed. Committee Member 4 thought the Band should take on more engagements. The Bandmaster said the Band should accept only the more prestige jobs but really up the fees. The Secretary was worried about high fees combined with low attendance at engagements. The Librarian thought less engagements would mean better attendance.

Committee Member 2 thought the Band should advertise for more players. This was carried unanimously and was an effective red herring regarding engagements which seemed to be left that the Band would take on more jobs or that the Band would take on less jobs thus satisfying everybody.

"Right, we will move on to the next item which is Instruments, Music and Uniforms," announced the Chairman. "Anybody got anything to say on this."

The Librarian made a request for more Music Stands to be purchased. At one time the Band had more stands than players but the former seemed to have a secret life of their own. They would all appear at one Fête say, but by the day of the next engagement one or two had slipped away never to be seen again. So over the year quite a number managed to escape. It was agreed that the Band should buy some more and try to hold on to them. Committee Member 2 persuaded the Committee that six new uniforms should be ordered for the up and coming youngsters of the Band. The Treasurer turned white as he tried to work out whether there was enough money in the funds.

New pieces of music was mentioned. We need more modern stuff said one. We can't play what we've got said another. Matter unresolved.

The Bandmaster made a plea for less talking in the bandroom during practice especially when he was attempting to give guidance to one section. Whether this had any effect is doubtful as most of the Committee Members were still talking amongst themselves about the last subject.

The Chairman said there had been a good discussion and he would move on to Any Other Business.

A new-comer to both the Band and the Committee made the suggestion that the Band should organise a Christmas Concert, sell tickets and make a lot of money. Older members of the Committee could remember previous attempts to do just that. Some could even remember a memorable occasion when the audience just out-numbered the Band. However it was decided to have another try in December in the newly built large Community Centre. The whole idea got off to a magnificent start when Committee Member 2, who was also Principal Cornet, announced she wouldn't be able to attend and the Assistant Secretary and Tenor Horn player said she would be giving birth to her second child at the time. Despite these set-backs it was decided to press on.

As no one could think of Any Other Business and some had developed a condition which could only be satisfied at the nearest Local the last item was reached.

This was the Date of next Meeting. Some consulted their diaries, others looked blank and a number of different conversations broke out between the Members so it was agreed between the Chairman and Secretary that the next meeting would take place at some unspecified date in the future.

"Meeting closed at 9-15pm" called the Chairman above the noise.

"Beige is nice." muttered Committee Member 1.

by Dennis H. Guile, November 1992

With grateful thanks to Maureen Guile who supplied the text.

Interlude Inter-Band Relations:
The Heathfield Band Family Tree

One of the most positive aspects of brass banding is the almost universal pass it offers players to move freely between ensembles. Musicians will rally round to help each other, and the only real hint of (very friendly) rivalry is when they attempt to out-perform one another at contests (though in practice bands from neighbouring communities are generally well-matched in terms of ability). "You're talking about village syndrome. All the villages around the area, they all share their players," explains Frank Francis, bandmaster at Heathfield during the early Nineties. "We were swapping over all the time. If you all had a gig on the same day, you had to put up with what you had." There thus exists an intricate web – an extended family – of musicians, and it is through such ties that Heathfield Band has become especially close to some bands whilst falling out with others. This chapter explores some of those relationships.

Warbleton & Buxted Band

Since its earliest days, the Band's closest bond has undoubtedly been with Warbleton & Buxted Band, based just a few miles from Heathfield in the picturesque village of Rushlake Green. Warbleton & Buxted Band is very much a younger sibling, an amalgamation of Warbleton Brass Band (founded in 1896) and the Buxted Brass Band (founded ca. 1907–10).[1] Its close

356

proximity to Heathfield meant that the two bands would regularly share players, and sometimes perform together in public, and in 1929 Heathfield even lent Warbleton its side drum to take to a contest.[2] "Warbleton have always been our best friends," says George Mepham jnr. (interviewed in 1981), whose father was a founding member of the Warbleton Band and an early member at Heathfield. Keith Pursglove adds: "I have always enjoyed the lovely welcome and friendship shown towards players that come along from other bands. There was always a very close relationship between Warbleton and Heathfield, both bands had 'second band' players from each other."

However, despite being part of an "organisational brotherhood," Peter Cornford believes that neighbouring community bands continue to guard their individualism in a manner akin to tribalistic football teams: "I remember in the 1980s when Warbleton players came periodically to help out Heathfield that there was always tension when they were asked to wear HSB red jackets. They wanted to maintain their Warbleton identity by continuing to wear their blue jackets!" The bands are so intertwined that, occasionally, journalists have unwittingly muddled the pair in press reports.[3]

At Heathfield's Hospital Parades in the early 1900s, the two bands would lead separate processions to converge at Heathfield Station, before massing together to play outside The Crown Hotel.[4] The bandmembers would also join forces, sometimes with players from the Dallington and Battle bands, at the Dallington Hospital Parade.[5] And at the unveiling of the Heathfield War Memorial in 1922, Warbleton played during the laying of the wreaths whilst Heathfield accompanied the Parish Church Choir.[6]

Throughout the Twenties, the pair would also share musical duties at British Legion events and, in the Thirties, they could often be seen together at Sussex bonfire parades. In 1930 the two ensembles performed a joint concert in the grounds of Spring Lodge (home to Heathfield Band's president F. Howard Martin), and in 1931 they would accompany a host of other bands and Friendly Societies through the streets of Eastbourne, to raise money for local hospitals.[7] In 1934, at a united service for Warbleton Hospital Parade, Heathfield Band played the hymns whilst Warbleton "Prize" Band performed the test piece which had recently won it a contest, after which the pair gave various selections together.[8] They also played (alongside Burwash Band) at the 1066 Commemoration Fair at Battle in May 1966, and would combine again in 1970 for Heathfield's RAFA Fete.[9] In addition, during the late

Seventies, Warbleton Band assisted Heathfield at the town carnival, as bass player Jeff Collins recalls: "Warbleton Band had just got a brand new Eb bass for me and it put a dent in it when we started countermarching and I collided with Bob [Lee]'s side drum!" In July 1979 the two bands marched in a spectacular grand parade at Calais, alongside about thirty other bands from across Europe,[10] and in 1996 members of Heathfield Band were invited to help Warbleton celebrate its centenary, whilst several members of Warbleton would be on hand to reciprocate at Heathfield's 125th anniversary concert in 2013.

There has also been plenty of personnel switching between the two bands. In 1932, as Heathfield were struggling to recruit a new bandmaster, it approached a Mr. Buss about taking on the role. This would almost certainly have been Warbleton's bandmaster (and clarinettist) Mr. Fred Buss, who had formerly been a member at Heathfield and who would assist it from time to time. Other possible candidates are his brother James Buss jnr., or father James Buss snr.[11] The proposal did not come to fruition, but it does illustrate the close relationship between the two bands. Shortly after leaving Heathfield in 1960, Bert Wise found himself conducting the Warbleton Band, whilst just a few years later, suffering from low membership, Heathfield would propose that the bands amalgamate (though accounts vary as to why or by whom this proposal was rejected).[12] During the Eighties, Warbleton's former bandmaster Dick Turner would return to Heathfield to take the baton, after an absence of several decades.

Callenders Band

In the early 1950s, Heathfield Band became friendly with the championship band, Callenders, whose bandmaster was an adjudicator at the annual Tunbridge Wells Festival. Looking for novel ways to raise funds, the secretary of Heathfield Band Arthur Frost approached Callenders with a view to putting on a joint concert. This took place in October 1952, at the Secondary School in Cade Street (now Heathfield Community College) which was hired for just one guinea (about £30 today). The concert would be a great success, generating over £27 in ticket sales (about £800 today) and the initiative was repeated in 1953 and 1954.[13] Callenders were based in Erith, Kent (now part of Greater London), so members of both bands would rendezvous before the evening concerts to enjoy a pub dinner together. "Callenders were good to Heathfield Band," believes Gordon Neve, whilst George Mepham jnr. adds: "They came to give concerts in aid of our instrument fund and then presented a new euphonium to Cyril Leeves. They had a flood and so sent a lot of their damaged music to us."

Uckfield Concert Brass

Heathfield Band would also maintain a friendship with Uckfield Concert Brass. The pair appeared alongside one another at numerous hospital parades and bonfire celebrations during the first half of the twentieth century and in 1963 Heathfield Band even donated its spare uniform jackets to Uckfield's learner players.[14] More recently, in 2009, the two massed together for the final Cliffe procession of the evening at Lewes Bonfire. The only march cards both bands had in common were Slaidburn and Sussex By The Sea, but the initiative was so successful that it would be repeated the following year, with the joint repertoire enlarged to include Colonel Bogey, Blaze Away, Imperial Echoes and Standard of St. George. The Uckfield-Heathfield massed band has remained a fixture at every Lewes Bonfire since. In addition, in 2013 the pair teamed up for the final parade of the evening at Uckfield Bonfire, resulting in a massed band of 55 musicians marching through the High Street.[15] These annual get-togethers are now an eagerly anticipated tradition for members of both bands.

Frothblowers

In the summer of 1972, Heathfield Band trombonist Bob Lee would form a small busking outfit – a band within a band – which he was to christen The Frothblowers. It was initially put together as a support band for one event, but proved such a success that it continued, in various guises, well into the 1990s. One of its first engagements was a RAFA Donkey Derby in Broad Oak: "The Frothblowers, an oddly attired offshoot of the Heathfield Silver Band, set up their stands outside the beer tent where the audience showed their appreciation by sending their donations tinkling into a china receptacle," reports one local newspaper.[16] The receptacle in question was, in fact, an old, handle-less chamber pot!

Although the Frothblowers' profits would be passed on to Heathfield Band, there were occasional misgivings concerning the use of its instruments and music, and some bandmembers worried that the "competition" might affect the parent band's prospects. "I played with them on many occasions," remembers Peter Cornford. "The group was not made up exclusively of HSB players. We were invitees of Bob put together ad hoc depending on what the event was." Jeff Collins adds: "I played Eb bass for them. There was a couple

Frothblowers, 1972.

of cornet players, Bob on trombone or sometimes, if he'd got a trombone player but was stuck for drums, Bob would play drums." Many of the Frothblowers' gigs took place at local pubs, such as The Star and The Prince of Wales in Heathfield. "If there was a pub that would have us for the evening, we'd play in there, we'd just keep playing until we run out of beers," says Jeff, whilst Peter adds: "It was driven and organised by Bob Lee, who proudly liked his beer and enjoyed gathering a few playing friends around him to play in pub gardens, free of the need to behave as would normally be expected as an ambassador of the Heathfield Silver Band." The Frothblowers would also play at Heathfield retirement home, Heffle Court, and at venues as far afield as Broad Oak and Burwash. "There was a continuous sense that we were somehow pulling a fast one," continues Peter. "The playing was unquestionably substandard (and worsened as the beer intake increased), everything casual, nothing agreed, no VAT, instruments and music 'borrowed' from the Band. Just good, plain, innocent clean fun. I'm not sure you could get away with it these days!"

Edenbridge Town Band

In 1970, Heathfield Silver Band would successfully team up with Edenbridge Town Band, to play at the international brass band parade in Calais.[17] This pairing was repeated several times over the coming years, including at the Prince of Wales, Heathfield, in 1975 (presumably as part of the Heathfield Carnival), and for Edenbridge Carnival in 1977. The minutes also note that

Heathfield Band hoped to obtain the assistance of Edenbridge for Lewes Bonfire that year.[18] The bands evidently got on well, as Edenbridge even invited members of Heathfield to attend its social in 1978.[19]

Vines Cross Modern / Wealden Brass

In early 1979, an internal disagreement resulted in several members of Heathfield Band being expelled, and others leaving in protest. The split resulted in the formation of Vines Cross Modern Brass (now Wealden Brass). But what was the reason for such unrest? Sue Sutton, one of those who left, reveals that the choice of music was in fact the underlying cause: "It was horrible. So old-fashioned, so dreary," she says. "All this new stuff was coming out and they wouldn't buy it. There was about six of us [who] left, all on corner instruments like lead cornet, trombone and that. We were so fed up because they wouldn't get updated a bit. We'd be sitting in a pub playing and they'd get a test piece out or something!" Sue's husband, fellow former bandmember Dave Sutton, elaborates: "At that time, Brighouse and Rastrick started doing a lot of modern stuff – Floral Dance was one of them, one of the shows as well – things like that were coming out and they wouldn't entertain them. We were suggesting that we had a second band that did the modern stuff and people played in both if they wanted to. It was trying to keep them together and develop the two styles. At the meeting that was being put forward, somebody out and out trashed it and said, 'They've gotta go!' "

Crowborough Town Band

For a time from the late 1980s, a close bond was formed between Heathfield Band and Crowborough Town Band, both of which were struggling to recruit new members. They had previously appeared together at hospital carnivals during the Thirties and would have crossed paths on the contesting scene (where Crowborough had been highly successful until the late Fifties). By the mid-Nineties, the pair would be working together closely. In 1994 they staged a joint Christmas Concert in Heathfield, and a combined trip to France was planned for the following spring, although this appears to have been abandoned at the eleventh hour. However, the pair would appear together that August, during the anniversary celebrations of VJ Day, at Goldsmiths Recreation Ground in Crowborough. The clerk to the town council would later write to Heathfield Band: "I have received much good comment on the quality of the music and I hope that your members enjoyed the evening as much as we did."[20] Sadly, just a few years later, Crowborough Town Band was forced to wind up.

Tavistock Town Band

In 1993 John Sherlock (brother of Richard and son of Ernie, both long-serving members of Heathfield Band) was now conducting Tavistock Town Band in Devon, and he suggested staging reciprocal gigs between the two town bands.[21] The idea was warmly greeted by all concerned and a twinning concert was held at the Heathfield Community Centre in Sheepsetting Lane, in October 1993. "They decided that an exchange would be fun – so Tavistock went to Heathfield first," remembers Caroline Leverett. "My dad and I were both in Tavistock Town Band and stayed with Sarah Leeves' family." In April 1994 Heathfield Band travelled to Devon for a long weekend, and the bands were reunited for a concert at Tavistock Town Hall. In 2006, members of Tavistock Band would make a return to Heathfield and, keen to experience the Sussex bonfire tradition, marched with Heathfield Band at Mayfield.

Sidmouth Town Band

Another link with Devon was formed in 2000. "For two years running, we did a trip down to Sidmouth where we joined up with Sidmouth Town Band," explains bass player and former bandmaster Jeff Collins. "We would go to their Friday night rehearsal and then play a Sunday afternoon concert on Sidmouth Bandstand. We did that in 2000 with Richard [Sherlock] conducting and then I conducted the one in 2001. It was arranged by our soprano cornet player, who'd got friends and relatives down in Sidmouth. He'd been talking to the bandmaster down there and got the idea of going. We had a couple of years of good concerts. We'd be all massed together, we just about had enough room on the bandstand! Their bandmaster would take one half of the entertainment and Heathfield's bandmaster would take the other half. There was some confusion on the one I conducted. We'd got into about the third number and this group of people turned up and it was the local Presbyterian Church or something expecting to do their songs of praise. Apparently Sidmouth Band hadn't double-checked that they hadn't got another booking on the bandstand, but seeing as we were seated and already playing we won the day!"

Seaford Silver Band

During the Nineties, a symbiotic link would develop with Seaford Silver Band after its secretary, Alan Jones, wrote to Heathfield Band suggesting that they foster a closer working relationship. "We were two community bands playing similar music a lot of the time," explains Dr. Isla Sitwell, conductor of Seaford Band. "Heathfield is a market town with a more rural identity than Seaford, but we both existed to play for 'town' or 'civic' events and at the usual fetes and garden parties." The novel nature of Heathfield Band's country engagements (such as the Heathfield Show) and Sussex bonfire parades, and the younger makeup of the Band, would therefore prove attractive to many of Seaford Band's musicians.

Conversely, many of Heathfield's players were to benefit from attending extra rehearsals and engagements with Seaford Silver Band. Once a fortnight an entourage of its younger players, encouraged by Frankie and tenor horn veteran Ted Lee, would make a forty-mile round trip to practice in the tiny seaside town. On one occasion, they were surprised and delighted to be presented with a vibraphone by Seaford Band player Mick Vise.[22] In 2005 Seaford would make another generous donation to Heathfield, this time to its bandroom extension fund, and in 2006 members of both bands made a joint trip to Seaford's twin town Bönningstedt in Germany. A wunderschön time was had by all.

On occasions when the Heathfield Band's conductor was unavailable, Isla Sitwell would sometimes step in to take the baton. His earliest, and most memorable, experience of conducting Heathfield was at Eastbourne Bandstand sometime in the early Nineties. "A few of us had been invited along to swell the numbers and I was playing second trombone," recalls Isla. "Suddenly, their conductor was stricken by a stomach upset and had to dash to the toilets." Frankie adds: "We all sat there thinking, Where's our conductor gone?!" Isla continues: "There was a bit of a silence and John Rossall [a member of Seaford Band and stalwart Sussex brass bander] put me forward to conduct. I don't think the Heathfield Band knew that I was then doing some conducting so they looked a bit scared! The next number on the programme was Sarah Leaves playing a euphonium solo, Bless This House, and they all got more scared. She played it beautifully, as you would expect, and their conductor returned for the next number."

Harmonie Concert Band

As was the case with the Vines Cross offshoot, differences of opinion would again lead to a number of members, including Frankie and her daughter Danielle, stepping away from the Band in 2007. "They were convinced we were leaving to start our own band," explains Danielle. "That was never our intention but in the end we did start our own band, a completely different one, and more importantly one run by only Mum and I so we didn't have to answer to anyone else." The name Harmonie was thus aptly-chosen. "It does make me sad though," adds Danielle. "I spent over fifteen years in that Band [Heathfield] and it ended so badly. It was hard to leave it behind but it had to be done, and it opened up a new chapter." Frankie (speaking in 2013) says: "We did a role reversal because Danielle was the brass player and I was the conductor at Heathfield. Now she's the conductor and I play the horn! We're a concert band: we have flutes, oboes, clarinets, bassoons, saxophones, and all the brass instruments as well. We were trying to decide where we were going to set our band up and [former members of Heathfield Band] Sue Sutton and her husband Dave organised that we could hire the Horam Scout Hut. Both play in our band and they are very supportive of us." Harmonie Band was well-received by the community but it would sadly be wound-up in August 2020, as Danielle re-evaluated her priorities in the wake of the covid-19 epidemic. She has since relocated to Wales.

Wadhurst Brass Band

Heathfield Band's most recent joint initiative would be a concert with Wadhurst Brass Band, which raised almost £2,500 for Cancer Research UK in April 2017. It was organised by David Healy, deputy conductor of Wadhurst Band, in memory of his grandmother who died of the disease. "That concert I did for her, really," explains David. "She was the reason that my sisters and I got music lessons because she gave our parents the money to do so. She would come from north London to every Wadhurst Band concert to see her grandchildren play!" But how did the collaboration come about? "When I was a teenager, about sixteen or seventeen, my good friend [former bandmember] Tim Fermor used to get me along to bonfire marches and I always remembered Heathfield Silver Band to have a welcoming presence," says David. "We were bands of a similar standard and, where Wadhurst lacked, Heathfield could bump up our sections, and vice versa. We couldn't have asked for a better conductor than Sarah [Leeves] to work with. She had so much to offer my band, especially as she has proper training and qualifications! She was an absolute delight to work with, an incredible educator and conductor with so much knowledge to share. I felt it was a real 50/50 effort on the bands' part. I always think of Heathfield Band fondly."

The brass band spirit of friendliness and mutual support endures to this day. Perhaps the beauty of, and key to, successful inter-band relationships is that they are a logical extension of the banding ethos: to work together in the music-making process sharing knowledge, support, and experience. Above all, such relationships can provide even greater enjoyment to our pursuit of bringing arts and entertainment to the wider community. Heathfield Band's extended family is large, but it will continue to grow.

---

[1] Bourke, J., 1996. *The History of a Village Band 1896-1996*. Heathfield: Warbleton and Buxted Band

[2] Minutes, 13th April 1929

[3] Press Release, Frankie Lulham, 11th April 2005

[4] e.g. Kent & Sussex Courier, 19th Sept 1902; Sussex Express, 9th September 1905

[5] Sussex Express, 29th August 1908 & 22nd July 1910

[6] Sussex Express, 27th January 1922

[7] e.g. Sussex Express, 1st August 1930 & 10th November 1933; Eastbourne Gazette, 26th August 1931

[8] Sussex Express, 18th May 1934

[9] Cornford, P., 1981. Personal Archive and Interviews; Kent & Sussex Courier, 25th September 1970

[10] Cornford, P., 1981

[11] Minutes, 7th December 1932

[12] Minutes, 26th November 1963

[13] Kent & Sussex Courier, 30th October 1953 & 8th October 1954

[14] Minutes, 26th November 1963

[15] Sussex Express, 13th September 2013

[16] Cutting, source unknown

[17] Cutting, source unknown

[18] Minutes, 6th August 1975 & 13th July 1977

[19] Minutes, 25th January 1978

[20] Correspondence, D. Harris to Band Secretary, 1st September 1995

[21] Minutes, 1st February 1993

[22] Press Release, Frankie Lulham, 25th October 2004

2010s Amateur Banding Today

Heathfield Silver Band, February 2014

Change, as we have seen, is an inevitable and necessary part of Heathfield Band's continuing journey. The Band of today may be characterised as a legacy institution aspiring to be relevant in the twenty-first century. As such, there has recently been a push to modernise its ethos and values, and yet commemoration of the past continues to play an important part in the Band's activities. During the decade, there would be celebrations for the centenary of Armistice and the Queen's 90th birthday, and Heathfield Band's 125th anniversary in 2013. In 2010, secretary Anna Farley would resign after 35 years with the Band. In addition, it mourned the passing of several long-term members: Tim Fermor and Cedric "Sid" Forward in 2010, drummer Ken Burchett in 2012, and Ted Lee, in 2020.

Having been musical director a decade before, Richard Sherlock could once again be seen in the role. The Band was a stable and happy one, with around thirty playing members including a handful of new recruits and the outlook was extremely positive. Camaraderie was also good, in part due to regular team-building exercises such as quiz nights, barbeques and Christmas dinners. The engagements programme for 2010 included a wide variety of prominent gigs, a tour of the Rhineland was imminent, and the year would begin with a flourish of publicity as the Sussex Express printed an early photograph and asked the question, "Does the Band still exist?"[1]

After an absence of two decades, the Heathfield Pancake Races would return in February 2010, taking place on a stretch of road between Old Heathfield and Cade Street. Championed by Ann Kenward and the Band's chairman Richard Leeves, the event raised money for Demelza and other local charities. The town band was naturally on hand to support the event, as was a large crowd of spectators and pancake-flippers of all ages.[2] "I have never seen so many smiling faces in the rain," says Richard Leeves. "Everyone was happy, […] there's no doubt we will do it again next year."[3] Indeed, the Band returned to the races in 2011 and 2012.

Richard Sherlock would lead the Band in its overdue return to Germany in April 2010, when it made a tour of the Rhineland. "We spent five days travelling to and from the area, playing at three venues, sightseeing and generally having a good time. Personally the most notable event being the concert held in the Marble Hall in Bad Ems," reports Richard.[4] The Band also performed at the Loreley Besuchetzentrum and the Rüdesheim Marktplatz, and was generally well-received by the locals (see *Continental Adventures: The Band Tour*).

Heidi Watkins leads the St. George's Day Parade, Seaford, April 2010.
Photograph supplied by Heidi Watkins.

Leading the St. George's Day Scout Parade in Seaford would be next on the Band's busy agenda, followed by Heathfield's own Cuckoo Fair, for which the organisers encouraged residents to assemble and display scarecrows promoting the event. The Band played a prominent part in the campaign, producing its own Bandsman Scarecrow which received a proposal of marriage from the Flower Scarecrow. The couple could soon be seen courting in the window of a local bakery![5] The Band would create another scarecrow the following year.

The HSB Cuckoo Fair Scarecrow in fine company, April 2010.
Photograph supplied by Keith Pursglove.

Other engagements for 2010 included regulars such as Heathfield Agricultural Show, All Saints Church Fête, and the Framfield Show, and Summer Fayres at Charleston Manor and Crowborough. In addition, the Band appeared for the final time at Heathfield Carnival, now organised by the Rotary Club in aid of St. Wilfred's Hospice. "They couldn't get the support," says Ted Lee (interviewed in 2013), his wife, Clarice, adding: "They said there was nobody interested to make it work, which was a shame, 'cause people used to really turn out for that." Unusually for such a high-profile engagement, the Band did not wear their uniform jackets. "It was so hot they didn't put uniforms on," recalls Ted. The Band also attended Le Marché, a private wedding function, and an impressive seven bonfire parades, in addition to performing at Eastbourne Bandstand. Later in the year there was Burwash Remembrance Parade, carolling outside local supermarkets and at All Saints Church in Old Heathfield, the Uckfield Bonfire Society Christmas Parade, and concerts at Horam Preschool and Heathfield's State Hall. On Christmas Eve, a new tradition would begin with its first Christingle Service at the Union Church (whose Vicar Mark Welch and his wife Sarah both played trombone with the Band).

This industrious run of successful engagements, combined with excellent team spirit among most bandmembers, was still not be enough to please everybody. One recent recruit complained: "The committee needs to be restructured. Things run very unorganised because Richard takes on too much […]. Practices are rushed through and pieces put to one side as there is no time to rehearse them, we often run through pieces for no reason whatsoever [and] we know all the music in the main pad now."[6] After some deliberation, the committee responded with a lengthy rebuttal to the grievances: "The Band is a village band with a mix of players from all walks of life, all ages and all abilities. As such it has to be recognised that not all members of the Band do know all the music and so do need to rehearse the items on a rotational basis. The Band has seen good growth and retention in its membership over the last few years which is, on the whole, due to Richard's love of and commitment to the Band."[7]

The 2010 bonfire season would also see some controversy as attention was drawn to the legal and moral issues of paying players to attend Lewes Bonfire.[8] Although the engagement is a highly lucrative one, such payments nevertheless constitute a significant chunk of the Band's earnings. "On the one hand we have been […] bemoaning the need to gain sponsorship and fundraise, and yet we are about to pay out potentially £2000 (equivalent to the fee from 13 fêtes)," writes one concerned bandmember.[9] It was argued that the payments were unconstitutional and also unfair to members who were not present, while the main counter-concern was that, without payments, fewer players would be inclined to attend such a demanding engagement.[10] By way of a compromise, payments were offered to those who wished to receive them, and members balloted for their opinions.

Nevertheless, despite overwhelmingly positive feedback regarding the ceasing of payments, there would be noticeably fewer players in attendance the following year.

Even despite these practical and administrative issues, 2011 was another successful year for the Band, which was buoyed considerably by a flourish of grants and donations. These were largely the result of a fundraising effort by Rue Butcher (the mother of junior bandmember Charlotte), and would enable the purchase of a gazebo and a new set of wet-weather coats.[11] A revised constitution was also adopted, to help clarify issues surrounding the future payment of expenses to players.

It is interesting to note that Richard Sherlock would keep the future of the Band foremost in his mind, planning player development not just months, but sometimes years, in advance. He was especially keen to progress younger players through the ranks, as is demonstrated in the minutes for November 2010: "Joe Pert is a promising young player and [Richard] would like to give him the opportunity to take Abigail de Bruin's place on flugel when she leaves for university in a few years' time. To this end, Richard would like to purchase either a 'reasonable' new flugel or second hand flugel [...], so that Joe can gain confidence before Abigail leaves."[12] Richard's forethought allowed for a more stable player line-up with built-in contingencies to handle unforeseen circumstances.

Lacklustre musical progress would begin to set in by the Summer of 2011, possibly due to overly-rapid attempts to introduce a more challenging repertoire. Richard would therefore bring in guest conductors to tutor the Band.[13] The first was Dennis Wilby who, in addition to being a well-known contest adjudicator, had previously conducted bands such as Grimethorpe and James Shepherd Versatile Brass. The second was Ian Stewart, whom Richard knew as the conductor of Lewes, Glynde & Beddingham Band, but who had also been the school bandmaster at Kneller Hall and the bandmaster of the Queen's Own Hussars. The tutoring would rapidly pay off, as Richard observes: "The Band sounded particularly good at Eastbourne. The Band is sounding the best it has for many years."[14]

Over the course of 2011, the Band would take part in a number of special events. In April, Heffle Court Nursing Home held a street party to celebrate the wedding of William and Kate, Duke and Duchess of Cambridge. In June, the Band took part in Sussex Day Celebrations at Chapel Green in Crowborough, alongside a dance troupe, a school choir and Mr. Topples' Puppet Show![15] There would also be Summer fêtes at Waldron and Fairwarp, a *Traditional Afternoon* concert on Eastbourne Bandstand, marching at Hailsham Carnival, and the Heathfield British Legion's Poppy Party, which would commence with a parade through the High Street. As the year progressed, there would be prestigious appearances at Hever Castle, Remembrance and bonfire parades, and a busy Christmas season, which included candlelit carol services at the All Saints and Kings churches in Heathfield. In addition, the Band's annual Christmas Concert made a return to the Heathfield Community Centre in Sheepsetting Lane.

Variability is the word which best describes 2012's engagement programme, during which the Band would return to Hever Castle and Eastbourne Bandstand, and appear in a music video for pop group Keane. However, it took on fewer engagements overall, perhaps due to difficulties producing a balanced line-up of musicians. There was certainly some alarm when three cornet players were "poached" by Battle Town Band. "They are valued and important members of HSB and it is hoped their loyalties remain with us as their first band," state the minutes.[16] Disappointingly, and most surprisingly, the Band did not appear at any celebrations for the Queen's Diamond Jubilee. "It just seems to have slipped this last year," Richard Sherlock concedes.

HSB receives a generous donation from Barclays Bank, May 2012.
Photograph supplied by Kent & Sussex Courier.

HSB 125th Anniversary Concert, Heathfield Community Centre, July 2013.

(Back Rows, L–R) ?, Adam Kearley, ?, ?, Mark Welch, Lucy Clements, Eric Kemp, Andy Bullivent, Abigail de Bruin, Claire Slinn Hawkins, Georgia Waddington, Trevor Gomersall, Simon Emberley, Lewis Rich, Richard Sherlock (bandmaster), Paul?, John Justo, ?, ?, Sarah Leeves, Jack de Bruin, ?, Steven Anderson.
(Front Row, L–R) Cath Gosden, Joe Pert, ?, ?, Cheryl Goodsell, Sarah Welch, Richard Ayres, Debbi Bailey, ?, Angela Benson, Charlotte Butcher, Emily Rich, Mostyn Cornford, Ted Lee, Anna Farley, Mel de Bruin, Mallory Hansford, Kerry Pert, Ben Crisford, Alex "Taff" Emberley.

Photograph supplied by Kent & Sussex Courier.

"We've probably got about ten that can play to a good standard – a couple of those are very good – and we've got some that are struggling a little bit, but we try and encourage them where we can. We've tried recruiting, [but] I'm gonna have to just cut back a little bit on some of the things we do. It's very difficult when you've been playing slightly harder music for so many years and then you've gotta draw the reins in a bit, try and give those who aren't moving up through the Band a bit more confidence to move forward."

Energies would now be directed towards the Band's forthcoming 125th anniversary, dubbed *The 125*, in an attempt to give members something positive to focus on. After an initial brainstorming session, it was agreed that an all-day, community-focussed, family-friendly event would be the best way to celebrate.[17] It was planned for the Summer of 2013 and the Band's Facebook page would advertise it thus: "Everyone is welcome to this free event which […] definitely has a local feel to it. With stalls outside and inside, musical entertainment in the afternoon from Heathfield Community College, a licensed bar, a Hog Roast, attractions including land orbing, a photo competition, huge raffle and plenty more, it will be a fun event. The Band will give an open air concert in the evening […] do come along with a picnic."[18] Local churches, schools and other institutions were invited, and the Fire Brigade and Red Cross also agreed to attend.[19] Fundraising began in earnest and major donors would include Barclays Bank, Barratt Homes, and the Co-operative Society. Enough money was raised to purchase a new set of music stand banners and publish a written history of the Band (the abandoned 2013 book).

Young and old would thus enjoy a day to remember and a fitting showcase for the Band, as the sun shone gloriously down at Heathfield Community Centre on 6th July 2013. There was music for everyone, from pop-folk group *Remnant* and acoustic duo *Everything Fundamental*, to Batucada drumming, a Swing Band, a Brass Ensemble, and even Acappella. There was a merry-go-round and a bouncy castle, demonstrations from St. John Ambulance, a display of Harley Davidsons, slow bike racing, and even a magician. And, for the centrepiece evening concert, Heathfield Band was augmented by friends and former members who came to join the celebrations. "Heathfield Silver Band trumpeted its 125 years of music-making with a rousing performance on Saturday," reports the Kent & Sussex Courier. "The 44-piece brass band rounded off a fun day at the town's community centre with a two-hour set of crowd pleasers."[20] The repertoire ranged from traditional classics such as *The Lonely Mill* and *Sussex By The Sea* (applauded so loudly that an encore was required), to modern favourites such as *Pirates Of The Caribbean* and *Mission Impossible*.[21] The proceeds of the day were donated to St. John Ambulance and *Heathfield Works!* (a local charity which promotes vocational opportunities for young people).[22]

Heathfield Cuckoo Fair, April 2013.
Photograph supplied by Sarah Tate Photography.

Other Spring and Summer engagements for 2013 included the Cuckoo Fair, All Saints Church Fête, Heathfield Agricultural Show, Hever Castle, Charleston Summer Fayre, Le Marché, and Windlesham Manor. However, having guided the Band triumphantly through its anniversary celebrations, Richard Sherlock would now step away to concentrate on his playing career with the Lewes, Glynde & Beddingham Band. Bass trombonist, Richard Ayres (speaking in 2018), explains: "Richard was very much a band person, he had played right from a lad. He was quite a good motivator and he conducted well enough, but I think he always would have rather have played." Keith Pursglove adds: "Richard had the opportunity to play the euphonium [for] a good contesting band and, of course, he shone with that, because he's primarily a player."

Unfazed by Richard's departure, the Band did not miss a beat. Sarah Leeves proudly took the baton in September 2013, and her first task as musical director was to lead it through the busy bonfire season. It would then segue seamlessly into Burwash Remembrance Parade, followed by a hectic Christmas season, which included a candlelit service at Kings Church, open-air carolling at the Co-Op, Union Church's Christingle Service, and the Band's annual concert at the Community Centre, where it has become a tradition to present memorial cups to bandmembers for notable contributions and achievements.

Most of Heathfield's major events have continued to be patronised by the Band in recent years, as have venues further afield, such as the Ashburnham Country Fair and Eastbourne Bandstand. Special engagements have included carolling at Batemans, celebrations of the Queen's 90th birthday (which would comprise a concert at Rushlake Green followed by a street party at Heffle Court), a joint concert with Wadhurst Brass Band, and a "Summer Soirée" at Heathfield's State Hall. In addition, the Band have played at St. Richard's Church, Windlesham Manor, Horam Farm, Heathfield and Ringmer community colleges, a plethora of Summer fêtes, and the Heathfield Summer Festival.

Also largely unchanged are the Band's seasonal commitments. It continues to appear at Burwash Remembrance Parade and a range of Sussex Bonfires. From 2015, its popular annual Christmas Concert has returned to the more centrally-located State Hall. Richard Ayres describes 2018's offering thus:

"The concert itself was presented 'café-style' with most of our audience able to sit at tables with their mince pies, mulled wine, tea, and later, raffle prizes to hand. It was very well attended and well received. I did wonder on what pretext some of our audience had been brought in; just before our first piece, the nice lady sitting next to my wife asked her where the choir was. [...] I wonder what went through her mind when instead of relaxing to the refined overture of Handel's masterpiece she was treated to an enthusiastic rendering of *Sussex by the Sea!*"[23]

Bonfire Societies' Carol Service, Uckfield, December 2013.
Photograph supplied by UckfieldNews.com.

Remembrance of the centenary of the Great War would begin in earnest in 2014, with a *Silent Night* carol service at All Saints Church in Old Heathfield, and a concert and picnic at Heathfield Community College for the Friends of All Saints. In 2015 the Band marched at Batemans and in June 2018 it played for the British Legion's Armed Forces Day at Crowborough. In November 2018 the centenary of Armistice was marked nationwide by a series of local "Battle's Over" celebrations. Heathfield's would take place at Cade Street, where there was a full day of music and dance and, in the evening, "a moving performance by a bagpiper, the excellent Heathfield Silver Band, [...] and the Heathfield Army Cadets, who were an integral part of the formal lighting of the beacon and reading the names of the fallen."[24] With the passing of the few remaining veterans of the Great War, this was an especially poignant occasion to be a part of, representing perhaps the final major commemoration of its kind.

Regretfully, many vestiges of the old Band have now also gone forever. In 2019, under the direction of a largely new committee, the rules and constitution were completely rewritten to be more in keeping with the modern world. But new ways and new ideas have led to many changes of personnel. 2018 saw the retirement of long-term librarian Ted Lee and the replacement of treasurer Mostyn Cornford. Chairman Richard Leeves resigned the following year and drummer Eric "Animal" Kemp stepped away in 2020. The sudden loss of so many of the Band's elders, the bastions of its long-held traditions, has undoubtedly resulted in an entity somewhat divorced from its roots. The institution has evolved.

Young players have recently suffered from cutbacks to brass tuition in schools, so the Band's recruitment and development strategy has become a more targeted and structured affair. In addition to the training band, now dubbed *First Class Brass*, a lesson group for complete beginners has also been re-established. "In the lesson group you will learn the basics of holding and blowing your chosen instrument, as well as the fundamentals of reading music, working alongside similarly placed learners of all ages," states the Band's website.[25] "The Training Band comprises learners who have progressed from The Lesson Band and are learning to play ensemble pieces. [...] You'll learn how to make your music fit in with that of others, how to blend with other musicians, and work as a team." In addition, in May 2019

Carolling at Heathfield Co-Op, December 2013.
Photograph supplied by Jim Still.

377

the Band was fortunate enough to be awarded a £500 grant by East Sussex County Council, to assist with the costs of tutoring newcomers. Hopefully, this reinvigorated approach to training will provide a steady stream of new players for the future.

Most encouraging of all, under Sarah's leadership the Band has been a happy, productive and sociable group, holding regular barbeques, picnics, quiz nights and an annual Christmas dinner. She has always aimed to have a positive, yet realistic, influence on members. "It's the players' Band, every player has an important role to play," says Sarah. "The bandmaster is there to choose the music, to select the right pieces for their abilities, to choose the right style pieces for the occasion. You have to be chirpy, as charismatic as you can, and make people laugh and smile. The bandmaster is just there to wave the stick, really, to serve the Band and to be the face of the Band."

Evolution has been a constant companion and an inextricable part of the Band's existence, and with a committee whose number one objective is to modernise, just where does it stand today? "You look around and you see big towns like Crowborough have lost their band, small little villages like Five Ashes used to have one, Buxted used to have one, and they've all gone," reflects Keith Pursglove. "I want the Band to survive and I want the Band to grow, [but] I think that the main emphasis should be the traditional and the local side of what the Band is about." Former president, Geoff Pickering (interviewed in 2013), adds: "My impression has always been that the majority are happy with just being a village band and playing for functions, and the bonfire things bring in some cash. I think the majority want it to be just what it is, they don't want to change it." But perhaps the final thoughts on the matter should belong to Sarah: "It's nice 'cause when you come along and you conduct, it just feels quite pressure-free, really. You don't feel like you've got a whole load of people in front of you with all different feelings on how it should be done. They just basically wanna have a good blow, have a good laugh, and enjoy their hobby."

---

[1] Sussex Express, 8th January 2010

[2] Kent & Sussex Courier, 26th February 2010

[3] ibid

[4] Minutes, 8th February 2011

[5] Minutes, 7th June 2010

[6] Minutes, 5th July 2010; Correspondence, Band Chairman to Dave Mildren, 8th July 2010

[7] Correspondence, Band Chairman to Dave Mildren, 8th July 2010

[8] Correspondence, Phil Barham to Band Chairman, 4th November 2010

[9] ibid

[10] Minutes, 15th November 2010

[11] Correspondence, Diana Francis to Rue Butcher, 23rd March 2011; Minutes, 6th June 2011

[12] Minutes, 15th November 2010

[13] Minutes, 9th May 2011

[14] Minutes, 11th July 2011

[15] Correspondence, Caroline Miles to Band Secretary, 4th April 2011

[16] Minutes, 9th July 2012

[17] Minutes, 8th May 2012 & 9th July 2012

[18] HSB Facebook Page, 2012

[19] Minutes, 8th October 2012

[20] Kent & Sussex Courier, 12th July 2013

[21] ibid; Sussex Express, 12th July 2013; see also www.youtube.com/watch?v=tNfA-aBxvEY&t=49s

[22] Sussex Express, 13th December 2013

[23] Heathfield Magazine, February 2019

[24] Heathfield Magazine, February 2019

[25] Heathfieldsilverband.com, 2019. *Learn to Play a brass instrument in Heathfield*. [online] Available at: <www.heathfieldsilverband.com/learn-to-play>

MEMBERS of NOTE...

Ted Lee
tenor horn, 1952–2018,
librarian, 1956–2018,
honorary life member,
SCABA long service award.

by Keith Pursglove

The brass banding world has lost a true gentleman following the passing of Ted Lee on Tuesday 28 July. The sadness was compounded for Ted's family with the death of Clarice, Ted's wife, just a few days later. Ted was a remarkable man who had the patience of a saint. He started his banding life with the Heathfield Silver Band in 1952 and remained a member until 2018. Clarice supported Ted throughout his banding life and we are all sure it was that support that allowed Ted to give the Band so much time and energy.

Ted first took my son David under his wing when he was ten years old and the impression he left on him remains to the present day. Ted never judged anyone on their age or ability; he just saw potential. David is a grown man now, but still plays with Warbleton Brass Band when he's back in Sussex and still talks fondly of Ted. My relationship with Ted started when he offered to teach me to play. You see Ted would, through gentle persuasion, encourage parents to "have a go" and that was how I was hooked; a decision I'm sure he regretted sometimes, but in his true character he persevered. Ted became a good friend and when I became assistant librarian we would spend many hours talking about his life in banding and the changes he had seen.

The impact Ted had on those he taught cannot be underestimated. He gave so much and asked for nothing in return. Those he helped on their way in banding can be counted in the hundreds. Even if Ted could see there was little hope of someone ever playing he would still encourage them with equal enthusiasm. Ted's biggest regret and sadness was when he was unable to march at the Sussex Bonfire processions, but even then he would turn up with the march pads and spare jackets.

I moved to Warbleton Brass Band some years ago only to find Ted had, over the years, made a similar impact there. It wasn't long before many had a tale to tell of how Ted had helped the Band on so many occasions. There were few at Warbleton who hadn't played alongside Ted and after receiving the sad news of his passing many remarked that "he was one of a kind and a true friend". The principle cornet player at Warbleton, Martin Buss, had particularly fond memories as he was Ted's apprentice when he left school. He remained good friends and enjoyed the countless opportunities they had to play together either when Ted would help Warbleton or Martin would play with Heathfield.

In 2006 Ted was presented with a plaque celebrating 60 years' service to banding by the president of SCABA (Southern Counties Amateur Bands Association). Due to his loyal and long service to the Heathfield Silver Band he was made an honorary vice president.

In 2007 Ted was made a full life member, an honour he wore with pride. Even when Ted had to stop playing completely due to his health he would still actively contribute whenever he could. He would always turn up at every AGM to cast his vote and for a while just sit and listen to the Band practice. So we all say goodbye to Ted, thank you for everything you gave to your community and the kindness you showed the hundreds of budding brass band players over the last 70 years.

Ted accepting SCABA long service award.

Photo supplied by Mostyn Cornford.

This tribute originally appeared in Heathfield Magazine in October 2020. It is reprinted by kind permission of the editor.

Coda The Story Continues…

The thoroughly modern HSB in shirtsleeves at Eastbourne Bandstand, July 2018.
(Back Row, L–R) Trevor Gomersall, Duncan Fisher, Tom Gower, Eric Kemp,
Dave Croxon, Kenneth Hammond, Andy Bullivent, Sarah Leeves.
(Middle Row, L–R) Gareth Burrows, Georgia Waddington, Vicky Noble,
Pippa Maynard, Imogen Burrows, John Justo, Mark Learey.
(Front Row, L–R) Mostyn Cornford, Dave Meakins, Charlotte Butcher, Georgia Brown, Louis Thain,
Rachel Ticehurst, Katherine Hills, Susan Ellis, Mallory Hansford, Torstein Strandness.

This book is, in many respects, a love story. It is about the love members feel for the brass banding world, for the music, for their community, and for one another. This love sustains the extended Band family through thick and thin, through the bad times as well as the good.

When I joined the Band in 2013, I had already known it for a long time. I had been a guest player at school fêtes and country manor houses, and carolled with it at Christmas. However, despite working in Heathfield for sixteen years, I had somehow never become a member. But the town must possess some powerful rural charm, for no sooner had I left my job there than I immediately found myself back again, this time as a part of the Heathfield Silver Band. Sarah Leeves, one of my favourite Sussex banders, was taking over as its new musical director, and my fondness for the Band family would compel me to become its regular bass trombonist. I, too, fell in love.

The incredible life of the Heathfield Band practically guaranteed that a written history would one day materialise and by 2018 I felt that the time was finally right. I embarked on the project as an archaeologist, for that is my day job, and I approached it as such, expecting to find fragments of information with which to construct an informed, if generalised, narrative. What I actually uncovered was a wonderful surprise. I was able to capitalise on my training to avoid getting bogged down in the manifold unknowns and instead used every available clue to answer the seemingly endless list of questions.

We are now 130 years removed from the Band's inception, over a hundred years from the devastation of the Great War and the creation of its committee, ninety years from the formation of the new Heathfield Silver Band, over eighty years from the Second World War, seventy years from its heyday on the contesting scene, fifty years from the beginnings of the modern Band, and thirty years from its brief experiment as a wind band. And yet the spirit of its past continues to permeate the bandroom. The Band's story remains, plain for all to see, through news reports, archive documents, and the recorded anecdotes of its members. By synthesising these rich sources, we are now able to witness the whole story in vivid detail. We can muse over its triumphs and its failures, and even its raison d'etre. We can say, without doubt, that it remains a symbiotic part of the community, with each offering something of value to the other. The Band has given a sense of belonging, a shared purpose, and an extended family to its hundreds of members, many of whom can count their association in terms of decades. Few ever really leave, even when life takes them in a new direction. The Band has grown in step with Heathfield, providing a reassuring continuity reaching back to the very beginnings of the modern town.

Whilst many changes have occurred since the 1880s, there are many fundamental aspects which remain the same. The town's independent, rural identity endures and continues to be celebrated in annual events such as the Cuckoo Fair and the Heathfield Show. More recent innovations, such as Le Marché, now complement the older traditions. Hospital Parades may now be a distant memory, but the Sussex Bonfire Parades and local carnivals continue the charitable fundraising spirit. All these facets of Heathfield's identity owe a great debt to the town band.

Sarah Leeves conducting at the Half Moon Inn, Cade Street, July 2019.
Photograph by Tony Withers.

Many amateur bands were established in the nineteenth century by grass-roots, working-class people such as Heathfield Band's founders Edward Bean and Fred Adams. As such, they functioned mainly within that socio-economic system. It is worth noting that each and every major bust-up in the Band's existence has essentially been the result of tensions between the traditional and the modern aspects of the amateur brass movement. Today the class boundaries are more blurred, and this social shift has resulted in a rethink of the ethos and core values of the town band. Fundraising is more inward-looking, the recruitment and teaching of youngsters more commercially-minded, and the choice of engagements more selective. However, the enjoyment of music-making in such a setting continues to entice new generations to join the Band. The objective of bringing music and music appreciation to the community remains its core goal and the pleasure obtained from this endeavour is plain to see on the faces of its players. It will be interesting to chart its continuing progress in the fast-paced world of the twenty-first century.

Today the Band stands on the shoulders of giants. Even as its committee and members gaze towards a bold new horizon, they would do well to remember that they are but temporary custodians of a beloved social institution. It is their duty to honour those who came before, the people who gave their time, energy, enthusiasm, and sometimes practically their souls, to maintain and protect that institution. Times have changed, music has evolved, and the town has grown significantly, but the essence of the Band must never be lost. It should first and foremost remain a force for bringing people together, for supporting the community, and for introducing new generations to the magical world of music-making. Long may it endure.

Select Bibliography

BBP, 2019. The National Rules of the National Brass Band Championships of Great Britain & The BBP Registry Rules.

Bourke, J., 1996. *The History of a Village Band 1896-1996*. Heathfield: Warbleton and Buxted Band.

Diniejko, A., 2014. *A Chronology Of Social Change And Social Reform In Great Britain In The Nineteenth And Early Twentieth Centuries* [online]. Available at: <www.victorianweb.org/history/socialism/chronology.html>.

Foord, F., 1982. *The Development Of The Tilsmore Area Of Waldron Parish From 1874*. Heathfield: F. Foord.

Galloway, S., McIldowie, P., Pryce, R. and Williams, J., 2008. *Old Heathfield And Cade Street*. Heathfield: Old Heathfield and Cade Street Society.

Gillet, A. and Russell, B., 1990. *Around Heathfield in old photographs*. Stroud: A. Sutton.

Hailstone, A., 1987. *The British Bandsman Centenary Book*. Baldock: Egon.

Herbert, T., 2000. *The British Brass Band: A Musical and Social History*. Oxford: Oxford University Press.

Herbert, T., 2000. Nineteenth-Century Bands: Making a Movement. In: T. Herbert, ed., *The British Brass Band: A Musical and Social History*. Oxford: Oxford University Press: 10–67.

Hind, H., 1934. *The Brass Band*. London: Hawkes & Son.

Hindmarsh, P., 2000. Building a Repertoire: Original Compositions for the Brass Band, 1913–1998. In: T. Herbert, ed., *The British Brass Band: A Musical and Social History*. Oxford: Oxford University Press: 245–277.

Holman, G., 2018. Brass Bands of the British Isles: a historical directory [online]. Available at: <https://gavinholman.academia.edu>.

Horne, n.d. The Past and Future of Brass Bands [online]. Available at: www.bandsman.co.uk/downloads/history.pdf.

Litchfield, N. and Westlake, R., 1982. *The volunteer artillery, 1859-1908*. Nottingham: Sherwood.

Munt, B., 1958. Bonfire. In: B. Pugh, ed., *Bonfire Night in Lewes* (2011). London: MX Publishing Ltd, pp.50–69.

Myers, A., 2000. Instruments and Instrumentation of British Brass Bands. In: T. Herbert, ed., *The British Brass Band: A Musical and Social History*. Oxford: Oxford University Press: 155–186.

Pugh, B., 2011. *Bonfire Night in Lewes*. London: MX Publishing Ltd.

Pryce, R., 1996. *Heathfield Park: A Private Estate and a Wealden Town*. Heathfield: Roy Pryce.

Roll of Honour, 2021. Sussex [online]. Available at: <www.roll-of-honour.com/Sussex/Heathfield.html>.

Roper, J., 2015. The Ad Hoc Calendarized: on the basis of November 5th effigy-burning in southern England). *Western folklore*, [online] 74(2 (Spring 2015), pp.161–183. Available at: <www.jstor.org/stable/24550793>.

Russell, B., 2004. *From Heathfield to East Hoathly*. Leyburn: Tartarus.

Russell, D., 2000. 'What's Wrong with Brass Bands?': Cultural Change and the Band Movement, 1918–c.1964. In: T. Herbert, ed., *The British Brass Band: A Musical and Social History*. Oxford: Oxford University Press: 68–121.

Walker, N., 2018. *Here Dead We Lie*. CreateSpace Independent Publishing Platform.

Index

1066 Commemoration Fair 208, 357
125th anniversary (see also *The 125*) 10, 12, 17, 358, 366, 372, 373
1812 Overture 18, 140
1st Heathfield Scout Group 274
20th Sussex Battalion 148
29th Divisional Band 52
2nd Royal Fusiliers 52
2nd Suite in F Major 108, 140
2nd Sussex Artillery Band 24, 214
2nd Sussex Artillery Volunteers Band 13, 20
2nd Sussex RGA 27
2nd Sussex Volunteer Artillery Corps 26
999 Emergency Services Weekend 276, 303

A

Abide With Me 135
Aces High 140
The Acrobat 296
Adagio from Spartacus 346
Adams, C. 35
Fred Adams 22, 23, 30, 89, 184, 384
AGM (see also general meeting) 71, 85, 91, 152, 176, 183, 277, 298, 345, 381
Agricultural Hall 45, 49, 89, 91, 283
Air Cadets 150
Air Force 173
Air on a G-String 107
Air Training Corps (see also ATC) 37, 150
Alamein Memorial 151
Alderman Fred Taylor Bowl 109
William Cleverley Alexander 47
Alexandra Palace 97
Alexandra Park 206
Alexandra Road 42, 45, 89, 94, 149, 150, 153, 176, 194, 239, 251, 260, 282, 283, 284, 293
All Hail The Power Of Jesus' Name 67
All In The April Evening 137, 140
All People That On Earth Do Dwell 67, 135
All Saints & St Richard's Primary School 22
All Saints Church (see also Parish Church) 22, 45, 55, 61, 66, 70, 90, 119, 120, 152, 174, 238, 274, 282, 311, 335, 339, 341, 345, 368, 369, 371, 375, 376
Amarillo 140
Amazing Grace 156
Christine Ambuchi 202, 207
Stanley Ambuchi 103, 202, 207
American Pie 141
Amorette 84, 98, 136
Amparito Roca 137, 337
Anchored 134
Ancient Order of Foresters 25, 62, 118
Steven Anderson 332, 372
Charles Antram 62
Arabian Fair 208
Armed Forces Day 376
Armistice Parade 84, 327
Army and Navy Supply Stores 36
Arnhem 317, 344

Malcolm Arnold 109, 137
Around the World in Eighty Days 207
Arthur Jarvis Memorial Trophy 104, 208
Artillery Band 24, 52, 214
Artillery Volunteers 13, 20, 33, 45, 133, 160, 282
Arts Council of England 311
Ashburnham Country Fair 375
Assembly Hall, Tunbridge Wells 38, 40, 102
Association of Cyclists 276
Association of the Royal Army Service Corps 176
ATC (see also Air Training Corps) 6, 14, 37, 148, 150, 152, 154, 215
Auld Lang Syne 49, 133
Autumn Contest 101, 108
The Avenue 42
Edwin Axell 90, 99
Ern Axell 99
Aylesham Challenge Cup 106
Richard Ayres 12, 16, 41, 142, 168, 288, 291, 298, 310, 372, 375

B

Burt Bacharach 143
Duncan Bachelor 268
Bad Ems 257, 367
Debbi Bailey 372
Bert Baker 126
George Baker 65, 66
Janet Baker 252, 253, 256, 268, 300, 304
Sam Baker 126
Louise Baldwin 307
Eric Ball 101
Ballerina 216
Band of 129 (Tunbridge Wells) Squadron 166
Band of Hope 284
Band of the Royal Corps of Signals 141
Band of the Territorial Army Unit, the 58th Sussex Field Brigade, Royal Artillery 150
Band of TS Spartan 250
Banditenstreiche 141
Bandology 137, 329
Bandroom Reopening 221, 291
Will Banfill 302
Bank of England 12
Barclays Bank 371, 373
Barcombe 154, 164, 166, 349
Barfield 66
Barley Mow 36
Barnardo's 276
Barratt Homes 373
John Barratt 141, 305, 306
Graham Barton 102, 284, 292
Mr. Barton 55
Mick Bassett 20
Batemans 276, 303, 375, 376
Mike Batt 141
Battle of Britain Day 176, 206
Battle of Hastings 103, 207
Battle of Loos 65

Battle of Poelcappelle 66
Battle Road 342
Battle Town Band 371
Battle's Over 376
BBC 164, 317, 319, 338, 339
Edward Bean 6, 10, 20, 22, 23, 24, 26, 30, 35, 44, 46, 49, 65, 66, 80, 87, 98, 99, 136, 151, 184, 247, 283, 384
Walter Bean 42
The Beatles 138, 143
Beautiful Britain 99, 136
Graham Beeney 103
Beethoven 101, 102, 137
Messrs. Beevers 36
Angela Benson 372
Frank Bernaerts 138
Besses o'the Barn 46
Besson 77
Bexhill Corporation 205
Herbert Bignall 316
Sir Oswald Birley 343
Black Dyke Mills 97, 242, 321, 326
Blackboys Inn 176
Blackboys British Legion 176
Doug Blackford 292, 345
Blaenwern 108
Graham Bland 103, 172, 207, 242
Jackie Bland 103, 202, 207
Janice Bland 103, 202, 205, 207
Lloyd Bland 6, 102, 103, 105, 106, 130, 131, 147, 172, 175, 178, 182, 188, 202, 203, 206, 207, 209, 210, 215, 232, 233, 237, 268, 284
Sue Bland 202, 204, 206, 207, 215
Bless This House 363
Bohemian Rhapsody 18
The Bold Gendarmes 140, 251
Boosey & Hawkes 71, 77
Boppard 258
Borough Bonfire Society 165
Borough Commercial Square Bonfire Society 166
Bouquet de Paris 140, 251, 252
E.W. Bourne 316
Bowley 316
Brass Band Nationals (see also National Brass Band Finals and Nationals) 96
Brass Band News 97
Brassed Off 205
Bray of Heathfield 35, 80
Lesley Bray 40, 238
The Brewers Arms 188, 209
Brighouse & Rastrick 361
Brighton & Hove Albion 206
Brighton Pavilion 339
Brighton Spastics 276
Brill Brass 345
The British Bandsman 48, 63, 133, 285, 386
British Empire 120
British Legion 82, 84, 89, 90, 91, 119, 120, 122, 125, 135, 151, 153, 177, 206, 274, 342, 357, 371, 376
British Red Cross 126, 151, 165, 316
British Telecom (see also BT) 198, 300
Broad Oak Village Hall 335
Paula Brooks 19

Brotherhood and Sisterhood 87, 88, 91, 282
Brotherhood Orchestra 91, 136
Ant Brown 153
Georgia Brown 307, 310, 382
Roy Chubby Brown 256
Tom Brown 153
BT (see also British Telecom) 301
Michael Bublé 143
Buckingham Palace 46, 293, 322
Danielle Budden (see also Danielle Lulham)291, 314, 320
Andy Bullivent 372, 382
Sid Bunce/Bunch 126, 151
Harold Burchett 80
Ken Burchett 366
Gareth Burrows 382
Imogen Burrows 382
H.G. Burtson 118
Burwash Band 357
Burwash Church of England Men's Society, 65
Burwash Common Provident Society 24
Burwash Nursing Association 91
Burwash Remembrance Parade 347, 369, 375
Fred Buss 65, 358
James Buss Snr. 358
Martin Buss 381
Charlotte Butcher 17, 224, 372, 382
Rue Butcher 370
Buxted Brass Band 161, 356

C
Cade Street 20, 22, 24, 30, 46, 49, 56, 58, 64, 65, 66, 81, 82, 88, 90, 91, 119, 124, 133, 140, 149, 236, 274, 282, 283, 289, 342, 358, 367, 376, 384, 386
Cade Street Drill Hall 46, 49, 64, 119
Lady Caffyn 335, 339, 349
Sir Edward Caffyn 184, 208, 243, 270
Arthur Caiger 91
Calais 233, 249, 250, 358, 360
Caledonian Market 208
Call of the Sea 101, 137
The Call of Youth 137
Callenders (Electric Cables) Band 71, 186, 358, 359
Calverley Grounds 97
A. Calvers 134
Cambridge 133, 370
Camelot 310
Camilla, Duchess of Cornwall 322
Campaign Against Consumption 62
Bill Campbell 316
Can Can (see also Orpheus) 252, 337
Cancer Research UK 364
Captain Jack 341
Carlisle 43, 108
Carnival Queen 161
Carols by Candlelight 341
Carousel 207
Carry On 88, 135, 196, 338
Caste 61
Alan Catherall 139
Catholic Church 158, 159
Cavalleria Rusticana 207, 238
CBS Television 164

Index

Cedric Forward Cup 281
Chailey Heritage Foundation 240
Channel Four Television 321
Chanson d'Amour 138
Charlie Chaplin 82
Charleston Manor 142, 218, 343, 345, 368
Charleston Summer Fayre 375
Chatham Winter Festival 104
The Cheeky Girls 339
Mr. Cheeseman 86
chicken-fattening 30, 31, 179
Chicken-Fatters' Band 13
Bob Childs 337, 338
Chitty Chitty Bang Bang 207
Christie Challenge Trophy 14, 98, 100, 121
Christingle 369, 375
Christmas Carol Concerts 341
Christmas Concert 17, 219, 220, 224, 275, 304, 306,
    335, 337, 340, 344, 355, 361, 371, 375
Christmas Fayre 172, 174, 179, 185, 188, 191, 202,
    210, 241, 275, 298, 339
Church of England Men's Society, 64, 65
The Church 47, 48, 63, 64, 74, 87, 119, 132, 159, 166,
    208, 271, 330, 341
Reverend Clark 117
Classic FM 139
Lucy Clements 224, 372
Cliffe Bonfire Society 163, 167, 206, 288, 341
Co-Op/Co-operative Society 288, 375, 373, 377
Cockleshell Heroes 344
Coldstream Guards 34, 66
John Collier 103
Frank Collins 118
Jeff Collins 138, 139, 220, 252, 304, 305, 306, 309,
    310, 311, 334, 358, 359, 362
Maurice Collins 173
Sara Collins 310
Colonel Bogey 142, 250, 253, 256, 272, 327, 359
Commercial Square 154, 164, 166, 233
Community Centre 140, 304, 335, 342, 355, 362, 371,
    372, 374, 375
Community Dividend Award 288
Community Land 140
Congress Theatre 341
Connaught Gardens 334
Kenneth Cook 110
Sylvia Cook 308
S. Cope 134
Copthorne Recreation Ground 100
Corn Exchange 102
Alison Cornford 216, 268
Esme Cornford 189, 190
Mostyn Cornford 7, 12, 18, 58, 168, 190, 216, 221,
    224, 243, 246, 255, 268, 276, 285-286, 289, 291,
    292, 303, 304, 308, 310, 318, 320, 340, 349, 372,
    377, 382
Peter Cornford 10, 12, 17, 39, 58, 73, 75, 103, 105,
    106, 107, 114, 116, 121, 123, 131, 138, 141, 146,
    156, 165, 166, 170, 173, 189, 191, 198, 199, 212,
    215, 216, 226, 230, 234, 236, 237-238, 239, 240,
    242, 249, 266, 268, 269, 270, 272, 273, 274, 277,
    284, 285, 286, 317, 319, 357, 359
"Tich" Cornford 316
Coronation 46, 60, 61, 62, 117, 122, 123, 160, 176, 177
Cory Band 8

Country Life 104
Courier (see also Kent & Sussex Courier) 40, 85, 99,
    103, 106, 108, 163, 166, 186, 187, 190, 208, 218,
    219, 235, 241, 250, 272, 273, 275, 320, 334, 347,
    348, 371, 372, 374
Court Meadow 159
Colonel Courthope 85
covid-19 158, 165
Tony Cresswell 108
Ben Crisford 372
Roy Crompton 262, 268, 285
Cross-in-Hand Choir 175
Cross-in-Hand Foresters 48
Cross-in-Hand Horse Show 87
Cross-in-Hand Hotel 49, 118
Cross-in-Hand British Legion 152, 175, 176
Cross-in-Hand Primary School 216
Cross-in-Hand Show 151
Cross-in-Hand Victory Show 152
Cross-in-Hand Women's Club 62
Crowborough Bonfire 163, 346
Crowborough Silver Band 101
Crowborough Silver Prize Band 160
Crowborough Town Band 250, 251, 280, 300, 309, 361
The Crown Hotel 21, 25, 55, 177, 357
Crown of Victory 46, 133
The Crown 21, 25, 34, 55, 130, 177, 357
Dave Croxon 382
Crystal Palace 45, 96, 97, 131, 136
Cuckoo Fair 179, 218, 335, 342, 345, 348, 368, 374,
    375, 383
Cuckoo Lady of Heffle Fair 249
Cuckoo Line (see also Cuckoo Trail) 21, 141
Cuckoo Line Calypso 141
Cuckoo Trail (see also Cuckoo Line) 233
Mr. Curtis 44
G. Cuthbert 24, 214

D
Daft Punk 142, 251
Daily Herald Contest/Festival 102, 172, 178
Daisy Tearooms 199
Dallington Hospital Parade 357
Roger Daltrey 317, 318, 320
The Dambusters 344
Dances from Terpsichore 109
Emily Irene Dann 79
Gerald Dann 40, 103, 268
Lesley Dann 16, 38, 165, 183, 202, 207
Jasper Darvill 142
David of the White Rock 109
Ted Davis 240
Dawn of Spring 100
Jim Dawson 268
De La Warr Pavilion 205, 276, 303, 334
Dead March 56, 135
Death or Glory 142
Abigail de Bruin 370, 372
Jack de Bruin 372
Mel de Bruin 372
Deep Harmony 101
Demelza 342, 367
John "Taff" Denison 268, 277, 306

Frankie Dettori 308
A Devon Fantasy 105
Charles Dickens 303
Dickensian Market 191, 275
Phil Dickenson 40
Dieppe 63, 250, 269
David Dimbleby 293, 319, 320, 321
Harry Dinnage 90, 172
Mr. Dinnage 44
Divertimento 105, 138
Dome (Brighton) 102
Dorking Contest 101
Dover 250
Down at the Old Bull and Bush 140
Down the Vale 136
Downland Suite 137
Dragon's Green Suite 108
Drill Hall 24, 26, 45, 46, 49, 64, 88, 90, 91, 119, 133, 282
Dave Dunk 40, 103
Dunkirk 149, 274
Dunkirk Veterans Association 274
J.W. Durrant 150, 152, 215

E

East Grinstead and District Guild of Church Bell Ringers 267
East Grinstead Music Festival 105
East Hoathly Bonfire 341
East Hoathly Hospital Parade 2, 23, 33
East Hoathly Show 47
East Sussex Association for the Blind 176
East Sussex County Council 378
East Sussex County Youth Brass Band 310
East Sussex Wind Orchestra 310
Eastbourne Bandstand 299, 303, 308, 310, 338, 343, 345, 363, 369, 371, 375, 382
Eastbourne Football Club 276
Eastbourne Gazette 26
Eastbourne Music Festival 107
Eastbourne Rotary Club 341
Eastbourne Scottish Pipers 91
Eastbourne Silver Band 250, 341
Edelweiss 329
Edenbridge Carnival 360
Edenbridge Town Band 249, 360
Alan Edwards 317
Jimmy Edwards 317
Edward Elgar 136
Susan Ellis 382
Mrs. Elphick 102
Roy Elphick 6, 40, 102, 103, 156, 172, 173, 187, 189, 202, 268, 284
Elvira Madigan 138
Alex "Taff" Emberley 372
Simon Emberley 372
Emjays 339
Empire Marketing Board 120
Empire Shopping Week 120
English Country Garden 140
English Folk Songs Suite 106, 138
The English Maiden 101, 137
Entry of the Gladiators 319

Erfurt 253, 255
Errey's 191, 283
Eton Boating Song 134
Everything Fundamental 374
Experience Corps 339

F

FA Cup Final 105
Facebook 373
Fairies 230
Fairlight Artillery Volunteers Brass Band 13
Fanfare and Hymn Repton 109
Fanfare for a Common Man 142
Fanfare for the Common Band 142
Anna Farley (see also Anna Lee) 10, 18, 105, 108, 205, 208, 240, 241, 242, 253, 270, 292, 298, 304, 310, 366, 372
Graham Farley 7, 240, 257, 298, 309, 310, 344
Mark Farley 271
Farmer's Boy 140
Max Farrow 268
Fasching 252, 253
Father Christmas 188, 202, 241, 275, 298, 341
Guido Fawkes/Guy Fawkes 25, 121, 159, 160, 210
Tim Fermor 364, 366
Alan Fernie 108, 139
Festival of Britain 176
Fight the Good Fight 135
Final Countdown 18, 139
Finlandia 196, 228
Fire Brigade 118, 373
Fireman Sam 307
First Class Brass 377
Duncan Fisher 382
P. Fitzgerald 134
Five Ashes Carnival 161
Cyril Fletcher 319, 320
Fletching Bonfire 159, 317
Fletching Bonfire Society 159
Floral Dance 138, 319, 361
flu epidemic 66
Folkestone Contest 109
Eric Ford 80
Fordcombe Fête 268, 273, 303
The Forest Chief 100, 136
Forges Les Eaux 251, 335
Forty Fathoms 140
Cedric "Sid" Forward 7, 280, 281, 292, 310, 302, 344, 366
Framfield Flower Show 42, 47, 61, 134, 316, 368
Frank Francis 76, 107, 140, 141, 160, 167, 203, 217, 220, 242, 252, 253, 300, 301, 302, 305, 336, 356
Gary Francis 12
Mrs. Francis 283
Archduke Franz Ferdinand 63
Fred Richardson Cup 315
French Comedy 141
Albert French 40
Freudenberg 253
Friends of Demelza Hospice for Children 342
Friends of Heathfield Silver Band 192
J. Frisby of Uckfield 20
Arthur Frost 6, 70, 80, 90, 91, 99, 119, 123, 126, 149, 358

Frothblowers 171, 359, 360
Julius Fucik 319
Eunice Funnell 146
Gerald Funnell 103

G

Shineen Galloway 10, 12
Garnkirk Brass Band 13
Gems of Evergreen Memory 100
Gems of Song 133
General Meeting 95, 178, 241, 242, 243, 284, 346
Get Lucky 142, 251
Ghyll Road 282, 298
Gibraltar Arms Slate Club 48
Gibraltar Tower 47, 66, 236
Gilbert Foyle Challenge Bowl 109
Gilbert Foyle Trophy 108
Glastonbury 101, 137
Glorious Fifth 158
Go To Sea 134
The Golden Age 99, 136
Goldsmith's College 212
Goldsmiths Recreation Ground 361
Trevor Gomersall 372, 382
Goodnight, Beloved 136
Cheryl Goodsell 223, 304, 307, 310, 372
J. Gorringe 20
Cath Gosden 372
Goudhurst Legion 176
Tom Gower 382
GPO (see also British Telecom) 198, 205, 212, 213
GPO Staff Magazine 198, 205
Grandfather's Clock 140
The Grange 65, 81
Great Depression 96, 116, 126
The Great Escape 142
Great Exhibition 176
Great War 6, 18, 22, 30, 34, 42, 52, 60, 62, 64, 65, 66, 68, 85, 97, 120, 134, 135, 142, 148, 149, 150, 160, 161, 184, 376, 383
Green Brothers Factory 149
Francis Greenaway 42, 65
Baroness Sally Greengross 339
Greenway Fruit Farm 240
Greenwood 98, 99, 100, 101, 103, 104, 134, 136, 137
Edward Gregson 137
Grieg's Last Spring 225
Grieg's Spring 277
Grimethorpe 242, 370
Grosvenor Hotel, 307
Grosvenor House Hotel 338
Ground Force 337
Mr. Groves 66
Guides 119, 176, 208, 274, 342
Ben Guile 40, 75, 103, 202, 203, 206, 207, 208, 212, 216, 233, 234, 237, 250, 261, 268, 269, 273, 287
Dennis Guile 7, 12, 40, 103, 198, 202, 204, 206, 207, 243, 268, 271, 285, 287, 304, 311
Maureen Guile 170, 188, 189, 190, 206, 240, 253, 255, 268, 271, 330, 355
Sue Guile 40, 268
Wendy Guile (see also Wendy Holloway) 40, 156, 203, 271
Sam Gurr 20, 33, 44

H

The H.S.B. 142
Hadlow Down Club Day 48
Hadlow Down Hospital Parade 34, 54-55
Hadlow Down School 22, 62, 80
Hadlow Down Show 82
Alec Haffenden 126
Ben Haffenden 20, 23, 44, 151
Earl Haig 120
Hailsham & Vines Cross Band (see also Vines Cross Modern Brass and Wealden Brass) 269
Hailsham Bonfire 218
Hailsham Brass Band 53
Hailsham Carnival 273, 371
Hailsham Drum & Fife Band 66
Hailsham Orchestra 53
Hailsham Road 55, 65, 125, 171, 175
Half Moon Inn 22, 24, 25, 140, 225, 384
James "Jim" Hall 103, 204, 206, 207
Kenneth Hammond 382
Hampton Court 98, 136
Hand and Sceptre 97
Handel 102, 376
Mallory Hansford 372, 382
Hard Times 67, 303
Herbert Harmer 20, 44
William Harmer 20, 32, 44, 62
Harmonie Concert Band 363
Harmony Aces Dance Band 126
Philip Harper 6, 8, 9, 12
Nelson Harriett 35, 80, 232
Tina Harris 202
Al & Bob Harvey 316
Harvey's Brewery 168
Hastings Festival 104, 234
Hawkes & Son 74, 78, 386
Hawks Farm School 335
Fireman Hayward 55
David Healy 363
Heath Robinson 165
Heathfield Talking Newspaper 240
Heathfield Agricultural Show (see also Heathfield Show) 25, 47, 118, 219, 272, 303, 304, 310, 338, 368, 375
Heathfield and District Lions 39
Heathfield and Waldron Ambulance 88, 161
Heathfield and Waldron Ambulance Fund 88
Heathfield and Waldron Community Association 270, 342
Heathfield and Waldron Parish Council 288
Heathfield Army Cadets 376
Heathfield ATC Band 14, 150
Heathfield Band Supporters' Club (see Supporters' Club)
Heathfield Benefit Association 25
Heathfield Bonfire Association 164
Heathfield Bonfire Parade 175
Heathfield Brass Band 13, 20, 24, 33, 35, 44, 49, 61, 63, 67, 80, 86
Heathfield Brass Band, Lanarkshire 13
Heathfield Brass Band, Somerset 13
Heathfield Brotherhood and Sisterhood 88, 91
Heathfield Carnival 18, 174, 234, 236, 246, 270, 273, 360, 368

Heathfield Choral Society 141, 334
Heathfield Community Centre 140, 362, 371, 372, 374
Heathfield Community College 342, 358, 373, 376
Heathfield Comrades 82
Heathfield County Secondary School 177
Heathfield Cricket Week 49
Heathfield Drill Hall 26
Heathfield Drum and Fife Band 13
Heathfield Equitables Juniors' Treat 49
Heathfield Equitables Juvenile Treat 81
Heathfield Fire Service 271
Heathfield Fire Station 140, 235, 338
Heathfield First Magazine 289
Heathfield Flower Show 81, 82, 118
Heathfield Football Club 87
Heathfield Friendly Brass Band 14
Heathfield Friendly Societies Hospital Committee 87
Heathfield Friendly Societies Brass Band 14
Heathfield High Street 118, 191, 219, 335, 339, 342
Heathfield Horticultural Show 272
Heathfield Hospital Parade 34, 47, 54, 55, 56, 64, 66, 82, 88, 91, 133
Heathfield Hospital Sports Carnival 91, 316
Heathfield Hospital Sunday 118
Heathfield Hotel 176
Heathfield House 49, 62, 70, 87, 335
Heathfield Junior Equitables' Treat 82
Heathfield Library 270
Heathfield Lions 287
Heathfield Local History Society 212
Heathfield Lodge of Oddfellows 25
Heathfield Marching Band 13
Heathfield Merrymakers Jazz Orchestra 87
Heathfield Nautical Training Corps Band 234
Heathfield Parish Council 86, 117
Heathfield Park 20, 25, 47, 56, 62, 66, 67, 85, 91, 174, 189, 236, 387
Heathfield Park Cricket Ground 56, 66, 67, 91
Heathfield Poultry Keepers 145
Heathfield Prize Band 14, 80, 98
Heathfield Rat and Sparrow Club 134
Heathfield Recreation Hall 61, 87, 126
Heathfield Round Table 235, 272
Heathfield Show (see also Heathfield Agricultural Show) 171, 233, 301, 302, 335, 345, 363, 383
Heathfield Silver Prize Band 14, 15, 99
Heathfield Silver Youth Band 223
Heathfield Sports Day 88
Heathfield Station 27, 174, 357
Heathfield Stoolball Team 186
Heathfield Talking Newspaper Fête 319
Heathfield Tobacco Fund 64
Heathfield Tower 49, 61, 65, 66, 80, 117, 118, 153, 164, 176, 239
Heathfield Tower Cricket Ground 49, 61
Heathfield Tower Nurseries 66
Heathfield Tower Post Office 65
Heathfield Town Band 13
Heathfield United 37, 49, 79, 81, 188
Heathfield United Football Club 49, 79, 81, 188
Heathfield Volunteer Brass Band 13, 45, 48
Heathfield War Memorial 357

Heathfield Wildlife Park 236
Heathfield Wines Stores 217
Heathfield Works! 374
Heathfield's own Band 10, 13, 30
Heathfield Red Cross Hall 271, 275
Heffle Court 59, 360, 370, 375
Heidelberg Castle 252
Hell's Kitchen 321, 346
A.D. Hellier & Co. 99
Hellingly School 302
Hellingly School's Parent Teacher Association 302
Mervin Hemsley 99
Trevor Herbert 77
Herstmonceux Band 52
Hever Castle 371, 375
Hiawatha 98, 136
higglers 83
Highland Cathedral 299, 344
Katherine Hills 382
Harold C. Hind 73, 75, 76
Adolf Hitler 120, 161
HMS Warbleton 63
Jeff Hobden 6, 102, 126, 130, 151, 172, 209, 238
A Holiday Suite 101, 137
Sid Hollands 99
Steve Holloway 94, 271
Wendy Holloway (see also Wendy Guile) 94, 138, 165, 183, 189, 191, 208, 235, 237, 240, 242, 317
Paul Holmwood 310
Gustav Holst 108, 136
The Holy City 140
Holy Cross Church 341
Home Guard 53, 148, 149, 150
Home, Sweet Home 27
Hooe Band 204
Hootenanny 138, 140
Alfred Hopkins 65, 66
Horam Carnival 164
Horam Farm 375
Horam Flower Show 273
Horam Preschool 369
Horam Road 204
Horam Village Hall 264
Horsham Contest 149
Horsted Place Hotel 342
Hospital Jack 55
Houses of Parliament 159
How Lovely it Was 136
F. Howard Martin 56, 84, 86, 87, 88, 90, 91, 98, 117, 184, 357
HSB March 141, 142
Humble-Crofts Cup Final 37, 119
Fred Hunt 12, 32, 85, 99, 204, 242, 277
Lee Hunt 2, 12
Hurst 91, 342
Hurst Green Recreation Ground 176

I
I Do Like to be Beside the Seaside 140
I See the Moon 196
I'm 21 Today 140
Imperial Echoes 100, 359
The Improvers 221, 223

Index

Dave Imray 256
John Ireland 136
It's A Knockout 209
It's A Long Way To Tipperary 64

J

Jack Cade pub 81
Barry Jackson 306, 307
Gordon Jacob 137
Major Jaeger 208
R.C. James 118
Bill Jarvis 35
Peter Jarvis 103
Jesu Lover of My Soul 135
Jogalong 141
John Brown's Body, 136
Alan Jones 310, 345, 362
Tim Jones 310
Jubilation 49, 133
Jubilee 104, 122, 123, 140, 176, 239, 240, 338, 371
Junior Equitables' Annual Treat 61
John Justo 372, 382

K

Karneval Club Rheingauviertel 252
Keane 13, 318, 320, 371
Adam Kearley 40, 340, 372
Ivy Keel 47
Myra & Ken Keeley 145
Keep the Home Fires Burning 136
Tom Kelly 7, 40, 105, 183, 230, 237, 238, 241, 266, 269, 285, 319
Eric "Animal" Kemp 7, 332, 333, 372, 377, 382
Ross Kemp 308
Kent & Sussex Courier (see also Courier) 40, 106, 108, 187, 235, 241, 272, 275, 334, 347, 371, 372, 374
Ann Kenward 367
The Kicking Donkey 317
King and I 139
King Edward II 342
King Edward VII 46
King Edward VIII 122
King George V 52, 60, 61, 122, 160
Jack King 6, 31, 40, 88, 94, 98, 99, 141, 215, 234, 241
Jenny King 260, 268
Kings Church 339, 375
Kings Cross Band 46
Rudyard Kipling 276
Arch Knapp 35, 56, 80
Laurie Knapp 103, 172, 202, 268, 304
Kneller Hall 301, 370
Captain J.G. Knight 26

L

La Cenerentola 133
La Reine 133
La Traviata 56, 136
Labour 21, 66, 266
Labour Battalion 66
Ladies' Committee 188, 189, 191, 205
Ladies' Entertainment for Mothers of the Ecclesiastical Parish of Burwash Weald 61
Lady Diana Spencer (see also Princess Diana) 271
Lakedown Trout Fishery 317
Land Army 122

Land of Hope and Glory 120, 136, 140, 164
Mr. Langdale 49
Stella Langdale 62
Gordon Langford 139
Abigail Lasham 310
Vicky Lasham 310
Last of the Summer Wine 138
Last Post 19, 88, 119, 131, 135, 161, 210, 342
Latona 133
Eric Latter 126
Ken Latter 126
Laurel & Hardy 341
Michael Laurent 98, 99, 136
The Lazy Trumpeter 140
Le Duc 100, 104, 136
Le Marché 140, 142, 208, 251, 289, 332, 335, 337, 338, 345, 349, 369, 375, 383
Leadenhall Market 23
League of Mercy 54
Mark Learey 2, 9, 12, 382
Anna Lee (see also Anna Farley) 261, 268, 271
Bob Lee 6, 7, 12, 40, 59, 102, 103, 170, 172, 188, 197, 202, 229, 234, 239, 240, 241, 253, 261, 264, 268, 271, 284, 292, 296, 302, 311, 359, 360
Clarice Lee 233
Ted Lee 7, 18, 19, 40, 103, 138, 146-147, 165, 172, 173, 177, 178, 186, 188, 195, 202, 215, 217, 220, 234, 237, 240, 241, 252, 263, 268, 270, 274, 285, 292, 304, 310, 319, 339, 344, 363, 366, 368, 372, 377, 380
Cyril Leeves 6, 32, 36, 40, 88, 102, 103, 114, 126, 145, 149, 165, 202, 215, 232, 235, 237, 246, 268, 359
Jennifer Leeves 298, 309
Richard Leeves 168, 225, 292, 304, 333, 341, 367, 377
Sarah Leeves 17, 18, 32, 76, 107, 110, 142, 168, 217, 222, 226, 237, 253, 257, 280, 293, 302, 304, 306, 307, 310, 337, 338, 362, 372, 375, 382, 384
The Lesson Band 377
Stephen Lester 241
Leukaemia Research Fund 232
Caroline Leverett 362
Lewes Academy of Music 343
Lewes Bonfire 163, 165, 168, 233, 288, 341, 359, 361, 369
Lewes, Glynde & Beddingham Band 347, 370, 375
Light A Life 339
Lingfield Silver Band 332
Little London Farm 62
Little Suite For Brass 109
Sidney Lock 99, 116
London Pride 136
The Lonely Mill 374
Lord Mayor's Hungarian Appeal Fund 165
Lord of the Dance 335
Loreley Besuchetzentrum 367
Lottery (see also National Lottery) 77, 141, 220, 225, 287, 298, 300, 309, 310, 311
Love Not 26
low pitch 75
Lowry 138
E.V. Lucas 159
Danielle Lulham (see also Danielle Budden) 142, 304, 310, 345
Frankie Lulham 10, 17, 19, 32, 39, 107, 140, 142, 148, 165, 167, 218, 221, 251, 280, 287, 291, 298, 302, 304, 310, 314, 315, 319, 320, 321, 322, 335, 337, 340, 343

Lustspiel 138
Vera Lynn 316
M
The Magnificent Seven 76
Majestical 133
Malvern Suite 140
Mamma Mia 140
Marching Through Georgia 136
Margie 250
Marksburg Castle 258
Mary Poppins 139, 207
Match Stalk Men 138
Ray Maulkin 343
Mayfield Band (see also Mayfield Brass Band) 99, 122, 146, 167, 314, 344
Mayfield Bonfire 163
Mayfield Brass Band (see also Mayfield Band) 56
Mayfield Carnival 341
Mayfield Drum and Fife Band 25, 159
Mayfield Hospital Parade 61, 82
Mayfield Silver Band 103, 166, 198
Mayfield telephone exchange 198
Mayfield Xaverian College 49, 61
Pippa Maynard 382
Mayor of Calais 249, 250
Maypole 176
Bob Mayston 40, 338
Pauline McIldowie 12
Dave Meakins 382
mechanical music 44, 117, 126
George Mepham Jnr. 6, 26, 35-36, 54, 73, 78, 84, 85, 89, 97, 100, 101, 102, 124, 135, 152, 161, 164, 173, 178, 185, 187, 357, 358
George Mepham Snr. 6, 23, 35, 52, 65, 78, 80, 91, 94, 99, 119, 126, 149, 151, 161
Horace Mepham 35, 80, 136
Meridian TV 339
Merrydown Cider 309
The Merrydown Heathfield Silver Band 309
Roger Meyer 206
Mid Sussex Brass 167
Mignonne 101, 102, 137
Dave Mildren 142
Mill Road 234
George Miller 138, 150, 171
Adam Milward 310
Mission Impossible 374
Fred Mitchell 35, 65, 80
Jack Mitchell 6, 26, 35, 42, 49, 58, 65, 71, 80, 81, 88, 89, 90, 99, 102, 119, 124, 126, 134, 136, 147, 149, 150, 151, 161, 172, 175, 178, 234, 249, 287
John Mitchell 18, 20, 27, 44, 45, 63, 65, 66
Eric Mockford 99
Modegiska 136
Molly Malone 258
Peter Monk 141
Mood Indigo 138
Dr. Gerald Moore 236
Henry Moore 236
A Moorside Suite 136, 140
Harry Mortimer 146
Mozart 138
Ms. Heathfield 208

Ms. RAFA 234
The Muppet Show 333
H. Musgrave 88
Music Works 339
Benito Mussolini 161
Mutton Hall Hill 31
My Colleen 46, 133
My Fair Lady 140
My Guiding Star 133
A. Myers 77, 387
Myfanwy 140
N
Nabucodonosor 138
National Anthem 62, 66, 119, 133
National Association of Brass Band Conductors 178
National Brass Band Championships of Great Britain 73, 386
National Brass Band Finals (see also Brass Band Nationals and Nationals) 125
National Health Service 47, 56, 57
National Lottery (see also Lottery) 77, 141, 220, 298, 300, 309, 310, 311
National School 22, 25, 67, 282
National Schools' Brass Band Association 137
National Service (Armed Forces) Act 148
National Youth Band 152
National Youth Wind Orchestra of Great Britain 310
Nationals (see also National Brass Band Finals and Brass Band Nationals) 96, 97
Natural Gas Fields of England 45
Nazis 121, 149, 253
Nearer My God To Thee 62
Alan Neve 126
Gordon Neve 14, 18, 36, 37, 38, 54, 74, 88, 99, 101, 119, 124, 126, 146, 147, 149, 166, 261, 268, 277, 283, 358
New Year 49, 60, 87, 88, 133, 260, 353
Newick Bonfire Society 104, 233
Kay Newnham 80
Vicky Noble 382
Norman Norris 208
Stan Nye 99, 215
O
O Canada 342
O Come all ye Faithful 175
O God, Our Help In Ages Past 67, 135
O, Valiant Hearts 135
The Observer 13, 318
Oh What A Beautiful Morning 344
Oklahoma 344
Old Comrades 140, 274
Old Drill Hall 88, 90, 91
Old Empire Celebration 276
Old Folks' Fund 165
Old Heathfield 20, 22, 30, 42, 45, 70, 80, 119, 124, 152, 212, 238, 264, 274, 282, 288, 289, 311, 335, 339, 341, 367, 369, 376, 386
Old Memories 134
Jessie Oliver 42, 80
One Moment in Time 140
Onward Christian Soldiers 135
Orpheus (see also Can Can) 140, 251
Our Flat 88

Our Village Band 6, 78, 114, 144, 145, 146
Overture to an Epic Occasion 101

P

Pack up you troubles 136
Paddington Green 276
Jim Paine 35, 44
Pancake Races 268, 276, 304, 367
Pantiles 97, 276
Paris 140, 249, 251, 252
Parish Church (see also All Saints) 21, 25, 45, 49, 54, 55, 61, 64, 82, 119, 120, 151, 306, 357
Parish Church Choir 82, 357
Parish Committee 23, 30
Parish Council 35, 86, 117, 118, 287, 288
Parish Magazine 22, 23, 27
Park House 45
George Patterson 252, 257, 300
Peace Celebrations 152
Peace Day 66
Pedal Pusher 337
Pendine 138, 296
Pennybridge College 79
Percorini 134
Joe Pert 370, 372
Kerry Pert 372
G.R. Pettett 20
Charles Pettitt/C.E. Pettitt 14, 20, 23, 24, 33, 34, 35, 42, 44, 46, 49, 63, 65, 80, 89, 91, 98, 99, 119, 126, 150
Phoney War 148
Geoff Pickering 257, 258, 284, 341, 378
Alec Piper 99
Pirates of Penzance 98, 136, 207
Pirates of the Caribbean 341, 374
Plaisir d'Amour 251
Plaza Cinema 179
Polegate Gala 209
The Police Band 37
Pop Rock! 109
Pope 160
Post Horn Gallop 340
Praetorius 109
Presbyterian Church 362
Pride of the Forest 103
Prince and Princess Michael of Kent 322
Prince Charles/Prince of Wales 150, 164, 166, 174, 239, 240, 271, 322, 360
Prince George 25
Prince Philip 322
Princess Alice Hospital 47, 54, 66
Princess Diana (see also Lady Diana Spencer) 311
Princess Mary of Teck 25
Protestant Martyrs 159
Proud Hearts 142
Punnetts Town Football Team 82
Keith Pursglove 12, 16, 40, 163, 218, 220, 223, 246, 255, 257, 288, 318, 346, 357, 368, 375, 378, 380

Q

Queen Elizabeth II 176, 322
Queen of Angels 136
Queen Victoria 44
Queen's Own Hussars 370

R

Rachmaninov's Prelude 138
RAF 206, 234, 344
RAF Association 206, 234
RAFA Donkey Derby 359
RAFA Fête 357
Railway Hotel 136
Arthur Ralph (see also Arthur Relf) 124
Charlie Ralph 99
Mrs. Ralph 124
Gordon Ramsay 320, 321, 346
Rangers' Ground 97
RASC 176
Real English Apple Fair 276
Recollections of Beethoven 101, 137
Recreation Ground 54, 82, 88, 100, 117, 153, 161, 164, 171, 176, 177, 186, 234, 239, 361
Recreation Hall 35, 45, 49, 60, 61, 80, 87, 90, 91, 120, 122, 126, 179
Red Cross 126, 151, 165, 271, 275, 316, 373
The Regiment Comes 49
Reichstag 121
Arthur Relf (see also Arthur Ralph) 35
Mr. Relf 20
Remembrance 19, 88, 90, 91, 119, 135, 138, 150, 151, 152, 161, 176, 206, 216, 233, 274, 305, 309, 335, 341, 342, 347, 369, 371, 375, 376
Remembrance Day 119, 151, 152, 176, 206, 233
Remembrance Parade 91, 119, 216, 347, 369, 375
Remembrance Sunday 88, 305
Remnant 15, 374
Reveille 19, 26, 119, 133, 135, 161, 342
Rhapsody on Negro Spirituals 104, 137
Rhineland 366, 367
Rhyl Band 146
Emily Rich 372
Lewis Rich 372
Albert Richardson 316
Fred Richardson 7, 142, 291, 302, 304, 310, 314, 315, 344
William Rimmer 102, 134, 135, 136
Ringmer Bonfire Society 161
Ringmer Contest 109, 110, 345
Roadrunners 272
Bob Roberts 20, 35, 44, 80
George Roberts 65, 116
Thomas William Robertson 61
Arthur Rodgers 89, 90, 98, 116, 136, 215, 282
Roller Skating Carnival 49, 60
Roman Catholic Church 158
Romeo and Juliet 102, 137
Trevor Rood 40, 103, 207, 242
Rose and Crown 159
Rose Bloom 134
John Rossall 363
Rotary Club 241, 341, 368
Rotherfield Bonfire 166, 273, 309
Rouen 66
H. Round 101, 134, 135
Round House School 42
Royal Corps of Signals 141, 305, 306
Royal Corps of Signals Association Band 305

Royal Corps of Signals Staff Band 305
Royal Engineers 65, 233, 239, 274, 303, 322
Royal Garrison Artillery 27
Royal National Lifeboat Institution 347
Royal Navy Old Comrades 274
Royal Northern College of Music 338
Royal Sussex Regiment 34, 65, 151
Rüdesheim am Rhein 255, 257
Rule Britannia 25, 133, 140
Runt in Tun 166
Alice Jane Rusbridge 30
Rushlake Green 56, 63, 119, 356, 375
Ken Russell 18, 100, 102, 147, 150, 151, 152, 165,
   175, 186, 204, 284, 285, 317
Rustic Festival 136

S
Sabbatarian 47, 48
Safroni 100
Salvation Army 120, 125, 132, 142, 280, 344
Santa Claus 170, 174, 210
Satinstown Farm 118, 120
George Saunders 309, 340
Stephen Saunders 22, 214
Save all Your Kisses for Me 138
Adolph Sax 72
Saxhorn family 73
SCABA (see also Southern Counties Amateur Bands
   Association) 97, 100, 101, 110, 146, 177, 281, 314,
   344, 381
SCABA Autumn Contest 101
Scarlet Serenaders 123
Scats 145
Scouts 119, 176, 208, 216, 274, 342
Seaford Silver Band 167, 337, 362, 363
Seahaven Scouts 342
Seaside Road 233
Second World War 14, 18, 37, 43, 53, 56, 71, 100, 122,
   130, 146, 148, 151, 161, 215, 240, 253, 314, 344,
   383
Sedlescombe Flower Show and Country Fayre 308
Seeboard 156
Seven Sisters Marathon 272, 303, 335
Severn Suite 136
Julia/Julie Seymour 40, 94
Sheepsetting Lane 118, 304, 335, 342, 362, 371
Ernie Sherlock 344, 345
John Sherlock 305, 362
Richard Sherlock 77, 110, 223, 224, 257, 306, 310, 332,
   334, 345, 346, 349, 366, 367, 370, 371, 372, 375
Shoreham Lifeboat Appeal 347
Sidmouth Bandstand 362
Sidmouth Town Band 334, 362
Edrich Siebert 137, 178
Silent Night 376
Silent Worship 138
Silver Moonlit Winds are Blowing 136
Mr. Sinden 44
Dr. Isla Sitwell 337, 363
Sky Farm 61
Slaidburn 140, 166, 326, 359
Sleeping Beauty 189
Claire Slinnhawkins 372
Slow Melody Contest 106, 107

Mike Smith 167, 255, 256, 310, 339
Socialist International Movement 85
Soldier Hero 64
The Soldier's Tale 133
Soldiers' Comforts Fund 126, 316
Solitaire 140, 346
Song of Wales 101, 137
Songs of Gallant Wales 136
Songs of Other Days 133
Songs of Praise 334, 362
Sons of the Brave 142
The Sound of Music 139
South African Anglo-Boer 27, 120
Southdown Band 229
Southdown Drum and Fife Band 91
Southern Counties Amateur Bands Association (see
   also SCABA) 97, 177, 381
Southern Counties Band Contest 71
Sovereign Light Café 318
Sovereign Radio 339
Spanish Eyes 328
The Spirit of Youth 98, 136
Spring Contest 100, 101, 108
Spring Festival 106
Spring Gardens School 267
Spring Lodge 56, 84, 87, 91, 357
St. Andrew's Variations 108, 109, 140
St. Barnabas (Kensington) Choral and Operatic Society
   88
St. Bartholomew's/St. Bart's Church 118, 289
St. Bede's School 166, 272
St. Dunstan's 81
St. George 120, 233, 238, 274, 342, 345, 359, 367, 368
St. George's Day Parade 238, 274, 342, 345, 367
St. Helen's Park Preservation Society 276
St. Hilda's 97
St. John Ambulance, 374
St. Mark's Church 271
St. Mary's Church 176, 345
St. Mary's School 266, 267
St. Phillips Church Choir 65
St. Phillips Church 65
St. Richard's Church 79, 90, 153, 202, 271, 282, 375
St. Richard's Church Building Fund 90
St. Richard's Hall 101, 174, 175, 188, 241
St. Richard's Primary School 22, 339
St. Richards Church Whit Monday Fête 118
St. Wilfred's Hospice 339, 368
Stand up, Stand Up For Jesus 67
Freddie Stanford 103, 268
Star Inn 25, 49, 55, 84, 289
Star Wars 138, 220
The Star 25, 34, 49, 55, 84, 124, 220, 289, 360
Start Out lesson group 226
State Hall 45, 49, 174, 185, 219, 340, 369, 375
Station District 62, 80
Station Road 26, 45, 46, 120, 185, 251, 282
Fred Stephens 20, 44
Stephenson's Operatic Silver Band 14
Ian Stewart 370
A.E. Stickells, Cranbrook 44
Stonegate School 275

Index

Torstein Strandness 382

Streat and Westmeston Summer Fête 316

Sturdy Firm 84

Arthur Sullivan 98, 134

Summer Festival 104, 375

Supporters' Club 37, 153, 172, 174, 175, 184, 185, 187, 188, 189, 192, 284

Sussex Air Ambulance 347

Sussex Bonfires 6, 158, 159, 160, 164, 166, 168, 309, 375

Sussex by the Sea 65, 140, 142, 159, 164, 166, 207, 250, 272, 327, 330, 337, 359, 374, 376

Sussex Day 219, 371

Sussex Express 24, 36, 47, 48, 60, 63, 65, 66, 67, 80, 82, 85, 86, 89, 90, 91, 117, 118, 120, 123, 125, 159, 175, 185, 272, 273, 283, 318, 321, 322, 339, 367

Sussex Hospital 6, 47, 54, 56, 57

Sussex in Silver 141

Sussex Newspapers 126, 172, 218

Dave Sutton 40, 103, 203, 206, 216, 217, 242, 361

Sue Sutton 40, 101, 103, 130, 147, 165, 182, 202, 203, 204, 205, 206, 215, 236, 317, 361, 364

T

TA (see Territorial Army)

Taff (see also John "Taff" Denison) 268, 277, 306, 326, 327, 328, 329, 330

Take It From Here 317

Tancredi 137

Tanners Manor 91

Maurice Tate 316

Sarah Tate 12, 219, 374

Tavistock Town Band 362

Tavistock Town Hall 362

Les Taylor 35

Tchaikovsky 137

Tennessee 144

Territorial Army 120, 141, 149, 150, 160, 300, 301

Louis Thain 382

That's Life 319

Margaret Thatcher 199, 269

Theobalds Green 171

There'll Always Be An England 159, 166

The Thin Red Line 136, 260

Bert Thompson 14, 37, 40, 55, 74, 80, 81, 82, 83, 86, 89, 97, 99, 103, 122, 124, 130, 136, 161, 233, 268

Len Thorne 6, 78, 114, 145, 146

Three Songs Without Words 104

Chris Threlfall 268

David/Dave Threlfall 7, 106, 107, 138, 199, 241, 266, 268, 269, 272, 275, 276, 277, 278, 296, 319

Nicholas Threlfall 267, 268, 272

Sarah Threlfall 216, 268

Rachel Ticehurst 382

Tilsmore Common 151

Tilsmore Recreation Ground 88

Tipperary 64, 136

RMS Titanic 62

toffing 123

Stan Tomlin 316

Mr. Topples' Puppet Show 371

Jayne Torvill 318, 320

Tottingworth Park 61, 65, 66, 78

Tour de Heathfield 309

Tower Recreation Ground 117, 153, 164, 176, 239

Tower Street 171

Trading4U 45, 191, 283

Training Band 39, 202, 215, 216, 217, 218, 219, 221, 222, 223, 224, 225, 226, 237, 341, 346, 377

trustees 42, 70, 182, 284, 292

tuberculosis 62

Tunbridge Wells Advertiser 40, 106

Tunbridge Wells Amateur Band Federation 70, 97, 104, 176, 249

Tunbridge Wells Band Festival (see Tunbridge Wells Festival)

Tunbridge Wells Contest 14, 31, 35, 42, 79, 87, 88, 91, 103, 116, 121, 122, 136, 153, 174, 207

Tunbridge Wells Federation (see Tunbridge Wells Amateur Band Federation)

Tunbridge Wells Festival 84, 97, 99, 100, 103, 104, 358

Tunbridge Wells Hospital 54, 156

Tunbridge Wells Marching Band 251

Dick Turner 102, 141, 172, 260, 267, 268, 276, 277, 358

Twinkle Twinkle, Little Star 217

Two Dogs Heathfield Silver Band 309

Two Folk Songs: Avenging and Bright and Early One Morning 110

Private W.E. Tyler 64

U

Uckfield Band 38

Uckfield Bonfire 163, 167, 218, 275, 341, 359, 369

Uckfield Bonfire Carol Service 167

Uckfield Bonfire Society 341, 369

Uckfield Concert Brass 166, 359

Uckfield Hospital Carnival 121

Uckfield Lions 223, 341

Uckfield Town Band 160

The Ugly Duckling 76

Una Paloma Blanca 138

Union Church 45, 223, 225, 275, 369, 375

Frank Upfield 35, 80, 87, 99, 117, 119, 121, 122

George Upfield 80

Lleyland Upfield 35

Mrs. T. Upfield 35

Sam Upfield 35

Sylvia Upfield 122, 202

Tom Upfield 35, 65

V

Vaughan Williams 106

Versatile Brass 242, 370

Gerald Vickers 268

The Viking 100

The Village Chimes 133

The Village Gala 136

Vines Cross Modern Brass (see also Hailsham & Vines Cross Band and Wealden Brass) 361

Vines Cross Post Office 275

Vines Cross Wheeler 267

Gilbert Vintner 137

Mick Vise 363

VJ Day 309, 361

Voice of the Guns 142

Volunteer Artillery Corps 26, 27

Volunteer Training Corps/VTC 64, 65

W

Georgia Waddington 372, 382

Wadhurst Brass Band 100, 280, 344, 364, 375
Wadhurst Contest 99
Wadhurst Drum & Fife Band 250
Waldron British Legion 84, 89, 91, 119, 151
Waldron British Legion's Sports Day 119
Waldron Carnival 152, 164
Waldron Fête 346
Waldron Hospital Parade 55
Waldron British Legion 120
Waldron Merrymakers Dance Band 161
Waldron Parish Council 287, 288
Waldron Remembrance Day Parade 151, 152
Waldron Thorns 174
Waldron War Memorial 88
Stephen Walkley 109
Wall Street Crash 116
William Wallace 134
War Memorial 43, 56, 66, 82, 88, 90, 91, 119, 120, 151, 152, 161, 177, 357
War of the Worlds 346
Warbleton & Buxted Band 204, 208, 233, 234, 250, 276, 356
Warbleton Band 56, 147, 160, 357, 358
Warbleton Brass & Reed Band 56, 123
Warbleton Brass Band 52, 133, 356, 380, 381
Warbleton Hospital Parade 56, 87, 357
Warbleton Prize Band 89, 357
Warrior Square 141, 233
Washington Grays 208
Water Music 102
Heidi Watkins 19, 163, 167, 255, 349, 367
Tom Watts 314
We Wish You A Wombling Merry Christmas 141
Wealden Brass (see also Vines Cross Modern Brass and Hailsham & Vines Cross Band) 361
Wealden Consort 347
Wealden District Council 287
Wealden Talking News (see also Heathfield Talking Newspaper) 240
Wealden Works! 318
wedding 17, 25, 62, 233, 238, 271, 322, 334, 369, 370
The Wedding March 238
Mark Welch 225, 369, 372
Sarah Welch 372
Welcome Mission 118
Welcome Stranger Inn 20
Madame Edith Welling 316
Paul Wells 268
The Welsh Guards 322
Dave Wenham 103, 202, 209
West Sussex Gazette 83
Western Front 65, 149
Whack-o! 317
Eric Wheale 99
Mr. Wheale 89
Trix Wheale 99
The Whistling Bandsman 130, 209
Whit Monday Contest 100
White Rock Pavilion 103
White Rock Theatre 189, 207
Flossie White 70
Whitehouse Lane 88

Herbert Whitely 48
Susan Whiting 103
Whitstable Scout Band 250
Wiesbaden 190, 252, 253, 255, 256, 257, 298, 301, 304, 309
Dennis Wilby 370
William and Kate, Duke and Duchess of Cambridge 370
William Hill's Interiors 342
Wimshurst Trophy 104
Windlesham Manor 375
Windmill Hill Place 26
Winemakers' Association 276
Winter Festival 104
Bert Wise 6, 37, 38, 76, 100, 101, 102, 123, 125, 126, 146, 147, 148, 150, 152, 153, 154, 156, 161, 173, 174, 175, 178, 179, 182, 185, 187, 203, 215, 234, 268, 314, 358
Terry Wogan 138
The Wombling Song 141
Charlie Woodgate 35, 80, 126
Norman Wragg 277
Denis Wright 101, 134, 135, 137
Wright & Round 134
Wright & Round Music Journal 134
Wright and Round Liverpool Journal 135
Wyngate Temperance 97
Y
Yamaha 75
Ye Merry Monarch 133
Cyril Yorath 178
The Young Brigade 133
The Young in Heart 104
Youngman 108
Youth Centre 342
YouTube 319, 362